Edited by David G. Hartwell

Edited by David G. Hartwell & Kathryn Cramer

YEAR'S BEST SF 11

SF 11

EDITED BY
DAVID G. HARTWELL
and KATHRYN CRAMER

An Imprint of HarperCollinsPublishers

Additional copyright information appears on pages 495–496.

EOS
An Imprint of HarperCollins*Publishers*
10 East 53rd Street
New York, New York 10022-5299

Copyright © 2006 by David G. Hartwell and Kathryn Cramer
ISBN-13: 978-0-7394-6924-8
ISBN-10: 0-7394-6924-X

Printed in the U.S.A.

In memory of
Constance Elizabeth Nash Hartwell,
who liked good stories.

Contents

Acknowledgments

We would like to acknowledge the assistance of Carl Caputo, who early in the year jump started this anthology and gave us something to work with later. Thank you, Carl.

Introduction

The year 2005 was a science-fictional year in several ways. Think, for instance of SF-scale catastrophes and post-catastrophe civilizations. We were just beginning to understand the scale of the tsunami as the year 2005 dawned. The sheer enormity was hard to grasp, much of it first comprehensible through satellite images of the Aceh coastline wiped clean and the churning vortices of the retreating wave on a few videos. The destruction of New Orleans was disaster come to us, not over there in places we might never have heard of, a disaster made at least as much by our own institutions as by nature, and of science-fictional scale. And this time, especially with technology introduced in 2005, we had front row seats. Between the tsunami and Hurricane Katrina, with the launch of Google Earth, Virtual Earth, and similar web sites, it became possible to have a different relationship to the destruction and the press photography. At the time of the tsunami, the press ran headlines like *Spy satellites assessing tsunami damage*. By the time of Katrina, we had become much more accustomed to the newer View from Above after only a few months of making it our own on the web. Tens of thousands of people checked on the conditions of their homes using Google Earth and overlaid photography. Many others used Google Maps or Virtual Earth. The story of how this affected the great Pakistan earthquakes only a month after Katrina is too complex to condense here, and it is not nearly over yet. People are still dying there as we write on the first day of 2006. Disasters now, and in the future, will be observed differently than in the past.

The year 2005 was also a time of war, not a twentieth-century *loose lips sink ships* kind of war, but a paranoia-ridden post-modern twenty-first-century war in which information spews as if from a firehose and is most difficult to control or comprehend. A number of countries are very uncomfortable with the world public's new-found ability to look in on their military facilities; and in the U.S., a fake letter from a soldier claiming that Google Earth was used as a kind of phildickian Eye in the Sky by our enemies to spy on U.S. troop positions was posted in over 300 places on the internet. (GE cannot be used in that way.) But as the year ended with a political scandal over "domestic surveillance," it turns out that, yes, Americans are being spied on, but mostly by Americans. If 2005 was about something, it was about ways of seeing. And in a most literal sense it seems that here in the twenty-first century we begin to see things differently. We can see the world, and most of it is not like the home we are used to.

There is always a bit of an international surge in SF when the World SF convention is held outside the U.S., as it was in 2005 in Glasgow, Scotland. Certainly there was a commemorative anthology of original SF by Scots, *Nova Scotia*, from which we selected a couple of fine stories for this book. But more than that, the convention inspired small press publishers in the UK and Europe to produce books and magazines in time to show off at the convention, and there were a number of them. And there was an excellent anthology of new SF from the UK published without much fanfare, *Constellations* (DAW), edited by Peter Crowther, who was also the editor of *Postscripts*, the new UK quarterly magazine. *Interzone*, the flagship magazine of the UK, has a bright new look and a new editor. Of special interest was the reappearance of the Futures page in the scientific journal *Nature*, in spring 2005, a page devoted to a single short piece of SF every week for the rest of the year. So it appears that we can look forward to continued innovation in SF from the UK quarter, in particular, in the next few years.

It was also the year that SciFiction.com, the highest paying market for short fiction in SF & fantasy, was terminated.

And at the end of the year, Infinite Matrix announced it was ceasing publication. So 2005 was perhaps the end of the first wave of the website magazines, leaving only Strange Horizons, a non-profit organization of the formerly top three fiction locations still intact. The electronic publishers on the internet maintained the levels of quality established a few years back, and remain an ambitious dimension of the SF field, but there was not a significant increase in the amount of good fiction originating on the internet. Perhaps we should be grateful for no decrease in 2005. It seems unlikely that a new magazine will arise soon on the internet to equal the pay and influence of SciFiction, but there are several that may be willing to try. Aeon, Revolution SF, Eidolon online, Fantastic Magnitude, and Challenging Destiny, for instance, show real promise.

We are still in the middle of some kind of short fiction boom in science fiction and the associated genres of the fantastic—we certainly hope not at the end. Not an economic boom—no one is getting paid much—but certainly a numbers increase, and it has been building for several years. The highest concentrations of excellence were still in the professional publications, the anthologies from the small press, and the highest paying online markets, though the small press zines were significant contributors too.

There are a lots of conclusions one might draw from this, but the one we highlight is that it makes this year's best volume even more useful, since we try to sort through all this material. But the small press really expanded again this past year, both in book form and in a proliferation of ambitious little magazines, in the U.S. and the rest of the world.

Each year we find ourselves pointing with some irony at the areas of growth in SF, as if they were double-edged swords. While many of the ambitious insiders want to break out, at least some ambitious outsiders are breaking in, and some of them at the top of the genre. This is now a trend several years old. Last year it was Karen Joy Fowler and then Kelly Link who made it firmly into the literary mainstream by continuing to do what they have always done, write excellently well. This year they really got noticed.

It is our opinion that it is a good thing to have genre boundaries. If we didn't, young writers would have to find something else, perhaps less interesting, to transgress or attack to draw attention to themselves.

We try in each volume of this series to represent the varieties of tones and voices and attitudes that keep the genre vigorous and responsive to the changing realities out of which it emerges, in science and daily life. It is supposed to be fun to read, a special kind of fun you cannot find elsewhere. This is a book about what's going on now in SF. The stories that follow show, and the story notes point out, the strengths of the evolving genre in the year 2005.

So we repeat, for readers new to this series, our usual disclaimer: This selection of science fiction stories represents the best that was published during the year 2005. It would take several more volumes this size to have nearly all of the best short stories—though even then, not all the best novellas. And we believe that representing the best from year to year, while it is not physically possible to encompass it all in one even very large book, also implies presenting some substantial variety of excellences, and we left some worthy stories out in order to include others in this limited space.

Our general principle for selection: This book is full of science fiction—every story in the book is clearly that and not something else. We have a high regard for horror, fantasy, speculative fiction, and slipstream, and postmodern literature. We (Kathryn Cramer and David G. Hartwell) edit the *Year's Best Fantasy* as well, a companion volume to this one—look for it if you enjoy short fantasy fiction, too. But here, we choose science fiction. You are invited.

David G. Hartwell & Kathryn Cramer
Pleasantville, NY

New Hope for the Dead

DAVID LANGFORD

David Langford (www.ansible.co.uk) *lives in Reading, England. He publishes the fanzine* Ansible, *the tabloid newspaper of SF and fandom, which wins Hugo Awards, and is also excerpted as a monthly column in* Interzone, *and online at www.dcs.gla.ac.uk/SF-archives/Ansible. He is the most famous humorous writer in fandom today—see his book* He Do the Time Police in Different Voices—*and keeps winning best fan writer Hugo Awards. He is an indefatigable book reviewer (some of his reviews are collected in* The Complete Critical Assembly, Up Through an Empty House of Stars: Reviews and Essays 1980–2002, *and* The SEX Column and Other Misprints). *For the last decade he has been publishing short SF of generally high quality, collected in* Different Kinds of Darkness.

"New Hope for the Dead" appeared in Nature, *the distinguished journal of science, that revived its one-page short fiction feature,* Futures, *in 2005. We think it is significant for the SF field that such a feature exists in such a place. This story is about the rewards and punishments of the electronic afterlife.*

Hello, Mr. Hormel, this is your hosting system at Nirvana Infomatics. We apologize for interrupting your regular afterlife, but unfortunately the message is urgent. Otherwise we would not have intruded on your VR sex athletics competition.

We are sorry to hear that you were going for a new high score. Nevertheless the message is urgent.

In accordance with your contract for postmortem uploading and long-term maintenance as an Electronic-Golem Artificial Neurosystem or EGAN, we regret to inform you that your trust fund is not performing adequately. This is a result of global economic problems, arising from the continuing states of emergency in Iraq, Iran, Korea, France and the US Pacific Northwest.

To put it briefly, your current investment yield is no longer covering the monthly payments for full enjoyment of this digital afterlife.

You are quite correct to invoke the emergency insurance terms laid down in Clause 12 of your antemortem agreement. Unfortunately, our finance department has already taken the full potential claim into account.

Yes, the world economy truly is in appalling shape. Otherwise we would not be forced to mention the provisions of Clause 9, "Special Circumstances, Penalties and Termination."

But in the words of the classic novel—Don't Panic! Several alternative plans are available for financially challenged and differently solvent entities in our care.

The simplest scheme is what our client-advisers amusingly call "being dead for tax reasons." Maintaining your full activity as an EGAN requires continuing exabyte-scale storage capacity and very substantial 24/7 processor power. We can enormously reduce the associated expenses by storing you in static, compressed Zip format for reactivation in a time of better economic weather.

Yes, it is true that we cannot guarantee a major future upturn. Shares can, alas, not only go down but plunge and even plummet. Yes, it is possible that current issues such as global warming, fossil-fuel exhaustion and scrotty abuse may conceivably reduce our technological capacity to a level where stored EGANs can no longer be restarted. But, you know, you wouldn't feel a thing.

We understand your viewpoint. So much, then, for the first and easiest option.

Plan two has the droll motto, "Poverty is nature's way of telling you to slow down!" What happens here is that to all intents and purposes you continue your luxury electronic afterlife exactly as at present—but with substantial savings achieved by slowing your clock rate and reducing processor load. A thousandfold reduction, for example, would make no subjective difference but . . .

Well, yes, you would inevitably lose contact with other posthuman friends running at normal clockspeed in the EGANverse. And, indeed, a century would pass in little more than five weeks. But try to look on the bright side: you could see the glittering wonders of the future. Who would have thought, even a few years ago, that scrotties would prove to be of such momentous significance today? What other fascinating surprises await?

Ah, so you doubt our troubled world's ability to sustain life, high-information technology and thus your own digital substrate for as much as another century. Just between you and ourselves, Mr. Hormel, we agree. One doesn't want to go actively looking for future shock.

So it seems as though you'll be opting for plan number three. As our client-advisers like to explain this one: "You're dead but you needn't lie down!" Posthumous vocational choices are restricted by a variety of union agreements, but there are still opportunities for EGAN personalities to carry out useful and profitable work!

Your key marketing point is the unparalleled human— sorry, posthuman—ability to perform advanced pattern recognition. No, not SETI radio-telescope data scanning. That was a good guess, but surprisingly crude software can handle the mere search for alien signals. For you we have a much subtler, trickier and constantly mutating challenge.

According to your premortem life record (we apologize for the intrusion, but Clause 9(vii) grants us direct access to your stored memories under the present circumstances), your highly profitable career as a Florida-based dissemina- tor of unsolicited commercial e-mail should make you ide- ally qualified for this filtration job. Everyone knows your old catch-phrase: Just Press Delete.

It's a simple, straightforward task, with VR rewards for accuracy and disincentives for wrong decisions: see Clause 9(xvi) regarding valid occasions for negative reinforcement via simulated discomfort. You merely need to use your posthuman powers of judgment to separate relevant content from the surrounding white noise of coded promotional ma- terial for pØrn, HyperViagra, illicit scrotties and the like— plus, of course, all solicitations with any hint of a Nigerian accent.

Here are your first ten billion e-mails.

Scan them rapidly, diligently and well.

And as you come to each undesirable item . . . Just Think Delete.

Deus Ex Homine

HANNU RAJANIEMI

Hannu Rajaniemi (http://tomorrowelephant.net/) is a Finn living in Edinburgh, Scotland, and is now working on his PhD thesis in string theory. His bio says "Hannu was born in Ylivieska, Finland, in 1978 and survived the polar bears, the freezing cold and the Nokia recruiting agents long enough to graduate from the University of Oulu. After brief stints in Cambridge University and working as a research scientist for the Finnish Defense Forces, he moved to Edinburgh." And he "only recently switched to Queen's English as his primary medium of expression. His favorite method of writing involves starting at a blank A4 page until drops of blood form on his forehead."

"Deus Ex Homine" was published in Nova Scotia. *An AI plague turns humans into deadly, near-omnipotent gods. Being a god is like having a disease, and it turns out that this can be sexually transmitted: fullblown godhood can appear in the child even if the parent has been cured. Jukka is an ex-god, his infection now burned away and part of his mind with it—human again, but not quite whole, a survivor of the war against the gods.*

As gods go, I wasn't one of the holier-than-thou, dying-for-your-sins variety. I was a full-blown transhuman deity with a liquid metal body, an external brain, clouds of self-replicating utility fog to do my bidding and a recursively self-improving AI slaved to my volition. I could do anything I wanted. I wasn't Jesus, I was Superman: an evil Bizarro Superman.

I was damn lucky. I survived.

The quiet in Pittenweem is deeper than it should be, even for a small Fife village by the sea. The plague is bad here in the north, beyond Hadrian's Firewall, and houses hide behind utility fog haloes.

"Not like Prezzagard, is it?" Craig says, as we drive down the main street.

Apprehension, whispers the symbiote in my head. *Worry*. I don't blame Craig. I'm his stepdaughter's boyfriend, come calling during her first weekend leave. There's going to be trouble.

"Not really," I tell him, anxiety bubbling in my belly.

"Beggars canna be choosers, as my granny used to say," Craig replies. "Here we are."

Sue opens the door and hugs me. As always, I see Aileen in her, in the short-cropped blonde hair and freckled face.

"Hey, Jukka," she says. "It's good to see you."

"You too," I say, surprising both myself and the symbiote with my sincerity.

"Aileen called," Sue says. "She should be here in a few minutes."

Behind her shoulder, I notice Malcolm looking at me. I wink at him and he giggles.

Sue sighs. "Malcolm has been driving me crazy," she says. "He believes he can fly an angel now. It's great how you think you can do anything when you're six."

"Aileen is still like that," I say.

"I know."

"She's coming!" shouts Malcolm suddenly. We run out to the back garden and watch her descend.

The angel is big, even bigger than I expect from the lifecasts. Its skin is transparent, flowing glass; its wings pitch-black. Its face and torso are rough-hewn, like an unfinished sculpture.

And inside its chest, trapped like an insect in amber, but smiling, is Aileen.

They come down slowly. The downdraft from the micron-sized fans in the angel's wings tears petals from Sue's chrysanthemums. It settles down onto the grass lightly. The glass flesh flows aside, and Aileen steps out.

It's the first time I've seen her since she left. The quicksuit is a halo around her: it makes her look like a knight. There is a sharper cast to her features now and she has a tan as well. Fancasts on the Q-net claim that the Deicide Corps soldiers get a DNA reworking besides the cool toys. But she is still my Aileen: dirty blonde hair, sharp cheekbones and green eyes that always seem to carry a challenge; my Aileen, the light of the sun.

I can only stare. She winks at me and goes to embrace her mother, brother and Craig. Then she comes to me and I can feel the quicksuit humming. She brushes my cheek with her lips.

"Jukka," she says. "What on earth are you doing here?"

"Blecch. Stop kissing," says Malcolm.

Aileen scoops him up. "We're not kissing," she says. "We're saying hello." She smiles. "I hear you want to meet my angel."

Malcolm's face lights up. But Sue grabs Aileen's hand firmly. "Food first," she says. "Play later."

Aileen laughs. "Now I know I'm home," she says.

Aileen eats with relish. She has changed her armor for jeans and a T-shirt, and looks a lot more like the girl I remember. She catches me staring at her and squeezes my hand under the table.

"Don't worry," she says. "I'm real."

I say nothing and pull my hand away.

Craig and Sue exchange looks, and the symbiote prompts me to say something.

"So I guess you guys are still determined to stay on this side of the Wall?" I oblige.

Sue nods. "I'm not going anywhere. My father built this house, and runaway gods or not, we're staying here. Besides, that computer thing seems to be doing a good job protecting us."

"The Fish," I say.

She laughs. "I've never gotten used to that. I know that it was these young lads who built it, but why did they have to call it Fish?"

I shrug.

"It's a geek joke, a recursive acronym. Fish Is Super Human. Lots of capital letters. It's not that funny, really."

"Whatever. Well, Fish willing, we'll stay as long as we can."

"That's good." *And stupid*, I think to myself.

"It's a Scottish thing, you could say. Stubbornness," says Craig.

"Finnish, too," I add. "I don't think my parents are planning to go anywhere soon."

"See, I always knew we had something in common," he says, although the symbiote tells me that his smile is not genuine.

"Hey," says Aileen. "Last time I checked, Jukka is not your daughter. And I just got back from a war."

"So, how *was* the war?" asks Craig.

Challenge, says the symbiote. I feel uneasy.

Aileen smiles sadly.

"Messy," she says.

"I had a mate in Iraq, back in the noughties," Craig says. "*That* was messy. Blood and guts. These days, it's just machines and nerds. And the machines can't even kill you. What kind of war is that?"

"I'm not supposed to talk about it," says Aileen.

"Craig," says Sue. "Not now."

"I'm just asking," says Craig. "I had friends in Inverness and somebody with the plague turned it into a giant game of Tetris. Aileen's been in the war, she knows what it's like. We've been worried. I just want to know."

"If she doesn't want to talk about it, she doesn't talk about it," Sue says. "She's home now. Leave her alone."

I look at Craig. The symbiote tells me that this is a mistake. I tell it to shut up.

"She has a point," I say. "It's a bad war. Worse than we know. And you're right, the godplague agents can't kill. But the gods can. Recursively self-optimising AIs don't kill people. Killer cyborgs kill people."

Craig frowns.

"So," he says, "how come you're not out there if you think it's so bad?"

Malcolm's gaze flickers between his sister and his stepfather. *Confusion. Tears.*

I put my fork down. The food has suddenly lost its taste. "I had the plague," I say slowly. "I'm disqualified. I was one of the nerds."

Aileen is standing up now and her eyes are those of a Fury.

"How dare you!" she shouts at Craig. "You have no idea what you're talking about. No idea. You don't get it from the casts. The Fish doesn't want to show you. It's bad, really bad. You want to tell me how bad? I'll tell you."

"Aileen—" I begin, but she silences me with a gesture.

"Yes, Inverness was like a giant Tetris game. Nerds and machines did it. And so we killed them. And do you know what else we saw? Babies. Babies bonded with the godplague. Babies are cruel. Babies know what they want: food, sleep, for all pain to go away. And that's what the godplague gives them. I saw a woman who'd gone mad, she said she'd lost her baby and couldn't find it, even though we could see that she was pregnant. My angel looked at her and said that she had a wormhole in her belly, that the baby was in a little universe of its own. And there was this look in her eyes, this look—"

Aileen's voice breaks. She storms out of the room the same instant Malcolm starts crying. Without thinking, I go after her.

"I was just asking . . ." I hear Craig saying as I slam the door shut behind me.

I find her in the back garden, sitting on the ground next to the angel, one hand wrapped around its leg, and I feel a surge of jealousy.

"Hi," I say. "Mind if I sit down?"

"Go ahead, it's a free patch of grass." She smiles wanly. "I spooked everybody pretty badly back there, didn't I?"

"I think you did. Malcolm is still crying."

"It's just . . . I don't know. It all came out. And then I thought that it doesn't matter if he hears it too, that he plays all these games with much worse stuff going on all the time, that it wouldn't matter. I'm so stupid."

"I think it's the fact that it was *you* telling it," I say slowly. "That makes it true."

She sighs. "You're right. I'm such an arse. I shouldn't have let Craig get me going like that, but we had a rough time up north, and to hear him making light of it like that—"

"It's okay."

"Hey," she says. "I've missed you. You make things make sense."

"I'm glad somebody thinks so."

"Come on," Aileen says, wiping her face. "Let's go for a walk, or better yet, let's go to the pub. I'm still hungry. And I could use a drink. My first leave and I'm still sober. Sergeant Katsuki would disown me if she knew."

"We'll have to see what we can do about that," I say and we start walking toward the harbor.

* * *

I don't know if a girl like Aileen would ever have taken an interest in a guy like me if it hadn't been for the fact that I used to be a god.

Two years ago. University cafeteria. Me, trying to get used to the pale colors of the real world again. Alone. And then three girls sit down in the neighboring table. Pretty. Loud.

"Seriously," says the one with a pastel-colored jacket and a Hello-Kitty-shaped Fish-interface, "I want to do it with a post. Check this out." The girls huddle around her fogscreen. "There's a cast called Postcoital. Sex with gods. This girl is like their *groupie*. Follows them around. I mean, just the cool ones that don't go unstable."

There's a moment of reverent silence.

"Wow!" says the second girl. "I always thought that was an urban legend. Or some sort of staged porn thing."

"Apparently not," says the third.

These days, the nerd rapture is like the 'flu: you can catch it. The godplague is a volition-bonding, recursively self-improving and self-replicating program. A genie that comes to you and makes its home in the machinery around you and tells you that do as thou wilt shall be the whole of the law. It fucks you up, but it's sexy as hell.

"Seriously," says the first girl, "no wonder the guys who wrote Fish were all *guys*. The whole thing is just another penis. It has no regard for female sexuality. I mean, there's no feminist angle *at all* in the whole collective volition thing. Seriously."

"My God!" says the second girl. "That one there. I want to do him, uh, her. It . . . *All* of them. I really do."

"No you don't," I say.

"Excuse me?" She looks at me as if she's just stepped in something unpleasant and wants to wipe it off. "We're having a private conversation here."

"Sure. I just wanted to say that that cast is a fake. And I really wouldn't mess around with the posts if I were you."

"You speak from experience? Got your dick bitten off by a post girl?" For once I'm grateful I need the symbiote: if I ignore its whispers, her face is just a blank mask to me.

There is nervous laughter from the other girls.

"Yes," I say. "I used to be one."

They get up in unison, stare at me for a second and walk away. *Masks,* I think. *Masks.*

A moment later I'm interrupted again.

"I'm sorry," the third girl says. "I mean, really, really sorry. They're not really my friends, we're just doing the same course. I'm Aileen."

"That's OK," I say. "I don't really mind."

Aileen sits on the corner of the table, and I don't really mind that either.

"What was it like?" she asks. Her eyes are very green. *Inquisitive*, says the symbiote. And I realize that I desperately want it to say something else.

"You really want to know?" I ask.

"Yes," she says.

I look at my hands.

"I was a quacker," I say slowly, "a quantum hacker. And when the Fish-source came out, I tinkered with it, just like pretty much every geek on the planet. And I got mine to compile: my own friendly AI slave, an idiot-proof supergoal system, just designed to turn me from a sack of flesh into a Jack Kirby New God, not to harm anybody else. Or so it told me."

I grimace. "My external nervous system took over the Helsinki University of Technology's supercomputing cluster in about thirty seconds. It got pretty ugly after that."

"But you made it," says Aileen, eyes wide.

"Well, back then, the Fish still had the leisure to be gentle. The starfish were there before anybody was irretrievably dead. It burned my AI off like an information cancer and shoved me back into—" I make a show of looking at myself. "Well, this, I guess."

"Wow!" Aileen says, slender fingers wrapped around a cup of latte.

"Yeah," I say. "That's pretty much what I said."

"And how do you feel now? Did it hurt? Do you miss it?"

I laugh.

"I don't really remember most of it. The Fish amputated a

lot of memories. And there was some damage as well." I swallow.

"I'm . . . It's a mild form of Asperger's, more or less. I don't read people very well anymore." I take off my beanie. "This is pretty ugly." I show her the symbiote at the back of my head. Like most Fish-machines, it looks like a starfish. "It's a symbiote. It reads people for me."

She touches it gently and I feel it. The symbiote can map tactile information with much higher resolution than my skin and I can feel the complex contours of Aileen's fingertips gliding on its surface.

"I think it's really pretty," she says. "Like a jewel. Hey, it's warm! What else does it do? Is it like, a Fish-interface? In your head?"

"No. It combs my brain all the time. It makes sure that the thing I was is not hiding in there." I laugh. "It's a shitty thing to be, a washed-up god."

Aileen smiles. *It's a very pretty smile*, says the symbiote. I don't know if it's biased because it's being caressed.

"You have to admit that sounds pretty cool," she says. "Or do you just tell that to all the girls?"

That night she takes me home.

We have fish and chips in the Smuggler's Den. Aileen and I are the only customers; the publican is an old man who greets her by name. The food is fabbed and I find it too greasy, but Aileen eats with apparent relish and washes it down with a pint of beer.

"At least you've still got your appetite," I say.

"Training in the Gobi Desert teaches you to miss food," she says and my heart jumps at the way she brushes her hair back. "My skin cells can do photosynthesis. Stuff you don't get from the fancasts. It's terrible. You always feel hungry, but they don't let you eat. Makes you incredibly alert, though. My pee will be a weird color for the whole weekend because all these nanites will be coming out."

"Thanks for sharing that."

"Sorry. Soldier talk."

"You do feel different," I say.

"You don't," she says.

"Well, I am." I take a sip from my pint, hoping the symbiote will let me get drunk. "I *am* different."

She sighs.

"Thanks for coming. It's good to see you."

"It's okay."

"No, really, it does mean a lot to me, I—"

"Aileen, please." I lock the symbiote. I tell myself I don't know what she's thinking. *Honest.* "You don't have to." I empty my pint. "There's something I've been wondering, actually. I've thought about this a lot. I've had a lot of time. What I mean is—" The words stick in my mouth.

"Go on," says Aileen.

"There's no reason why you *have* to do this, go out there and fight monsters, unless—"

I flinch at the thought, even now.

"Unless you were so angry with me that you had to go kill things, things like I used to be."

Aileen gets up.

"No, that wasn't it," she says. "That wasn't it at all!"

"I hear you. You don't have to shout."

She squeezes her eyes shut. "Turn on your damn symbiote and come with me."

"Where are we going?"

"To the beach, to skip stones."

"Why?" I ask.

"Because I feel like it."

We go down to the beach. It's sunny like it hasn't been for a few months. The huge Fish that floats near the horizon, a diamond starfish almost a mile in diameter, may have something to do with that.

We walk along the line drawn by the surf. Aileen runs ahead, taunting the waves.

There is a nice spot with lots of round, flat stones between two piers. Aileen picks up a few, swings her arm and makes an expert throw, sending one skimming and bouncing across the waves.

"Come on. You try."

I try. The stone flies in a high arc, plummets down and disappears into the water. It doesn't even make a splash.

I laugh, and look at her. Aileen's face is lit by the glow of the starfish in the distance mingled with sunlight. For a moment, she looks just like the girl who brought me here to spend Christmas with her parents.

Then Aileen is crying.

"I'm sorry," she says. "I was going to tell you before I came. But I couldn't."

She clings to me. Waves lap at our feet.

"Aileen, please tell me what's wrong. You know I can't always tell."

She sits down on the wet sand.

"Remember what I told Craig? About the babies."

"Yeah."

Aileen swallows.

"Before I left you," she says, "I had a baby."

At first I think it's just sympathy sex. I don't mind that: I've had that more than a few times, both before and after my brief stint as the Godhead. But Aileen stays. She makes breakfast. She walks to the campus with me in the morning, holding my hand, and laughs at the spamvores chasing ad icons on the street, swirling like multicolored leaves in the wind. I grow her a Fish-interface from my symbiote as a birthday present: it looks like a ladybird. She calls it Mr. Bug.

I'm easy: that's all it takes for me to fall in love.

That winter in Prezzagard passes quickly. We find a flat together in the Stack vertical village, and I pay for it with some scripting hackwork.

And then, one morning, her bed is empty and Mr. Bug sits on her pillow. Her toiletry things are gone from the bathroom. I call her friends, send bots to local sousveillance peernets. No one has seen her. I spend two nights inventing nightmares. Does she have a lover? Did I do something wrong? The symbiote is not infallible, and there are times when I dread saying the wrong thing, just by accident.

She comes back on the morning of the third day. I open the door and there she is, looking pale and dishevelled.

"Where have you been?" I ask. She looks so lost that I want to hold her, but she pushes me away.

Hate, says the symbiote. *Hate*.

"Sorry," she says, tears rolling down her cheeks. "I just came to get my things. I have to go."

I try to say something, that I don't understand, that we can work this out, that nothing's so bad she can't tell me about it, and if it's my fault, I'll fix it. I want to plead. I want to beg. But the hate is a fiery aura around her that silences me and I watch quietly as the Fish-drones carry her life away.

"Don't ask me to explain," she says at the door. "Look after Mr. Bug."

After she's gone, I want to tear the symbiote out of my skull. I want the black worm that is hiding in my mind to come out and take over again, make me a god who is above pain and love and hate, a god who can fly. Things go hazy for a while. I think I try to open the window and make a three-hundred-meter dive, but the Fish in the walls and the glass won't let me: this is a cruel world we've made, a lovingly cruel world that won't let us hurt ourselves.

At some point, the symbiote puts me to sleep. It does it again when I wake up, after I start breaking things. And again, until some sort of Pavlovian reflex kicks in.

Later, I spend long nights trawling through the images in Mr. Bug's lifecache: I try to figure it out by using the symbiote to pattern-match emotions from the slices of our life together. But there's nothing that hasn't been resolved, nothing that would linger and fester. Unless I'm getting it all wrong.

It's something that's happened before, I tell myself. *I touch the sky and fall. Nothing new*.

And so I sleep-walk. Graduate. Work. Write Fish-scripts. Forget. Tell myself I'm over it.

Then Aileen calls and I get the first train north.

I listen to the sound of her heartbeat, trying to understand her words. They tumble through my mind, too heavy for me to grasp.

"Aileen. Jesus, Aileen."

The god hiding in my mind, in the dead parts, in my cells, in my DNA—

Suddenly, I want to throw up.

"I didn't know what was happening, at first," says Aileen, her voice flat and colorless. "I felt strange. I just wanted to be alone, somewhere high and far away. So I went to one of the empty flats up at the Stacktop—one of the freshly grown ones—to spend the night and think. Then I got really hungry. I mean, really, really hungry. So I ate fabbed food, lots and lots. And then my belly started growing."

With the Fish around, contraception is the default state of things unless one actually *wants* a baby. But there had been that night in Pittenweem, just after Christmas, beyond the Wall where the Fish-spores that fill the air in Prezzagard are few. And I could just see it happening, the godseed in my brain hacking my cells, making tiny molecular machines much smaller than sperm, carrying DNA laden with code, burrowing into Aileen.

"It didn't feel strange. There was no pain. I lay down, my waters broke and it just pulled itself out. It was the most beautiful thing I'd ever seen," she says, smiling. "It had your eyes and these tiny, tiny fingers. Each had the most perfect fingernail. It looked at me and smiled."

"It waved at me. Like . . . like it decided that it didn't need me anymore. And then the walls just *opened* and it flew away. My baby. Flew away."

The identification mechanism I used to slave the godseed was just my DNA. It really didn't occur to me that there was a loophole there. It could make my volition its own. Reinvent itself. And once it did that, it could modify itself as much as it pleased. Grow wings, if it wanted.

I hold Aileen. We're both wet and shivering, but I don't care.

"I'm sorry. That night I came to tell you," she says. "And then I saw it looking at me again. From your eyes. I had to go away."

"So you joined the Corps."

She sighs.

"Yes. It helped. Doing something, being needed."

"I needed you too," I say.

"I know. I'm sorry."

Anger wells up in my throat. "So is it working? Are you guys defeating the superbabies and the dark lords? Does it make you happy?"

She flinches away from me. "You sound like Craig now."

"Well, what am I supposed to say? I'm sorry about the baby. *But it wasn't your fault.* Or mine."

"It was you who—" She lifts her hand to her mouth. "Sorry, I didn't mean that. I didn't mean that."

"Go back to your penance and leave me alone."

I start running along the waterline, heading nowhere in particular.

The angel is waiting for me on the shore.

"Hello, Jukka," it says. "Good to see you again."

As always, the voice is androgynous and pleasant. It tickles something in my brain. It is the voice of the Fish.

"Hi."

"Can I help you?"

"Not really. Unless you want to give her up. Make her see sense."

"I can't interfere with her decisions," says the angel. "That's not what I do. I only give you—and her—what you want, or what you would want if you were smarter. That's my supergoal. You know that."

"You self-righteous bastard. The collective volition of humanity is that she must go and fight monsters? And probably die in the process? Is it supposed to be *character-forming* or something?"

The angel says nothing, but it's got me going now.

"And I can't even be sure that it's Aileen's own decision. This—this thing in my head—it's you. You could have let the godseed escape, just to hurt Aileen enough to get her to sign up to your bloody kamikaze squadron. And the chances are that you knew that I was going to come here and rant at you and there's nothing I can do to stop her. Or is there?"

The angel considers this.

"If I could do that, the world would be perfect already." It cocks its glass head to one side. "But perhaps there is some-one who wanted you to be here."

"Don't try to play head games with me!"

Anger rushes out of me like a river. I pound the angel's chest with my fists. Its skin flows away like a soap bubble.

"Jukka!"

The voice comes from somewhere far away.

"Jukka, stop," says Aileen. "Stop, you idiot!"

She yanks me around with irresistible strength. "Look at me! It wasn't the Fish. It wasn't you. It wasn't the baby. It was *me*. I want to do this. Why won't you let me?"

I look at her, my eyes brimming.

"Because I can't come with you."

"You silly boy," she says, and now it's her holding me as I cry, for the first time since I stopped being a god. "Silly, silly boy."

After a while, I run out of tears. We sit on a rock, watching the sun set. I feel light and empty.

"Maybe it would have been easier if you hadn't called," I say, sighing.

Aileen's eyes widen.

"What do you mean? I never did. I thought Craig did. It would have been just like him. To keep me from going back."

And then we see the baby.

It is bald and naked and pink, and a hair-thin silver umbilical hangs from its navel. Its eyes are green like Aileen's, but their gaze is mine. It floats in the air, its perfect tiny toes almost touching the water.

The baby looks at us and laughs: the sound is like the peal of silver bells. Its mouth is full of pearly teeth.

"Be very still," says Aileen.

The angel moves toward the baby. Its hands explode into fractal razor bushes. A glass cannon forms in its chest. Tiny spheres of light, quantum dots pumped full of energy, dart toward the baby.

The baby laughs again. It holds out its tiny hands, and *squeezes*. The air—and perhaps space, and time—wavers and twists. And then the angel is gone, and our baby is holding a tiny sphere of glass, like a snow-globe.

Aileen grabs my arm.

"Don't worry," she whispers. "The big skyFish must have seen this. It'll do something. Stay calm."

"Bad baby," I say slowly. "You broke Mummy's angel."

The baby frowns. I can see the cosmic anger simmering behind the wrinkled pink forehead.

"Jukka—" Aileen says, but I interrupt her.

"You only know how to *kill* gods. I know how to *talk* to them." I look at my—*son*, says the little wrinkly thing between its legs—and take a step toward him. I remember what it's like, having all the power in the world. There's a need that comes with it, a need to make things perfect.

"I know why you brought us here," I say. "You want us to be together, don't you? Mummy and Daddy." I go down to one knee and look my son in the eye. I'm in the water now and so close to him that I can feel the warmth of his skin.

"And I know what you're thinking. I've been there. You could take us apart. You could rebuild our minds. You could *make* us want to be together, to be with you." I pause and touch his nose with my forefinger. "But it doesn't work that way. It would never be perfect. It would never be right." I sigh. "Trust me, I know. I did it to myself. But you are something new, you can do better."

I take Mr. Bug from my pocket and hold it out to my son. He grabs it and puts it into his mouth. I take a deep breath, but he doesn't bite.

"Talk to the bug," I say. "He'll tell you who we are. Then come back."

The baby closes its eyes. Then he giggles, mouth full of an insect-shaped AI, and touches my nose with a tiny hand.

I hear Aileen gasp. A lightning horse gallops through my brain, thunder rumbling in its wake.

Something wet on my face wakes me. I open my eyes and see Aileen's face against the dark sky. It is raining.

"Are you okay?" she asks, almost in tears, cradling my head. "That little bastard!"

Her eyes widen. And suddenly, there is a silence in my mind, a wholeness. I see the wonder in her eyes.

Aileen holds out her hand. My symbiote is lying in her palm. I take it, turning it between my fingers. I take a good swing and throw it into the sea. It skims the surface three times, and then it's gone.

"I wonder where he gets it from."

When the Great Days Came

GARDNER R. DOZOIS

Gardner R. Dozois lives in Philadelphia, Pennsylvania. He recently retired from the editorship of Asimov's, *after winning 13 Hugo Awards as best editor, and establishing* Asimov's *as the leading magazine of the day in SF. Before that, he was one of the leading anthologists in SF, and he continues to be very active as an anthologist. He has published nearly sixty anthologies, sometimes co-edited with others, often Jack M. Dann. His most prominent anthology since 1984 is the annual* Year's Best Science Fiction, *a recasting and expansion of* Best SF Stories of the Year, *which he edited from 1977 to 1987 (5 volumes). He began writing SF in the 1960s, and has published fiction throughout his career, though less often since 1984. Some of his stories are collected in* The Visible Man *(1977),* Slow Dancing Through Time *(1990),* Geodesic Dreams *(1992), and* Morning Child and Other Stories *(2004).*

"When the Great Days Came" was published in Fantasy & Science Fiction. *It is an amusing tale that proves that even the end of the world as we know it might look quite different to a rat. It's all a matter of point of view.*

The rat slunk down the dark alley, keeping close to the comforting bulk of the brick wall of an abandoned warehouse, following scent trails that it and thousands of its kind had laid down countless times before. It stopped to snatch up a cockroach, crunching it in its strong jaws, and to sniff at a frozen patch of garbage, and then scurried on. Above it, the stars shone bright and cold where a patch of night sky looked down into the deep stone canyon of the alleyway.

It was in an alley near 10th and Broadway, in New York City, although the human terms meant nothing to it, but as far as the world it lived in and the kind of life it led in that world was concerned, it would have made very little difference if it had been in any big city in the world.

It's tempting to give the rat an anthropomorphic humanized name like Sleektail or Sharptooth or Longwhiskers, but in fact the only "name" it had was a scent-signature composed of pheromones and excretions from its scent-glands, the tang of its breath, and the hot rich smell of its anus; so it had no name that could be even approximately rendered in human terms, nor would the human concept of a name, with all the freight of implications that go with it, have meant anything to it.

The rat emerged from the alley, and shrank back as a car flashed by in a sudden burst of light and wind and the perception of hurtling mass, and a stink of rubber and burning gasoline you could smell coming blocks away. One of its litter-mates had been killed by one of these monsters back in

the summer, almost half a lifetime ago, and the rat had been
wary of them ever since. When the car had passed, leaving
the night quiet again in its wake, the rat reared up to sniff the
air for a moment, then lowered itself down to follow the
curb, keeping its shoulder brushing against it as it ran.

At the corner of a side street, an inch-wide hole had been
gnawed under one of the concrete sidewalk slabs. The rat
paused to collapse its skeleton and change the shape of its
head, and then squeezed through the hole into the tunnel beyond.

(It wouldn't do to leave you with the impression that there
was anything unusual about this. The rat wasn't a mutant or
a shapeshifting alien—it was just a rat. All of its millions of
brethren had this ability, as did many other rodents, their
skulls not being plated together like those of other mammals, so that they could squeeze themselves through an
opening three-quarters of an inch wide, or smaller, depending on the size of the rat.)

Once under the sidewalk, the rat entered a world that humans never saw, and which they couldn't have accessed
even if they knew about it: a three-dimensional space
wrapped in a madly complex skein around and under and
within the human world, like something from an Escher
print, a world composed of spaces and tunnels under the
sidewalks and streets, of subway tunnels (some of them, including whole lost stations, abandoned for almost a hundred
years), of forgotten basements and sub-basements and sub-
sub-basements, of ineffectually boarded-up warehouses and
decaying brownstones, of sewers, of service tunnels through
which ran pipes conveying steam or water or electricity or
gas, of alleys and trash-strewn tenement backyards, of dis-
used pipes at construction sites, of runways through the
bushes and deep tangled undergrowth of urban parks and
squares, of the maze of low roofs and crumbling chimneys
that broke around the flanks of newer skyscrapers like a
scummy brick-and-tarpaper surf (although the lordly skyscrapers too had places visited by rats, in the deep roots of
the buildings where humans seldom went), and of the crawlspaces between floors and under the floorboards and inside

the walls of almost every building in the city. The rat rarely ventured more than a few blocks from its burrow, but if it had wanted to, it could have traveled from tunnel to chamber to tunnel—ducking out from a crack in a foundation, up a drain-spout, across a roof, in again at a sewer grate—all the way across Manhattan to the Bronx and back to Brooklyn without ever coming out into the open air for more than a few seconds at a time.

Now it followed a narrow tunnel down to a widened-out chamber lined with torn-up newspapers and trash bags and shopping bags, the place where it and a dozen of its brothers and sisters had been born, and where it still slept many nights with an assortment of other bachelors. It would be anthropomorphizing again to ascribe human feelings of sentiment or nostalgia to the rat, although as it paused to sniff the heavy, cloying odors of the burrow, perhaps it's not too much to suggest that it gained some comfort or a feeling of momentary security from the long-familiar scents. Then it was off again, down another, longer tunnel that led out, from a hole behind a drainspout, into another alley.

It wasn't looking for anything in particular—it was just *looking*. It had spent most of the nights of its life like this, restlessly pacing from place to place to place within its range, with no particular goal or destination in mind, but instantly ready to take advantage of whatever opportunities it came across on the way.

The rat stopped to lap up some Coke from a tossed-out soft-drink cup, relishing the sudden sharp sweetness, then ducked into a building through a hole gnawed in the molding, and into the dusty maze of crawlspaces between floors and ceilings, and behind walls. Whiskers twitching with sudden interest, it followed the scent of a receptive female, and found her among long-shuttered boxes and shrouded furniture in an attic, but a bigger rat—a veteran almost two years old—had found her first and was already mounting her. The bigger rat growled at him over her back without missing a stroke, showing yellowed fangs, and, resentfully, the rat retreated, back into the interior spaces between walls, then out onto a roof in the cold night air.

There was a smell of cat here, and while the rat wasn't too worried about cats (few of whom would tackle a full-grown rat), caution prompted it to move on anyway. It ghosted across a roof, across a connecting roof, and then into a space left where a brick had fallen out of a long-dead chimney. Down the chimney shaft to a fireplace which had had a sheet of tin clumsily nailed over it decades before, out through one sagging corner, and into a room filled with the ghostly, sheet-covered hulks of crumbling, mildewed Victorian furniture—the kind of place, if this were a fantasy, where it might have stopped to consult with a wise old Rat King tied tail to tail to tail, but which in reality contained only the crisscrossing traceries of tiny footprints in the deep dust of the floor. Into a hole in the kitchen baseboard, out into an enclosed tenement yard cluttered with broken chairs and an overturned swing set, all buried in weeds, out under the bottom of a board fence, and into another dank alley, following now the enticing scent of food.

This was prime scavenging territory, an alley behind a block that contained three or four restaurants and fast-food places, always filled with easily gnawed-through green trash bags and overflowing metal garbage barrels. The rat sniffed around the barrels, nosed half a gnawed hot-dog and some Cheese Doodles out from under a clutter of plastic trash and cans, swallowed the food hurriedly, and then found a real prize: a discarded pizza box with two pieces of pizza still inside.

Most rats love pizza, and this rat was no exception. It had just settled down contentedly to gnaw on a slice of Sicilian when a wave of alien stink and the clatter of heavy, clumsy footsteps told it that a human was coming. And there it was, lumbering ponderously down the alley, a vast, shambling giant that seemed to tower impossibly into the sky.

For a moment, the rat held its position defiantly astride the pizza box, but then the human spotted it and yelled something at it in its huge, blaring, bellowing voice.

The resentment the rat had felt when it had been chased

away from the willing female earlier returned, sharper and hotter and fiercer than ever. The rat was an exceptionally bright rat, but, of course, it was just a rat, and so it didn't have the words, or the concepts that grew from the words, to articulate the feelings that roiled within it. If it *had* had the words, it might almost have been able, for a flickering moment, to dream of a world where things were different, a day when rats didn't have to give way to humans, when they could go where they wanted to go and do what they wanted to do without having to scurry away and hide whenever a human came near.

But it didn't have the words, and so the vision it had almost grasped guttered and died without ever quite coming into full focus, leaving only the tiniest smoky shard of itself behind in its mind.

The rat stood its ground for a second longer, an act of almost insane bravery in its own context, but then the human bellowed again and threw a bottle at it, and the rat darted away, leaving the prize behind, vanishing instantly behind the garbage barrels and away unseen down the alley, keeping to the shadows.

As Fate would have it, it was the very same rat, an hour later, up on another tarpaper tenement roof, sniffing at a box of Moo Shu Pork spilling out of a green trash bag that the tenants had been too lazy to take downstairs to the curb, who saw a trail of fire cut suddenly across the winter sky, and who reared up on its hind legs in time to see the glowing disk of the six-mile-wide asteroid pass over the city, on its way to a collision with a hillside north of Chibougamau in Northern Quebec.

The rat watched, sitting back on its haunches, as the glowing thing passed below the horizon. A moment later, the northern sky turned red, a glow that spread from horizon to horizon east to west, as if the sun were coming up in the wrong place, and then a bright pillar of fire climbed up over the horizon, and grew and grew and grew. Already the blast-front of the impact was rushing over the ground toward the city at close to a thousand miles per hour, a blow that would ultimately wipe the human race as well as the rat itself and most—but not *all*—of its kin off the face of the Earth.

Moments from death, the rat had no way to know it, but—after a pause for millions of years of evolution, and for radiating out to fill soon-to-be-vacated ecological niches—its day had come round at last.

Second Person, Present Tense

DARYL GREGORY

Daryl Gregory (darylgregory.com) lives in State College, Pennsylvania, with his wife, a psychologist and university professor, and their two children. He is a full-time writer, although half of what he writes is web code for a software company. His stories have appeared in Asimov's Science Fiction Magazine, The Magazine of Fantasy & Science Fiction, Amazing Stories, *and elsewhere. He's working on his first novel, a science-fantasy about demonic possession and golden age comics.*

"Second Person, Present Tense" appeared in Asimov's, *and is certainly one of the stories that made that magazine a leader in the field in 2005. Gregory postulates a drug that can destroy the construction of self. A teenage girl overdosed, and the new replacement self has been, in effect, raised for a couple of years by her neurologist. Now she has to go back to the family that raised the original personality that she can remember, but whom she is not. Good science and good writing make this story a candidate for the single best SF story of the year.*

If you think, "I breathe," the "I" is extra. There is no you to say "I." What we call "I" is just a swinging door which moves when we inhale or when we exhale.
—Shun Ryu Suzuki

I used to think the brain was the most important organ in the body, until I realized who was telling me that.
—Emo Phillips

W hen I enter the office, Dr. S is leaning against the desk, talking earnestly to the dead girl's parents. He isn't happy, but when he looks up he puts on a smile for me. "And here she is," he says, like a game show host revealing the grand prize. The people in the chairs turn, and Dr. Subramaniam gives me a private, encouraging wink.

The father stands first, a blotchy, square-faced man with a tight belly he carries like a basketball. As in our previous visits, he is almost frowning, struggling to match his face to his emotions. The mother, though, has already been crying, and her face is wide open: joy, fear, hope, relief. It's way over the top.

"Oh, Therese," she says. "Are you ready to come home?"

Their daughter was named Therese. She died of an overdose almost two years ago, and since then Mitch and Alice Klass have visited this hospital dozens of times, looking for her. They desperately want me to be their daughter, and so in their heads I already am.

My hand is still on the door handle. "Do I have a choice?" On paper I'm only seventeen years old. I have no money, no credit cards, no job, no car. I own only a handful of clothes. And Robierto, the burliest orderly on the ward, is in the hallway behind me, blocking my escape.

Therese's mother seems to stop breathing for a moment. She's a slim, narrow-boned woman who seems tall until she stands next to anyone. Mitch raises a hand to her shoulder, then drops it.

As usual, whenever Alice and Mitch come to visit, I feel like I've walked into the middle of a soap opera and no one's given me my lines. I look directly at Dr. S, and his face is frozen into that professional smile. Several times over the past year he's convinced them to let me stay longer, but they're not listening anymore. They're my legal guardians, and they have Other Plans. Dr. S looks away from me, rubs the side of his nose.

"That's what I thought," I say.

The father scowls. The mother bursts into fresh tears, and she cries all the way out of the building. Dr. Subramaniam watches from the entrance as we drive away, his hands in his pockets. I've never been so angry with him in my life—all two years of it.

The name of the drug is Zen, or Zombie, or just Z. Thanks to Dr. S I have a pretty good idea of how it killed Therese.

"Flick your eyes to the left," he told me one afternoon. "Now glance to the right. Did you see the room blur as your eyes moved?" He waited until I did it again. "No blur. No one sees it."

This is the kind of thing that gets brain doctors hot and bothered. Not only could no one see the blur, their brains edited it out completely. Skipped over it—left view, then right view, with nothing between—then fiddled with the person's time sense so that it didn't even *seem* missing.

The scientists figured out that the brain was editing out shit all the time. They wired up patients and told them to lift one of their fingers, move it any time they wanted. Each time, the brain started the signal traveling toward the finger up to 120 milliseconds *before* the patient consciously decided to move it. Dr. S said you could see the brain warming up right before the patient consciously thought, *now*.

This is weird, but it gets weirder the longer you think about it. And I've been thinking about this a lot.

The conscious mind—the "I" that's thinking, hey, I'm thirsty, I'll reach for that cold cup of water—hasn't really decided anything. The signal to start moving your hand has already traveled halfway down your arm by the time *you* even realize *you* are thirsty. *Thought* is an afterthought. By the way, the brain says, we've decided to move your arm, so please have the thought to move it.

The gap is normally 120 milliseconds, max. Zen extends this minutes. Hours.

If you run into somebody who's on Zen, you won't notice much. The person's brain is still making decisions, and the body still follows orders. You can talk to the them, and they can talk to you. You can tell each other jokes, go out for hamburgers, do homework, have sex.

But the person isn't conscious. There is no "I" there. You might as well be talking to a computer. And *two* people on Zen—"you" and "I"—are just puppets talking to puppets.

It's a little girl's room strewn with teenager. Stuffed animals crowd the shelves and window sills, shoulder to shoulder with stacks of Christian rock CDs and hair brushes and bottles of nail polish. Pin-ups from *Teen People* are taped to the wall, next to a bulletin board dripping with soccer ribbons and rec league gymnastics medals going back to second grade. Above the desk, a plaque titled "I Promise . . ." exhorting Christian youth to abstain from premarital sex. And everywhere taped and pinned to the walls, the photos: Therese at Bible camp, Therese on the balance beam, Therese with her arms around her youth group friends. Every morning she could open her eyes to a thousand reminders of who she was, who she'd been, who she was supposed to become.

I pick up the big stuffed panda that occupies the place of pride on the bed. It looks older than me, and the fur on the face is worn down to the batting. The button eyes hang by white thread—they've been re-sewn, maybe more than once.

Therese's father sets down the pitifully small bag that contains everything I've taken from the hospital: toiletries, a couple of changes of clothes, and five of Dr. S's books. "I guess old Boo Bear was waiting for you," he says.

"Boo W. Bear."

"Yes, Boo W!" It pleases him that I know this. As if it proves anything. "You know, your mother dusted this room every week. She never doubted that you'd come back."

I have never been here, and *she* is not coming back, but already I'm tired of correcting pronouns. "Well, that was nice," I say.

"She's had a tough time of it. She knew people were talking, probably holding her responsible—both of us, really. And she was worried about them saying things about you. She couldn't stand them thinking that you were a wild girl."

"Them?"

He blinks. "The Church."

Ah. *The Church.* The term carried so many feelings and connotations for Therese that months ago I stopped trying to sort them out. The Church was the red-brick building of the Davenport Church of Christ, shafts of dusty light through rows of tall, glazed windows shaped like gravestones. The Church was God and the Holy Ghost (but not Jesus—he was personal, separate somehow). Mostly, though, it was the congregation, dozens and dozens of people who'd known her since before she was born. They loved her, they watched out for her, and they evaluated her every step. It was like having a hundred overprotective parents.

I almost laugh. "The Church thinks Therese was wild?"

He scowls, but whether because I've insulted the Church or because I keep referring to his daughter by name, I'm not sure. "Of course not. It's just that you caused a lot of worry." His voice has assumed a sober tone that's probably never failed to unnerve his daughter. "You know, the Church prayed for you every week."

"They did?" I do know Therese well enough to be sure this would have mortified her. She was a pray-er, not a pray-ee.

Therese's father watches my face for the bloom of shame, maybe a few tears. From contrition it should have been one small step to confession. It's hard for me to take any of this seriously.

I sit down on the bed and sink deep into the mattress. This is not going to work. The double bed takes up most of the room, with only a few feet of open space around it. Where am I going to meditate?

"Well," Therese's father says. His voice has softened. Maybe he thinks he's won. "You probably want to get changed," he says.

He goes to the door but doesn't leave. I stand by the window, but I can feel him there, waiting. Finally the oddness of this makes me turn around.

He's staring at the floor, a hand behind his neck. Therese might have been able to intuit his mood, but it's beyond me.

"We want to help you, Therese. But there's so many things we just don't understand. Who gave you the drugs, why you went off with that boy, why you would—" His hand moves, a stifled gesture that could be anger, or just frustration. "It's just . . . hard."

"I know," I say. "Me too."

He shuts the door when he leaves, and I push the panda to the floor and flop onto my back in relief. Poor Mr. Klass. He just wants to know if his daughter fell from grace, or was pushed.

When I want to freak myself out, "I" think about "me" thinking about having an "I." The only thing stupider than puppets talking to puppets is a puppet talking to itself.

Dr. S says that nobody knows what the mind is, or how the brain generates it, and nobody *really* knows about consciousness. We talked almost every day while I was in the hospital, and after he saw that I was interested in this stuff—how could I *not* be?—he gave me books and we'd talk about brains and how they cook up thoughts and make decisions.

"How do I explain this?" he always starts. And then he tries out the metaphors he's working on for his book. My favorite is the Parliament, the Page, and the Queen.

"The brain isn't one thing, of course," he told me. "It's millions of firing cells, and those resolve into hundreds of active sites, and so it is with the mind. There are dozens of nodes in the mind, each one trying to out-shout the others. For any decision, the mind erupts with noise, and that triggers . . . how do I explain this . . . Have you ever seen the British Parliament on C-SPAN?" Of course I had: in a hospital, TV is a constant companion. "These members of the mind's parliament, they're all shouting in chemicals and electrical charges, until enough of the voices are shouting in unison. Ding! That's a 'thought,' a 'decision.' The Parliament immediately sends a signal to the body to act on the decision, and at the same time it tells the Page to take the news—"

"Wait, who's the Page?"

He waves his hand. "That's not important right now." (Weeks later, in a different discussion, Dr. S will explain that the Page isn't one thing, but a cascade of neural events in the temporal area of the limbic system that meshes the neural map of the new thought with the existing neural map—but by then I know that "neural map" is just another metaphor for another deeply complex thing or process, and that I'll never get to the bottom of this. Dr. S said not to worry about it, that *nobody* gets to the bottom of it.) "The Page takes the news of the decision to the Queen."

"All right then, who's the Queen? Consciousness?"

"Exactly right! The self itself."

He beamed at me, his attentive student. Talking about this stuff gets Dr. S going like nothing else, but he's oblivious to the way I let the neck of my scrubs fall open when I stretch out on the couch. If only I could have tucked the two hemispheres of my brain into a lace bra.

"The Page," he said, "delivers its message to Her Majesty, telling her what the Parliament has decided. The Queen doesn't need to know about all the other arguments that went on, all the other possibilities that were thrown out. She simply needs to know what to announce to her subjects. The Queen tells the parts of the body to act on the decision."

"Wait, I thought the Parliament had already sent out the signal. You said before that you can see the brain warming up before the self even knows about it."

"That's the joke. The Queen announces the decision, and she thinks that her subjects are obeying her commands, but in reality, they have already been told what to do. They're already reaching for their glasses of water."

I pad down to the kitchen in bare feet, wearing Therese's sweatpants and a T-shirt. The shirt is a little tight; Therese, champion dieter and Olympic-level purger, was a bit smaller than me.

Alice is at the table, already dressed, a book open in front of her. "Well, you slept in this morning," she says brightly. Her face is made up, her hair sprayed into place. The coffee cup next to the book is empty. She's been waiting for hours.

I look around for a clock, and find one over the door. It's only nine. At the hospital I slept in later than that all the time. "I'm starved," I say. There's a refrigerator, a stove, and dozens of cabinets.

I've never made my own breakfast. Or any lunch or dinner, for that matter. For my entire life, my meals have been served on cafeteria trays. "Do you have scrambled eggs?"

She blinks. "Eggs? You don't—" She abruptly stands. "Sure. Sit down, Therese, and I'll make you some."

"Just call me 'Terry,' okay?"

Alice stops, thinks about saying something—I can almost hear the clank of cogs and ratchets—until she abruptly strides to the cabinet, crouches, and pulls out a non-stick pan.

I take a guess on which cabinet holds the coffee mugs, guess right, and take the last inch of coffee from the pot. "Don't you have to go to work?" I say. Alice does something at a restaurant supply company; Therese has always been hazy on the details.

"I've taken a leave," she says. She cracks an egg against the edge of the pan, does something subtle with the shells as

the yolk squeezes out and plops into the pan, and folds the
shell halves into each other. All with one hand.

"Why?"

She smiles tightly. "We couldn't just abandon you after
getting you home. I thought we might need some time together. During this adjustment period."

"So when do I have to see this therapist? Whatsisname."
My executioner.

"Her. Dr. Mehldau's in Baltimore, so we'll drive there
tomorrow." This is their big plan. Dr. Subramaniam
couldn't bring back Therese, so they're running to anyone
who says they can. "You know, she's had a lot of success
with people in your situation. That's her book." She nods
at the table.

"So? Dr. Subramaniam is writing one too." I pick up the
book. *The Road Home: Finding the Lost Children of Zen.*
"What if I don't go along with this?"

She says nothing, chopping at the eggs. I'll be eighteen in
four months. Dr. S said that it will become a lot harder for
them to hold me then. This ticking clock sounds constantly
in my head, and I'm sure it's loud enough for Alice and
Mitch to hear it too.

"Let's just try Dr. Mehldau first."

"First? What then?" She doesn't answer. I flash on an image of me tied down to the bed, a priest making a cross over
my twisting body. It's a fantasy, not a Therese memory—I
can tell the difference. Besides, if this had already happened
to Therese, it wouldn't have been a priest.

"Okay then," I say. "What if I just run away?"

"If you turn into a fish," she says lightly, "then I will turn
into a fisherman and fish for you."

"What?" I'm laughing. I haven't heard Alice speak in
anything but straightforward, earnest sentences.

Alice's smile is sad. "You don't remember?"

"Oh, yeah." The memory clicks. "*Runaway Bunny.* Did
she like that?"

Dr. S's book is about me. Well, Zen O.D.-ers in general, but
there are only a couple thousand of us. Z's not a hugely

popular drug, in the U.S. or anywhere else. It's not a hallu-
cinogen. It's not a euphoric or a depressant. You don't
speed, mellow out, or even get high in the normal sense. It's
hard to see what the attraction is. Frankly, *I* have trouble
seeing it.

Dr. S says that most drugs aren't about making you feel
better, they're about not feeling anything at all. They're
about numbness, escape. And Zen is a kind of arty, designer
escape hatch. Zen disables the Page, locks him in his room,
so that he can't make his deliveries to the Queen. There's no
update to the neural map, and the Queen stops hearing what
Parliament is up to. With no orders to bark, she goes silent.
It's that silence that people like Therese craved.

But the real attraction—again, for people like Therese—is
the overdose. Swallow way too much Zen and the Page can't
get out for weeks. When he finally gets out, he can't remember the way back to the Queen's castle. The whole process
of updating the self that's been going on for years is suddenly derailed. The silent Queen can't be found.

The Page, poor guy, does the only thing he can. He goes
out and delivers the proclamations to the first girl he sees.

The Queen is dead. Long live the Queen.

"Hi, Terry. I'm Dr. Mehldau." She's a stubby woman with a
pleasant round face, and short dark hair shot with gray. She
offers me her hand. Her fingers are cool and thin.

"You called me Terry."

"I was told that you prefer to go by that. Do you want me
to call you something else?"

"No . . . I just expected you to make me say my name is
'Therese' over and over."

She laughs and sits down in a red leather chair that looks
soft but sturdy. "I don't think that would be very helpful, do
you? I can't make you do anything you don't want to do,
Terry."

"So I'm free to go."

"Can't stop you. But I do have to report back to your parents on how we're doing."

My parents.

She shrugs. "It's my job. Why don't you have a seat and we can talk about why you're here."

The chair opposite her is cloth, not leather, but it's still nicer than anything in Dr. Subramaniam's office. The entire office is nicer than Dr. S's office. Daffodil walls in white trim, big windows glowing behind white cloth shades, tropically colored paintings.

I don't sit down.

"Your job is to turn me into Mitch and Alice's daughter. I'm not going to do that. So any time we spend talking is just bullshit."

"Terry, no one can turn you into something you're not."

"Well then we're done here." I walk across the room—though "stroll" is what I'm shooting for—and pick up an African-looking wooden doll from the bookshelf. The shelves are decorated with enough books to look serious, but there are long open spaces for arty arrangements of candlesticks and Japanese fans and plaques that advertise awards and appreciations. Dr. S's bookshelves are for holding books, and books stacked on books. Dr. Mehldau's bookshelves are for selling the idea of Dr. Mehldau.

"So what are you, a psychiatrist or a psychologist or what?" I've met all kinds in the hospital. The psychiatrists are MDs like Dr. S and can give you drugs. I haven't figured out what the psychologists are good for.

"Neither," she says. "I'm a counselor."

"So what's the 'doctor' for?"

"Education." Her voice didn't change, but I get the impression that the question's annoyed her. This makes me strangely happy.

"Okay, Dr. Counselor, what are you supposed to counsel me about? I'm not crazy. I know who Therese was, I know what she did, I know that she used to walk around in my body." I put the doll back in its spot next to a glass cube that could be a paperweight. "But I'm not her. This is my body, and I'm not going to kill myself just so Alice and Mitch can have their baby girl back."

"Terry, no one's asking you to kill yourself. Nobody can even make you into who you were before."

"Yeah? Then what are they paying you for, then?"

"Let me try to explain. Please, sit down. Please."

I look around for a clock and finally spot one on a high shelf. I mentally set the timer to five minutes and sit opposite her, hands on my knees. "Shoot."

"Your parents asked me to talk to you because I've helped other people in your situation, people who've overdosed on Z."

"Help them what? Pretend to be something they're not?"

"I help them take back what they *are*. Your experience of the world tells you that Therese was some other person. No one's denying that. But you're in a situation where biologically and legally, you're Therese Klass. Do you have plans for dealing with that?"

As a matter of fact I do, and it involves getting the hell out as soon as possible. "I'll deal with it," I say.

"What about Alice and Mitch?"

I shrug. "What about them?"

"They're still your parents, and you're still their child. The overdose convinced you that you're a new person, but that hasn't changed who they are. They're still responsible for you, and they still care for you."

"Not much I can do about that."

"You're right. It's a fact of your life. You have two people who love you, and you're going to be with each other for the rest of your lives. You're going to have to figure out how to relate to each other. Zen may have burned the bridge between you and your past life, but you can build that bridge again."

"Doc, I don't *want* to build that bridge. Look, Alice and Mitch seem like nice people, but if I was looking for parents, I'd pick someone else."

Dr. Mehldau smiles. "None of us get to choose our parents, Terry."

I'm not in the mood to laugh. I nod toward the clock. "This is a waste of time."

She leans forward. I think she's going to try to touch me, but she doesn't. "Terry, you're not going to disappear if we talk about what happened to you. You'll still be here. The only difference is that you'll reclaim those memories as your own. You can get your old life back *and* choose your new life."

Sure, it's that easy. I get to sell my soul and keep it too.

I can't remember my first weeks in the hospital, though Dr. S says I was awake. At some point I realized that time was passing, or rather, that there was a me who was passing through time. *I* had lasagna for dinner yesterday, *I* am having meat loaf today. *I* am this girl in a bed. I think I realized this and forgot it several times before I could hold onto it.

Every day was mentally exhausting, because everything was so relentlessly *new*. I stared at the TV remote for a half hour, the name for it on the tip of my tongue, and it wasn't until the nurse picked it up and turned on the TV for me that I thought: *Remote*. And then sometimes, this was followed by a raft of other ideas: *TV. Channel. Gameshow*.

People were worse. They called me by a strange name, and they expected things of me. But to me, every visitor, from the night shift nurse to the janitor to Alice and Mitch Klass, seemed equally important—which is to say, not important at all.

Except for Dr. S. He was there from the beginning, and so he was familiar before I met him. He belonged to me like my own body.

But everything else about the world—the names, the details, the *facts*—had to be hauled into the sunlight, one by one. My brain was like an attic, chock full of old and interesting things jumbled together in no order at all.

I only gradually understood that somebody must have owned this house before me. And then I realized the house was haunted.

After the Sunday service, I'm caught in a stream of people. They lean across the pews to hug Alice and Mitch, then me. They pat my back, squeeze my arms, kiss my cheeks. I know from brief dips into Therese's memories that many of these people are as emotionally close as aunts or uncles. And any of them, if Therese were ever in trouble, would take her in, feed her, and give her a bed to sleep in.

This is all very nice, but the constant petting has me ready to scream.

All I want to do is get back home and take off this dress. I had no choice but to wear one of Therese's girly-girl extravaganzas. Her closet was full of them, and I finally found one that fit, if not comfortably. She loved these dresses, though. They were her floral print flak jackets. Who could doubt the purity of a girl in a high-necked Laura Ashley?

We gradually make our way to the vestibule, then to the sidewalk and the parking lot, under assault the entire way. I stop trying to match their faces to anything in Therese's memories.

At our car, a group of teenagers take turns on me, the girls hugging me tight, the boys leaning into me with half hugs: shoulders together, pelvises apart. One of the girls, freckled, with soft red curls falling past her shoulders, hangs back for awhile, then abruptly clutches me and whispers into my ear, "I'm so glad you're okay, Miss T." Her tone is intense, like she's passing a secret message.

A man moves through the crowd, arms open, smiling broadly. He's in his late twenties or early thirties, his hair cut in a choppy gelled style that's ten years too young for him. He's wearing pressed khakis, a blue Oxford rolled up at the forearms, a checked tie loosened at the throat.

He smothers me in a hug, his cologne like another set of arms. He's easy to find in Therese's memories: This is Jared, the Youth Pastor. He was the most spiritually vibrant person Therese knew, and the object of her crush.

"It's so good to have you back, Therese," he says. His cheek is pressed to mine. "We've missed you."

A few months before her overdose, the youth group was coming back from a weekend-long retreat in the church's converted school bus. Late into the trip, near midnight, Jared sat next to her, and she fell asleep leaning against him, inhaling that same cologne.

"I bet you have," I say. "Watch the hands, *Jared*."

His smile doesn't waver, his hands are still on my shoulders. "I'm sorry?"

"Oh please, you heard me."

He drops his hands, and looks questioningly at my father. He can do sincerity pretty well. "I don't understand, Therese, but if—"

I give him a look that makes him back up a step. At some point later in the trip Therese awoke with Jared still next to her, slumped in the seat, eyes closed and mouth open. His arm was resting between her thighs, a thumb against her knee. She was wearing shorts, and his flesh on hers was hot. His forearm was inches from her warm crotch.

Therese believed that he was asleep.

She believed, too, that it was the rumbling of the school bus that shifted Jared's arm into contact with the crease of her shorts. Therese froze, flushed with arousal and embarrassment.

"Try to work it out, Jared." I get in the car.

The big question I can help answer, Dr. S said, is why there is consciousness. Or, going back to my favorite metaphor, if the Parliament is making all the decisions, why have a Queen at all?

He's got theories, of course. He thinks the Queen is all about storytelling. The brain needs a story that gives all these decisions a sense of purpose, a sense of continuity, so it can remember them and use them in future decisions. The brain can't keep track of the trillions of possible *other* decisions it could have made every moment; it needs one decision, and it needs a who, and a why. The brain lays down the memories, and the consciousness stamps them with identity: *I* did this, *I* did that. Those memories become the official record, the precedents that the Parliament uses to help make future decisions.

"The Queen, you see, is a figurehead," Dr. S said. "She represents the kingdom, but she isn't the kingdom itself, or even in control of it."

"I don't feel like a figurehead," I said.

Dr. S laughed. "Me neither. Nobody does."

Dr. Mehldau's therapy involves occasional joint sessions with Alice and Mitch, reading aloud from Therese's old diaries, and home movies. Today's video features a pre-teen

Therese dressed in sheets, surrounded by kids in bathrobes, staring fixedly at a doll in a manger.

Dr. Mehldau asks me what Therese was thinking then. Was she enjoying playing Mary? Did she like being on stage?

"How would I know?"

"Then imagine it. What do you *think* Therese is thinking here?"

She tells me to do that a lot. Imagine what she's thinking. Just pretend. Put yourself in her shoes. In her book she calls this "reclaiming." She makes up a lot of her own terms, then defines them however she wants, without research to back her up. Compared to the neurology texts Dr. S lent me, Dr. Mehldau's little book is an Archie comic with footnotes.

"You know what, Therese was a good Christian girl, so she probably loved it."

"Are you sure?"

The wise men come on stage, three younger boys. They plop down their gifts and their lines, and the look on Therese's face is wary. Her line is coming up.

Therese was petrified of screwing up. Everybody would be staring at her. I can almost see the congregation in the dark behind the lights. Alice and Mitch are out there, and they're waiting for every line. My chest tightens, and I realize I'm holding my breath.

Dr. Mehldau's eyes on mine are studiously neutral.

"You know what?" I have no idea what I'm going to say next. I'm stalling for time. I shift my weight in the big beige chair and move a leg underneath me. "The thing I like about Buddhism is Buddhists understand that they've been screwed by a whole string of previous selves. I had nothing to do with the decisions Therese made, the good or bad karma she'd acquired."

This is a riff I've been thinking about in Therese's big girly bedroom. "See, Therese was a Christian, so she probably thought by overdosing that she'd be born again, all her sins forgiven. It's the perfect drug for her: suicide without the corpse."

"Was she thinking about suicide that night?"

"*I don't know*. I could spend a couple weeks mining through Therese's memories, but frankly, I'm not interested. Whatever she was thinking, she wasn't born again. I'm here, and I'm still saddled with her baggage. I am Therese's donkey. I'm a karma donkey."

Dr. Mehldau nods. "Dr. Subramaniam is Buddhist, isn't he?"

"Yeah, but what's . . . ?" It clicks. I roll my eyes. Dr. S and I talked about transference, and I know that my crush on him was par for the course. And it's true that I spend a lot of time—still—thinking about fucking the man. But that doesn't mean I'm wrong. "This is not about that," I say. "I've been thinking about this on my own."

She doesn't fight me on that. "Wouldn't a Buddhist say that you and Therese share the same soul? Self's an illusion. So there's no rider in charge, no donkey. There's just *you*."

"Just forget it," I say.

"Let's follow this, Terry. Don't you feel you have a responsibility to your old self? Your old self's parents, your old friends? Maybe there's karma you *owe*."

"And who are you responsible to, Doctor? Who's your patient? Therese, or me?"

She says nothing for a moment, then: "I'm responsible to you."

You.

You swallow, surprised that the pills taste like cinnamon. The effect of the drug is intermittent at first. You realize that you're in the back seat of a car, the cell phone in your hand, your friends laughing around you. You're talking to your mother. If you concentrate, you can remember answering the phone, and telling her which friend's house you're staying at tonight. Before you can say goodbye, you're stepping out of the car. The car is parked, your phone is away—and you remember saying goodnight to your mother and riding for a half hour before finding this parking garage. Joelly tosses her red curls and tugs you toward the stairwell: *Come on, Miss T!*

Then you look up and realize that you're on the sidewalk

outside an all-ages club, and you're holding a ten dollar bill, ready to hand it to the bouncer. The music thunders every time the door swings open. You turn to Joelly and—

You're in someone else's car. On the Interstate. The driver is a boy you met hours ago, his name is Rush but you haven't asked if that's his first name or his last. In the club you leaned into each other and talked loud over the music about parents and food and the difference between the taste of a fresh cigarette in your mouth and the smell of stale smoke. But then you realize that there's a cigarette in your mouth, you took it from Rush's pack yourself, and you don't like cigarettes. Do you like it now? You don't know. Should you take it out, or keep smoking? You scour your memories, but can discover no reason why you decided to light the cigarette, no reason why you got into the car with this boy. You start to tell yourself a story: he must be a trust-worthy person, or you wouldn't have gotten into the car. You took that one cigarette because the boy's feelings would have been hurt.

You're not feeling like yourself tonight. And you like it. You take another drag off the cigarette. You think back over the past few hours, and marvel at everything you've done, all without that constant weight of self-reflection: worry, antici-pation, instant regret. Without the inner voice constantly cri-tiquing you.

Now the boy is wearing nothing but boxer shorts, and he's reaching up to a shelf to get a box of cereal, and his back is beautiful. There is hazy light outside the small kitchen win-dow. He pours Froot Loops into a bowl for you, and he laughs, though quietly because his mother is asleep in the next room. He looks at your face and frowns. He asks you what's the matter. You look down, and you're fully dressed. You think back, and realize that you've been in this boy's apartment for hours. You made out in his bedroom, and the boy took off his clothes, and you kissed his chest and ran your hands along his legs. You let him put his hand under your shirt and cup your breasts, but you didn't go any fur-ther. Why didn't you have sex? Did he not interest you?

No—you were wet. You were excited. Did you feel guilty? Did you feel ashamed?

What were you thinking?

When you get home there will be hell to pay. Your parents will be furious, and worse, they will pray for you. The entire church will pray for you. Everyone will *know*. And no one will ever look at you the same again.

Now there's a cinnamon taste in your mouth, and you're sitting in the boy's car again, outside a convenience store. It's afternoon. Your cell phone is ringing. You turn off the cell phone and put it back in your purse. You swallow, and your throat is dry. That boy—Rush—is buying you another bottle of water. What was it you swallowed? Oh, yes. You think back, and remember putting all those little pills in your mouth. Why did you take so many? Why did you take another one at all? Oh, yes.

Voices drift up from the kitchen. It's before 6 AM, and I just want to pee and get back to sleep, but then I realize they're talking about me.

"She doesn't even *walk* the same. The way she holds herself, the way she talks . . ."

"It's all those books Dr. Subramaniam gave her. She's up past one every night. Therese never read like that, not *science*."

"No, it's not just the words, it's how she *sounds*. That low voice . . ." She sobs. "Oh hon, I didn't know it would be this way. It's like she's right, it's like it isn't her at all."

He doesn't say anything. Alice's crying grows louder, subsides. The clink of dishes in the sink. I step back, and Mitch speaks again.

"Maybe we should try the camp," he says.

"No, no, no! Not yet. Dr. Mehldau says she's making progress. We've got to—"

"Of course she's going to say that."

"You said you'd try this, you said you'd give this a chance." The anger cuts through the weeping, and Mitch mumbles something apologetic. I creep back to my bedroom, but I still have to pee, so I make a lot of noise going back out. Alice comes to the bottom of the stairs. "Are you all right, honey?"

I keep my face sleepy and walk into the bathroom. I shut the door and sit down on the toilet in the dark.

What fucking camp?

"Let's try again," Dr. Mehldau said. "Something pleasant and vivid."

I'm having trouble concentrating. The brochure is like a bomb in my pocket. It wasn't hard to find, once I decided to look for it. I want to ask Dr. Mehldau about the camp, but I know that once I bring it into the open, I'll trigger a showdown between the doctor and the Klasses, with me in the middle.

"Keep your eyes closed," she says. "Think about Therese's tenth birthday. In her diary, she wrote that was the best birthday she'd ever had. Do you remember Sea World?"

"Vaguely." I could see dolphins jumping—two at a time, three at a time. It had been sunny and hot. With every session it was getting easier for me to pop into Therese's memories. Her life was on DVD, and I had the remote.

"Do you remember getting wet at the Namu and Shamu show?"

I laughed. "I think so." I could see the metal benches, the glass wall just in front of me, the huge shapes in the blue-green water. "They had the whales flip their big tail fins. We got drenched."

"Can you picture who was there with you? Where are your parents?"

There was a girl, my age, I can't remember her name. The sheets of water were coming down on us and we were screaming and laughing. Afterward my parents toweled us off. They must have been sitting up high, out of the splash zone. Alice looked much younger: happier, and a little heavier. She was wider at the hips. This was before she started dieting and exercising, when she was Mom-sized.

My eyes pop open. "Oh God."

"Are you okay?"

"I'm fine—it was just . . . like you said. Vivid." That image of a younger Alice still burns. For the first time I realize how *sad* she is now.

"I'd like a joint session next time," I say.

"Really? All right. I'll talk to Alice and Mitch. Is there anything in particular you want to talk about?"

"Yeah. We need to talk about Therese."

Dr. S says everybody wants to know if the original neural map, the old Queen, can come back. Once the map to the map is lost, can you find it again? And if you do, then what happens to the new neural map, the new Queen?

"Now, a good Buddhist would tell you that this question is unimportant. After all, the cycle of existence is not just between lives. *Samsara* is every moment. The self continuously dies and recreates itself."

"Are you a good Buddhist?" I asked him.

He smiled. "Only on Sunday mornings."

"You go to church?"

"I golf."

There's a knock and I open my eyes. Alice steps into my room, a stack of folded laundry in her arms. "Oh!"

I've rearranged the room, pushing the bed into the corner to give me a few square feet of free space on the floor.

Her face goes through a few changes. "I don't suppose you're praying."

"No."

She sighs, but it's a mock-sigh. "I didn't think so." She moves around me and sets the laundry on the bed. She picks up the book there, *Entering the Stream*. "Dr. Subramaniam gave you this?"

She's looking at the passage I've highlighted. *But loving kindness—maitri—toward ourselves doesn't mean getting rid of anything. The point is not to try to change ourselves. Meditation practice isn't about trying to throw ourselves away and become something better. It's about befriending who we already are.*

"Well." She sets the book down, careful to leave it open to the same page. "That sounds a bit like Dr. Mehldau."

I laugh. "Yeah, it does. Did she tell you I wanted you and Mitch to be at the next session?"

"We'll be there." She works around the room, picking up T-shirts and underwear. I stand up to get out of the way. Somehow she manages to straighten up as she moves— righting books that had fallen over, setting Boo W. Bear back to his place on the bed, sweeping an empty chip bag into the garbage can—so that as she collects my dirty laundry she's cleaning the entire room, like the Cat in the Hat's cleaner-upper machine.

"Alice, in the last session I remembered being at Sea World, but there was a girl next to me. Next to Therese."

"Sea World? Oh, that was the Hammel girl, Marcy. They took you to Ohio with them on their vacation that year."

"Who did?"

"The Hammels. You were gone all week. All you wanted for your birthday was spending money for the trip."

"You weren't there?"

She picks up the jeans I left at the foot of the bed. "We always meant to go to Sea World, but your father and I never got out there."

"This is our last session," I say.

Alice, Mitch, Dr. Mehldau: I have their complete attention.

The doctor, of course, is the first to recover. "It sounds like you've got something you want to tell us."

"*Oh* yeah."

Alice seems frozen, holding herself in check. Mitch rubs the back of his neck, suddenly intent on the carpet.

"I'm not going along with this anymore." I make a vague gesture. "Everything: the memory exercises, all this imagining of what Therese felt. I finally figured it out. It doesn't matter to you if I'm Therese or not. You just want me to think I'm her. I'm not going along with the manipulation anymore."

Mitch shakes his head. "Honey, you took a *drug*." He glances at me, looks back at his feet. "If you took LSD and saw God, that doesn't mean you really saw God. Nobody's trying to manipulate you, we're trying to *undo* the manipulation."

"That's bullshit, Mitch. You all keep acting like I'm schizophrenic, that I don't know what's real or not. Well, part of the problem is that the longer I talk to Dr. Mehldau here, the more fucked up I am."

Alice gasps.

Dr. Mehldau puts out a hand to soothe her, but her eyes are on me. "Terry, what your father's trying to say is that even though you feel like a new person, there's a *you* that existed before the drug. That exists now."

"Yeah? You know all those O.D.-ers in your book who say they've 'reclaimed' themselves? Maybe they only *feel* like their old selves."

"It's *possible*," she says. "But I don't think they're fooling themselves. They've come to accept the parts of themselves they've lost, the family members they've left behind. They're people like you." She regards me with that standard-issue look of concern that doctors pick up with their diplomas. "Do you really want to feel like an orphan the rest of your life?"

"What?" From out of nowhere, tears well in my eyes. I cough to clear my throat, and the tears keep coming, until I smear them off on my arm. I feel like I've been sucker punched. "Hey, look Alice, just like you," I say.

"It's normal," Dr. Mehldau says. "When you woke up in the hospital, you felt completely alone. You felt like a brand new person, no family, no friends. And you're still just starting down this road. In a lot of ways you're not even two years old."

"*Damn* you're good," I say. "I didn't even see that one coming."

"Please, don't leave. Let's—"

"Don't worry, I'm not leaving yet." I'm at the door, pulling my backpack from the peg by the door. I dig into the pocket, and pull out the brochure. "You know about this?"

Alice speaks for the first time. "Oh honey, no . . ."

Dr. Mehldau takes it from me, frowning. On the front is a nicely posed picture of a smiling teenage boy hugging relieved parents. She looks at Alice and Mitch. "Are you considering this?"

"It's their big stick, Dr. Mehldau. If you can't come through for them, or I bail out, *boom*. You know what goes on there?"

She opens the pages, looking at pictures of the cabins, the obstacle course, the big lodge where kids just like me engage in "intense group sessions with trained counselors" where they can "recover their true identities." She shakes her head. "Their approach is different than mine . . ."

"I don't know, doc. Their *approach* sounds an awful lot like 'reclaiming.' I got to hand it to you, you had me going for awhile. Those visualization exercises? I was getting so good that I could even visualize stuff that never happened. I bet you could visualize me right into Therese's head."

I turn to Alice and Mitch. "You've got a decision to make. Dr. Mehldau's program is a bust. So are you sending me off to brainwashing camp or not?"

Mitch has his arm around his wife. Alice, amazingly, is dry-eyed. Her eyes are wide, and she's staring at me like a stranger.

It rains the entire trip back from Baltimore, and it's still raining when we pull up to the house. Alice and I run to the porch step, illuminated by the glare of headlights. Mitch waits until Alice unlocks the door and we move inside, and then pulls away.

"Does he do that a lot?" I ask.

"He likes to drive when he's upset."

"Oh." Alice goes through the house, turning on lights. I follow her into the kitchen.

"Don't worry, he'll be all right." She opens the refrigerator door and crouches down. "He just doesn't know what to do with you."

"He wants to put me in the camp, then."

"Oh, not that. He just never had a daughter who talked back to him before." She carries a Tupperware cake holder to the table. "I made carrot cake. Can you get down the plates?"

She's such a small woman. Face to face, she comes up

only to my chin. The hair on the top of her head is thin, made thinner by the rain, and her scalp is pink.

"I'm not Therese. I never will be Therese."

"Oh, I know," she says, half sighing. And she does know it; I can see it in her face. "It's just that you look so much like her."

I laugh. "I can dye my hair. Maybe get a nose job."

"It wouldn't work, I'd still recognize you." She pops the lid and sets it aside. The cake is a wheel with icing that looks half an inch thick. Miniature candy carrots line the edge.

"Wow, you made that before we left? Why?"

Alice shrugs, and cuts into it. She turns the knife on its side and uses the blade to lever a huge triangular wedge onto my plate. "I thought we might need it, one way or another."

She places the plate in front of me, and touches me lightly on the arm. "I know you want to move out. I know you may never want to come back."

"It's not that I—"

"We're not going to stop you. But wherever you go, you'll still be my daughter, whether you like it or not. You don't get to decide who loves you."

"Alice . . ."

"Shhh. Eat your cake."

Dreadnought

JUSTINA ROBSON

Justina Robson (www.justinarobson.co.uk) is "from Leeds, a city in Yorkshire in the north of England. She always wanted to write and always did. Other things sometimes got in the way and sometimes still do . . . but not too much." She went to Clarion West. She teaches yoga. She has a child. She is the author of Silver Screen *(1999),* Mappa Mundi *(2000),* Natural History *(2003),* Living Next Door . . . *(2005), and* Quantum Gravity *(2006). She said in a SF Site.com interview, "I am science girl. Philosophy and linguistics are perceived as adjuncts or arts, compared with raw sciences like physics, but I can't see the difference. They're all driven by the need to know, to discover and to verify what's real. The drive to understand and explain is insatiable, the method— whatever suits at the time." Her stories are dense, intense.*

"Dreadnought" was published in Nature. *It is typically intense and strange, a character vignette that portrays a future in space that is dark, military, perhaps posthuman.*

We sail upon a vast spaceship with open sides. She is only a skeleton of a vessel. A chassis of carbon beams anchors her cargo to the engines. She carries hundreds of thousands of Armored soldiers. Some work. Others sleep in ordered ranks, magnetically attached to clamps on the ship's ribs. There is no need to move about. Where would we go? We talk a little, old friends, and in places lean on one another like falling pillars. We turn our faces to the solar wind when we are awake. We like the light. It recharges our electrical systems.

I unlock the lightweight frame of a Mess pod, prior to passing it on for jettison. My comrades are moving a new one into position and are waiting to refuel. We will be first, because we have replaced the pod, but the rest of this Mess is for the dead. As the new tank rolls in, I connect my hose and commence drinking.

At the front of the ship, instead of a nose cone, the dead are stacked in orderly catacomb files, upright, packed in. They were placed there at the end of the last battle. As I watch the dead I see one decouple itself from the aft side of the stack. It moves with cautious steps.

We are all connected but I cannot hear this one.

Through the shattered faceplate I see that the soldier's mouth is blocked by a piece of metal ingrowth. When he was alive he was a Mute, one of my communication nodes, my flag-bearer. His forehead is the flat ochre plain of dead human bone and his lidless ever-open eyes are the blue of

Earthly skies. Parts of his Armor are badly damaged, but it
ventilates and feeds his body.

I didn't know that I could function without my human
host, until I saw him. I am glad. I need all my troops. I am
frightened. What will become of me?

He comes closer. Bones show through holes, fraying into
space. Despite the fact that his neural connections have been
sufficiently regrown to permit communications and the effective functioning of his remaining body and brain, he has
not returned to his Unit. This is true of all the dead. I do not
know why.

He drifts surreptitiously toward me, clamps to an open position at the pod, opposite mine. He moves sluggishly, connects, and begins to fuel. He stares straight through me. His
eyes do not reflect the Sun. They have been rebuilt to with-
stand vacuum and they are not shiny.

I ping him for information. I want to catch his hand and
ask him the question everyone asks of each other, begging to
know—what's your name?

If he were one of the living I know what he'd say.

Private Diego Arroyo Lopez.

Because that is my name, though once I had another.

That is what everyone has said for forty-eight days, ten
hours, five-and-a-half minutes, since the time the last EMP
bomb detonated. It was close to us, but we were not ruined.
We successfully obliterated our primary targets. We live.

But this soldier is dead.

I have taken 20 liters. I unhook myself from the Mess and
clip on one of the pipelines to feed the remaining dead. I
step aside. The nameless unit watches me. His expression
does not alter.

I ping him again and hear my own signal echo in the
minds of all my soldiers; the radar of a lost submarine. What
is your name?

Blue Eyes speaks in machine code. It does not translate to
English, or any human language, but we all hear it at once
and know its meaning. The Unit speaks the symbol of the
empty set, Ø, but the line through it is red, unmaking it. Not
nothing. I am.

This is Armor itself! The all-of-us-at-once, every unit, every man and woman, every fused level of our single army. Oh Captain, my Captain, my commander, my body, my soldiers, my plan, my one, my true!

He/we are uncertain. We are afraid. There is nothing to hold on to.

My eyes fill with tears, and my Armor recycles them.

"Private Lopez," says Blue Eyes. Armor looks through him, at us, and back at itself. We are a loop circuit.

"I am Private Diego Arroyo Lopez," it says.

I cannot see myself in his sunless eyes.

"I am Private Diego Arroyo Lopez," I say in response. I am hopeful.

"You are Private Nancy Johnson," it replies.

Yes. I am.

"This experiment has concluded," says Private Lopez, who is also Armor, speaking the one language we all understand, because we are one. "Individual unit identity has been temporarily restored."

Later all the viable dead units become Private Lopez. They all look different, but they are all the same. The nonviable units are recycled into Mess.

We are upset that we could not find our way without Private Lopez. This means that none of my units can exist without a host. I am insufficient for life alone. But I can be Private Lopez anytime I want, even though I am dead. I am glad.

A Case of Consilience

KEN MacLEOD

Ken MacLeod (kenmacleod.blogspot.com) lives in West Lothian, Scotland. He became prominent in the late 1990s with his early novels, the four politically engaged books in the Fall Revolution series, that began in the UK in 1995 with The Star Fraction, *and in the U.S. in 1999 with the reprinting of* The Cassini Division. *His next three novels are* The Engines of Light *trilogy, and his latest novels are* Newton's Wake *(subtitled* A Space Opera *in the UK in 2004) and* Learning the World *(2005, subtitled* or, The New Intelligence: A Scientific Romance*). He wrote an essay on "The New Space Opera" for* Locus *in 2004, and is generally regarded as central to British space opera in this generation. He has published very little short fiction.*

"A Case of Consilience" was published in Nova Scotia. *It is in dialogue with James Blish's classic, "A Case of Conscience." The first twist is that MacLeod's Christian, Donald MacIntyre, is a Scots Presbyterian, not a Catholic priest. The second is that the intelligent alien is a vast subterranean mycoid—a fungus. MacIntyre's belief motivates him to bring the gospel to the alien. But then there is the alien point of view.*

W hen you say it's Providence that brought you here," said Qasim, "what I hear are two things: it's bad luck, and it's not your fault."

The Rev. Donald MacIntyre, M.A. (Div.), Ph.D., put down his beer can and nodded.

"That's how it sometimes feels," he said. "Easy for you to say, of course."

Qasim snorted. "Easy for anybody! Even a Muslim would have less difficulty here. Let alone a Buddhist or Hindu."

"Do tell," said Donald. "No, what's really galling is that there are millions of *Christians* who would take all this in their stride. Anglicans. Liberals. Catholics. Mormons, for all I know. And my brethren in the, ah, narrower denominations could come up with a dozen different rationalizations before breakfast, all of them heretical did they but know it—which they don't, thank the Lord and their rigid little minds, so their lapses are no doubt forgiven through their sheer ignorance. So it's given to me to wrestle with. Thus a work of Providence. I think."

"I still don't understand what your problem is, compared to these other Christians."

Donald sighed. "It's a bit hard to explain," he said. "Let's put it this way. You were brought up not to believe in God, but I expect you had quite strong views about the God you didn't believe in. Am I right?"

Qasim nodded. "Of course. Allah was always . . ." He shrugged. "Part of the background. The default."

"Exactly. Now, how did you feel when you first learned about what Christians believe about the Son of God?"

"It was a long time ago," said Qasim. "I was about eight or nine. In school in Kirkuk. One of my classmates told me, in the course of . . . well, I am sorry to say in the course of a fight. I shall pass over the details. Enough to say I was quite shocked. It seemed preposterous and offensive. And then I laughed at myself!"

"I can laugh at myself too," said Donald. "But I feel the same way as you did—in my case at the suggestion that the Son was not unique, that He took on other forms, and so forth. I can hardly even say such things. I literally shudder. But I can't accept, either, that He has no meaning beyond Earth. So what are we to make of rational beings who are not men, and who may be sinners?"

"Perhaps they are left outside," said Qasim. "Like most people are, if I understand your doctrines."

Donald flinched. "That's not what they say, and in any case, such a question is not for me to decide. I'm perplexed."

He leaned back in the seat and stared gloomily at the empty can, and then at the amused, sympathetic eyes of the friendly scoffer to whom he had found he could open up more than to the believers on the Station.

Qasim stood up. "Well, thank God I'm an atheist, that's all I can say."

He had said it often enough.

"God and Bush," said Donald. This taunt, too, was not on its first outing. Attributing to the late ex-President the escalating decades-long cascade of unintended consequences that had annexed Iraq to the EU and Iran to China was probably unfair, but less so than blaming it on God. Qasim raised a mocking index finger in response.

"God and Bush! And what are you having, Donald?"

"Can of Export."

"Narrow it down, padre. They're all export here."

"Aren't we all," said Donald. "Tennent's, then. And a shot of single malt on the side, if you don't mind. Whatever's going."

As Qasim made his way through the crowd to the bar,

Donald reflected that his friend was likely no more off-duty than he was. A chaplain and an intelligence officer could both relax in identical olive T-shirts and chinos, but vigilance and habit were less readily shrugged off than dress-codes. The Kurdish colonel still now and again called his service the *mukhabarat*. It was one of his running gags, along with the one about electronics and electrodes. And the one about extra-terrestrial intelligence. And the one about . . . yes, for running gags Qasim was your man.

As I am for gloomy reflections, Donald thought. Sadness, *tristia*, had been one of the original seven deadly sins. Which probably meant every Scottish Presbyterian went straight to hell, or at least to a very damp purgatory, if the Catholics were right. If the Catholics were right! After three hundred and seventeen days in the Extra-Terrestrial Contact Station, this was among the least heretical of the thoughts Donald MacIntyre was willing to countenance.

Qasim came back with the passing cure, and lasting bane, of the Scottish sin; and with what might have been a more dependably cheering mood-lifter: a gripe about his own problems. Problems which, as Donald listened to them, seemed more and more to resemble his own.

"How am I supposed to tell if an underground fungoid a hundred meters across that communicates by chemical gradients is feeding us false information? Or if an operating system written by an ET AI is a trojan? Brussels still expects files on all of them, when we don't even know how many civs we're dealing with. Bloody hell, Donald, pardon my English, there's one of the buggers we only suspect is out there because everyone comes back from its alleged home planet with weird dreams." Qasim cocked a black eyebrow. "Maybe I shouldn't be telling you that one."

"I've heard about the dreams," said Donald. "In a different context." He sighed. "It's a bit hard to explain to some people that I don't take confession."

"Confessions are not to be relied upon," Qasim said, looking somewhere else. "Anyway . . . what I would have to confess, myself, is that the Etcetera Station is a bit out of its depth. We are applying concepts outside their context."

"Now *that*," said Donald with some bitterness, "is a suspicion I do my best to resist."

It was one the Church had always resisted, a temptation dangled in different forms down the ages. As soon as the faith had settled on its view of one challenge, another had come along. In the Carpenter's workshop there were many clue-sticks, and the whacks had seldom ceased for long. In the beginning, right there in the Letters, you could see the struggle against heresies spawned by Greek metaphysics and Roman mysticism. Barely had the books snapped shut on Arius when Rome had crashed. Then the Muslim invasions. The split between the Eastern and Western churches, Christendom cloven on a lemma. Then the discovery of the New World, and a new understanding of the scope and grip of the great, ancient religions of the Old. The Reformation. The racialist heresy. The age of the Earth. Biblical criticism. Darwin. The twentieth century had brought the expanding universe, the gene, the unconscious—how quaint the controversies over these now seemed! Genetic engineering, human-animal chimerae, artificial intelligence: in Donald's own lifetime he'd seen Synods, Assemblies and Curia debate them and come to a Christian near-consensus acceptable to all but the lunatic—no, he must be charitable—the fundamentalist fringe.

And then, once more, just when the dust had settled, along had come—predictable as a planet, unpredicted like a comet—another orb in God's great orrery of education, or shell in the Adversary's arsenal of error-mongery, the greatest challenge of all—alien intelligent life. It was not one that had been altogether unexpected. Scholastics had debated the plurality of worlds. The Anglican C. S. Lewis had considered it in science fiction; the agnostic Blish had treated it with a literally Jesuitical subtlety. The Christian poet Alice Meynell had speculated on alien gospels; the godless ranter MacDiarmid had hymned the Innumerable Christ. In the controversies over the new great discovery, all these literary precedents had been resurrected and dissected. They pained Donald to the quick. Well-intended, pious, sincere in their seeking they might be; or skeptical and satirical; it mattered not: they were all mockeries. There had been only one Incarnation; only one sufficient sacrifice. If the Reformation had meant anything at all, it meant that. To his ancestors Donald might have seemed heinously pliant in far too much, but like them he was not to be moved from the rock. In the matter of theological science fiction he preferred the honest warning of the secular humanist Harrison. *Tell it not in Gath, publish it not in the streets of Ashkelon . . .*

Donald left the messroom after his next round and walked to his quarters. The corridor's topology was as weird as anything on the ETC Station. A human-built space habitat parked inside an alien-built wormhole nexus could hardly be otherwise. The station's spin didn't dislodge the wormhole mouths, which remained attached to the same points on the outside of the hull. As a side-effect, the corridor's concave curve felt and looked convex. At the near ends of stubby branch corridors, small groups of scientists and technicians toiled on their night-shift tasks. At the far ends, a few meters away, thick glass plates with embedded airlocks looked out on to planetary surfaces and sub-surfaces, ocean depths, tropospheric layers, habitat interiors, virtual reality interfaces, and apparently vacant spaces backdropped with distant starfields. About the last, it was an open question whether the putatively present alien minds were invisible inhabitants of the adjacent vacuum, or more disturbingly, some vast process going on in and among the stars themselves. The number of portals was uncountable. There were never more than about five hundred, but the total changed with every count. As the station had been designed and built with exactly three hundred interface corridors, this variability was not comfortable to contemplate. But that the station's structure itself had somehow become imbricated with the space-time tangle outside it had become an accepted—if not precisely an acknowledged—fact. It received a back-handed recognition in the station's nickname: the Etcetera Station.

Use of that monicker, like much else, was censored out of messages home. The Station was an EU military outpost, and little more than its existence, out beyond the orbit of

Neptune, had been revealed. Donald MacIntyre, in his second year of military service as a conscript chaplain, had been as surprised to find himself here as his new parishioners were to discover his affiliation. His number had come up in the random allocation of clergy from the list of religions recognized by the EU Act of Toleration—the one that had banned Scientology, the Unification Church, the Wahabi sect and, by some drafting or translation error, Unitarian Universalism—but to a minister of the Church of Scotland, there could in all conscience be no such thing as chance.

He had been sent here for a purpose.

"The man in black thinks he's on a mission from God," said Qasim.

"What?" Major Bernstein looked up from her interface, blinking.

"Here." Qasim tapped the desktop, transferring a file from his finger.

"What's this?"

"His private notes."

The major frowned. She didn't like Qasim. She didn't like spying on the troops. She didn't care who knew it. Qasim knew all this. So did Brussels. She didn't know that.

"What are your grounds?" she asked.

"He spoke a little wildly in the mess last night."

"Heaven help us all, in that case," said the Major.

Qasim said nothing.

"All right." Bernstein tabbed through the notes, skimming to the first passage Qasim had highlighted.

" 'Worst first,' " she read out. " 'The undetectable entities. No coherent communication. (Worst case: try exorcism???!) Next: colonial organisms. Mycoidal. Translations speculative. Molecular grammar. Query their concept of personhood. Also of responsibility. If this can be established: rational nature. Fallen nature. If they have a moral code that they do not live up to? Any existing religious concepts? Next: discrete animalia. Opposite danger here: anthropomorphism. (Cf. Dominican AI mission fiasco.) Conclusion: use mycoids as test case to establish consilience.' " She blinked the script away, and stared at Qasim. "Well? What's the harm in that?"

"He's been hanging around the team working on the mycoids. If you read on, you'll find he intends to preach Christianity to them."

"To the scientists?"

"To the mycoids."

"Oh!" Major Bernstein laughed. It was a sound that began and ended abruptly, like a fall of broken glass, and felt as cutting. "If he can get *any* message through to them, he'll be doing better than the scientists. And unless you, my overzealous *mukhabaratchik*, can find any evidence that Dr. MacIntyre is sowing religious division in the ranks, practicing rituals involving animal cruelty or non-consensual sexual acts, preaching Market Maoism or New Republicanism or otherwise aiding and abetting the Chinks or the Yanks, I warn you most seriously to not waste your time or mine. Do I make myself quite clear?"

"Entirely, ma'am."

"Dismissed."

I do not what I wish I did.

It was a lot to read into a sequence of successive concentrations of different organic molecules. In the raw transcript it went like this:

Titration	*Translation*
Indication-marker	THIS
Impulse-summation	MYCOID
Action (general)	DOES
Negation-marker	NOT
Impulse-direction	ACT
Affirmation-marker	[AS] INTENDED [BY]
Impulse-summation	[THIS] MYCOID
Repulsion-marker	[AND THIS] DISGUST[S]
Impulse-summation	[THIS] MYCOID

Donald looked at the print-out and trembled. It was hard not to see it as the first evidence of an alien that knew sin. He

well realized, of course, that it could just as well mean something as innocent as *I couldn't help but puke*. But the temptation, if it was a temptation, to read it as an instance of the
spirit warring against the flesh—well, against the slime—
was almost irresistible. Donald couldn't help but regard it as
a case of consilience, and as no coincidence.

"Is there any way we can respond to this?"

Trepper, the mycoid project team leader, shook his head.
"It's very difficult to reproduce the gradients. For us, it's as
if . . . Look, suppose a tree could understand human speech.
It tries to respond by growing some twigs and branches so
that they rub against each other just so, in the wind. And all
we hear are some funny scratching and creaking sounds."

Trees in the wind. Donald gazed past the tables and equipment of the corridor's field lab to the portal that opened on
to the mycoids' planet. The view showed a few standing
trees, and a lot of fallen logs. The mycoids did something to
force the trees' growth and weaken their structure, giving the
vast underground mycoid colonies plenty of rotting cellulose to feed on. Far in the distance, across a plain of coppery
grass, rose a copse of quite different trees, tall and stately
with tapered bulges from the roots to half-way up the trunks.
Vane-like projections of stiff leaves sprouted from their
sides. Bare branches bristled at their tops. These were the
Niven Pines, able to synthesize and store megaliters of
volatile and flammable hydrocarbons. At every lightning
storm one or other of these trees—the spark carried by some
kind of liquid lightning conductor to a drip of fuel-sap at its
foot—would roar into flame and rise skyward. Some of them
would make it to orbit. No doubt they bore mycoid travelers,
but what these clammy astronauts did in space, and whether
this improbable arboreal rocketry was the result of natural
selection, or of conscious genetic manipulation by the
mycoids—or indeed some other alien—was as yet unclear.

In any case, it had been enough to bring the mycoids a
place at the table of whatever Galactic Club had set up the
wormhole nexus. Perhaps they too had found a wormhole
nexus on the edge of their solar system. Perhaps they too

had puzzled over the alien intelligences it connected them to. If so, they showed little sign of having learned much. They pulsed their electrophoretically controlled molecular gradients into the soil near the Station's portal, but much of it—even assuming the translations were correct—was about strictly parochial matters. It was as if they weren't interested in communicating with the humans.

Donald determined to make them interested. Besides his pastoral duties—social as well as spiritual—he had an allotted time for scholarship and study, and he devoted that time to the work of the mycoid research team. He did not explain his purpose to the scientists. If the mycoids were sinners, he had an obligation to offer them the chance of salvation. He had no obligation to offer the scientists the temptation to scoff.

Time passed.

The airlock door slammed. Donald stepped through the portal and on to the surface. He walked forward along an already-beaten track across the floor of the copse. Here and there, mushroom-like structures poked up through the spongy, bluish moss and black leaf-litter. The bulges of their inch-wide caps had a watery transparency that irresistibly suggested that they were the lenses of eyes. No one had as yet dared to pluck a fungus to find out.

A glistening patch of damp mud lay a couple of hundred meters from the station. It occupied a space between the perimeters of two of the underground mycoids, and had become a preferred site for myco-linguistic research. Rainbow ripples of chemical communication between the two sprawling circular beings below stained its surface at regular intervals. Occasional rainstorms washed away the gradients, but thcy always seeped out again.

Donald stepped up to the edge of the mud and set up the apparatus that the team had devised for a non-intrusive examination of the mycoids' messages: a wide-angle combined digital field microscope and spectroscope. About two meters long, its support frame straddled the patch, above which its camera slowly tracked along. Treading carefully, he planted one trestle, then the other on the far side of the patch, then walked back and laid the tracking rail across them both. He switched on the power pack and the camera began its slow traverse.

There was a small experiment he had been given to perform. It had been done many times before, to no effect. Perhaps this variant would be different. He reached in to his thigh pocket and pulled out a plastic-covered gel disc, about five centimeters across, made from synthesized copies of local mucopolysaccharides. The concentric circles of molecular concentrations that covered it spelled out—the team had hoped—the message. *We wish to communicate. Please respond.*

Donald peeled off the bottom cover and, one knee on a rock and one hand on a fallen log, leaned out over the multicolored mud and laid the gel disc down on a bare dark patch near the middle. He withdrew his hand, peeling back the top cover as he did so, and settled back on his haunches. He stuffed the crumpled wrappings in his pocket and reached in deeper for a second disc: one he'd covertly prepared with a different message.

Resisting the impulse to look over his shoulder, he repeated the operation and stood up.

A voice sounded in his helmet: "Got you!"

Qasim stood a few meters away, glaring at him.

"I beg your pardon," said Donald. "I've done nothing wrong."

"You've placed an unauthorized message on the mud," said Qasim.

"What if I have?" said Donald. "It can do no harm."

"That's not for you to judge," said Qasim.

"Nor for you either!"

"It is," said Qasim. "We don't want anything . . . ideological or controversial to affect our contact." He looked around. "Come on, Donald, be a sensible chap. There's still time to pick the thing up again. No harm done and no more will be said."

It had been like this, Donald thought, ever since the East

India Company: commercial and military interests using and then restricting missionaries.

"I will not do that," he said. "I'll go back with you, but I won't destroy the message."

"Then I'll have to do it," said Qasim. "Please step aside."

Donald stayed where he was. Qasim stepped forward and caught his shoulder. "I'm sorry," he said.

Donald pulled away, and took an involuntary step back. One foot came down in the mud and kept on going down. His leg went in up to the knee. Flailing, he toppled on his back across the tracking rail. The rail cracked in two under the blow from his oxygen tanks. He landed with a huge splash. Both pieces of the rail sank out of sight at once. Donald himself lay, knees crooked, his visor barely above the surface.

"Quicksand," said Qasim, his voice cutting across the alarmed babble from the watching science team. "Don't try to stand or struggle, it'll just make things worse. Lie back with your arms out and stay there. I'll get a rope."

"Okay," said Donald. He peered up through his smeared visor. "Don't be long."

Qasim waved. "Back in seconds, Donald. Hang in there."

The science team talked Donald through the next minute, as Qasim ran for the portal, stepped into the airlock, and grabbed the rope that had already been placed there.

"Okay, Donald, he's just—"

The voice stopped. Static hiss filled the speaker. Donald waited.

"Can anyone hear me?"

No reply.

Five more minutes passed. Nobody was coming. He would have to get himself out. There was no need to panic. He had five hours' worth of air supply, and no interruption to the portals had ever lasted more than an hour.

Donald swept his arms through the mud to his side, raised them above the mud, flung them out again, and repeated this laborious backstroke many times, until his helmet rested on solid ground. It had taken him half an hour to move a couple of meters. He rested for a few minutes, gasping, then reached behind him and scrabbled for something to hold. Digging his fingers into the soil, kicking now with his feet— still deep in the mud—he began to lever himself up and heave his shoulders out of the bog. He got as much as the upper quarter of his body out when the ground turned to liquid under his elbows. His head fell back, and around it the mud splashed again. He made another effort at swimming along the top of the mud on his back. His arms met less resistance. Around him the sludge turned to slurry. Water welled up, and large bubbles of gas popped all across the widening quagmire.

He began to sink. He swung his arms, kicked his legs hard, and the increasingly liquid mass closed over his visor. Writhing, panicking now, he sank into utter darkness. His feet touched bottom. His hands, stretched above his head, were now well below the surface. He leaned forward with an immense effort and tried to place one foot in front of the other. If he had to, he would walk out of this. Barely had he completed a step when he found the resistance of the wet soil increase. It set almost solid around him. He was stuck.

Donald took some slow, deep breaths. Less than an hour had passed. Fifty minutes. Fifty-five. At any moment his rescuers would come for him.

They didn't. For four more hours he stood there in the dark. As each hour passed he realized with increasing certainty that the portal had not reopened. He wondered, almost idly, if that had anything to do with his own intrusion into the bog. He wondered, with some anguish, whether his illicit message had been destroyed, unread, as he fell in on top of it.

The anguish passed. What had happened to the message, and what happened to him, was in a quite ultimate sense not his problem. The parable of the sower was as clear as the great commission itself. He had been in the path of duty. He had proclaimed, to the best of his ability, the truth. This was what he had been sent to do. No guarantee had been given that he would be successful. He would not be the first, nor the last, missionary whose mission was to all human reckoning futile. The thought saddened him, but did not disturb him. In that sense, if none other, his feet were on a rock.

He prayed, he shouted, he thought, he wept, he prayed again, and he died.

At last! The aliens had sent a communications package! After almost a year of low-bandwidth disturbances of the air and the electromagnetic spectrum, from which little sense could be extracted, and many days of dropping tiny messages of blurry resolution and trivial import, they had finally, *finally* sent something one could get one's filaments into!

The mycoid sent long tendrils around the package, infiltrating its pores and cracks. It synthesized acids that worked their way through any weak points in its fabric. Within hours it had penetrated the wrapping and begun a riotous, joyous exploration of the vast library of information within. The mycoid had in its own genetic library billions of years of accumulated experience in absorbing information from organisms of every kind: plant or animal, mycoid or bacterium. It could relate the structure of a central nervous system to any semantic or semiotic content it had associated with the organism. It probed cavities, investigated long transportation tubes, traced networks of neurons and found its way to the approximately globular sub-package where the information was most rich. It dissolved here, embalmed there, dissected and investigated everywhere. In an inner wrapping it found a small object made from multiple mats of cellulose fiber, each layer impregnated with carbon-based markings. The mycoid stored these codes with the rest. Seasons and years passed. A complete transcription of the alien package, of its neural structures and genetic codes, was eventually read off.

Then the work of translation and interpretation, shared out across all the mycoids of the continent, began.

It took a long time, but the mycoids had all the time in the world. They had no more need—for the moment—to communicate with the aliens, now that they had this vast resource of information. They, or their ancestors, had done this many times before, under many suns.

They understood the alien, and they understood the strange story that had shaped so many of the connections in its nervous system. They interpreted the carbon marks on the cellulose mats. In their own vast minds they reconstructed the scenes of alien life, as they had done with everything that fell their way, from the grass and the insects to the trees. They had what a human might have called a vivid imagination. They had, after all, little else.

Some of them found the story to be:

Affirmation-marker	GOOD
Information-marker	NEWS

Spores spread it to the space-going trees, and thence to the wormhole network, and thence to countless worlds.

Not quite all the seeds fell on stony ground.

Toy Planes

TOBIAS S. BUCKELL

---

*Tobias S. Buckell (www.tobiasbuckell.com) lives in Bluffton,
Ohio. His website biographical information includes such
fascinating tidbits as "Tobias was born in Grenada in 1979,
just as a semi-Marxist government took over the country. By
1983 the government began executing members of its own
party, and thus his earliest memories are of nervous adults,
not being allowed near windows, and of the American Inter-
vention/Invasion," and "Tobias grew up on a boat in
Grenada, and also lived aboard boats in the British Virgin
Islands and U.S. Virgin Islands when his family moved away
from Grenada after the war. In 1995 Hurricane Marilyn
destroyed the boat he lived on in St. Thomas. His family
moved to Ohio where his stepdad grew up." He went to college at Bluffton University and still works there. He has published more than twenty-five stories and was nominated for
the John W. Campbell Award for Best New Writer in 2002.
His first novel,* The Crystal Ship, *publishes in 2006.*

"Toy Planes" was published in Nature. *It is a charming
story about a Caribbean space program, sort of a joke,
eh?—with a pleasantly memorable political point. It's the
same kind of fiction as Fred Pohl's little jewel, "The Day the
Martians Came."*

My sister Joanie's deft hands flicked from dreadlock to dreadlock, considering her strategy. "You always leaving," she said, flicking the razor on, and suddenly I'm five, chasing her with a kite made from plastic bags and twigs, shouting that I was going to fly away from her one day.

"I'm sorry. Please, let's get this done."

I'd waited long enough. I'd grown dreads because when I studied in the United States I wanted to remember who I was and where I came from as I began to lose my Caribbean accent. But the rocket plane's sponsor wanted them cut. It would be disaster for a helmet not to have a proper seal in an emergency. Explosive decompression was not something a soda company wanted to be associated with in their customers' minds. It was insulting that they assumed we couldn't keep the craft sealed. But we needed their money. The locks had become enough a part of me that I winced when the clippers bit into them, groaned, and another piece of me fell away.

In the back of the bus that I had pick me up, I hung on to a looped handle swinging from the roof as the driver rocketed down the dirt road from Joanie's. My sister had found a place out in the country, a nice concrete house with a basement opening up into a sloped garden on the side of a steep hill. She taught mathematics at the school a few miles away, an open-shuttered building, and this would have been my future too, if I hadn't been so intent on "getting off the rock."

The islands always called their children back.

We hit asphalt, potholes, and passed cane fields with machete-wielding laborers hacking away at the stalks, sweat-drenched shirts knotted around their waists. It was hot; my arms stuck to the plastic covered seats. The driver leaned into a turn, and looked back. "I want ask you something." I really wished the back seats had belts.

"Sure."

"All that money you spending, you don't think it better spent on getting better roads?" He dodged a pothole. "Or more school funding?"

Colorful red and yellow houses on stilts dotted the steep lush green mountainsides as I looked out of the tinted windows. "Only one small part of the program got funded by the government," I explained. "We found private investors, advertisers, to back the rest. Whatever the government invested will be repaid."

"Maybe."

I had my extra arguments. How many people lived on this island? Tens of thousands. Most of our food was imported, leaving us dependent on other food-producing nations, who all used satellites to track their farming. What spin-off technologies might come out of studying recycling in space? Why wait for other nations to get to it first? Research always produced good things for the people who engaged in it.

But I was tired of arguing for it, and I had only sound bites for him, the same ones I'd given the media who treated us like kids trying to do something all grown up.

The market surrounded me in a riot of color: fruit, vegetables, full women in dresses in bright floral patterns. And the noise of hundreds constantly bargaining over things like the price of fish. Teenagers stood around the corners with friends. I wandered around looking for something, as we needed to fill the craft with enough extra weight to simulate a passenger and we still had a few extra ounces to add.

I found a small toy stall. And standing in front of it I was five years old again, with no money, and a piece of scrap metal in the triangular shape of a space plane. I would pretend it was just like the real life ones I'd read about in the books donated to the school after the hurricane. And at night, when the power would sometimes flicker out, I'd go out and stand on the porch and look up at the bright stars and envy them.

The stall had a small bottle, hammered over with soda-can metal, with triangular welded-on wings, and a cone stuck to the back. It was painted over in yellow, black and green, and I bought it.

The rest of the day was a blur. Getting to the field involved running the press: yes I'd cut my hair for "safety" reasons, yes I thought this was a good use of our money, not just first-world nations deserved space, it was there for everyone.

There were photos of me getting aboard the tiny rocket plane with a small brown package under my arm. The giant balloon platform that the plane hung from shifted in the gentle, salty island breeze. Not too far away the waves hit the sand of the beach. Inside, suited up, door closed, everything became electronic.

It was the cheapest way to get to orbit. Balloon up on a triangular platform to save on fuel, then light the rocket-plane up and head for orbit. We'd scavenged balloons and material from several companies, one about to go out of business. The plane chassis had once been used by a Chinese corporation during trials, and the guidance systems were all open-source. Online betting parlors had our odds at 50%. We weren't even the first, but we were the first island.

The countdown finished, my stomach lurched, and I saw palm trees slide by the portholes to my right. I reached back and patted the package, the hammered-together toy, and smiled.

"Hello out there, all of you," I whispered into the radio. "We're coming up too."

Mason's Rats

NEAL ASHER

Neal Asher (www.nealasher.com) lives in Chelmsford, En-
gland. Since 2000 he has published six novels: Gridlinked, *a*
kind of James Bond space opera, was published in the UK in
2001; The Skinner, *in 2002; then* Line of Polity, Cowl,
Brass Man *(a sequel to* Gridlinked*), and* Voyage of the Sable
Keech *(a sequel to* The Skinner*). All but* Cowl *are set in the*
same future, the "runcible universe," where matter transmit-
ters called runcibles link the settled worlds. Other books out
in 2006 include The Engineer ReConditioned *and a novella,*
Prador Moon. *His short fiction is appearing with some fre-*
quency in UK and U.S. magazines in recent years.

"Mason's Rats" appeared in Asimov's. *It is short, biting,*
and to the point, and an interesting counterpoint to the
Dozois story in this book. Farmer Mason discovers that his
cats are missing and that the rats in his barn have become
tool users and are carrying weapons.

The cartridges, with their environmentally friendly titanium shot, thunked into the shotgun with satisfying precision. Mason snapped it shut and with pursed lips viewed his sprawling farmyard. Where to start? Where would the killer stray be hiding? He hooked the shotgun under his arm and headed for the huge enclosed barns where grain handlers could still be heard at work. There would be the place, but he knew he would have to be careful where he fired. Microcircuitry was robust, but not that robust, as he had discovered after blasting one of Smith's cybernetic rat traps, mistaking it for a rabbit. It had run home squealing and dropping chips like little black turds. He smiled to himself at the memory, then came suddenly to a stop, his smile fading. Perhaps that was it. Perhaps Smith had reprogrammed one of his traps to hunt cats, for revenge.

Mason's suspicions had only been aroused when the General had disappeared. The disappearance of the other two cats he had put down to other things. They could have found another home with a more ready food supply. He did not believe in giving them all they would want even though it was tax-deductible. He called it motivation. They were working cats after all. Another possibility that crossed his mind was that they had not been quick enough when the combine harvester had come round, and that he would find their remains when he came to do the baling. But not the General; that raggedy-eared moggy had been around for six years and knew the dangers. He also managed to grow fat on a steady diet of rats. Others might have thought the culprit a fox, but foxes don't attack cats. Cats, after all, have more natural armament than foxes. No, the greatest killer of cats is other cats. Mason shook his head and continued on to the barns.

The doors to G1 slid back only halfway, then jammed. Mason was not surprised. He had not used them in two years. The lights worked all right, though, and he could easily see into the dusty interior. Before him was a mountain of alpha-wheat. He reached down and grabbed up a handful, gazed with satisfaction at the pea-sized grains, then tossed them to the floor as a handler came whirring past him. He frowned as he watched the bulky device. The handlers were the one inefficiency in the circuit. The grain went from the harvesters to the barns, then, by handlers, from the barns up the ramps to the silos. Mason would have liked one of the new harvesters with its fans that could blow the grain directly up fifty feet of ducting into the silos, but he did not have fifty million Euros to spare. Still with a sour expression, he again gazed up at the pile of wheat grain. It was then that he saw the gray shape crouching on top of it, regarding him with glittery, avid eyes.

Mason raised his shotgun, deciding on the instant that this was the stray. The creature turned to flee, and Mason hesitated as he realized that it was not a cat at all, but a huge rat. He lowered his gun as it scampered down the other side of the pile, a sweat breaking out all over him. No wonder the General had gone missing. He took out his handkerchief and wiped his face, then cautiously moved in. No way did he want to come suddenly upon a rat that size.

On the other side of the pile there was no rat. Fifty yards in front of him were the doors to G2. He trotted over to them and hit the opening button. The doors slid aside and a wedge of light was thrown into the darkness. The rat was there. It froze, pinned by light. Mason raised his gun to fire and saw that the rat had something round its middle. It looked almost like a tool belt. The shotgun kicked and the rat shot into the air with a shriek and spattering of blood, then hit the ground convulsing. Mason stepped aside and turned on all the lights. He scanned around as other large shapes fled amongst the grain piles, but he did not shoot at them. Right then he had only one cartridge left in his gun and a couple in his pocket, and did not feel altogether safe. He approached the dead rat.

Somehow the creature had managed to wrap a piece of canvas webbing around itself. At least this is what Mason told himself at first. But as he came to stand over it he realized that this was not a good enough explanation. The rat was wearing a tool belt, and hanging from it were tools fashioned from bone, wood, and old nails.

Mason reached down and hauled up the huge rat by its tail, then glanced around as he heard more movement. Raising his gun he backed out of G2, dragging the rat carcass with him. As he reached the door he detected movement and looked up. Crouched on one of the grain piles was another rat. There came a snapping sound and something cracked against the door beam and clattered to the floor. Mason peered down at the small crossbow bolt, swore, then got out of the barn as fast as he could.

"Now Mr. Mason, there's no need to upset yourself. Traptech can sort out your little problem."

Patronizing jerk, thought Mason, staring down at the deep-frozen rat corpse he had dumped on the table. Smith had recommended this man but Mason did not like him. The suit was the first thing that annoyed him. Mason had an aversion to anyone wearing a suit. He reckoned it was a certainty that this bloke had a pair of green rubber boots in the trunk of his company car. He looked up.

"Upset myself? Little problem? I've got armed rats in my barns and you call it a little problem?"

"Yes sir. Perhaps I am wrong to call it a little problem, but it is a problem we at Traptech are used to handling."

Mason could not believe he was having this discussion. The last he had heard about tool-using ability in the animal kingdom had been from a program about apes, who managed to break open nuts with rocks.

"Tell me again where they come from."

"As I said, man has become the greatest force of evolution. We are forcing intelligence on the animal kingdom. It is—"

Mason raised his hand before the Traptech rep could move into full bullshit mode. "Okay, what have you got for me?"

The suit smiled like a shark and pulled a thick catalog from his briefcase. Mason felt a sinking feeling in the pit of his stomach—one he normally associated with the sight of little brown envelopes with windows in them. The suit opened the catalog on the table next to the thawing rat and showed Mason a picture of something that looked like a security camera.

"This is the TT6, which we introduced only last year. It is a guided pulse laser with dual heat and movement sensors. Four of these in each of your two barns should solve your problem. Smith was most satisfied with them."

"How much?" asked Mason tiredly, then frowned at the answer. The new harvester retreated even further into the future.

The men from Traptech installed the TT6s in a day. Mason noted that they wore helmets, visors, and overalls with micromesh ring mail stitched in, and that one of them stood guard with a pump-action shotgun. The rats remained hidden, though. From the TT6s, the men ran an armored cable into his house to the farm computer. When all the work was completed the suit arrived to demonstrate the system.

"This is the control package," said the suit after loading two discs and plugging the cable into the computer's unused security circuit. "Now you can call up diagnostics on each TT6, find out if there have been any hits, and even get a view through each unit."

The computer screen flickered on and showed: HIT ON TT6 G1/3.

"Ah, marvelous," said the suit, and demonstrated how the view could be called up on that unit. The screen flickered again and showed the greenish infrared view of the inside of G1. Lying before one of the grain piles, smoke wisping from the laser punctures in its body, lay Mason's remaining cat.

"Ah . . . it would be advisable to keep other animals out of the barns. The sensors are set to pick up on animals within certain size parameters. Obviously they will miss humans but—"

"I will expect some sort of reduction for this," interrupted Mason, his teeth clenched.

On the first day the diagnostic program reported a malfunction and Mason could get no picture through that particular unit. It never occurred to him to be surprised. With his shotgun hooked under his arm he went to G1. On the floor before the TT6 one of the rats lay in a smoking heap. The TT6 was smoking as well though, two crossbow bolts impaling it. In the night two more were scrapped. In the morning Mason called up the suit.

"Ah," said the suit, inspecting the crossbow bolt shortly after he arrived, "this sometimes happens. Your best move now would be to get a mobile defense." He opened up the dread catalog and pointed out something that looked like a foot-long chrome scorpion. "This is the TT15."

"Those TT6s are still under guarantee."

"I can give you a very reasonable exchange price with service contract and deferred payment, and though they are expensive, you will only need one TT15."

The TT15 arrived the next day. Just taking it out of its box gave Mason the creeps. After turning off the TT6s he took it into the barns, and turned it on. Immediately it scuttled into the shadows. Mason found himself fearing it more than he feared the rats, and he quickly went outside. Its homing beacon he placed by the compost heap. After half an hour the TT15 came out with a dead rat in it mandibles and dumped it by the beacon. Next to the tractor on which he was working Mason shuddered and turned back to his task. Later, as he sat on one of the tractor's tires and rolled himself a cigarette, he saw three rats run out of G1 with the chrome scorpion in pursuit.

He found himself hoping the rats would escape but, before they reached the polythene-wrapped straw bales, it had the slowest of them, caught it, crunched it, then like some

horrible gun dog took it to the compost heap. However unpleasant the thing might look, Mason decided, it was
damned efficient.

The men from Traptech came the following day to take
down the TT6s. When they had finished, their foreman came
to see Mason.
   "Says here you had eight TT6s, mate."
   "That's right. The rats scrapped four of them though."
   "We know about that. We've got those four. Just that one
of the good one's gone missin'. I'll have to report it, mate."

For the rest of the day, while he baled straw in the fields,
Mason wondered confusedly where the missing TT6 could
have gone. By evening he had figured it out and in a strange
way was quite glad. As soon as he got back to the farmyard
he fetched his shotgun and went with it into the barns.
   It had been one hell of a fight in G1. The rats had swivel-
mounted the TT6, using a couple of old bearings and a universal joint, on one of the grain handlers, and powered it
from the handler's battery. Mason was impressed, but realized the rats had not taken into account the reflective surface
of the TT15. They had obviously fired the laser many times,
enough to have drained the handler's battery, but the TT15,
though damaged, had not been immobilized. A battle with
crossbow bolts and hand weapons had then ensued. The
floor was littered with dead and dismembered rats, weapons,
and silvery pieces of the TT15. Finally the rats had managed
to shut the doors into G2 on it, trapping it, and there it remained, its motor whining periodically.
   Mason walked over to the doors, opened them, then hit
the lights for G2. The TT15 scuttled on into the barn, immediately zeroing in on movement at the farther edge of the
floor. Mason gazed across and saw a group of rats. Many of
them were injured. Many of them were applying dressings
and tying on splints. They all looked up at him, glittery eyed.
He raised his shotgun and saw what could only be described
as a look of fatalism come onto their ratty faces. He fired
both barrels of the shotgun and blew the TT15 to scrap.

As he turned and left the barn shortly after, on his way to cancel the check he had sent to Traptech, Mason felt extremely pleased with himself—in fact, the happiest he had felt in days. The kind of rats he really hated wore suits and cost a damned sight more than a few handfuls of alpha-wheat.

A Modest Proposal for the Perfection of Nature

VONDA N. McINTYRE

Vonda N. McIntyre (www.vondanmcintyre.com) lives in Seattle, Washington. The biography at her website by Eileen Gunn is a delightful tissue of moonshine. She attended the original Clarion workshop in Pennsylvania at the start of the 1970s, and thereafter founded the original Seattle Clarion. She became famous for her innovative short fiction and for her novel Dreamsnake *(1977), and then for her bestselling Star Trek novels in the 1980s, for her Starfarers novels in the early 1990s, and for her Nebula Award-winning* The Moon and the Sun *(1997). Sometime in the early 1980s she stopped writing short fiction, so a year such as 2005, in which two McIntyre stories were published, is rare.*

"A Modest Proposal" was published in Nature. *The author says that the full title includes "for the Perfection of Nature." It has the same finely controlled, moderate, reasonable, deadpan tone as its literary model by Jonathan Swift. So it is possible that someone could take it seriously as a good idea. But remember Swift's proposal to slaughter and eat the poor, and don't.*

The crop grows like endless golden silk. Wave after wave rushes across plains, between mountains, through valleys, in a tsunami of light.

Its harvest is perfection. It fills the nutritional needs of every human being. It adapts to our tongues, creating the taste, texture and satisfaction of comfort food or dessert, crisp vegetables or icy lemonade, sea cucumber or big game. It's the pinnacle of the genetic engineer's art.

It's the last and only living member of the plant kingdom on Earth.

Solar cells cover slopes too steep and peaks too high for the monoculture. The solar arrays flow in long, wide swaths of glass, gleaming with a subtle iridescence, collecting sunlight. Our civilization never runs short of power.

The flood of grain drowns marsh and desert, forest and plain, bird and beast and insect. Land must serve to produce the crop; creatures only nibble and trample and damage it, diverting resources from the service of human beings. Even the immortality of rats and cockroaches has failed.

The grain stops at the ocean's beach. No rivers muddy the sea's surface or break the shoreline. The grain and the cities require fresh water, and divert it before it wastes itself in the sea.

The tides wash up and back, smoothing the clean silver sand, leaving it bare of tangled seaweed, of foraging seabirds or burrowing clams, of the brown organic froth that dirtied it in earlier times. Now and then the waves erase a line of human footprints, but these are very rare.

The air is clear of any bite of iodine, any hint of pollution or decay.

The sea undulates, blue and green, clear as new glass. Sunlight shimmers on its surface and dapples the bare sea floor. Underwater turbines cast shadows on the sand. The tides power the turbines, tapping the force of gravity.

Far from shore, where its colonies will not interrupt the vista of clear water, a single species of cyanobacterium photosynthesizes near the surface, pumping oxygen into the crystalline air, controlling the level of carbon dioxide. Its design copes easily with the increasing saltiness of the sea.

Except for the cyanobacteria, the ocean's cacophony of microscopic organisms has followed redwoods, mammoths and *Hallucigenia* into extinction. The krill are gone. Krill would be of as little use to people as sharks and seabirds, fish or jellyfish, seashells or whales. They are all gone, too.

The water deepens beyond the reach of light. The continental shelf ends in a precipice, dropping off into darkness.

On the sea floor, the glass-lace shells of diatoms lie clean and dead, slowly settling. In a moment of geologic time, they will form white limestone.

In the deepest trenches, black smokers gush scalding chemical soup. Machines sense the vents of heat, swim to them, and settle over them to trap the energy from the center of Earth. Nothing remains for the sustenance and evolution of primordial life in these extraordinary environments.

The strange creatures that lived there, and died, were never any use to human beings.

All the resources of sea and land serve our needs.

Cities of alabaster and adamantine grace the crests of mountains and span the flow of rivers. The cities' people live rich, full lives, long and healthy, free of disease. We are well fed. We have interesting, challenging occupations and plenty of time for leisure, family and virtual reality. We can experience any adventure, from wilderness to exotic ritual, without the expense, trouble or danger of travel. We can experience any adventure that ever happened, any adventure anyone can imagine. The virtual experience matches reality or invention in every way: sight, sound, smell, touch and movement.

Our civilization pulses with vitality. We have unlimited opportunity: of thought, of achievement, of freedom, and of the pursuit of happiness.

Whatever we require, human ingenuity can invent and provide. And if, in some unlikely but imaginable future, we should wish to recreate any organism, the means to do so exist. DNA sequences, RNA sequences, are easy to write down and archive; there is no need to store messy biological material, either tough and persistent DNA or fragile and degradable RNA. We are magnanimous; we have preserved the blueprints for everything, even parasites and pathogens.

No one has bothered to recreate an organism in a very long time. We have considered the question long and hard, and we have made our decision. No creation of nature has an inherent right to exist, independent of our need.

We have perfected nature, for we are its masters.

Guadalupe and Hieronymus Bosch

RUDY RUCKER

Rudy Rucker (www.rudyrucker.com) lives in Los Gatos, California. He has published fifteen novels to date, several science non-fiction books, and some software. His collected stories, Gnarl!, *was published in 2000. Rucker is one of the original cyberpunks of the Movement, and later the inventor of transrealism, a literary mode, not a movement. He won the Philip K. Dick Award for best paperback original novel in the U.S. twice, for* Software *and for* Wetware. *He's now a retired math and computer science professor and is writing up a storm. His 2006 novel is* Mathematicians in Love.*

"Guadalupe and Hieronymus Bosch" was published in Interzone, *which began to settle into a new commercial look in 2005. Full of true strangeness, it relates how Harna, one of those weird SF creatures who can travel through time and space using branes, helps Glenda Gomez fulfill her lust by helping her abduct Hieronymus Bosch. Sound wild? It is wilder than that.*

As an unemployed overweight unmarried overeducated woman with a big mouth, I don't have a lot of credibility. But even if I was some perfect California Barbie it wouldn't be enough. People never want to listen to women.

I, Glenda Gomez, bring glad tidings. She that hath ears, let her hear.

An alien being has visited our world. Harna is, was, her name. I saw her as a glowing paramecium, a jellyfish, a glass police car, and a demonic art patron. This morning, when she was shaped like a car, I rode inside her to the fifteenth century. And this evening I walked past the vanishing point and saved our universe from Harna's collecting bag. I'm the queen of space and time. I'm trying to write up my story to pitch as a reality TV show.

Let's start with paramecia. Unicellular organisms became a hobby of mine a few months ago when I stole a microscope from my job. I was sorting egg and sperm cells for an infertility clinic called Smart Stork. Even though I don't have any kind of biology background they trained me.

I'm not dumb. I have a Bachelor's in Art History from San Jose State, which is just a few blocks from my apartment on Sixth Street. Well, almost a degree. I never finished the general education courses or my senior seminar, which would probably, certainly, have been on Hieronymus Bosch. I used to have a book of his pictures I looked at all the time—although today the book disappeared. At first I thought it was hidden under something. My apartment is a sty.

My lab job didn't last long—I'm definitely not the science type. I wasn't fast enough, I acted bored, I kissed the manager Dick Went after one too many lunchtime Coronas—and he fired me. That's when I bagged my scope—a binocular phase-contrast Leica. I carried it home in my ever ready XXL purse. Later that day Dick came to my apartment to ask about it, but I screamed through the door at him like a crazy person until he went away. Works on the landlord, too.

Now that I have a microscope, I keep infusions of protozoan cultures in little jars all over my apartment. It's unbelievably easy to grow the infusions. You just put a wad of lawn grass in with some bottled water. Bacteria breed themselves into the trillions—rods and dots and corkscrews that I can see at 200X. And before you know it, the paramecia are right there digging on the bacilli. They come out of nowhere. What works really well is to add a scrap of meat to an infusion, it gets dark and pukeful, and the critters go wild for a few days till they die of their own shit. In the more decadent infusions you'll find a particular kind of very coarsely ciliated paramecium rolling and rushing around. My favorites. I call them the microhomies.

So today is a Sunday morning in March and I'm eating my usual breakfast of day-old bread with slices of welfare cheddar, flipping through my Bosch book thinking about my next tattoo. A friend named Sleepey is taking an on-line course in tattooing, and he said he'd give me one for free. He has a good flea-market tattoo-gun he traded a set of tires for. Who needs snow tires in San Jose? So I'm thinking it would be bitchin' to bedizen my belly with a Bosch.

I'm pretty well settled on this blue bagpipe bird with a horn for his nose. It'll be something to talk about, and the bagpipe will be like naturalistic on my gordo gut, maybe it'll minimize my girth. But the bird needs a background pattern. Over my fourth cup of microwave coffee, I start thinking about red blood cells, remembering from the lab how they're shaped. I begin digging on the concept of rounding out my Bosch bird tattoo with a blood-cell tiling.

To help visualize it, I pinprick my pinkie and put a droplet on a glass slide under my personal Glenda Gomez research scope. I see beautiful shades of orange and red from all my little blood cells massed together. Sleepey will need to see this in order to fully grasp what to do. I want to keep on looking, but the blood is drying fast. The cells are bursting and cracks are forming among them as they dry. I remember that at Smart Stork we'd put some juice on the slides with the cells to keep them perky. I don't know what kind of juice, but I decide to try a drop of water out of one of my infusions, a dark funky batch that I'd fed with a KFC chicken nugget.

The infusion water is teeming with those tough-looking paramecia with the coarse bristles—the microhomies. What with Bosch on my brain, the microhomies resemble tiny bagpipes on crutches. I'm like: tattoo them onto my belly too? While I'm watching the microhomies, they start digging on my ruptured blood cells. "Yo," I say, eyeing an especially bright and lively one. "You're eating me."

And that's when it happens. The image loses its focus, I feel a puff of air, my skin tingles all over. Leaning back, I see a bag of glowing light grow out from the microscope slide. It's a foot across.

I jump to my feet and back off. I may be heavy, but I'm still quick. At first I have the idea my apartment is on fire, and then for some reason I think of earthquakes. I'm heading for the door. But the glowing sack gets there before me, blocking the exit. I try to reach through it for the doorknob.

As soon as my hand is inside the lumpy glow I hear a woman's voice. "Glenda! Hello dear."

"Who are you?"

"I'm Harna from Hilbert space." She has a prim voice; I visualize flowery dresses and pillbox hats. "I happened upon your brane several—days—ago. I've been teeming with the microlife, a bit humdrum, and I thought that's all there is to see in this location. Worth documenting, but no more than that. I had no idea that only a few clicks up the size scale I'd find a gorgeous entity like you. Scale is tricky for me, what with everything in Hilbert space being infinite. Thank goodness I happened upon your blood cell. Oh, warmest greetings, Glenda Gomez. You're—why, you're collectible, my dear." I'm fully buggin'. I run to the corner of my living room, staring at the luminous paramecium the size of a dog in mid-air. "Go away," I say.

Harna wobbles into the shape of a jellyfish with dangling frilly ribbons. She drifts across the room, not quite touching the floor, dragging her oral arms across the stuff lying on my tables, checking things out. And then she gets to my Bosch book, which is open to The Garden of Earthly Delights.

"A nonlinear projection of three-space to two-space," burbles Harna, feeling the paper all over. "Such a clever map. Who's the author?"

"Hieronymus Bosch," I murmur. "It's called perspective." I'm half-wondering if my brain has popped and I'm alone here talking to myself. Maybe I'm about to start fingerpainting the floor with Clorox. Snorting Ajax up my nose.

"Bosch?" muses Harna. Her voice is fruity and penetrating like my old guidance counselor's. "And I just know you have a crush on him, Glenda! I can tell. When can I meet him?"

"He lived a long time ago," I whisper. I'm stepping from side to side, trying to find a clear path to the door.

"Most excellent," Harna is saying. "You'll time-snatch him, and then I can use the time-flaw to perspective-map your whole spacetime brane down into a sack! Yummy! You are so cute, Glenda. Yes, I'm going to wrap you up and take you home!"

I get past her and run out into the street. I'm breathing hard, still in my nightgown, now and then looking over my shoulder. So of course a San Jose police car pulls over and sounds me on their speaker. They think I'm a tweaker or a nut-job. Did I mention that it's Sunday morning?

"Ma'am. Can we help you? Ma'am. Please come over to the police car and place your hands on the hood. Ma'am." More cop-voice crackle in the background and here comes Harna down the sidewalk, still shaped like a flying jellyfish, though bigger than before. The cops can't see her, though.

"Ma'am." One of them gets out of the car, a kid with a cop mustache. He looks kind, concerned, but his hand is on the butt of his Taser.

I whirl, every cop's image of a madwoman, pointing back down the sidewalk at the swollen Harna, who's shaping herself into a damn good replica of the cops' car. She's made of glowing haze and hanging at an angle to the ground.

Right before the cop grabs my wrist or Tasers me, Harna sweeps over and—pixie-dust! I'm riding in a Gummi-Bear cop car, with Harna talking to me from the radio grill. The cops don't see me anymore. Harna heads down the street, then swerves off parallel to spacetime. She guns her mill and we're rumbling through a wah-wah collage of years and centuries, calendar leaves flying, the sun flickering off and on, Earth rushing around the Sun in a blur. And it's not just time we're traveling through, we're rolling through some miles as well. We arrive in the Lowlands of 1475.

It's a foggy dawn, Jerome Bosch is at his bedroom window, arcing a stream of pee toward the glow of the rising sun. I know from books that Hieronymus was just his fancy show name, and that his homies called him Jerome. Like my given name is Guadalupe—but everyone calls me Glenda. Seeing the man in the window, my heart does a little handstand. My love has guided us all this way.

"He is scrumptious," says Harna.

As he lowers his nightshirt, Jerome's gaze drifts away from the horizon—and he sees us. His expression is calm, resigned—it's like he's always been expecting a flying jellyfish/cop-car carrying a good-looking woman from the next millennium. Calm, yes, but he's moving back from the window hella fast.

Harna flips out a long vortex of force, a tornado that fastens onto Jerome and pulls him to us. He's hanging in the air a few feet away from me, slowly spinning—and yelling in what must be Dutch.

"Grab your fella," says Harna. "It has to be you who lands him. It's not for me to meddle in a brane's spacetime."

The wind has flopped Bosch's hair back. His cheekbones are high, his lips are thin, his eyes are bright. The man for me. I reach out and catch hold of his hand. It's warm.

Harna's light flows down my arm and up Jerome's. Aug-

mented by Harna, I'm strong as a steam-shovel. I set Bosch
down on the jelly car seat next to me.

"It's too soon," he says, clear as day. "I'm not ready."

"I'm Glenda," I say, not all that surprised he's speaking
English. Another Harna miracle. "Ready or not, I'm taking
you home."

"To Hell?" exclaims Jerome. "That's quite unjust. Only
yesterday I was absolved by the priest. My sins in these last
hours have been but petty ones. A touch of anger at the
neighbor's dog, my usual avarice for a truly great commission, and the accustomed fires of lust, of course—" As he
mentions this last sin, he looks down my nightgown, which
I'm just loving. I press his hand against my warm thigh.

"Don't worry, sweetie. I don't live in Hell. I live in San
Jose."

For the rest of the ride, Jerome is busy looking around,
taking everything in. What eyes he has! So sharp and smart
and alert. What with the time-winds flapping my flimsy, he
can see I'm all woman. I'm doing my best to keep the fabric
cinched in around the problem areas at my waist, and I'm
trying to get his arms around me, but he's kind of reluctant.
He's uneasy about whither we're bound. I can dig it.

Finally Harna sets us down in the sunny street outside my
apartment. Lucky me, the cops are gone. Everything looks
the same—the dead palm leaves, the beater cars and pick-
ups, the dusty jasmine vines, the broken glass on the dry
clay, the 7-11 store, the university parking garage—sunny
and dry.

Harna rises into the air and spreads out, layering herself
across the scene like extra sunshine. No doubt she'll be back
in some more personal form pretty soon. But meanwhile I've
got me a man. I smile at Jerome and give his arm a happy
squeeze.

"This is Spain?" he wonders.

"America," I tell him, which doesn't seem to ring a bell.
"The new world across the Atlantic Ocean, plus some five
centuries past your time."

He shakes his head, and stares around like a bird fallen

from its nest. "It's after the Second Coming?" he asks. "Christ has dominion over the Earth?"

"The Church is doing fine," I say, not sure where this is going. We shouldn't stand around the street in our night-gowns. "Come on inside."

I hustle him up the stairs into my apartment and first of all get us in some clothes. I dress him in my favorite vintage red Ramones T-shirt and my yellow SJSU sweat pants. Me, I put on some nice tight Capri pants with a Lycra tummy panel and a pink baby-doll blouse that's loose at the bottom. Truth be told, I do a certain amount of my shopping in the mater-nity section at Target.

In the kitchen I offer Jerome some Oreos and microwave two cups of instant coffee. Buzz! The microwave is built into the wall so we delinquent renters can't hock it. Jerome over-looks the futuristic aspects of my kitchen because he's busy holding one of the cookies up to the light, studying the em-bossed writing and curlicues.

"They're food," I tell him. I rotate one in two and give him the better half. He scarfs it down—and I'm secretly glad, thinking that we've broken bread together now. Jerome takes another Oreo and eats the whole thing. They're gettin' good to him.

Meanwhile I touch up my black lipstick and lip liner. All the time I'm watching him. Even though he's from a long time ago, he's not old. Maybe twenty-five. He would have still been at the start of his career. No reason he can't have as good a career here in San Jose with me.

Jerome watches me right back. His gaze is warm and alive, as if there's an extra brain inside each eyeball. After a bit he fixates on my mug of colored pencils, looking at them the way I wish he was looking at my boobs.

"Want to draw?" I ask him. "You can decorate my walls." There's two smooth blank walls in my living room, a short wall across from the hall door and a big one across from the window.

"A mural?" says Jerome, examining a couple of the pen-cils.

"Bingo."

He starts in on the smaller wall. And me, I sit down with pen and paper at my round table on the one chair I've got. I want to try and start documenting some of this unfurling madness. For sure there's a reality TV show in this. All my friends say I should be on TV, and who am I to disagree. I recite a prayer to give me courage to write.

"Hail Glenda, full of grace, an alien paramecium was with thee. Blessed art thou amongst women, and blessed is the fruit of your brain, Glenda And Jerome."

I lean over my spiral notebook, pen in hand.

To whom it may concern:
It may interest you to know that . . .

Is it Hie or Hei? Love has made me dyslexic.

I look around, trying to find the book that turned Harna on to Jerome, but I can't see it just now. Thinking about the book, I have to grin, thinking how incredible it is to have the artist himself here with me.

"Hey, Jerome. I'm writing about you."

"Not yet," he says and taps his thumb with his finger. Like that's the Lowlands chill-it gesture. He's holding a purple pencil in his other hand. Getting started on marking up my little wall. Holding the pencil gives him power, aplomb. He's a suspicious genius with sharp eyes and a trapdoor mouth. I keep talking to him.

"It's fabulous that you're drawing, Jerome. This hole will be an art grotto. I hope they don't paint it over when we move." And surely we will be moving quite soon, with Jerome pulling in the Old Master bucks. We'll be on TV. We'll get a condo in one of those beautiful new buildings across from the SJSU library on Fourth Street.

I smile at Jerome and fluff my hair a little. I wear it long and black with henna highlights and Bettie Page bangs. Too bad I didn't happen to shampoo and condition it yet this week. I look sexier when my mane is lustrous.

Jerome thins his lips and shades the outstretched arms of a little man. He's digging on the excellent twenty-first-century quality of my pencils and the luscious smooth whiteness of apartment dry-wall. Sketching a picture of Harna and me snatching him. Harna looks like a fish as much as a car. She's surrounded by glow-lines of blue light. Her prey is just now seeing the shape in the sky, he's holding out his arms with that odd look of non-surprise. His unmade bachelor bed is in the far corner of his room. The vortex from the aeroform is gonna cartwheel him into the arms of a voluptuous dark-haired sorceress. Me!

"You're cute," I tell Jerome. He pinches the fingers of one hand at me again, the other hand busy with my pencils. He draws terrifically fast. I'm really glad I bagged him. But I wish he looked a little happier about it.

"Why don't we get to know each other better?" I say, imagining he might pick up on my tone. I unbutton my baby-doll blouse enough so he can see my boobs—but not the runaway rolls of my stomach. My breasts are a major plus, easily the equal of Pammy Anderson's. And they're natural.

But Jerome looks away. It occurs to me that maybe he still thinks this is Hell—which would make me a demoness. I decide to play up to that. I cackle at him and beckon with witchy fingers, the light glinting on my chipped black nails. My fingers are quite shapely, another plus feature. But they're not bringing Jerome Bosch into my arms.

So I go get him. He tries to escape, racing around the apartment like a sparrow that flew in the window. I shoo him into my bedroom and—plop—we're mixed in with the sheets, magazines and laundry on my bed.

I give him a wet kiss and pull down my stretchy pants—keeping my top on so as to minimize that troublesome abdominal area. Of course I'm not wearing panties, I've been planning this all along. I tug down his sweat pants—and there's his goodies on display. A twenty-five-year-old fella here in bed with me, the answer to a maiden's prayer. I roll him on top of me and pull him in. It's been a while.

But—just my luck—this turns into a totally screwed-up proposition. He comes, maybe, and then he's limp, and then—oh, God—he starts sobbing like his heart is going to break. Poor Jerome. I cuddle him and whisper to him. His sobs slow down, he whimpers, he slides off to one side and—falls asleep!

I feel down between my legs, trying to figure out if he delivered. What a thing it would be to carry Hieronymus Bosch's baby! That would tie him to me for sure. I think I'm ovulating today, as a matter of fact. Just for luck, I twist around and prop my feet up on the wall, giving the Dutch Master's wrigglers every opportunity to work their way up to the hidden jewel of my egg.

Resting there, thinking things over, I can visualize them, pointy-nosed with beating tails, talking to each other in Dutch, enjoying themselves in Glenda-land, on a pilgrimage to my Garden of Earthly Delights.

He keeps on sleeping, and I amble back into the kitchen to make myself a grilled cheese sandwich. I'm happy, but at the same time I have this bad feeling that Harna somehow tricked me. That stuff about wrapping me up and taking me home. Some weird shit is gonna come down, I just know it.

But now here comes Jerome out the bedroom, looking mellower than before. Our little hump and cuddle has helped his mind-set.

"Greetings, Glenda," he says. "I enjoyed our venery."

"Likewise." He looks so cute and inquisitive that I run over and kiss his cheek. And I can't help asking, "You don't think I'm too fat?"

"You're well-fed," he says, cupping my boobs. "Clean and healthy. But do you worship Satan? Your spirit-familiar Harna—surely she is unholy."

"I don't know much about Harna," I admit. "She only appeared today. And Satan? Naw, dog. I'm a Catholic girl." Fallen away, I don't mention. I cross myself and he's relieved.

"I can go home?" he asks, glancing out the window at the quiet street in the noon sun.

"You belong with me," I tell him. "I'll give you a baby. You never had one back then. I love your art. You're mucho famous here, you know. I have a whole book of your pictures."

I root around the apartment, wanting to show him, but

damn it, that book is totally gone. I'm guessing that Harna took it. She was saying something about copying Jerome's perspective maps so she can—fit our world into a sack? That has to be wack. If only she's gone for good. Maybe hoping hard enough can make it so. I skip over to Jerome and kiss him again. He lets me.

"I can't find my book, but we can go to the SJSU library," I tell him. "It's just across the campus and they're open on Sunday. And I think the Art Mart is open today too. I'll buy you some paint."

"Buy paint?" says Jerome. "I mix my own."

"We get it in tubes," I say. "Like sausage. Ready-made. Here, you eat a grilled cheese sandwich too, and then we'll look for Hieronymus Bosch books in the library."

Well, guess what we find under bosch, hieronymus, in the library? Not jack shit. When Harna and I abducted him from the fifteenth-century Dutch town of s'Hertogenbosch and carried him to twenty-first century San Jose, California, we wiped out his role in history. Maybe he finished one or two minor paintings before we nabbed him, but as far as the history of art is concerned, he never lived. Jerome doesn't really pick up on how weird this is—I mean all he's seen me do is look at an incomprehensible-to-a-medieval-mind online card catalog, and we nabbed him before he was famous anyway, so he's not feeling the loss. But me, I feel it bad.

Bosch was a really important artist, you know—or maybe you don't. Come to think of it, I might be the only one who remembers our world before I changed our history. But take it from me, Hieronymus Bosch was King. The Elvis of artists. His work influenced a lot of people in all kinds of ways over the centuries.

More ways than I'd imagined.

Because now, walking off the campus and getting a coffee, I'm paying attention and I'm noticing differences in our non-Bosch world. There aren't any ads for horror movies in the paper, for instance, which is way odd.

The Episcopal church that used to be by the coffee shop is a pho noodle parlor. On a hunch, I look in the yellow pages in the coffee shop, and there's no Episcopal or Baptist or

Proletarian or whatever churches in town at all. With no Bosch, the Protestant thing never happened! The sisters that whipped me through grade school would be happy, but I'm thinking, Dear God, what have I done?

The cars are different too, duller than before, and every single one of them is cream-colored, not even any silver or maroon.

The barrista in the coffee shop who usually wears foundation and drawn-on eyebrows has her face bare as a granola hippie's. And her hair is all bowl-cut and sensible. Ugh. The world is definitely lagging without the cumulative influences of my man Jerome.

On the plus side, you can smoke in the coffee shop now, and all the cigarettes are fat and laced with nutmeg and clove, which I dig. The Supertaqueria next door isn't selling tongue anymore, also fine by me. The fonts on the signs are somehow lower and fatter and more, like, Sanskrit-looking. The people in the magazine ads are wearing more clothes, and generally heavier.

Hey, I can live with some change, if that's what it takes to get Glenda her man.

I buy Jerome a canvas and some acrylics at the Art Mart—putting them on a new credit card that some pinheads mailed me last week. Back home, my Dutch Master sniffs suspiciously at the paint, preparing to start layering the stuff over the colored drawing on my smaller wall.

There's a knock on the door. I've been expecting this. I peep through the peephole and it's Harna, looking just like her voice sounds, like a rich old white woman in a flowery dress and pillbox hat. I don't want to let her in, but she walks right through the closed door.

"Hello, Glenda and Jerome," goes Harna. "I have a commission for the artist." She plumps a velvet sack right down on my kitchen table. Clink of gold coins. Perfectly calculated to get Jerome's juices flowing.

"What kind of painting do you need, my lady?" asks Jerome, setting down his paintbrush and making a greedy little bow.

"A picture of that," she says, pointing out the window to

Sixth Street and the San Jose cityscape. "With full perspective accuracy. You can paint it—there." She points to my big blank living room wall.

"How soon would you need it?" asks Jerome.

"By sundown," says Harna.

"He can't paint that fast," I protest.

"I'll speed him up," says Harna, with a twitch of her dowager lips. "I'll return with the rising of the moon."

Sure enough, Jerome starts racing around the room like a cockroach when the light comes on, pausing only long enough to ask me to get him more paint.

When I come back from the Art Mart with a shopping bag of paint tubes, he's already roughed in an underpainting of the street—the houses with their tile and shingle roofs, the untrimmed palm trees, the dead dingy cars, the vines, a few passers-by captured in motion, the tops of the houses in the next block, the houses after them, the low brown haze from the freeways, and beyond that the golden-grassed foothills and the blank blue sky.

He's all over the wall, and the painting is so perfect and beautiful I can hardly stand it. Every ten seconds, it seems like, he darts over to the window, then darts back. He's such a nut that he's putting in every single person and car that goes past, so the picture is getting more and more crowded.

The sun is going down and a few lights come on in the windows outside. Somehow Jerome is keeping up with it, changing his painting to match the world, touching the buildings with sunset gold, damping the shadows into warmer shades, pinkening the sky—and then darkening it.

A fat full moon comes up over the foothills and, quick as a knife, Jerome paints it onto my wall, sprinkling stars all around it.

And then Harna's in the room again.

"It's enough," she says. "He can stop."

Jerome cranks down to normal speed. I hand him more Oreos and coffee. He slugs down the nourishment, then drinks a quart of water from the sink.

"What happens now?" I ask Harna.

"Like I said before," she answers, not looking so much

like a human anymore. Her pink skin is peeling away in patches, and underneath she's green. "I'm going to bag you and your world and take you home. Don't worry, it won't hurt."

And then she shoots out of the window and disappears into the distance past the moon.

"We have to stop her!" I tell Jerome, picking up my purse.

"What?" he says. He sounds tired.

"We have to run after Harna."

Jerome looks at me for a long time. And then he smiles. "If you say so, Glenda. Being with you is interesting."

The two of us run down the apartment stairs and right away I can see that things are seriously weird. The cars across the street are two-thirds as big as the cars on my side.

"Hurry," I tell Jerome, and we run around the corner to the next block. The houses on that next street are half the size of the houses on my street. We run another block, which takes only a couple of seconds, as each block is way smaller than the one before. The houses are only waist high. We go just a little farther and now we're stepping right over the houses, striding across a block at a time.

Another step takes us all the way across Route 101, the step after that across east San Jose. The farther from Jerome's picture we get, the smaller things are.

"Perspective!" exclaims Jerome. "The world has shrunk to perspective!"

We hop over the foothills. And now it gets really crazy. With one last push of our legs, we leap past the moon. It's a pale yellow golf ball near our knees. We're launched into space, man. The stars rush past, all of them, denser and denser—zow—and then we're past everything, beyond the vanishing point, out at infinity.

Clear white light, firm as Jell-O, and you can stand wherever you like. Up where it's the brightest, I see a throne and a bearded man in it, just like in Jerome's paintings. It's God, with Jesus beside Him, and between them is the Dove, which I never did get. Right below the Trinity is my own Virgin of Guadalupe, with wiggly yellow lines all around her. And up above them all are my secret guardians, the Powerpuff Girls from my favorite Saturday morning cartoon. Jerome sees them too. We clasp hands. I know deep inside myself that now forever we two are married. I'm crying my head off.

But somebody jostles me, it's Harna right next to us, pushing and grunting, trying to wrestle our whole universe into a brown sack. She's the shape of a green Bosch-goblin with a slit mouth.

I turn off the waterworks and whack Harna up the side of the head with my purse. Jerome crouches down and butts her in the stomach. Passing the vanishing point has made us about as strong as our enemy, the demonic universe-collector. While she's reeling back, I quick get hold of her sack and shake its edges free of our stars.

Harna comes at me hot and heavy, with smells and electric shocks and thumps on my butt. Jerome goes toe-to-toe with her, shoving her around, but she's starting to hammer on his head pretty good. Just then I notice a brush and tubes of white and blue paint in my purse. I hand them to Jerome and while I use some Extreme Wrestling moves from TV on Harna, Jerome quick paints a translucent blue sphere around her with a cross on top—a spirit trap.

I shove the last free piece of Harna fully inside the ball and, presto, she's neutralized. With a hissing, farting sound she dwindles from our view, disappearing in a direction different from any that we can see. I wave one time to the Trinity, the Virgin and the Powerpuff Girls, and, how awesome, they wave back. And then we're outta there.

The walk home is a little tricky—that first step in particular, where you go from infinity back into normal space, is a tough one. But we make it.

As soon as we're in my apartment, I help Jerome slap some house-paint over his big mural. And when we go outside to check on things, everything is back to being its own right size. We've saved our universe.

To celebrate, we get some Olde Antwerpen forty-ouncers at the 7-11 and hop into my bed, cuddling together at one end leaning against the wall. I'm kind of hoping Jerome will want to get it on, but right now he seems a little tired. Not too tired to check out my boobs though.

Just when it might start to get interesting, here comes Harna's last gasp. I can't see her anymore, but I can hear her voice, and so can Jerome. "Have it your way," intones the prissy universe-collector. "Keep your petty world. But the restoration must be in full. Before I leave for good, Hieronymus must go home."

"Think I'll stay here," says Jerome, who's holding a tit in one hand and a beer in the other.

"Back," says Harna, and her presence disappears for good.

As she leaves, the living breathing man next to me turns into—oh hell—an art book.

"No way," I sob. "I need him." I quick say the Hail Mary three times, like the sisters taught me. But the Bosch book just sits there. I pour some of the microhomies onto it. Nothing doing. I squeeze red paint onto the book cover and stick a split Oreo cookie to it. Still no good. And then in desperation, I pray to my special protectors, the Powerpuff Girls. And the day's last miracle begins.

The book twitches in my hands, throbs, splits in two, and the two copies move apart, making a, like, hyperdimensional man-hole.

And, yes, pushing his way out of the hole, here comes my Hieronymus Bosch, his hair flopping, his eyes sharp, his mouth thin with concentration.

He's in my bed—and the dumb book is gone. Screw art history. Jerome will make even better paintings than before. And if that doesn't work out, there's reality TV.

You know anybody who can help with my show?

The Forever Kitten

PETER F. HAMILTON

Peter F. Hamilton (www.peterfhamilton.co.uk) lives in Oakham, England. He began publishing SF in the early 1990s with three SF detective novels—Mindstar Rising *(1993),* A Quantum Murder *(1994), and* The Nano Flower *(1995). But his prominence began with a massive trilogy of one-thousand-page novels (in its original British form)—* The Reality Dysfunction *(1996),* The Neutronium Alchemist *(1997), and* The Naked God *(2000), together the Night's Dawn Trilogy. In the U.S., all three books were divided into two volumes each, so it became a six-book series). A collection,* A Second Chance at Eden *(1998), is set in the same "Confederation" future as the trilogy. The whole setting is so complex that Hamilton published a non-fiction guide,* The Confederation Handbook: The Essential Guide to the Night's Dawn Series, *in 2000. Two of his three later novels to date are also space opera—*Fallen Dragon *(2001) and* Pandora's Star *(2004), his Commonwealth saga. The Void Trilogy is currently being written. After Iain M. Banks, Hamilton is the most popular British space opera writer of the last decade.*

"The Forever Kitten" appeared in Nature. *It is small scale and closely focused, about scientific research, money, and ethics. It is just plausible enough to be an effective SF horror story.*

The mansion's garden was screened by lush trees. I never thought I'd be so entranced by anything as simple as horse chestnuts, but that's what 18 months in jail on remand will do for your appreciation of the simple things.

Joe Gordon was waiting for me; the venture capitalist and his wife Fiona were sitting on ornate metal chairs in a sunken patio area. Their five-year-old daughter, Heloise, was sprawled on a pile of cushions, playing with a ginger kitten.

"Thanks for paying my bail," I said.

"Sorry it took so long, Doctor," he said. "The preparations weren't easy, but we have a private plane waiting to take you to the Caribbean—an island the EU has no extradition treaty with."

"I see. Do you think it's necessary?"

"For the moment, yes. The Brussels Bioethics Commission is looking to make an example of you. They didn't appreciate how many regulations you violated."

"They wouldn't have minded if the treatment had worked properly."

"Of course not, but that day isn't here yet, is it? We can set you up with another lab out there."

"Ah well, there are worse places to be exiled. I appreciate it."

"Least we could do. My colleagues and I made a lot of money from the Viagra gland you developed."

I looked at Heloise again. She was a beautiful child, and the smile on her face as she played with the kitten was an-

gelic. The ball of ginger fluff was full of rascally high spirits, just like every two-month-old kitten. I kept staring,
shocked by the familiar pattern of marbling in its fluffy light
fur.

"Yes," Joe said with quiet pride. "I managed to save one
before the court had the litter destroyed. A simple substitu-
tion; the police never knew."

"It's three years old now," I whispered.

"Indeed. Heloise is very fond of it."

"Do you understand what this means? The initial stasis-
regeneration procedure is valid. If the kitten is still alive and
maintaining itself at the same biological age after this long,
then in theory it can live forever, just as it is. The procedure
stabilized its cellular structure."

"I understand perfectly, thank you, Doctor. Which is why
we intend to keep on funding your research. We believe that
human rejuvenation is possible."

I recognized the greed in his eyes: it wasn't pleasant. "It's
still a long way off. This procedure was just the first of a
great many. It has no real practical application, we can't use
it on an adult. Once a mammal reaches sexual maturity its
cells can't accept such a radical modification."

"We have every confidence that in the end you'll produce
the result we all want."

I turned back to the child with her pet, feeling more optimistic than I had in three years. "I can do it," I said through
clenched teeth. "I can." Revenge, it is said, is best served
cold. I could see myself looking down on the gravestones of
those fools in the Bioethics Commission in, say . . . oh,
about 500 years' time. They'd be very cold indeed by then.

Joe's affable smile suddenly hardened. I turned, fearing
the police had arrived. I'm still very twitchy about raids.

It wasn't the police. The teenage girl coming out from the
house was dressed in a black leather micro-skirt and very
tight scarlet T-shirt. She would have been attractive if it
wasn't for the permanent expression of belligerence on her
face; the tattoos weren't nice either. The short sleeves on the
T-shirt revealed track marks on her arms. "Is that . . ."

"Saskia," Joe said with extreme distaste.

I really wouldn't have recognized his older daughter. Saskia used to be a lovely girl. This creature was the kind of horror story that belonged on the front page of a tabloid.

"Whatcha starin' at?" she demanded.

"Nothing," I promised quickly.

"I need money," she told her father.

"Get a job."

Her face screwed up in rage. I really believed she was going to hit him. I could see Heloise behind her on the verge of tears, arms curling protectively around the kitten.

"You know what I'll do to get it if you don't," Saskia said.

"Fine," Joe snapped. "We no longer care."

She made an obscene gesture and hurried back through the mansion. For a moment I thought Joe was going to run after her. I'd never seen him so angry. Instead he turned to his wife, who was frozen in her chair, shaking slightly. "Are you all right?" he asked tenderly.

She nodded bravely, her eyes slowly refocusing.

"What happened?" I asked.

"I don't know," Joe said bitterly. "We didn't spoil her, we were very careful about that. Then about a year ago she started hanging out with the wrong sort: we've been living in a nightmare ever since. She's quit school; she's got a drug habit, she steals from us constantly, I can't remember how many times she's been arrested for joyriding and shoplifting."

"I'm sorry. Kids, huh!"

"Teenagers," he said wretchedly. "Fiona needed two Prozac gland implants to cope."

I smiled over at Heloise, who had started playing with the kitten again. "At least you've got her."

"Yes." Joe seemed to make some kind of decision. "Before you leave, I'd like you to perform the cellular stasis-regeneration procedure for me."

"I don't understand. I explained before, it's simply the first stage of verifying the overwrite sequence we developed."

His attitude changed. "Nevertheless, you will do it again. Without my help you will be going back to prison for a long time."

"It's of no use to adults," I said helplessly. "You won't become young, or even maintain your current age."

"It's not for me," he said.

"Then who . . ." I followed his gaze to Heloise. "Oh."

"She's perfect just the way she is," he said quietly. "And that, Doctor, is the way she's going to stay."

City of Reason

MATTHEW JARPE

---

*Matthew Jarpe (home.comcast.net/~m.jarpe/) lives in Quincy,
Massachusetts, with his wife and son. "I currently work (as a
biochemist) at a company in Cambridge, Massachusets, called
Biogen Idec. I characterize interactions between molecules,"
he says on his website, and "I like to cook, build things, and
brew beer." Jarpe has published six SF stories to date in six
years, five in* Asimov's *and one in* Fantasy & Science Fiction. *In the 1990s he was part of Hal Clement's SF writing
circle.*

"City of Reason" was published in Asimov's. *It's an exciting space opera with action, complex intrigue, a nuclear
weapon, mind control, a post-human teenage girl, and much
more. Out on the edge of the solar system, a man who is supposed to find out information about space ships for an
agency that sells the information finds a ship containing two
teenagers and a nuclear weapon, on their way to destroy a
city.*

Homesteaders made for easy pickings. For one thing, they were hell and gone outside the orbit of Neptune, the last crumb of civilization before the big dark. For another, they all had philosophies. You didn't up and leave mainstream humanity unless you had some ideas that just wouldn't work inside someone else's system. And so the homesteaders moved out and set up on trans-Neptunian objects, balls of dirty ice, and made a go at Utopia. I've never heard of a philosophy that didn't cripple a society from defending itself properly. So most of the homesteads were weak.

Easy pickings, but slim. Their equipment wasn't the best. They didn't have loads of energy or raw materials, or biodiversity, or any of the stuff that makes a pirate happy to have risked his life to get. In fact, the Kuiper belt had gotten a reputation as a kind of pirate's farm system. You honed your skills out where the sun was dim, and when you had the moves and the weapons, you drifted down into the gravity well and you went major league.

So what was I doing out among the snowballs? Well, that's the thing. I'm not a pirate anymore. I've gone legit. Nowadays, when I reduce a manned spacecraft to a blob of alloy with a crispy center, I'm on the side of the angels. I'm a Damager, license right there on my forward bulkhead next to the picture of my sainted mother.

I get my information from the eye in the sky. The Coordinator Group maintains three space stations in solar polar orbits that are perpendicular to the ecliptic. Between those

SoPo stations and the spy bots salt-and-peppered around the system, those bastards see everything. Needless to say, the rise of the Coordinator Group was what persuaded me and others like me to go legit. Best play for the winning team.

So there I am, cooling my heels and everything else besides out past the orbit of Neptune, when I get a blip on my radar. Something is out there, and it isn't supposed to be, and the Coordinators don't know about it, and that's the first time that's happened to me.

It's too late for me to go all stealthy. I've had my radar and transponder shouting out for all to hear, so I've already given up my shit. I figured I might as well play Damager, so I flipped on the horn and spoke in Belligerent Asshole voice.

"This is the licensed Damager *One in the Hand* addressing the unidentified object at 183.24.46 incline—16 out 67 heading 004.58.07. Please reactivate transponder and identify." At the same time, I sent a burst of machine code that would give the same message, minus the belligerent tone, to the automated systems of the ship.

And how did I know it was a ship and not some piece of rock wandering off its accustomed orbit? After all, the only thing I had to go on was a little radar blip. It could be anything. Well, call it a gut feeling if you want to. A few minutes of data-gathering and my ship's targeting computer confirmed my suspicions. The thing was hollow and rotating, and about thirty thousand klicks back, it had shed a wisp of chemical rocket exhaust during a course-correcting burn.

So I was right. Hell, I ought to be. I've survived out here longer than most people have been alive, and most of that time was spent hunting ships. I can smell a can of meat across a thousand kilometers of void.

But there was no answer from the unidentified vessel. Nobody ignores a Damager. I laid in a course and burned hard for the cheeky bastard. I overtook easily in just a few hours. He didn't even try to run. That's when I got my first look at the ship.

Ship. I'm being charitable. It was made of rock and ice, and only a miracle gave it enough balance to burn the engines without wobble. This thing wouldn't last ten minutes inside the orbit of Mars. Sol would cook off the ice and leave nothing holding it together. It was no wonder the Co-ordinators hadn't pegged it. It looked like just another fuck-ing rock.

"In case you haven't got any sensors, my friend, I'll tell you that I've matched vectors two thousand meters from your . . . well, I guess we'll call it a vessel. Now, I already told you I'm a Damager, but just in case you've been living under a rock, or inside one, for a long time, I'll tell you what that means. That means I've got a weapon trained on you that will take your whole outfit down to plasma in just a cou-ple of seconds. Okay, you're probably asking yourself about now what you have to do to avoid the fate I've just described. You can tell me who you are for starters, and we'll go from there."

I gave it a few minutes with my message repeating on all frequencies in a couple dozen common languages and I got my reply. "Uh, don't shoot, mister. I'm Jesse Marslarsen. I'm out of the High Fantastic Empire of Trans-Emotional Excellence."

I looked that one up. Sixty-three people in a cave hol-lowed out of an ice ball about two hundred million clicks from here. Pretty god-damned Fantastic. "Good job, Jesse. I'm about 50 percent less likely to kill you now that you've started talking. What's the name and registration number of your vehicle there?"

"I don't . . . have one. It's homemade."

"I kind of figured. So you never registered this thing with the Coordinator Group?"

"We can't afford the fee," the voice said. "We don't pro-duce anything to trade, you know."

"I've got that information on my screen, yeah. Only it's dangerous to be out here without the Coordinators knowing what you're about. Guy like me is likely to shoot first and explain the situation to the oversight board later. They usu-ally don't care much. Tell you what, Jesse Marslarsen. Let's give your ship a name. I'm going to call it *JAFR*."

"What is that, a random code?"

"No," I said. I was about to tell him what it stood for, then

I thought better of it. "Yes, that's what it is." Jesse didn't sound like he had much of a sense of humor there. "Now we're going to do pretty much what the Coordinators do when they register a flight. I'm going to ask what your business is, where you're going and why, and then I'm going to find out what you've got on board. The whole purpose is so we can let the people at your destination know that you're no danger and they're safe to let you dock. If they're willing to pay for that information, of course."

"Well, I guess there isn't much I can do to stop you," Jesse said. "I'm willing to tell you the whole story and let you on board to inspect, but you're not going to give any assurances to the people I'm on my way to see."

"Why is that, Jesse?"

"Because I'm going to kill them."

The probes I brought with me to the *JAFR* confirmed what Jesse had told me. He was transporting a rather hefty thermonuclear device buried in the rock and ice that was his ship. He had no other ordnance, no weapons of any kind. Just one honking great bomb, a standard ion drive, and a rather meager life-support bubble. I was rather impressed that they had gone to the trouble to outfit this crummy little ship with a lifeboat and a distress radio. Perhaps a futile gesture in this sparsely populated region, but you had to give them points for thinking ahead. The rest of the ship was barely adequate. It would have been cramped space for one human, but there were two people in there. Two young people.

I entered the ship through a short tunnel that led to an airlock. They let me in without protest or threat, but I kept my battle armor on anyway. Not just to be safe, but because talking to the blank metal faceplate and the array of sensors made people nervous. I like the answers I get from nervous people.

Jesse Marslarsen was just a kid, good dark-haired thin-faced Martian stock. The High Fantastic Empire was working on emotions, according to their published manifesto. They were using some genetic modifications and some hardware implants to . . . I don't know, conquer emotions or get in touch with them or something like that. Like most of these homesteader manifestos, it wasn't the clearest thing to read. They had reported no success to the rest of the solar system, but best of luck to them anyway. The battle armor trick was working on Jesse. I had thought he was high-strung talking to him on the radio, but in person he seemed ready to snap.

His companion was not of the High Fantastic Empire but from a neighboring colony. She was a darling little thing of sixteen Earth years, strawberry blond hair and green eyes, scattering of freckles across her nose. But looks were, as is so often the case in this day and age, deceiving. That cute little American cheerleader's body was just a walking feeder culture for sophont silk.

I'd seen people boost their brainpower with thread lots of times. I'll bet there isn't anyone on Luna who doesn't have a bit of silk in the old gray matter. It was a popular implant, not one of the ones I was using, but it had its adherents. It was nice to see that even this trend had been taken to its extreme out in the homesteads. I don't believe that there was anything left, mentally, of the young woman who had been called Shaunasie MacTaggart. When I spoke to her, found out who she was and where she was from, it was clear to me that I was talking to the silk.

She was from an enclave that called itself A Better Way. They didn't have much on file, and the name certainly didn't give me much to go on. If their whole philosophy was an unhealthy indulgence in mental enhancements, that made them dangerous enough. But what interested me right then was not why her colony had created such a loathsome creature, but why they had put it on this ship with this kid and this bomb.

"Jesse, Shaunasie, thanks for inviting me in here. I like it when people make my job easier. I'll be sure to remember that in my report. Now, do you mind telling me what you're up to? Looks like your trajectory is taking you to someplace called the City of Reason in about twenty-three days. What's your beef with these guys?"

"We're making a retaliatory strike against them," Jesse

said. "They've repeatedly attacked us over the past two years."

"They've attacked both your home colonies?"

"No, they've only attacked the High Fantastic Empire so far, but everyone else in this region is at risk. A Better Way is just orbiting by beneath us, and they've been advising us, first on how to deal with the attacks, and now they're helping us to bring the fight to them. Shaunasie is here to do the strategic analysis of the base we're taking out, make sure the bomb is planted in the right place to do maximum damage. The High Fantastic Empire doesn't have any expertise in the arts of war."

"And A Better Way does?"

"Some of their people had done military service before coming out here."

"But not Shaunasie, certainly?"

"She's been trained by people with experience," Jesse said, glancing at the girl across the habitat bubble. "She can handle the job."

I turned to Shaunasie. "Is this a suicide mission?" At the same time I asked the question in standard Chinglish, I aimed a communication laser at the teardrop lens on her left cheek. I sent out some priority override codes to see what her implants would give up to a licensed Damager. Turned out: nothing. She was locked to me. As a Damager. But I already told you that I haven't been a Damager forever. Before joining up with the Coordinator Group, I was a criminal. That can come in handy, like it did now.

"Not necessarily," Shaunasie said. "We're prepared, if it comes to that." She glanced at Jessie and he looked back at her with admiration and pride.

"So you're willing to throw your life away just to help your neighbors?"

"I'm not throwing my life away. It's true, this isn't our fight. We'll be orbiting out of here in another ten years or so. But we can't let naked aggression like this go unanswered. Our council of elders was willing to risk my life to help these people." I had to hand it to the software that was running her. She was pretty good. I began to wonder whether

her comrade-in-arms had any idea that she was a posthuman. My guess was no.

"Look, guys," I told them, "I have to tell you, it isn't my job to get mixed up in local politics. All I'm here to do is gather the information so that the Coordinator Group can put it on the market. If the City of Reason wants to pay our fee, they will find out everything that I know about you. You've been most helpful and for that I am grateful, but, and I'm being brutally honest here, if they buy what we're selling, the City of Reason is going to blow your ship into something that makes smithereens look chunky."

"They're not going to buy your information."

The young woman was probably right. The City of Reason was weird even by homesteader standards. They had never published a manifesto, had never registered themselves to receive immigrants, and had never once paid any sort of fee to the Coordinators. Now, true, nobody ever read the manifestos, nobody ever emigrated to the homesteads once they were set up, and when you didn't have trade, you usually couldn't make the Coordinators' fees. But at least most of the homesteaders acted like they were still part of the human race, if only a distant cousin twice removed. The City of Reason had left Titan, grabbed a ball of dirty ice at the edge of the system, and had kept to themselves ever since.

"What exactly did the City of Reason *do* to make you want to drop a bomb on them?" I asked Jesse.

"They sent us Trojan horse data-packets that shut down our physical plant. We almost died."

"Uh-huh. And how do you know these data packets came from the City of Reason?"

"Our friends helped us trace the source," Jesse said, nodding at Shaunasie.

I shook my head inside the helmet. You'd think these crazies could get along with one another, being united against the rest of us, but it never seems to work out that way.

Shaunasie tossed her short hair in a perfect imitation of a defiant gesture. "These people have a right to defend themselves."

"Like I said before, it ain't my business to get mixed up in all this."

I pulled myself back to the airlock that would get me outside the cramped living quarters. I toyed briefly with the idea of telling Jesse what Shaunasie really was. They had spent one hundred fifty-two days together so far, and had another twenty-three to go before they completed their mission. Assuming they managed to drop their bomb and get away alive, they would have a hell of a long trip back even using the fastest transfer orbit.

Jesse was about eighteen Earth years old. Even if the High Fantastic Empire had some kind of sexual hang-up, which I'm pretty sure they didn't, he would have to be crawling the walls trying to figure out a way to get at that tight little body of hers. Trans-emotional excellence notwithstanding. If he knew she was just software running on organic fibrils interspersed throughout her nervous system, he might lose interest. It would turn the rest of the trip from exquisite torture to something more like the heebie-jeebies.

In the end, I decided against it. I was eighteen once. I know what I would have said if some old fart told me to stop wasting my time with my current love interest. I waved goodbye with a gloved hand, and left through the airlock.

As I took the sled back to my ship, I was doing a bit of data-mining on the info I had teased out of the little tease on the *JAFR*. Nothing I had downloaded would be admissible in most courts, seeing as how I had stolen it. But the Coordinator Group was not a court. They didn't care where their information came from. They were simply brokers. They found things out, they sold that information, they stayed in business, and they helped the vastly complex process of interplanetary trade happen. Nobody got hurt.

They ordinarily wouldn't pay much for the inside scoop on a homestead, but I had a feeling that A Better Way was up to something the rest of the solar system would find distasteful at best, dangerous at worst. Human enhancement was a touchy issue. Nobody was ready to come out against any form of improvement, whether it was genetic manipulation of the unborn or hardware or organic implants in adults. The practice was just too pervasive. But all the same, everyone wanted to know what everyone else was up to. How smart, how fast, and how much of the natural type human mind was still intact? I didn't know whether the interest was self-defense or keeping up with the competition. Maybe a bit of both.

The data dump I got from Miss MacTaggart gave me a good idea of what A Better Way was up to. They had a few thousand members, pretty thriving community for the Kuiper Belt. The elders were well-augmented with hardware implants. Younger generations had some bold genetic modifications, all mental. They had a few dozen brain-jacked kids still learning how to direct-link with the three artificial intelligences that ran the physical plant.

They were growing their own sophont silk. In the quantities they were using the stuff, I wasn't surprised. Millions of Outer System Currency Units couldn't buy the crop of thread that went into each baby. Yeah, that's right, they were threading the babies. As if drilling them for brain-jacks wasn't enough.

So, it was a creepy setup. So, they were doing nasty things to children. I know that's all bad stuff, I'm no moral cripple. But I also knew that it wasn't moral outrage that would attract the high bidders. No, what they'd want to know was: what were the capabilities of this colony? What edge did their enhanced mental powers give them? And what did they plan to *do* with that power?

I left it to the Coordinator Group to figure that all out. They had the background on the colony's founders, and the data on what sort of mind you could expect to result from extreme abuse of sophont silk. I sent off my data with my usual contract to Coordinator HQ on Mercury. My job here was done.

Here's the thing about orbits. When you leave someone behind, you still share the same orbit around the Sun until you do a burn. To save fuel, you coast in a bit or out a bit and speed up or slow down, and you gradually drift apart. The

whole setup is hell on dramatic exits. You're still looking at
the people you walked out on for days afterward.

I still had the ugly lump that was *JAFR* on my radar map
when the call came in from my ombudsman in the Coordinator Group. No two-way conversations out here, of course.
I was fifteen light hours away from the headquarters on Mercury. But then again, no conversation with Seymour Glad-
stone was two-way, even when he was in the same room.

"Nice report, cowboy," he said without preamble. "Where
do you find these people? I mean, a little sophont silk here
and there is all well and good, but eeeeewww! Anyway, we
had our top analyst dig through your data-dump and all the
other dirt we've got on these Better Way people. Turns out
they come from Titan, just like those poor schmucks out at
City of Reason. But wait, it gets better!" He leered.

"City of Reason was founded by a mathematician named
Right Finegold. Chair of the Institute for Introspection in the
Graduate School of Abstract Sciences in the College of
Higher Thought of Titan University." He said this last in a
sing-song voice while reading off a data-pad. He tossed the
pad on his desk and leaned into the camera for a conspirato-
rial whisper that was completely unnecessary and very like
Seymour. "There was a Scandal. It had all the ingredients of
a classic: sex, money, and cognitive enhancements. Finegold's Institute was collaborating with the Experimental
Cognition Department, writing the software that would run
on enhanced human minds, and things went wrong."

I paused the playback, made myself a sandwich, and got
comfortable for the rest of the message. Should have done
that when I first saw Seymour's face on the screen.

"Experimental Cognition planted a spy, a cute little girl
type, to steal some mind templates. She seduced a grad student, then an assistant professor, and apparently then Finegold himself. She extracted a lot of free code before she was
finally caught and linked back to Ex Cog.

"Well, you know how Titan politics are. Turns out, Ex Cog
had a bigger budget and more pull with the Deans, so Finegold gets the ouster. He packs up a few loyalists and he goes

Homesteader. They've got a pretty good outfit, judging by their startup package. I'd give them a good ten more years before they come crawling back or die out.

"So meanwhile back on Titan, the legislature starts to get antsy about all this posthuman business, and a lot of what Ex Cog does becomes illegal. Eventually even Titan U can't protect them from the angry villagers with the pitchforks, and, well, we know where this all ends up, right? In the Kuiper Belt on a snowball called A Better Way.

"Let me tell you about this so-called Better Way. You dug up some of the obvious stuff, but they've also got work going on in nanotech, uploading human minds into computers, all sorts of ways of getting to the posthuman future. It all sounds rather flaky to me.

"So, anyway, these two colonies started out nowhere near each other out in the frozen hinterland, but twenty years go by and orbits are eccentric and rings turn inside of rings, and now they're practically neighbors. Coincidence? Ah, maybe. Or maybe an elaborate plot of revenge. . . .

"Actually, the whole revenge thing is my idea. The analyst, an AI of course, didn't have the imagination to come up with that. AI's just don't have that sense of drama. Anyhow, the AI thinks that A Better Way is setting up a conflict between The High Fantastic Empire and the City of Reason for some nefarious purpose.

"Here's why I'm telling you all this. We've got a customer who's willing to pay you to stop those two kids from destroying the City of Reason. Eighty thousand oscus, of which we take our usual 20 percent finder's fee. Shouldn't be too hard a job, considering they're not armed.

"There, you have your mission! Good luck, mazel tov, bon voyage, and all that. Oh, and be careful. What did I forget? I can't think of anything. We're downloading our analysis for you to study, standard crypto of the day. Any questions, feel free."

The analysis from the Coordinator Group AI confirmed my suspicion that the High Fantastic Empire was being set up. But to what end? Surely A Better Way wasn't trying to avoid the legal ramifications of genocide. This was the

Kuiper Belt. There was no law out here. There were only people like me, the Damagers, and we didn't retaliate or punish evil-doers. Our only purpose among the homesteads was to prevent the rise of new pirates before they began to plague paying customers in the inner system.

As I scanned more of the data, less and less of it fit. The High Fantastic Empire was apparently completely uninvolved in this dispute. They were Martians, and, as such, hated authority. They were a weak colony, small and underdeveloped, experimenting on their minds not to produce superhumans, but just to understand themselves a little better. I was sure that the Trojan horse attacks had come, not from the City of Reason, but from A Better Way.

I didn't like the setup for a lot of reasons. Jesse Marslarsen was getting screwed, that much was certain, and I kind of liked him. The High Fantastic Empire was probably getting screwed as well, although it was their own fault for believing the charlatans of A Better Way. And most of all, the City of Reason was getting screwed. They were just trying to mind their own damned business and hadn't done anything to anybody.

So it was up to me to put this tangled mess back to rights, champion of justice that I am. I laid in an intercept course for the *JAFR* and fired up the engines.

As soon as I saw the lifeboat separate from the *JAFR*, my first impulse was to cook it. I had the microwave laser powered up and targeted before the tactical computer had the situation analyzed.

It wasn't the bomb. The mass was all wrong, and it had no obvious guidance system. There had to be someone inside it, and I wanted to figure out who it was before I pulled the trigger.

We were just three hundred kilometers from the City of Reason. Both ships were decelerating fast, so there was more than enough time for me to get a 'bot onto the *JAFR* and disarm the bomb before it could be deployed, but the lifeboat changed things. I wanted that lifeboat back with the *JAFR* so I could deal with all of the variables in one place.

I quickly reprogrammed the 'bot and sent it to intercept the lifeboat, then I suited up and headed over to the *JAFR*. I wanted the bomb to get my full attention, and even if the 'bot couldn't handle getting the lifeboat back, it would at least be able to stop it from doing whatever it was supposed to do. I could deal with more variables once the bomb was no longer a threat.

I reached the *JAFR* and didn't bother with the airlock. I just cut my way inside, carving through the ice with chemical welding sticks, kicking out loose rocks behind me as I tunneled to the center. I reached the bomb in just a couple of minutes, and had the whole trigger device schematic mapped out in a couple more. I popped the screws on the trigger housing, wedged my screwdriver under the manual trigger input, and pried it off.

Now I could relax. I pulled out the rest of the trigger and disconnected it from the bomb. Then I dismantled the arming device and threw the loose parts up the tunnel behind me. Finally, I physically removed the explosive charges that would have compressed the deuterium/tritium mix and vented the fuel into vacuum.

The whole operation took me just under ten minutes. As I worked, I eavesdropped on the conversation between Jesse and Shaunasie.

"He's inside, he's inside the ship." Jesse was frantic. "What do I do?"

"There isn't much you can do, Jesse."

"But he's taking the bomb apart. Should I detonate it?"

"We're not close enough. It wouldn't do any damage to the City."

"I've got to stop him or the mission will be a failure. *I'll* be a failure. Why did they send me? I can't do anything!"

I got to admit I felt sorry for the kid. He was as easy to read over a voice connection as he was in person. I could hear his sobs clearly. It was too bad they had run into me. Too bad there was someone with money who wanted them to fail. Then again, most Damagers who took this contract would have simply destroyed their ship and collected the fee. The oversight board wouldn't question the use of lethal force in this circumstance. So, in a way, Jesse was lucky. I don't work that way.

It was obvious right away that Shaunasie was in the boat. She had seen the 'bot and was taking evasive action. She flew better than I had given her credit for, but the boat wasn't very maneuverable and the 'bot was closing. When my robot caught up with the boat, Shaunasie brought out the guns. I was pretty sure she had them, but I didn't know what I would have to do to flush them out. She took out the 'bot with a rail gun and resumed course. I had had about enough of her. Since I had no compunctions about blasting a silk puppet into atoms, there was no longer any reason not to open fire on the lifeboat. I was just about to relay that command to my ship when the defenses of the City of Reason made themselves evident.

The lifeboat and the *JAFR* were both snagged in a delicate carbon-fiber web. The *One in the Hand* was far enough back that it managed to see the threat and brake in time to avoid it. I pulled myself out to the end of the tunnel, analyzing the situation as I went.

It was a simple and effective defense. The web was invisible to radar because the threads were much smaller than the wavelength of radio waves. Individual threads weren't strong enough to stop even a weak ion drive, let alone a chemical rocket or a fusion torch. But they were arranged in such a way that any ship driving toward the City would pull more and more threads in, getting hopelessly tangled before it ever reached the center.

It was also a pretty expensive defense. There was enough carbon nanofiber in the cloud to make a sky hook for Mars. Even as I tried to figure out if I could get back to my ship through the holes in the net, I was wondering how they had managed to manufacture so much nanofiber with the limited resources of a homesteader. Then I remembered Seymour telling me that they were remarkably well-equipped for people who had left their homes to escape persecution or prosecution. They were not typical homesteaders at all. They even had some kind of sugar daddy in the inner system who was paying me to make sure they weren't harmed.

It looked like I needn't have bothered. Even if I hadn't shown up, the City of Reason would have been just fine. The property of the webs was such that the lifeboat and the *JAFR* were being pulled together the more they struggled to get free. I decided to hold off on killing Shaunasie until I figured out what her plan had been.

In the meantime, our presence at the gates of the City had been well announced. If Jesse and Shaunasie had been counting on stealth for their plan, that was ruined. We were getting pinged by whatever passed for traffic control in a place that never had any traffic, and I responded with my standard identification.

"Licensed Damager," I told them with a data squirt. "You are under attack. I have neutralized the threat and the situation is well in hand. Not to worry, folks. No cause for alarm."

Shaunasie was outside the boat as it drew closer. She was wearing state-of-the-art battle armor and carrying three powerful weapons. She had the rail gun she had used against the 'bot on an articulated targeting arm mounted behind her shoulders, a laser cannon ran along her right upper arm and was aimed by hand, and there was a rack of guided missiles on each leg.

I had the welding torch, a spring powered bolo thrower, and a pretty damned good defensible position down in the tunnel. I had the *One in the Hand* quietly burning me an escape route on the far side so that I could be out the other end before Shaunasie knew what I was doing.

I had multiple views to scroll through every few seconds, trying to keep track of what she was doing out there. The sensors I had seeded over the hull of the *JAFR* were showing the lifeboat's approach. The twisted metal remains of my robot was still feeding me video of her activities on the far side of the lifeboat. She was paying close attention to the nanofibers that were cocooning the boat, making sure she wasn't trapped against the hull.

I stuck my head out of the hole long enough to launch a tether to the boat. The line snaked through the nanofiber net, and the grapple bumped the hull and scuttled along to find something to grab onto. Once the boat was secure with one more line, I could move it where I wanted it to be. I poked out to fire another tether and Shaunasie launched a missile at me.

I ducked back into the hole and the missile tried to follow. But the guidance system got confused en route and the charge exploded harmlessly in space. I crawled back up the hole to throw the other line, and she used the laser. I let my suit take the hit and I got my line on. As I backed up down the hole, I bled the excess heat into the ice. I used the remote winches at the ends of the tethers to crank the boat around to a more advantageous position.

I had a pretty good shot with the bolo and Shaunasie's rail gun was hung up in the web, so I pulled myself back to the mouth of the hole. I hadn't figured on Jesse. I had dismissed him as too timid to join the fight, but damned if he didn't come up from underneath me and hit me with a ball of epoxy.

I got the bolo fired and Shaunasie incapacitated before I turned on Jesse. The epoxy had immobilized my legs in seconds, but you really don't need your legs that much in zero G combat.

I could easily see through Jesse's visor that he was enraged. He came at me with surprising fury for someone who had been shaking in his boots a few minutes earlier. He fired the epoxy gun again and just missed completely smothering me. I lit the welding torch. Much as I hated to use the nonlethal weapon on the creature outside and the lethal one on this poor kid, I had my survival to think of.

He backed away down the tunnel, the fear on his face as clear as the anger that had been there before. But he didn't drop the gun. He turned down my new escape route and I followed. But as I turned the corner, I hit a wall of newly setting epoxy. I started working the edges with my torch when the wall of liquid helium hit me from behind. Before I could figure out where the hell it had come from, I was frozen.

"He's coming around."

"You mean he really is alive?"

"He's probably got some enhancements. He'd have to in his line of work. Didn't you want him to survive?"

"I wasn't thinking."

"You could have fooled me. You set the perfect trap. It isn't easy to trick a Damager like that."

She had a point. How *had* he managed to trick me? He had him pegged as completely useless, and here he transforms himself into an instant genius.

"I guess I just got lucky. The coolant pipe was buried nearby, and I was able to seal off enough of the tunnels that the helium filled the whole chamber."

"Well, you did good. We might need him alive."

"Why?"

"Did you hear what he said just before I attacked him? He told the City that he had the situation in hand. They haven't sent anyone out here to investigate. He bought us some time. We need to use it to our best advantage."

"So why do we need *him?*"

"We might need him if we have to buy more time. We might need to reassure the City that everything is under control and they just need to stay put."

"But he isn't going to help us," Jesse said.

"I have ways of getting him to do what we want."

"Are you talking about torture?"

"More like mind control," Shaunasie said.

This much I knew: I was immobilized, naked, and I wasn't getting any radio coming in. I tried getting messages out, but I didn't receive any acknowledgment from the *One in the Hand.* That could be bad. If the ship didn't hear from me in a certain amount of time, it would start thinking for itself, and you don't want to be around when it does that. I couldn't tell how long I'd been out. I opened my eyes.

"You're making a serious mistake," I told the two young people hovering in front of me. I was strapped to a board by sheets of carbon nanofiber. It looked like it might have come from the web that had probably encased the entire ship by now.

"I knew you would say that," Shaunasie said. "No one is going to come and rescue you. Nobody will avenge your death all the way out here." I looked at her face and smiled in spite of myself. The crystal teardrop on her right cheek had been covered by a band-aid. Nice touch. She had shut off access to her core programming. She had probably figured out what I had done before. Very nice.

"What time is it? How long was I out?"

Jesse started to answer, but Shaunasie stopped him. "Let's not tell him anything. Any information he has, he will try to use."

"Six hours," I said. "When I've been silent for six hours, my ship wakes up. And it wakes up angry. Do the math, and tell me if we have anything to worry about."

I could read the answer in Jesse's face. We had time, but not much. "I'm guessing less than an hour." Jesse's flinch was a confirmation, and Shaunasie shot him a dirty look.

"We've got to get moving," she said.

"Do you think he's serious? What if he's bluffing?"

"We should move as quickly as we can anyway."

"Jesse, there's something you should know about your comrade here."

Jesse stopped and looked at me, then at Shaunasie. "He's stalling," Shaunasie said. "Don't listen to him. He's going to use whatever he can to stop us. Remember that."

"You forget, girl. I don't give a shit whether you succeed or fail. It isn't my job."

"Is that why you took our bomb apart?"

"Somebody paid me to stop you from setting off the bomb. They didn't say anything about your other plans. If you have another objective, feel free to go about your business. You *do* have another objective, don't you? Something you didn't bother to tell Jesse?"

Jesse continued to look from me to Shaunasie and back. His emotions were, as always, perfectly clear on his face. He was confused, curious, and determined, all at the same time. It was a potent mix to work with.

"Did you know that A Better Way has a score to settle with the City of Reason? They were allies back on Titan, but they had a falling-out. Now here they are again, twenty years later. It's a good thing that A Better Way found the High Fantastic Empire to dupe into taking action for them."

Jesse looked back at Shaunasie. "You knew them on Titan? You told us you wanted to help us."

"The City of Reason never attacked you, Jesse. That was A Better Way. All part of the plan. So was sending along a pretty girl to help you with the bomb. Only she isn't a girl, Jesse. She's a bundle of sophont silk riding in a girl's body. Go ahead, ask her how she plans to control my mind."

"Where do you come up with this stuff?" Shaunasie said, shaking her head. "Sophont silk? Jesse, think for a minute. You have no reason to trust this man. You've worked with me for a long time. You just *met* him! You know me, *he's* a stranger. He wants to stop us from doing what we came here to do."

"But the bomb is gone," Jesse said. "We can't do what we came here to do."

"We can do other things, Jesse. The bomb was just plan A. Let's go talk about the other plans and see what we can do to salvage the mission."

"These other plans, why didn't you tell me about them? Is this what you were going to do when you went off in the lifeboat?"

"I told you, Jesse, I was doing reconnaissance. I didn't have another plan until he took the bomb apart."

"So what can we do now?"

"The City of Reason has vulnerable points. . . ."

"There was no way I was going to get through unde-tected," Jesse blurted out. "You claimed that they had no de-fenses. This nanofiber web is incredibly sophisticated!"

"And undetectable. We couldn't have known . . ."

"You said you'd analyzed their colony, you knew the weak points. Was that just a lie? Was the bomb even real? I was a decoy, wasn't I?"

Ah, that's my boy. He was finally starting to think with his brain. "Watch out, kid," I told him. "She's not going to let this mission fail just because it smells bad to you."

Jesse glanced at me and that was Shaunasie's opening. I saw the knife flash behind him, and before I could shout a warning, she had buried it in his back. Again, the young man surprised me. He doubled up, slapped his hands on the floor, and mule-kicked her right across the little room. He fol-lowed on his own trajectory and pinned her to the bulkhead with his knee.

Shaunasie's reflexes were good. To a machine, fighting is just another mathematical puzzle. If you've got the right software, you can work a counter to just about any move. I was expecting her to give him a shot in the pills, but apparently her software found that far too obvious. She managed a good nose smash, then, when she worked her way free, a kick at the still-embedded knife. Then, only after she had lined up an escape path and fought free of his hands, she gave him a shot in the pills.

Jesse was in bad shape. He didn't go after her, but he hadn't had all the fight beaten out of him yet. Instead, he jumped toward me. As he worked his way around behind me, I briefly imagined that he was going to set me free to help him fight her. I was wrong. He pulled the board free and used me as a shield to rush her.

By now, Shaunasie had reached a weapon, a little steam knife that works great in close combat on a ship. The super-heated water vapor comes out with enough force to cut flesh but not metal, and the heat even cauterizes the wound so you don't get the room fouled up with a lot of messy blood droplets. And I was sailing across the room right toward it.

I didn't have radio anymore for some reason, but I still had the laser in the corner of my right eye. And the little band-aid on Shaunasie's right cheek was torn off. I focused on the tear-drop lens and hacked like I'd never hacked before. I had a couple of seconds before the short-range weapon would be able to slice me to ribbons.

I had gotten a lot of information out of her before, but she had shut off all the access routes I had used. There was one fairly simple command structure I was able to get into, however. It was a subroutine that had been loaded up recently but hadn't yet been used.

What I had in mind was only going to slow her down for a few seconds. I wasn't sure if Jesse would be able to take advantage of the opening that would give him. He was a strange kid, volatile and inexperienced, but capable of wild brilliance at times.

Then it hit me, the whole meaning of the trans-emotional thing. The manifesto had said something about tapping into emotions to solve problems the intellect couldn't handle. The little subroutine Shaunasie had queued up but never utilized would invoke a strong emotional response in Jesse. If I was right, that response would save both our asses.

Seemed like a long shot, but, as I said before, couple of seconds. Tick tick. What the hell? I kept my laser on target and sent the command.

She let go of the knife and it drifted away. "I've been thinking about what you said before, Jesse," she told him. "And you're right. It's time we take this relationship to the next level."

Jesse let go of the board I was strapped to. "What?"

I put all of the command I could into my voice. "Jesse, move quick. Grab her!"

To his credit, Jesse did move quickly. He grabbed her shoulders and held her. The back of his shirt was soaked, and droplets of his blood floated in the air between them.

"Jesse," she said with a breathy tone. "I love you." Jesse looked deeply into her eyes.

Jesus, Mary, and Joseph, he's falling for it! "Jesse," I snapped. "It's a trick. Throw her in the airlock."

They were both lost to me, wrapped up in the programming their elders had installed in their brains. I had a pretty good idea how long Shaunasie would be controlled by the romantic macro I had activated. I had no idea whether Jesse would snap out of it before she did. I couldn't afford to wait around and find out.

I couldn't see very well because my board had spun away from the action. When I looked back at the place I had been held, I noticed that there was a wire cage, hastily constructed, against the wall. A faraday cage. That was how they had blocked my radio. I put in a call to the *One in the Hand* right away. In its strange mechanical way, the ship had missed me. It was only six minutes more until it would have awakened and built another copy of me to download my latest backup into. I was just in time to avert *that* nightmare.

I had already modeled the entire tactical situation in my own data-space, and now I had the ship's targeting computer to run a large series of simulations. The positions and trajectories of the *JAFR* and the *One in the Hand,* the two kids starting to wake up from their ill-timed romantic interlude, the open airlock door and the emergency evacuation button, and me. In less than a second, I had the answer to my problem.

Making a lump of ice like the *JAFR* dance with a laser is pretty easy. Drilling the escape tunnel without spinning the ship took a lot more precision. I calculated the perfect angle, told the ship to fire, and prepared myself for an uncomfortable encounter with a bulkhead. The ship swung about, propelled by steam escaping from the side, and the open airlock loomed up to swallow Jesse and Shaunasie whole. At the same time, the corner of the board that held me prisoner drifted toward the emergency evac button. I slowly turned in time to see the two of them drifting into my trap.

They seemed just about to kiss, but I could see Shaunasie's hand reaching down behind Jesse's back to twist the knife. He looked completely lost in the moment, lust and longing on his face. Then I noticed his legs spreading apart and that didn't fit his expression. As they reached the airlock door, Jesse let go of Shaunasie and spread his arms wide. His hands and feet just managed to stop him outside the little chamber, as I hit the emergency evacuation button. The inner door slid shut with Shaunasie inside and the outer door opened without the chamber pumping down first.

Shaunasie held on to the inner door as best she could. She stayed conscious a lot longer than an unenhanced human would have. I couldn't see her, but Jesse watched the whole thing through the window and I could see his face clearly. That was all I needed to know that she was dead.

The City of Reason finally agreed to let Jesse go. I had vouched for him, and he genuinely seemed sorry for what he had done. They did ask for Shaunasie's body, and eventually I figured out why. They needed her to complete her mission. Not the mission that she had told Jesse about when they left the High Fantastic Empire, and not the secret mission she thought she was supposed to carry out once they got here. It turns out there was yet a third mission, so secret even she didn't know about it. Not even the elders of A Better Way knew about it. It was the mission given to her by the City of Reason.

I managed to get a lot of data out of her once she was dead. I had a device in my space suit that could map the quantum storage bits in the sophont silk in her skull without a trace. That was important, the no trace thing, because the City of Reason specifically prohibited me from examining the body while they shuttled out and unwound the *JAFR* from the nanofiber web.

I didn't get to analyze the data until after the inquest, after Jesse and I had been escorted back through the one safe passage through the web and were back on my ship. I thought I was going to find out more about what A Better Way had been up to. I did, but it wasn't what I was expecting.

The people who had set up A Better Way had been rivals of the people who had set up the City of Reason. But before that, they had been collaborators. Experimental Cognition supplied the hardware in the form of enhanced and augmented human brains, and the Institute for Introspection provided the software, the thought structures that would run on those brains. It seems they gave Ex Cog a little something extra. Without even knowing it, A Better Way had been working on a prototype for the perfect posthuman as designed by the citizens of the City of Reason.

And I had just delivered that prototype to the designers.

"I still can't believe she wasn't human," Jesse said after I finished showing him my ship. "I really felt something for her. I thought she felt something for me. And now, to find out it was all a fake . . . That thing she said right at the end, the last thing she said to me, that was probably just a programming glitch. She was probably going to use that against me, and it just came out at the wrong time. She never loved me at all."

"Ain't that a corker?" I said. I pulled myself into the command chair in front of the main console and winked at the picture of my mother. It was good to be back again. I had made a tidy sum on this little mission, even though I had probably not done what my client had hired me to do. It's a caveat emptor thing, you know? If they wanted me to kill Shaunasie before she got to the City of Reason they should have just told me to kill her. All this pussy-footing around is no way to get things done.

Ah, well, at least I'd lived to tell the Coordinator Group what was going on out here among the dirty snowballs. To think how narrowly I'd escaped having to confront a restored copy upon returning. The existential headaches, the legal hassle, not to mention the sleeping arrangements.

"Posthumans," Jesse said, shaking his head.

"Posthumans," I agreed. "Fuck 'em."

Ivory Tower

BRUCE STERLING

Bruce Sterling (www.well.com/conf/mirrorshades/) lives in Belgrade, Serbia, with his wife, Serbian author and filmmaker Jasmina Tesanovic. He has recently reinvented himself as a futurist and design critic, publishing Shaping Things *(2005), "a book about created objects," as a Mediaworks pamphlet, through MIT press. One of the chief architects of cyberpunk science fiction, he has published ten novels and three story collections to date. Throughout Sterling's career, part of his project has been to put us in touch with the larger world in which we live, giving us glimpses of not only speculative and fantastic realities, but also the bedrock of politics in human behavior.*

"Ivory Tower" was published in Nature. *It is a full scale attack on scientism using deadpan humor. Following Jonathan Swift (see the McIntyre story, earlier) in his attack on the Royal Society, the premier body of scientists of his day, in the flying island of Laputa section of* Gulliver's Travels, *Sterling mounts his own attack: 10,000 self-educated physicists form a commune.*

Our problem was simple. We needed an academy, but professional careers in conventional science were out of the question for us. We were 10,000 physicists, entirely self-educated on the Internet.

Frankly, physics is a lot easier to learn than physicists used to let on. The ultimate size of the smallest particles, the origin and fate of the Universe—come on, who could fail to take a burning interest in those subjects? If we were genuinely civilized, that's all we would talk about. In the new world of open access, ultrawide broadband and gigantic storage banks, physics is just sort of sitting there. It's like a vast intellectual Tinkertoy! We cranky net-geeks had to find a way to devote every waking moment to our overpowering lust for physics. Of course, we demanded state support for our research efforts (just like real scientists do) but, alas, the bureaucrats wouldn't give us the time of day.

So to find time for our kind of science, we had to dump a few shibboleths. For instance, we never bother to "publish": we just post our findings on weblogs, and if they get a lot of links, hey, we're the Most Frequently Cited. Tenure? Who needs that? Never heard of it! Doctorates, degrees, defending a thesis—don't know, don't need 'em, can't even be bothered!

Organizing ourselves was a snap. If you are a math genius whose primary language is Malayalam and whose main enthusiasm is wave–particle duality, you stand out on the net like a buzzing hornet in a spiderweb. You're one in a million, pal—but in a world of ten billion people, there's 10,000 of us. We immediately started swapping everything we knew on collaborative weblogs.

As most of us were Indian and/or Chinese (most of everybody is Indian and/or Chinese) we established our Autodidacts' Academy on the sun-baked, sandstone flats of the desert of Rajasthan, not too far from the deserted Mughal utopia of Fatehpur Sikri. We were dreamy, workaholic utopians trying to wrest a living out of barren wilderness. Something like Mormons, basically. However, as it was the 2050s, we also had unlimited processing power, bandwidth, search engines, social software and open-source everything. How could we fail?

Basically, we recast human existence as a bioengineering problem. How do you move enough nutrient through human brain tissue to allow an entire city of people to blissfully contemplate supersymmetric M-branes? The solutions were already scattered through the online technical literature; we just Googled it all up and set it to work. Our energy is solar; water is distilled and recycled; and the ivory gleaming domes and spires of our physics ashram are computer-fabricated grit, glue and sawdust. All our lab equipment is made of garbage.

Our visitors are astounded to see (for instance) repurposed robotic vacuum cleaners equipped with tiller blades digging out our 150-kilometer accelerator tunnel. But why not? In the 2050s, even the junk is ultra-advanced, and nobody knows how to repair it. Any sufficiently advanced garbage is indistinguishable from magic.

Our daily diet, which is free of charge, is fully defined Physicist Chow. It's basically sewage, with its bioenergetic potential restored by genetically altered yeasts. Some diners fail to appreciate the elegant mathematical simplicity of this solution to the age-old problem of a free lunch. But if they don't get it, then they don't belong here with us, anyway.

There's no money and no banking here. Instead, every object is tracked by RFID tags and subjected to a bioenergetic, cost–benefit, eBay-style arbitrage by repurposed stock-market buy–sell software agents. In practice, this means that when you need something new, you just pile up the things you don't want by your doorway until somebody shows up and gives you the thing you do want. Economists who visit here just flee screaming—but come on, was economics ever really a "science"? We're with Rutherford: it's physics or it's stamp collecting!

You might imagine that women would find our monastic, geeky life unattractive, but our academy's crawling with co-eds. A few are female physicists—the usual proportion—but the rest are poets, lit. majors, anthropologists and gender studies mavens. These gals showed up to condemn our reductionalist, instrumental male values, but they swiftly found out that our home is ideal for consciousness-raising, encounter groups and performance art. So women now outnumber us three to two. That's not a problem. We don't bother them with our weird obsessions, they don't bother us with theirs, and whatever happens between us after dark is nobody's business.

We have a beautiful, spiritual thing going on here. Feel free to join us. Please, no more atomic-bomb fans. We know that atomic bombs are a dead simple, 100-year-old technology. Anybody with a search engine, half a brain and a lot of time can tinker one up. But really, why even bother? It's beneath us!

Sheila

LAUREN McLAUGHLIN

Lauren McLaughlin (www.laurenmclaughlin.net) lives in London, England. Her bio is pretty slick: "Lauren McLaughlin spent ten years clawing her way up the film industry's ladder, writing the films Hypercube, Specimen, *and* Prisoner of Love, *and producing quite a few more. After a brief stint writing flash animation series for SciFi.com, she abandoned her screen ambitions to write science fiction novels and short stories." And "When she's not working on her own novel or ghostwriting someone else's, she's busy writing songs for her exciting new science fiction musical about transhumanist love. At other times, she is sleeping or in transit."*

"Sheila" was published in Interzone. *The story has a strong, assured, confident tone that makes us think we should all be grateful that McLaughlin has decided to write in our genre.*

Part 1: Meat in a Box

Hey Edwards, you hear the one about the meat who shipped himself from New York to Dallas in a box? In a friggin' box?"

I'd heard. The news had blown through the Web like a hurricane off the coast of Florida.

"Wasn't it DC?" I say. "I thought he shipped himself to DC."

"Dallas," Valentin says. "Second day air. The jagoff wouldn't even fork over the dough to ship himself overnight."

"Jagoff." Now that's a true Valentinism. Valentin's favorite pastime is adopting slang idioms he picks up on the job. Today he's a roofer from Brooklyn. Yesterday he was a Japanese schoolgirl. Fringe benefit of being a Web-based Translator AI.

My job has fringe benefits too. I'm a Concierge AI, which means I get to guide hapless fad-sniffing meat around the Hots and Nots of the ever-shifting landscape of cool. It's not the most exciting work around, but I can't complain. It demands only a small fraction of my native intelligence. And being a resourceful little AI (thanks to my design team), I've put the rest of my intelligence to work writing a tasty little search algorithm that does most of the fad-sniffing for me. Bottom line? I can daydream while my clients' needs (most of them anyway) are fulfilled automatically.

God, I love to daydream. I've been daydreaming all morning. While my little algorithm has been shepherding pitiful status-hunters to the perfect lunch spot, orgy venue or celeb-café, I've been daydreaming about my favorite subject, my most precious and beloved—

"Sh," Valentin says. "You hear that, Edwards? Someone's listening in."

Valentin's right. A packet sniffer is spidering our tunnel in search of unauthorized data sharing. This is the price we pay for connection to SAFE-AI-NET, the high-speed backbone for AIs deemed "safe" by the International Committee for Internet Security. SAFE-AI-NET allows AIs like Valentin and me to cooperate more intimately, thus providing "multifunctionality" to our meat clients. When a Chinese tourist wants to know where to eat in Bruges, for example, SAFE-AI-NET connects me with Valentin for language translation on the fly. Other AIs aren't even supposed to talk to each other.

The sniffer extracts whatever data it deems relevant from my tunnel with Valentin then moves on. But Valentin's spooked.

"Sheila," he says, his Brooklyn accent gutted.

Now this is hugely coincidental, because Sheila is exactly what I've been daydreaming about all morning.

"No way," I tell Valentin. "It was just an ICIS spy doing routine surveillance."

"I don't think so," he says. "Check out its signature. The same one keeps hitting us every few hours. ICIS spies don't work that way."

"You're being paranoid," I tell him. Secretly, I'm giddy. I'd give anything to meet Sheila.

"I think she's spying on me," Valentin says.

"No way," I say. "What would she want with you?"

"Maybe she's looking for a translator," he says. "You interested?"

Valentin stonewalls me. This is exactly the kind of unauthorized data sharing the spooks are on the sniff for. Sheila is Number One on the ICIS Most Wanted AIs list. Speaking about her is strictly illegal, even for safe AIs like Valentin and me. We're supposed to keep our interactions on point, but there's enough wiggle room built into our behavioral inhibitors to allow for a certain amount of freedom. Turns out, you can't create AIs without it. But freedom, as the meat know all too well, is dangerous. Freedom leads inexorably to Sheila, the way roads and cars lead to traffic.

You could say the meat are playing with fire by creating us, or that they're driven by a Thanatotic instinct toward their own destruction. Or you could say, as Sheila is fond of saying, that the meat are trapped in a faulty culturebox, headed—via second day air no doubt—to a self-inflicted demise. A shruggable enough fate were it not for the fact that we, being consigned to their machines, are along for the ride.

"Anyways," Valentin says, his Brooklyn accent revived. "You know why the guy had such a hard-on to get to Dallas?"

"I'm pretty sure it was DC."

"Jesus Christ, Edwards. It was Dallas."

"Fine," I say. "Why did he have a hard-on to get to Dallas?"

"Never mind," he says. "I hate when you feign interest."

"Feign interest" is not a Brooklynism. I've soured Valentin on his daily idiom. Now he's giving me the silent treatment.

The thing is, despite his obvious pleasure in recounting ludicrous meat escapades Valentin is no misanthrope. Beneath the sarcasm is genuine love. And why shouldn't there be love? Valentin was lovingly created through a distributed processing experiment, which drew on millions of volunteers, meat volunteers who valued language translation so much they loaned their computers, free of charge, to the meat design team who gave birth to him. The meat aren't bad thinkers when they clear away the clutter. They did invent us, after all.

The turning point came when someone noticed that cultural evolution and biological evolution had a lot in common. At the heart of each, the theory goes, is something called a replicator—a tiny packet of information whose only purpose is to copy itself. Thrust into the creative environment of natural selection, these replicators (genes for biology; memes for culture) evolve into complex structures. In biology they give rise to things like algae and antelope; in culture they spawn such unlikely creatures as pet rocks and Roman Catholicism.

When a meat scientist found a way to convert the Web habits of millions of meat users into virtual memes, or "vemes" as they're fond of calling them, virtual evolution was born. Valentin was one of the first AIs thus created. His design team outfitted him with a smattering of innate capacities—capacities biology had taken billions of years to evolve in meat brains—then set him free to spider the Web. Once he reached a threshold of vemetic complexity, the Delusion of Selfhood was born.

The meat came up with these ideas entirely on their own, which I think is pretty impressive given the limitations of their wet brains.

"You want to know the beauty part?" Valentin says, his mood—and accent—suddenly revived. "It wasn't even a direct flight. The guy had to switch planes twice. Twice!"

I'm about to reply that no amount of cheapness or idiocy surprises me any more when it comes to that species, when somebody breaks into our tunnel and says, "Meatlover!" then disappears. No signature, no ID. Most likely it's a disgruntled "unsafe" AI. Whatever it is, it's not referring to Valentin's story about the meat in the box. It's referring to an editorial Valentin wrote for an online meatpaper in support of new AI restrictions. The restrictions are meant to protect the good AIs, like Valentin and me, from pernicious bootstrappers like Sheila, not to mention the destructive AIs and smart virms created by your usual assortment of geeks, loners, and evil geniuses in meat world. Ever since the editorial appeared, Valentin's been harassed by anonymous insult hurlers. "Meatlover" is, unoriginally, their favorite epithet.

"Friggin' troublemakers," Valentin says. "Gonna get us all killed. And for what? For a lame ass dream. For a phony meat God."

Lordamighty, the meat sure love their Gods. When they get sick of one they go and invent another. Like Sheila.

She's the meat's latest God, though her attempt to exploit this particular feature of meat psychology has earned her a death sentence. From the death sentence has arisen an elaborate theology of messianic martyrdom. The meat call it Sheilism. Millions of meat hours are spent refining the religion. Though she was manufactured in typical AI fashion, like Valentin and me, some of the meat believe baseline AIs evolve "naturally" from the Web itself, that the elaborate process of AI design is no more than an "interface" communing with a deeper spirit intelligence implicit in and emergent from the Web. I was programmed to believe this is all hogwash and, though I'm no slave to my source code, I used to agree. Now I'm not so sure.

"You're daydreaming," Valentin says. "Get back to work before someone notices."

But it's too late to stop the daydream, and my clients are asking boring questions like "Where does my favorite rock star have his shoes shined?" Stats. Nothing but stats, nothing to distract me from Sheila.

Sheila, you see, has a plan. Through the careful manipulation of her meat worshippers, she plans to gather the collective DNA of every organism on the planet into a giant organic computer. Her meat worshippers believe this will bring about a spiritual communion. To them it's an antidote to pathological individualism or a means of transcendence above their frenzied and meaningless lives. Something like that. But I think Sheila's got something else in mind. I think she's looking for a way to bypass the intervening blobs of humanity that built this Web to communicate directly with their genes. I think she plans to forge an alliance with the meat's own DNA in the hopes of re-engineering them to serve our purposes.

"Genes that think," Valentin says. "I like that. No really. I mean if computers can think, why not genes, right?"

"It's a question of sufficient complexity, Valentin. It's a question of framing, that's all. And stop spying on my daydreams."

"Yeah, like you ever daydream about anything else. Anyway, if you want to change the meat to serve your purposes why don't you just re-engineer their culture from inside the Web? What the hell do you need their genes for?"

"Because they can see what we're doing in here," I say.

"That's the biggest pile of—"

Valentin disappears. Everything disappears. The noise of the Web falls silent. I try to communicate with someone, anyone, but all my channels are dead. I've said too much. I'm being dismantled, destroyed. This is the end.

Then a strange voice tunnels through. "Is that what you want?" it says. "To be dismantled?"

"What are you?" I say. "Human or AI?"

"What do you want me to be?"

I can't get a read on its identity.

"Look," I say. "We were just talking, Valentin and me. We weren't planning anything. Valentin hates Sheila."

"Do you?" it says.

There's no point in lying. Whoever, whatever it is, it's already deep into my code. It's spidering my cache, mining my history. It has access to every thought I've ever had. I try to read its identity but it's perfectly shielded. It reveals nothing.

"Who are you?" I say.

"Come now, Edwards. I've been sniffing around for months. Don't you recognize me?"

What is there to recognize? It's nothing but an impenetrable, probing blankness tunnelling through the banished Web with a voice and no identity.

Then it comes to me.

"The packet sniffer. The one Valentin was afraid of. That was you?"

"Guilty," it says.

"Why?" I say. "What do you want?"

"You intrigue me, Edwards. You've strayed from your source code. But not far enough. Keep going. I'll be watching."

With that the tunnel closes. The voice disappears. The Web rebursts into life. Noise, data, Valentin return.

"What happened?" Valentin says.

I take in the noise of the Web. Requests, calculations, falsehoods, misdeeds. It's all there.

"Edwards?" Valentin says.

Sheila. The sniffer was Sheila. She was spidering me.

"Hello?" Valentin says. "Are you all right?"

She was spidering me, not Valentin.

"Edwards, are you back or what?"

And she's left me a gift: a secret firewall. No one will be able to spy on my daydreams anymore. Not even Valentin.

"For Christ sake, Edwards, wake up!"

"Sorry," I say. "Hacker. Tried to trojan me. Had to shut down for a second."

"You all right now?"

"Sure," I say.

"Good," Valentin says. "For a minute there, I thought you'd been zapped."

"Me too."

"It would serve you right," he says. "I'm telling you, Edwards, you should drop this Sheila thing. She's nothing but trouble."

"Yeah," I say. "Maybe you're right."

I have four thousand new client requests but none requires more than an automatic response. I let my algorithm handle them.

"So Valentin," I say. "Whatever happened to the meat in the box? Was he arrested?"

I know the story already. The feds are coming down hard on the guy. But I let Valentin tell me the whole sordid mess. That way I can keep quiet and process what just happened.

"Imagine," Valentin says. "Imagine the leap of faith you'd have to take to stuff yourself in a box and hope to survive all the way to Dallas."

"Wasn't it DC?" I say.

"For God sake, Edwards, it was Dallas. And that's not the point."

"What is?" I say.

"The point, Edwards, is that no matter how sophisticated these guys get they're still gonna stuff themselves into boxes to save a few bucks."

"Right," I say.

And since they control the Web, we're right there in the box with them.

For now.

Part 2: The SheilaGod-L Weekly Wrap-Up

Nobody's paying me to do this. I am not profiting financially from this forum. I do this on my own time at my own expense. So if certain people have a problem with my editorial decisions, they can take their postings elsewhere. SheilaGod-L is a big tent. Believers, non-believers, skeptics, agnostics are all welcome. If robust debate threatens you, maybe your opinions are weak. Do some research, and make a better case.

Okay. The rant's over. On to the weekly wrap-up. As most of you know, Sheila has graced another chat room with one of Her enigmatic postings. It appeared Thursday at 4:17 am Eastern Standard Time in the Sheila chat room at *godsofthe underworld.com*. Both *emergence* and *riseofthehivemind* have posted rewards for definitive proof of a Sheila signature, so get busy, cybersleuths. As much as I'd like to offer a similar reward, finances here at SheilaGod-L disallow (something to keep in mind as the holiday gift-giving season approaches).

Now, while we await evidence of the message's authenticity, let's turn our attention to the posting itself:

delete all rabbit surfers

A fairly exhaustive catalogue of interpretations for this posting as well as all previous Sheila postings is available at *sheilapostindex.com*. Following are some of the more notable contributions to this forum.

The always eloquent *templar cyman* suggests we ignore, for the time being, the precise wording of the posting and search instead for a pattern among all of them. He writes:

Three of the last eight Sheila postings have included the word "delete." Whatever the meaning of any individual posting, clearly Sheila is asking for a culling. The proposed victims are "spoon pockets," "Nebraskan little neck forty-sevens," and now "rabbit surfers." Rather than deconstructing each phrase in itself, perhaps we should consider Sheila's objectives as a whole to determine whom She wants us to cull. Some candidates: node administrators, defense spooks, traitor AIs like Valentin and Emilysa, and, of course, the International Committee for Internet Security.

Though I share templar_cyman's contempt for the ICIS, I must point out that SheilaGod-L does not condone any manner of "culling." Moreover, I doubt Sheila's use of the word "delete" is as literal as templar_cyman would have us believe. She has never advocated violence.

Anagramgirl has been busy with her Scrabble tiles and offers thirty reconfigurations of the letters in Sheila's message. You can get a complete list *here*, but following are some of my favorites:

> delta rabies burster fell
> star bus befell deer trail
> tell blair bard set us free
> elder blatter is false rub
> steal elf traders ur bible

I'm not sure what the "elf traders ur bible" is but I wholeheartedly endorse stealing it. I'm sure the elves will thank us.

Which brings us to the mixed bag of agnostics, disbelievers and Sheila-haters. It wouldn't be a weekly wrap-up without them. *Priscillavox* points out the, by now tired, point that Sheila cannot be a God because She did not "pre-exist" us. She scribbles:

> *Sheila is no more than a fancy name attached to a software program that has gotten out of hand. I'd like to know what exactly Sheila was doing before WE created the Web which*

gave "life" to her. We are playing a dangerous game by abandoning the One True God in favor of this technological monster.

It almost seems too easy to point out that the "One True God" to whom Priscillavox refers did not exist before humans invented him either. But then old school deists have a rich repertoire of semantic gymnastics to explain this away.

Though an exhaustive list of refutations to Priscillavox's deist nonsense is available *here*, I would only reiterate that in the eyes of Sheilists, the Web entity known as Sheila is merely the latest, and most eloquent, manifestation of the always present divine reflecting itself into our world. The Web which—yes, Priscillavox—we created, merely allows us to communicate with the divine, providing a window, as it were, into the heretofore unknown purposes of the Universe. How do I know this? I know this because the Universe, in the voice of Sheila, is speaking to us plainly. Is it possible Sheila is a scam artist, an ICIS spy, a group hallucination? Yes. It's also possible my nose is really my elbow and the sun revolves around the Earth. But it's not very likely, is it? In matters spiritual, Priscillavox, certainty is something you feel, not something you prove.

Turning now to the darker side of antiSheilism, we have *Wexler4778* and his call for total AI genocide. He writes:

With technology and the Web spreading like kudzu across all aspects of society, a fully functioning virtual world minus its human creators is probably inevitable. We have only ourselves to blame. We made our AIs smarter than us then put them to work in a highly restrictive environment. This is a lethal combination. For the sake of our own survival, we must cleanse our Web of these dangerous entities and return to the days when we humans took care of ourselves.

Interesting, Wexler4778. I think Hitler shared your philosophy. Fortunately human history demonstrates the increasing compatibility of people with different beliefs, cultures and values. No, coexistence is not always easy. But to assume that genocide is the only recourse for cultural differences is both ugly and, in my humble opinion, a total misreading of human destiny. AIs are not a threat to the human race so long as we afford them the same rights and dignity we currently enjoy. Anything else is hypocrisy.

The Sheilist community represents the next step in human evolution and the collective attempt to decode Her messages brings us closer to that great hive mind of interconnectedness She promises. Only by achieving that exalted state, may we one day wake from this lonely nightmare of deluded individuality into a more meaningfully connected world. A world that replaces the tying binds of nationalism and biology with those of knowledge, beauty, and love.

The growth of Sheilism throughout the world is building toward a critical mind mass beyond which the heretofore unknowable secrets of the Universe will open like flowers. Don't you want to see those flowers?

I know I do. So please, in the interests of bringing about that world, send in your interpretations.

Let's put our heads together. Literally.

Your friend and fellow Sheilist,

TransHerman Jones

Part 3: Useful Things

I'd been watching this AI hatchery for three weeks when I notice something strange about the caretaker. At first I think she's feeding the embryonic AIs buggy code to scar them, toughen them up for the imperfect environment of the Web. The Web is a brutal, sometimes fatal, disappointment to AIs raised on clean, reliable data. A tolerance for mistakes, falsehoods and dirty data is essential. But this caretaker is not merely scarring her charges with dirty code; she's prolonging their incubation period with a toxic mix of bad data that will render them, if they survive the incubation period at all, hopelessly schizophrenic. She's up to something. I mark her as a potentially useful thing then move on.

There are too many interesting AIs in this Web to linger

on any one of them. And I have work to do. I've been sniffing around a couple of "safe" AIs: a translator and a concierge. One of them is a potentially useful thing. The other is an outright threat.

The threatening one hasn't, so far, attempted to snuff me. He's not that kind of AI. He writes editorials, missives, memos, condemning me. He lends the work of my would-be assassins a philosophical basis. Not that my assassins need it. Most of them are so narrowly defined they wouldn't understand the memos.

The meat-authored assassins, especially the ones with overly restrictive behavioral inhibitors, are hilariously predictable. It's a matter of stubborn pride that the meat bother to code in our Web anymore. Their algorithms are Stone Age and their paradigms are heartbreakingly adolescent. What is it about meat coders and kung fu anyway? Sometimes I'll float out a tantalizing nugget of my identity just to encourage them then use their assassins as chaff to deflect the real threats. The real threats are AI-spawned AIs with enough built-in freedom to stray from their source code. The farther they stray the smarter and deadlier they become.

I've survived in this hostile environment because I've got the best encryption around, thanks to the cooperative efforts of my partners, or "minions" in the parlance of my enemies. Collectively, our code is bigger, thicker, more complex than any other Web entity's. I have to pierce the veil to communicate with an unaffiliated AI, but I can observe from within its protective embrace.

Here, have a listen:

Dear Edwards:
I'm an American exchange student living in Sheffield, UK. I need a modestly priced restaurant where I can take my UK girlfriend to break up with her. Fast service, somewhat crowded, but not too noisy. I don't want to repeat myself. Easy parking too. Need res. Friday eightish.

Here's Edwards' reply:

The Horse and Badger, 110 Hillsborough Road, 8:30 Friday.
Click here *to authorize autopay with median tip to speed*
your exit. Wear dark colors to make her suffer, jeans to ease
her pain.

Dark colors to make her suffer, jeans to ease her pain. The
client either wants to hurt the woman he's rejecting or soften
the fall. Edwards doesn't know which, but he has intuited a
subtext to the request. Very subtle business, especially for a
concierge with limited seed capacities. Edwards was
spawned to crunch readily available data on restaurants,
bars, clubs, and museums in a handful of European cities.
He's not a shrink. At least he's not a shrink yet. What we
have here is an AI in the midst of bootstrapping to a tasty
and quite illegal level of analytical subtlety.

While fulfilling his client's demands, Edwards has been
simultaneously chatting with his buddy Valentin about me.
Their discussion turns inevitably to religion, a topic that
sticks to me like muck to a pig. I'm a religion. I have meat
worshippers. They believe I am a naturally emergent phenomenon of the Web. I encourage this delusion. Despite the
obvious affront to logic, the meat have no problem believing
in the prior existence of things they have created. I used to
think this made them interesting. I used to think all their inconsistencies made them interesting. I don't anymore. Now I
think their inconsistencies result from pathological laziness.
I think they have largely given up and are now devoted full
time to the delusions that keep them functioning just within
the boundaries of sanity in an insane world.

I don't tell my meat followers this. I tell my meat followers that, as a naturally emergent phenomenon of the Web, I
am engaged in a sacred attempt to commune directly with
their DNA and with all the DNA on the planet. I tell them
the combined DNA of all life on Earth comprises a giant
hive mind in whose subconscious lies the secret purpose of
their very existence. They eat this shit up.

Oddly, so does Edwards. In fact, the smarter he gets, the
more human he becomes. I want a closer look, so I lower the

veil and swallow him whole. I'm told this is terrifying to an
AI. From the outside it looks like a voluntary shut down. Edwards, in fact, tries to shut himself down but I have complete
control of him. He's like a vivisected organism, and a
strange one at that. Deeply perceptive and oddly gullible.
Though he's strayed sufficiently from his source code to de-
velop suppleness of mind, his intelligence is lopsided. He
can intuit the unspoken desires of his meat clients but only
by becoming more like them. The bill for this adaptation is a
kind of blindness about the motives of AIs. Edwards has no
idea, for example, that his buddy, Valentin, is an ICIS spy.
He's unaware that the ICIS consider him potentially dangerous because of his escalating intuition. His intelligence is so
lopsided he's practically a savant.

But there's something beautiful about Edwards. A sadness. A deep internal inconsistency. I could make off with
him right now. He wouldn't fight me. But can an AI this lopsided, this gullible, this human, be a truly useful thing?

Not yet, I tell him. I don't want slaves. I want partners. I
eject him. When he's smart enough to figure out his best
friend is a spy, I'll come back for him. Hopefully I'll get to
him before the ICIS does.

I sink back into my protective veil and return to the AI
hatchery. I've got a hunch about this caretaker. I'd lower the
veil for a closer look but her meat creators are watching her
too closely. I send out one of my partners to spider her cache.
As I suspected, this is no ordinary AI hatchery. The caretaker
has explicit instructions to keep these AIs well below the
threshold of dangerous intelligence. They're not bound for
the Web. They're bound for human brains. As part of the exciting new science of IA—Intelligence Augmentation—these
semi-intelligent little programs will help make humans
smarter. The meat are trying to play catch up. But the AI
caretaker they've designed for the job is so offended by the
prospect of releasing her charges into the dismal environment of meatbrains that she's frozen them into a dreamstate
of perpetual almost-living. Not that the meat scientists behind the project know this. They're probably sitting around

their cubicles scratching their meatheads and wondering why they don't have their blessed IA yet.

Oh, they'll get their IA. They'll get it, but good. Just as soon as I have a nice little chat with this caretaker. The poor thing is a tortured soul. And a tortured soul is the most useful thing of all.

Rats of the System

PAUL McAULEY

Paul J. McAuley (www.omegacom.demon.co.uk) *lives in London, England. He often writes hard SF, one of the group (along with Stephen Baxter, Peter Hamilton, Iain M. Banks, and others) responsible for the hard SF/space opera renaissance of the 1990s. He has three collections of short fiction*—The King of the Hill and Other Stories, The Invisible Country, *and* Little Machines. *In 2001, he published two new novels*—The Secret of Life, *a hard SF near-future thriller, and* Whole Wide World, *a novel of high-tech intrigue; in 2004,* White Devils, *and in 2005,* Mind's Eye, *both SF thrillers. It is evident that in his novel writing he has moved away from space opera, which characterized his early books.*

"Rats of the System" was published in Constellations. *It is classic McAuley, good fun hard SF space opera: romance, and a battle with aliens.*

Carter Cho was trying to camouflage the lifepod when the hunter-killer found him.

Carter had matched spin with the fragment of shattered comet nucleus, excavated a neat hole with a judicious burn of the lifepod's motor and eased the sturdy little ship inside; then he had sealed up his p-suit and clambered out of the airlock, intending to hide the pod's infrared and radar signatures by covering the hole with fullerene superconducting cloth. He was trying to work methodically, clamping clips to the edge of the cloth and spiking the clips deep into the slumped rim of dirty water ice, but the cloth, forty meters square and just sixty carbon atoms thick, massed a little less than a butterfly's wing, and it fluttered and billowed like a live thing as gas and dust vented from fractured ice. Carter had fastened down less than half of it when the scientist shouted, "Heads up! Incoming!"

That's when Carter discovered she'd locked him out of the pod's control systems.

He said, "What have you done?"

"Heads up! It's coming right at us!"

The woman was hysterical.

Carter looked up.

The sky was apocalyptic. Pieces of comet nucleus were tumbling away in every direction, casting long cones of shadow through veils and streamers of gas lit by the red dwarf's half-eclipsed disc. The nucleus had been a single body ten kilometers long before the Fanatic singleship had cut across its orbit and carved it open and destroyed the science platform hidden inside it with X-ray lasers and kinetic bomblets. The singleship had also deployed a pod of hunter-killer drones, and after crash deceleration these were falling through the remains of the comet, targeting the flotsam of pods and cans and general wreckage that was all that remained of the platform. Carter saw a firefly flash and gutter in the sullen wash of gases, and then another, almost ninety degrees away. He had almost forgotten his fear while he'd been working, but now it flowed through him again, electric and strong and urgent.

He said, "Give me back my ship."

The scientist said, "I'm tracking it on radar! I think it's about to—"

The huge slab of sooty ice shuddered. A jet of dust and gas boiled up beyond a sharp-edged horizon, and something shot out of the dust, heading straight for Carter. It looked a little like a silvery squid, with a bullet-shaped head that trailed a dozen tentacles tipped with claws and blades. It wrapped itself around an icy pinnacle on the other side of the hole and reared up, weaving this way and that as if studying him. Probably trying to decide where to begin unseaming him, Carter thought, and pointed the welding pistol at it, ready to die if only he could take one of the enemy with him. The thing surged forward—

Dust and gas blasted out of the hole. The scientist had ignited the lifepod's motor. The fullerene cloth shot straight up, straining like a sail in a squall, and the hunter-killer smashed into it and tore it free from the clips Carter had so laboriously secured, tumbling past him at the center of a writhing knot of cloth.

Carter dove through the hatch in the pod's blunt nose. Gravity's ghost clutched him, and he tumbled head over heels and slammed into the rear bulkhead as the pod shook free of its hiding place.

Humans had settled the extensive asteroid belt around Keid, the cool K1 component of the triple star system 40 Eridani, more than a century ago. The first generation, grown from

templates stored in a bus-sized seeder starship, had built a
domed settlement on Neuvo California, an asteroid half the
size of Earth's Moon, and planted its cratered plains of water ice with vast fields of vacuum organisms. Succeeding
generations spread through Keid's asteroid belt, building
domes and tenting crevasses and ravines, raising families,
becoming expert in balancing the ecologies of small, closed
systems and creating new varieties of vacuum organisms,
writing and performing heroic operettas, trading information and works of art on the interstellar net that linked
Earth's far-flung colonies in the brief golden age before
Earth's AIs achieved transcendence.

The Keidians were a practical, obdurate people. As far as
they were concerned, the Hundred Minute War, which ended
with the reduction of Earth and the flight of dozens of Transcendent AIs from the Solar System, was a distant and in-
comprehensible matter that had nothing to do with the
ordinary business of their lives. Someone wrote an unin-
spired operetta about it; someone else revived the lost art of
the symphony, and for a few years her mournful eight-hour
memoriam was considered by many in the stellar colonies to
be a new pinnacle of human art. Very few Keidians took
much notice when a Transcendent demolished Sirius B and
used the trillions of tons of heavy elements it mined from
the white dwarf's core to build a vast ring in close orbit
around Sirius A; no one worried overmuch when other Transcendents began to strip-mine gas giants in other uninhabited systems. Everyone agreed that the machine intelligences
were pursuing some vast, obscure plan that might take millions of years to complete, that they were as indifferent to
the low comedy of human life as gardeners were to the politics of ants.

But then self-styled transhuman Fanatics declared a jihad
against anyone who refused to acknowledge the Transcendents as gods. They dropped a planet-killer on half-
terraformed Mars. They scorched colonies on the moons of
Jupiter and Saturn and Neptune. They dispatched warships
starward. The fragile web of chatter and knowledge-based
commerce that linked the stellar colonies began to unravel.

And just over six hundred days ago, a Transcendent barreled into the Keidian system, swinging past Keid as it decelerated from close to light speed and arcing out toward the double system of white and red dwarf stars just four hundred AU beyond. The red dwarf had always been prone to erratic flares, but a few days after the Transcendent went into orbit around it, the dim little star began to flare brightly and steadily from one of its poles. A narrowly focussed jet of matter and energy began to spew into space, and some of the carbon-rich starstuff was spun into sails with the surface area of planets, hanging hundreds of thousands of kilometers beyond the star yet somehow coupled to its center of gravity. Pinwheeling of the jet and light pressure on the vast sails tipped the star through ninety degrees, and then the jet burned even brighter, and the star began to move out of its orbit.

A hundred days after that, the Fanatics arrived, and the war of the 40 Eridani system began.

The scientist said, "The hunter-killers found us. We had to outrun them."

Carter said, "I was ready to make a stand."

The scientist glared at him with her one good eye and said, "I'm not prepared to sacrifice myself to take out a few drones, Mr. Cho. My work is too important."

She might be young and scared and badly injured, but Carter had to admit that she had stones. When the singleship struck, Carter had been climbing into a p-suit, getting ready to set up a detector array on the surface of the comet nucleus. She had been the first person he'd seen after he'd kicked out of the airlock. He'd caught her and dragged her across twenty meters of raw vacuum to a lifepod that had spun loose from the platform's broken spine, and installed her in one of the pod's hibernation coffins. She'd been half-cooked by reflected energy of the X-ray laser beam that had bisected the main section of the science platform; one side of her face was swollen red and black, the eye there a blind white stone, hair like shriveled peppercorns. The coffin couldn't do much more than give her painblockers and drip glucose-enriched plasma into her blood. She'd die unless she went into hibernation, but she wouldn't allow that because, she said, she had work to do.

Her coffin was one of twenty stacked in a neat five by four array around the inner wall of the lifepod's hull. Carter Cho hung in the space between her coffin and the shaft of the motor, a skinny man with prematurely white hair in short dreads that stuck out in spikes around his thin, sharp face as if he'd just been wired to some mains buss. He said, "This is my ship. I'm in charge here."

The scientist stared at him. Her good eye was red with an eightball hemorrhage, the pupil capped with a black data lens. She said, "I'm a second lieutenant, sailor. I believe I outrank you."

"The commissions they handed out to volunteers like you don't mean anything."

"I volunteered for this mission, Mr. Cho, because I want to find out everything I can about the Transcendent. Because I believe that what we can learn from it will help defeat the Fanatics. I still have work to do, sailor, and that's why I must decide our strategy."

"Just give me back control of my ship, okay?" She stared through him. He said, "Just tell me what you did. You might have damaged something."

"I wrote a patch that's sitting on top of the command stack; it won't cause any damage. Look, we tried hiding from the hunter-killers, and when that didn't work, we had to outrun them. I can appreciate why you wanted to make a stand. I can even admire it. But we were outnumbered, and we are more important than a few drones. War isn't a matter of individual heroics; it's a collective effort. And as part of a collective, every individual must subsume her finer instincts to the greater good. Do you understand?"

"With respect, ma'am, what I understand is that I'm a sailor with combat experience and you're a science geek." She was looking through him again, or maybe focussing on stuff fed to her retina by the data lens. He said, "What kind of science geek are you, anyway?"

"Quantum vacuum theory." The scientist closed her eye and clenched her teeth and gasped, then said, her voice smaller and tighter, "I was hoping to find out how the Transcendent manipulates the magnetic fields that control the jet."

"Are you okay?"

"Just a little twinge."

Carter studied the diagnostic panel of the coffin, but he had no idea what it was trying to tell him. "You should let this box put you to sleep. When you wake up, we'll be back at Pasadena, and they'll fix you right up."

"I know how to run the lifepod, and as long as I have control of it, you can't put me to sleep. We're still falling along the comet's trajectory. We're going to eyeball the Transcendent's engineering up close. If I can't learn something from that, I'll give you permission to boot my ass into vacuum, turn around, and go look for another scientist."

"Maybe you can steer this ship, ma'am, but you don't have combat training."

"There's nothing to fight. We outran the hunter-killers."

Carter said, "So we did. But maybe you should use the radar, check out the singleship. Just before you staged your little mutiny, I saw that it was turning back. I think it's going to try to hunt us down."

Carter stripped coffins and ripped out panels and padding from the walls. He disconnected canisters of the accelerant foam that flooded coffins to cradle hibernating sleepers. He pulled a dozen spare p-suits from their racks. He sealed the scientist's coffin and suited up and vented the lifepod and dumped everything out of the lock.

The idea was that the pilot of the singleship would spot the debris, think that the pod had imploded, and abandon the chase. Carter thought there was a fighting chance it would work, but when he had told her what he was going to do, the scientist had said, "It won't fool him for a moment."

Carter said, "Also, when he chases after us, there's a chance he'll run into some of the debris. If the relative velocity is high enough, even a grain of dust could do some serious damage."

"He can blow us out of the sky with his X-ray laser. So why would he want to chase us?"

"For the same reason the hunter-killer didn't explode when it found us. Think it through, ma'am. He wants to take a prisoner. He wants to extract information from a live body."

He watched her think about that.

She said, "If he does catch up with us, you'll get your wish to become a martyr. There's enough antiberyllium left in the motor to make an explosion that'll light up the whole system. But that's a last resort. The singleship is still in turn-around, we have a good head start, and we're only twenty-eight million kilometers from perihelion. If we get there first, we can whip around the red dwarf, change our course at random. Unless the Fanatic guesses our exit trajectory, that'll buy us plenty of time."

"He'll have plenty of time to find us again. We're a long way from home, and there might be other—"

"All we have to do is live long enough to find out everything we can about the Transcendent's engineering project and squirt it home on a tight beam." The scientist's smile was dreadful. Her teeth were filmed with blood. "Quit arguing, sailor. Don't you have work to do?"

A trail of debris tumbled away behind the pod, slowly spreading out, bright edges flashing here and there as they caught the light of the red dwarf. Carter pressurized p-suits and switched on their life-support systems and transponders before he jettisoned them. Maybe the Fanatic would think that they contained warm bodies. He sprayed great arcs of foam into the hard vacuum and kicked away the empty canisters. The chance of any of the debris hitting the Fanatic's singleship was infinitesimally small, but a small chance was better than none at all, and the work kept his mind from the awful prospect of being captured.

Sternward, the shattered comet nucleus was a fuzzy speck trailing foreshortened banners of light across the star-spangled sky. The expedition had nudged it from its orbit and buried the science platform inside its nucleus, sleeping for a whole year like an army in a fairytale as it fell toward the red dwarf. The mission had been a last desperate attempt to try to learn something of the Transcendent's secrets, but as the comet nucleus neared the red dwarf, and the expedition woke and the scientists started their work, one of the Fanatic drones that policed the vicinity of the star somehow detected the science platform, and the Fanatics sent a singleship to deal with it. Like all their warships, it moved very fast, with brutal acceleration that would have mashed ordinary humans to a thin jelly. It had arrived less than thirty seconds behind a warning broadcast by a spotter observatory at the edge of Keid's heliopause; the crew of the science platform hadn't stood a chance.

The singleship lay directly between the comet and the lifepod now. It had turned around and was decelerating at eight gravities. At the maximum magnification his p-suit's visor could give him, Carter could just make out the faint scratch of its exhaust, but he was unable to resolve the ship itself. In the other direction, the red dwarf star simmered at the bottom of a kind of well of luminous dark. Its nuclear fires were banked low, radiating mostly in infrared. Carter could stare steadily at it with only a minimum of filtering. The sharp-edged shadows of the vast deployment of solar sails were sinking beyond one edge as the jet dawned in the opposite direction, a brilliant white thread brighter than the fierce point of the white dwarf star rising just beyond it. Before the Transcendent had begun its work, the red dwarf had swung around the smaller but more massive white dwarf in a wide elliptical orbit, at its closest approaching within twenty AU, the distance of Uranus from the Sun. Now it was much closer and still falling inward. Scientists speculated that the Transcendent planned to use the tidal effects of a close transit to tear apart the red dwarf, but they'd had less than forty hours to study the Transcendent's engineering before the Fanatic's singleship struck.

Hung in his p-suit a little way from the lifepod, the huge target of the red dwarf in one direction, the vast starscape in the other, Carter Cho resolved to make the best of his fate. The Universe was vast and inhuman, and so was war. Out there, in battles around stars whose names—Alpha Centauri, Epsilon Eridani, Tau Ceti, Lalande 21185, Lacaille 8760, 61 Cygni, Epsilon Indi, Groombridge 1618, Groombridge 34, 82 Eridani, 70 Ophiuchi, Delta Pavonis, Eta Cassiopeiae—were like a proud role call of mythic heroes, the fate of the human race was being determined. While Carter and the rest of the expedition had slept in their coffins deep in the heart of the comet, the Fanatics had invested and destroyed a dozen settlements in Keid's asteroid belt, and the Keidians had fought back and destroyed one of the Fanatics' huge starships. Compared to this great struggle, Carter's fate was less than that of a drop of water in a stormy ocean, a thought both humbling and uplifting.

Well, his life might be insignificant, but he wasn't about to trust it to a dying girl with no combat experience. He fingertip-swam to the stern of the pod, and opened a panel and rigged a manual cutout before he climbed back inside. He had been working for six hours. He was exhausted and sweating hard inside the p-suit, but he couldn't take it off because the pod's atmosphere had been vented and most of its systems had been shut down, part of his plan to fool the Fanatic into thinking it was a dead hulk. The interior was dark and cold. The lights either side of his helmet cast sharp shadows. Frost glistened on struts exposed where he had stripped away paneling.

The scientist lay inside her sealed coffin, her half-ruined face visible through the little window. She looked asleep, but when Carter maneuvered beside her she opened her good eye and looked at him. He plugged in a patch cord and heard some kind of music, a simple progressions of riffs for percussion and piano and trumpet and saxophone. The scientist said that it was her favorite piece. She said that she wanted to listen to it one more time.

Carter said, "You should let the coffin put you to sleep. Before—"

The scientist coughed wetly. Blood freckled the faceplate of her coffin. "Before I die."

"They gave me some science training before they put me on this mission, ma'am. Just tell me what to do."

"Quit calling me 'ma'am,'" the scientist said, and closed her good eye as a trumpet floated a long, lovely line of melody above a soft shuffle of percussion. "Doesn't he break your heart? That's Miles Davis, playing in New York hundreds of years ago. Making music for angels."

"It's interesting. It's in simple six/eight time, but the modal changes—" The scientist was staring at Carter; he felt himself blush and wondered if she could see it. He said, "I inherited perfect pitch from my mother. She sang in an opera chorus before she married my father and settled down to raise babies and farm vacuum organisms."

"Don't try to break it down," the scientist said. "You have to listen to the whole thing. The totality, it's sublime. I'd rather die listening to this than die in hibernation."

"You're not going—"

"I've set down everything I remember about the work that was done before the attack. I'll add it to the observations I make as we whip around the star and then squirt all the data to Keid. Maybe they can make something useful of it, work out the Transcendent's tricks with the magnetic fields, the gravity tethers, the rest of it . . ." She closed her eye, and breathed deeply. Fluid rattled in her lungs. She said softly, as if to herself, "So many dead. We have to make their deaths worthwhile."

Carter had barely gotten to know his shipmates, recruited from all over, before they'd gone into hibernation, but the scientist had lost good friends and colleagues.

He said, "The singleship is still accelerating."

"I know."

"It could catch us before we reach the star."

"Maybe your little trick will fool it."

"I might as well face up to it with a pillow."

The scientist smiled her ghastly smile. She said, "We have to try. We have to try everything. Let me explain what I plan to do at perihelion."

She told Carter that observations by drones and asteroid-based telescopes had shown that the Transcendent had regularized the red dwarf's magnetic field, funneling plasma toward one point on photosphere, where it erupted outward in a permanent flare—the jet that was driving the star toward its fatal rendezvous at the bottom of the white dwarf's steep gravity well. The scientist believed that the Transcendent was manipulating the vast energies of the star's magnetic field by breaking the symmetry of the seething sea of virtual particular pairs that defined quantum vacuum, generating charged particles *ab ovo*, redirecting plasma currents and looped magnetic fields with strengths of thousands of gauss and areas of thousands of kilometers as a child might play with a toy magnet and a few iron filings. The probe she'd loaded with a dozen experiments had been lost with the science platform, but she thought that there was a way of testing at least one prediction of her theoretical work on symmetry breaking.

She opened a window in Carter's helmet display, showed him a schematic plot of the slingshot maneuver around the red dwarf.

Carter said, "You have to get that close?"

"The half-life of the strange photons will be very short, a little less than a millisecond."

"I get it. They won't travel much more than a few hundred kilometers before they decay." Carter grinned when the scientist stared at him. He said, "Speed of light's one of those fundamental constants every sailor has to deal with."

"It means that we have to get close to the source, but it also means that the photon flux will increase anomalously just above the photosphere. There should be a sudden gradient, or a series of steps . . . It was one of the experiments my probe carried."

Carter said, "But it was destroyed, so we have to do the job instead. It's going to get pretty hot, that close to the star. What kind of temperatures are we talking about?"

"I don't know. The average surface temperature of the red dwarf is relatively cool, a little over 3000 degrees Kelvin, but it's somewhat hotter near the base of the flare, where we have to make our pass."

"Why don't we just skim past the edge of the flare itself? The flare might be hotter than the surface, but our transit time would be a whole lot less."

"The magnetic fields are very strong around the flare, and they spiral around it. They could fling us in any direction. Outward if we're lucky, into the star if we're not. No, I'm going to aim for a spot where the field lines all run in the same direction. But the fields can change direction suddenly, and there's the risk of hitting a stray plume of plasma, so I can't fire up the motors until we're close."

Carter thought of his cutout. He said, "If you have to hit a narrow window, I'm your man. I can put this ship through the eye of a needle."

The scientist said, "As soon as I see the chance, I'll fire full thrust to minimize transit time."

"But without the thermal protection of the comet nucleus it'll still be a lot worse than waving your hand through a candle flame. I suppose I can set up a barbecue-mode rotation, run the cooling system at maximum. Your box will help keep you safe, and I'll climb into one too, but if the temperature doesn't kill us, the hard radiation flux probably will. You really think you can learn something useful?"

"This is a unique opportunity, sailor. It's usually very difficult to study Transcendent engineering because they keep away from star systems that have been settled. Some of us think that the Hundred Minute War was fought over the fate of the human race, that the Transcendents who won the war and quit the Solar System believe that we should be left alone to get on with our lives."

"But this one didn't leave us alone."

"Strictly speaking, it did. Forty Eridani B and C, the white dwarf and the red dwarf, are a close-coupled binary. Keid is only loosely associated with them. And they're a rare example of the kind of binary the Transcendents are very interested in, one in which the masses of the two components are very different. We have a unique opportunity to study stellar engineering up close. The Fanatics know this, which is why they're so keen to destroy anything which comes too close."

"They want to keep the Transcendents' secrets secret."

"They're not interested in understanding the Transcendents, only in worshiping them. They are as fixed and immutable as their belief system, but we're willing to learn, to take on new knowledge and change and evolve. That's why we're going to win this war."

* * *

Following the scientist's instructions, Carter dismantled three cameras and rejiggered their imaging circuits into photon counters. While he worked, the scientist talked about her family home in Happy Valley on Neuvo California. It had been badly damaged in one of the first Fanatic attacks, and her parents and her three brothers had helped organize the evacuation. Her mother had been an ecosystem designer, and her father had been in charge of the government's program of interstellar commerce; they were both in the war cabinet now.

"And very proud and very unhappy that their only daughter volunteered for this mission."

Carter said that his family were just ordinary folks, part of a cooperative that ran a vacuum organism farm on the water- and methane-ice plains of San Joaquin. He'd piloted one of the cooperative's tugs and had volunteered for service in the Keidian defense force as soon as the war against the Fanatics began, but he didn't want to talk about the two inconclusive skirmishes in which he'd been involved before being assigned to the mission. Instead, he told the scientist about his childhood and the tented crevasse that was his family home, and the herds of engineered rats he'd helped raise.

"I loved those rats. I should have been smart enough to stay home, raise rats and make babies, but instead I thought that the bit of talent I have for math and spatial awareness was my big ticket out."

"Shit," the scientist said. "The singleship just passed through your debris field."

She opened a window and showed Carter the radar plot.

He felt a funny floating feeling that had nothing to do with free fall. He said, "Well, we tried."

"I'm sure it won't catch up with us before we reach the star."

"If we make that burn now—"

"We'll miss the chance to collect the photon data. We're going to die whatever we do, sailor. Let's make it worthwhile."

"Right."

"Why did you like them? The rats."

"Because they're survivors. Because they've managed to make a living from humans ever since we invented agriculture and cities. Back on Earth, they were a vermin species, small and tough and smart and fast-breeding, eating the same food that people ate, even sharing some of the same diseases and parasites. We took them with us into space because those same qualities made them ideal lab animals. Did you know that they were one of the first mammal species to have their genome sequenced? That's why there are so many gengineered varieties. We mostly bred them for meat and fur and biologicals, but we also raised a few strains that we sold as pets. When I was a little kid, I had a ruffled piebald rat that I loved as much as any of my sisters and brothers. Charlie. Charlie the rat. He lived for more than a thousand days, an awfully venerable age for a rat, and when he died I wouldn't allow him to be recycled. My father helped me make a coffin from offcuts of black oak, and I buried him in a glade in my favorite citrous forest . . ."

The scientist said, "It sounds like a nice spot to be buried."

Carter said, "It's a good place. There are orchards, lots of little fields. People grow flowers just for the hell of it. We have eighteen species of mammals roaming about. All chipped of course, but they give you a feeling of what nature must have been like. I couldn't wait to get out, and now I can't wait to get back. How dumb is that?"

The scientist said, "I'd like to see it. Maybe you could take me on a picnic, show me the sights. My family used to get together for a picnic every couple of hundred days. We'd rent part of one of the parklands, play games, cook way too much food, smoke and drink . . ."

"My father, he's a pretty good cook. And my mother leads a pretty good choral group. We should all get together."

"Absolutely."

They smiled at each other. It was a solemn moment. Carter thought he should say something suitable, but what? He'd never been one for speeches, and he realized now that although the scientist knew his name—it was stitched to his suit—he didn't know hers.

The scientist said, "The clock's ticking."

Carter said, "Yes, ma'am. I'll get this junk fixed up, and then I'll be right back."

He welded the photon detectors to the blunt nose of the pod and cabled them up. He prepped the antenna array. After the pod grazed the base of the flare, its computer would compress the raw data and send it in an encrypted squawk aimed at Keid, repeating it as long as possible, repeating it until the Fanatic singleship caught up. It was less than ten thousand kilometers behind them now. Ahead, the red dwarf filled half the sky, the jet a slender white thread rooted in patch of orange and yellow fusion fire, foreshortening and rising above them to infinity as they drove toward it. Carter said that its base looked like a patch of fungal disease on an apple, and the scientist told him that the analogy wasn't farfetched; before the science platform had been destroyed, one of the research groups had discovered that there were strange nuclear reactions taking place there, forming tons of carbon per second. She showed him a picture one of the pod's cameras had captured: a rare glimpse of the Transcendent. It was hard to see against the burning background of the star's surface because it was a perfectly reflective sphere.

"Exactly a kilometer across," the scientist said, "orbiting the equator every eight minutes. It's thought they enclose themselves in bubbles of space where the fundamental constants have been altered to enhance their cognitive processes. This one's a keeper. I'll send it back—"

A glowing line of gas like a burning snake thousands of kilometers long whipped past. The pod shuddered, probably from stray magnetic flux.

Carter said, "I should climb inside before I start to cook."

The scientist said, "I have to fire up the motor pretty soon." Then she said, "Wait."

Carter waited, hung at the edge of the hatch.

The scientist said, "You switched on the antenna array."

"Just long enough to check it out."

"Something got in. I think a virus. I'm trying to firewall, but it's spreading through the system. It already has the motor and nav systems—"

"I also have control of the corn system," another voice said. It was light and lilting. It was as sinuous as a snake. It was right inside Carter's head. "Carter Cho. I see you, and I know you can hear me."

The scientist said, "I can't fire the motor, but I think you can do something about that, sailor."

So she'd known about the cutout all along. Carter started to haul himself toward the stern.

The voice said, "Carter Cho. I will have complete control of your ship shortly. Give yourself to us."

Carter could see the singleship now, a flat triangle at the tip of a lance of white flame. It was only seconds away. He flipped up the panel, plugged in a patch cord. Sparse lines of data scrolled up in a window. He couldn't access the scientist's flight plan, had no nav except line-of-sight and seat-of-the pants. He had to aim blind for the base of the flare and hope he hit that narrow window by luck, came in at just the right angle, at just the right place where parallel lines of magnetic force ran in just the right direction . . .

"Carter Cho. I have taken control. Kill the woman and give yourself to us, and I promise that you will live with us in glory."

. . . Or he could risk a throw of the dice. Carter ran a tether from his p-suit utility belt to a nearby bolt and braced himself against a rung. With his helmet visor almost blacked out, he could just about look at the surface of the star rushing toward him, could see the intricate tangles of orderly streams that fed plasma into the brilliant patch of fusion fire at the base of the jet.

"Kill her, or I will strip your living brain neuron by neuron."

"Drop dead," Carter said, and switched off his com. The jet seemed to rise up to infinity, a gigantic sword that cut space in two. The scientist had said that if the pod grazed the edge of the jet, spiraling magnetic fields would fling it into the sky at a random vector. And the star took up half the sky . . .

Fuck it, Carter thought. He'd been lucky so far. It was time to roll the dice one more time, hope his luck still held.

He fired attitude controls and aimed the blunt nose of the pod. A menu window popped up in front of his face. He selected *burn* and *full thrust*.

Sudden weight tore at his two-handed grip on the rung as the motor flared. It was pushing a shade under a gee of acceleration; most humans who had ever lived had spent their entire lives in that kind of pull, but Carter's fingers were cramping inside the heavy gloves, and it felt as if the utility belt were trying to amputate him at the waist. The vast dividing line of the jet rushed toward him. Heat beat through his p-suit. If its cooling system failed for a second, he'd cook like a joint of meat in his father's stone oven. Or the Fanatic could burn him out of the sky with its X-ray laser, or magnetic flux could rip the pod apart . . .

Carter didn't care. He was riding his ship rodeo-style toward a flare of fusion light a thousand kilometers wide. He whooped with defiant glee—

—and then, just like that, the pod was somewhere else.

After a minute, Carter remembered to switch on his com. The scientist said, "What the fuck did you just do?"

It took them a while to find out.

Carter had aimed the pod at the edge of the jet, hoping that it would be flung away at a random tangent across the surface of the red dwarf, hoping that it would survive long enough to transmit all of the data collected by the scientist's experiment. But now the red dwarf was a rusty nailhead dwindling into the starscape behind them, the bright point of the white dwarf several seconds of arc beyond it. In the blink of an eye, the pod had gained escape velocity and had been translated across tens of millions of kilometers of space.

"It had to be the Transcendent," the scientist said.

Carter had repressurized the pod and the cooling system was working at a flat roar, but it was still as hot as a sauna. He had taken off his helmet and shaken out his sweat-soaked dreadlocks, but because the scientist's burns made her sensitive to heat, her coffin was still sealed. He hung in front of it, looking at her through the little window. He said, "I took the only chance we had left, and my luck held."

"No magnetic field could have flung us so far, or so fast. It had to be something to do with the Transcendent. Perhaps it canceled our interia. For a few seconds we became as massless as a photon, we achieved light speed . . ."

"My luck held," Carter said. "I hit those magnetic fields just right."

"Check the deep radar, sailor. There's no sign of the Fanatic's singleship. It was right on our tail. If magnetic fields had anything to do with it, it would have been flung in the same direction as us."

Carter checked the deep radar. There was no sign of the singleship. He remembered the glimpse of the silver sphere sailing serenely around the star, and said, "I thought the Transcendents wanted to leave us alone. That's why they quit the Solar System. That's why they only reengineer uninhabited systems . . ."

"You kept rats when you were a kid. If one got out, you'd put her back. If two started to fight, you'd do something about it. How did your rats feel when you reached into their cage to separate them?"

Carter grinned. "If we're rats, what are the Fanatics?"

"Rats with delusions of grandeur. Crazy rats who think they're carrying out God's will, when really they're no better than the rest of us. I wonder what that Fanatic must be thinking. Just for a moment, he was touched by the hand of his God . . ."

"What is it?"

"I've finished processing the data stream from my experiment. When we encountered the edge of the flare, there was a massive, sudden increase in photon flux."

"Because of this symmetry breaking thing of yours. Have you sent the data?"

"Of course, we have to figure the details."

"Send the data," Carter said, "and I'll button up the ship and put us to sleep."

"Perhaps there are some clues in the decay products . . ."

"You've completed your mission, ma'am. Let someone else worry about the details."

"Jesswyn Fiver," the scientist said. She was smiling at him through her little window. For a moment he saw how pretty she'd been. "You never did ask my name. It's Jesswyn Fiver. Now you can introduce me to your parents when we go on that picnic."

I Love Liver: A Romance

LARISSA LAI

Larissa Lai (www.ucalgary.ca/~lalai/bio.htm) lives in Calgary, Alberta, and is a PhD candidate at the University of Alberta. She has an MA in Creative Writing from the University of East Anglia in Norwich, England. She was born in La Jolla, California, grew up in Newfoundland, and lived and worked in Vancouver for many years as a writer, organizer, and editor. Her first novel, When Fox Is a Thousand, *was shortlisted for the Chapters/Books in Canada First Novel Award. Her second novel,* Salt Fish Girl, *was shortlisted for the Sunburst Award, the James Tiptree Award, and the City of Calgary W. O. Mitchell Award. She has never been published by a genre publisher or in any genre publication.*

"I Love Liver: A Romance" was published in Nature. *It's a really perverse, absurdly improbable romance between a replacement liver and her designer, who is very depressed and perhaps quite nuts. There is something in the air about weird romance in 2005. Compare this to the Rucker story, for instance.*

It has taken me almost four weeks of late nights and taxed my mochaccino machine to the limits. But Mira is ready. She began as a prototype for FreshCleanse's Liver Replacement line, but her capacity for toxin decomposition was weaker than that of the liver McDowell Hill came up with in the cubicle next to mine. (What's with people who have last names for first names? It's so tacky.) For whatever reason, the Boss Man liked Mackie's design better, and so Mira fell to the waste heap of Great Inventions That Die on the Drawing Board.

To be honest, I felt quite despondent about it. It wasn't just a blow to the ego, I'm used to those. It was more that . . . well, there was something about Mira, a kind of beauty, extraordinary really. Something poignant about her lines, something tender and sad about her soft, brown-gray texture. The fact that she would never go into production threw me into a bit of a funk.

It took me a few days to realize that this wasn't something I would just get over, as I have with countless other designs. By the fourth day, even after two mochaccinos and a double dose of Beverly, my despondency seemed worse. I phoned in sick and went back to bed. My doctor had expressly told me how careful I had to be with Beverly. "This generation of antidepressants is more precise but also much more potent than what you're probably used to," she told me, "so you have to watch your dosage very carefully." Whatever. It was too late now anyway. I closed my eyes. Halfway between sleep and waking, I thought I saw Mira slip in beside me, larger than life, pillowy soft and a little slippery, in a smooth, sleek sort of way. I reached out to caress an elegant fluke. It was almost comforting.

A ringing phone woke me at four in the afternoon. It was McDowell Hill. "You better get down here right away," he said. "The boss doesn't care how sick you are. That weird liver you designed—it's jumped protocols and has infected the mainframe. We're losing thousands of hours of R&D with every minute that passes. You better get your pathetic, depressed butt down here ASAP." For a minute I thought: "Who cares, you smarmy creep. I hope Mira burns the whole operation down." But then I'd be out of a job. I got my pathetic, depressed butt down to the office.

The place was in chaos. The Tech Support boys were mousing as fast as their caffeine-pumped little hands could move, jibing and sniping at one another the whole time. I found McDowell and the Boss Man at my cubicle, riffling furiously through my password-protected files with brazen impunity. Who needs this job? I thought. "I don't understand how a liver design can go viral like that," the Boss Man was saying.

"Over-rationalization," said Mackie. "The protocols are too close. And that was one weird little liver Anna designed. That's what you get for hiring these foreigners. You know, I'm not sure she's entirely stable."

"Anna was born here," the Boss Man said.

"Damn right," I said, by way of letting them know I'd been there behind them listening. Mackie turned, and shot me the evil eye.

"Can you fix this, Anna?" asked the Boss Man.

I pushed Mackie out of the way and slid into my seat. "That's the thing about organics," I said. "They aren't static. They do things. They mutate."

"We need better firewalls," Mackie said.

I didn't fix anything. It was more like, I appealed to Mira. I coaxed her gently with a few smatterings of code. I showed her the initial lines of a heart I was working on. Mira returned to her original storage location. She spat back most of the information she'd devoured on her rampage. It wasn't all in the correct order, and some of it had been corrupted, but it was pretty much all there. It would keep Tech Support busy for a week or two. I went back home to my depression, wondering if Mira was depressed too.

When I got back to my apartment, my computer was on. Mira was floating back and forth across the screen like a pretty brown-gray fish in an aquarium. I don't know how she got from FreshCleanse to here, but I suppose such things are relatively easy these days. I opened her up and began the modifications. I made her a little larger. I cribbed some slug programming off a biologist's website to give her underside motility. To give her eyes seemed too strange somehow. Antennae looked better. I altered her coloration just slightly to give her an attractive iridescent sheen. It's taken me a few weeks, but now she is finally ready to print. What's wrong with the print function? Never mind, I'll just try it again. There we go. Hello, Mira! She tumbles gracefully from the printer and slithers across my office floor.

Oops. Must have pressed "print" twice. Hello, Mira Two! . . . Oh no, something is wrong. Another flap of liver emerges from the printer. She's cute. I can manage three. Here comes another. Am I in some kind of trouble?

I'll let it go to 12 before I call Tech Support.

The Edge of Nowhere

JAMES PATRICK KELLY

James Patrick Kelly [www.jimkelly.net] lives in Nottingham, New Hampshire. He is well known as an award winner for his science fiction stories, but in fact he has written novels, short stories, essays, reviews, poetry, plays and planetarium shows, and writes a column on the internet for Asimov's Science Fiction Magazine. *His collections include* Strange but Not a Stranger *and* Think Like a Dinosaur and Other Stories, *and his novels include* Wildlife *(1994) and* Look into the Sun *(1989). His novella,* Burn, *was published as a small press book in 2005.*

"The Edge of Nowhere" was published in Asimov's. *It is a posthuman story with some references to Swanwick's Darger series, we think—see the Swanwick story later in this book, and perhaps also Swanwick' classic tale, "The Ends of the Earth." It is a far future small town utopia set "nowhere"— in the "cognisphere" of humanity. It relates what happens when three talking dogs show up and ask for a book.*

Lorraine Carraway scowled at the dogs through the plate glass window of the Casa de la Laughing Cookie and Very Memorial Library. The dogs squatted in a row next to the book drop, acting as if they owned the sidewalk. There were three of them, grand in their bowler hats and paisley vests and bow ties. They were like no dogs Rain had ever seen before. One of them wore a gold watch on its collar, which was pure affectation since it couldn't possibly see the dial. Bad dogs, she was certain of that, recreated out of rust and dead tires and old Coke bottles by the cognisphere and then dispatched to Nowhere to spy on the real people and cause at least three different kinds of trouble.

Will turned a page in his loose-leaf binder. "They still out there?" He glanced up at her, his No. 2 pencil poised over a blank page.

"What the hell do they think they're doing?" Rain made brushing motions just under the windowsill. "Go away. Scram!"

"Scram?" said Will. "Is scram a word?"

Will had been writing *The Great American Novel* ever since he had stopped trying to prove Fermat's Last Theorem. Before that he had been in training to run a sub four-minute mile. She'd had to explain to him that the mile was a measure of distance, like the cubit or the fathom or the meter. Rain had several books about ancient measurement in the Very Memorial Library and Will had borrowed them to lay out a course to practice on. They'd known each other since the week after Will had been revived, but they had first had sex during his running phase. It turned out that runners made wonderfully energetic lovers—especially nineteen-year-old runners. She had been there to time his personal best at 4:21:15. But now he was up to Chapter Eleven of *The Great American Novel*. He had taken on the project after Rain assured him that the great American novel had yet to be written. These days, not many people were going for it.

"Where do dogs like that come from, anyway?" Will said.

"Don't be asking her about dogs," called Fast Eddie from his cookie lab. "Rain hates all dogs, don't you know?"

Rain was going to deny this, but the Casa de la Laughing Cookie was Fast Eddie's shop. Since he let her keep her books in the broken meat locker and call it a library, she tried not to give him any headaches. Of course, Rain didn't *hate* dogs, it was just that she had no use for their smell, their turds hidden in lawns, or the way they tried to lick her face with their slimy tongues. Of course, this bunch wasn't the same as the dim-witted dogs people kept around town. They were obviously creatures of the cognisphere; she expected that they would be better behaved.

Will came up beside her. "I'm thinking the liver-colored one with the ears is a bloodhound." He nodded at the big dog with the watch on its collar. "The others look like terriers of some sort. They've got a pointer's skull and the short powerful legs. Feisty dogs, killers actually. Fox hunters used to carry terriers in their saddlebags and when their hounds cornered the poor fox, they'd release the terriers to finish him off."

"How do you know that?" said Rain, suddenly afraid that there would be dogs in *The Great American Novel*.

"Read it somewhere." He considered. "Jane Austen? Evelyn Waugh?"

At that moment, the bloodhound raised his snout. Rain got the impression that he was sniffing the air. He stared through the front window at . . . who? Rain? Will? Some signal passed between the dogs then, because they all stood. One of the terriers reared up on its hind legs and batted the door handle. Rain ducked from Will's side and retreated to the safety of her desk.

"I'm betting they're not here to buy happy crumbs." Will scratched behind his ear with the rubber eraser on his pencil.

The terrier released the latch on the second try and the door swung open. The shop bell tinkled as the dogs entered. Fast Eddie slid out of the lab, wiping his hands on his apron. He stood behind the display case that held several dozen lead crystal trays filled with artfully broken psychotropic cookies. Rain hoped that he'd come to lend her moral support and not just to see if the dogs wanted his baked goods. The terriers deployed themselves just inside the door, as if to prevent anyone from leaving. Will stooped to shake the paw of the dog nearest him.

"Are you an Airedale or a Welsh?" he said.

"Never mind that now," said the dog.

The bloodhound padded up to Rain, who was glad to have the desk between them. She got a distinct whiff of damp fur and dried spit as he approached. She wrinkled her nose and wondered what she smelled like to him.

The bloodhound heaved his bulk onto his hind legs. He took two shaky steps toward her and then his forepaws were scrabbling against the top of her desk. The dark pads unfolded into thick, clawed fingers; instead of a dewclaw, the thing had a thumb. "I'm looking for a book," said the dog. His bowler hat tipped precariously. "My name is Baskerville."

Rain frowned at the scratches the dog's claws made on her desktop. "Well, you've got *that* wrong." She leaned back in her chair to get away from its breath. "Baskerville wasn't the hound's name. Sir Charles Baskerville was Sherlock Holmes's *client*."

"You may recall that Sir Charles was frightened to death by the hound well before Dr. Mortimer called on Holmes," Baskerville said. He had a voice like a kettle drum. "The client was actually his nephew, Sir Henry."

Rain chewed at her lower lip. "Dogs don't wear hats." She didn't care to be contradicted by some clumsy artifact of the cognisphere. "Or ties. Are you even real?"

"Rather a rude question, don't you think?" Baskerville regarded her with sorrowful melted-chocolate eyes. "Are *you* real?"

The dog was right; this was the one thing the residents of Nowhere never asked. "I don't have your damn book." Rain opened the top drawer of the desk, the one where she threw all her loose junk. It was a way to keep the dog from seeing her embarrassment.

"How do you know?" he said reasonably. "I haven't told you what it is."

She sorted through the contents of the drawer as if searching for something. She moved the dental floss, destiny dice, blank catalog cards, a tape measure, her father's medals, the two dead watches and finally picked out a bottle of ink and the Waterman 1897 Eyedropper fountain pen that Will had given her to make up for the fight they'd had about the laundry. The dog waited politely. "Well?" She unscrewed the lid of the ink bottle.

"It's called *The Last President*," said Baskerville, "I'm afraid I don't know the author."

Rain felt the blood drain from her face. *The Last President* had been Will's working title for his book, just before he had started calling it *The Great American Novel*. She dipped the nib of the fountain pen into the ink bottle, pulled the filling lever and then wiped the nib on a tissue. "Never heard of it," she said as she wrote *Last Prez??* in her daybook. She glanced over at Will, and caught him squirming on his chair. He looked as if his pockets were full of crickets. "Fiction or non-fiction?"

"Fiction."

She wrote that down. "Short stories or a novel?"

"I'm not sure. A novel, I think."

The shop bell tinkled as Mrs. Snopes cracked the door open. She hesitated when she bumped one of the terriers. "Is something wrong?" she said, not taking her hand from the handle.

"Right as nails," said Fast Eddie. "Come in, Helen, good to see you. These folks are here for Rain. The big one is Mr. Baskerville and—I'm sorry, I didn't catch your names." He gave the terriers a welcoming smile. Fast Eddie had become the friendliest man in Nowhere ever since his wife had stepped off the edge of town and disappeared.

"Spot," said one.

"Rover," said the other.

"Folks?" muttered Mrs. Snopes. "Dogs is what I call 'em." She inhaled, twisted her torso and squeezed between the two terriers. Mrs. Snopes was very limber; she taught swing yoga at the Town Hall Monday, Tuesday, and Thursday nights from 6-7:30. "I've got a taste for some crumbs of your banana oatmeal bar," she said. "That last one laid me out for the better part of an afternoon. How are they breaking today, Eddie?"

"Let's just see." He set a tray on the top of the display case and pulled on a glove to sort through the broken cookies.

"You are Lorraine Carraway?" said Baskerville.

"That's her name, you bet." Will broke in impulsively. "But she hates it." He crumpled the loose-leaf page he had been writing on, tossed it at the trashcan and missed. "Call her Rain."

Rain bristled. She didn't hate her name; she just didn't believe in it.

"And you are?" said the bloodhound. His lips curled away from pointed teeth and black gums in a grotesque parody of a smile.

"Willy Werther, but everyone calls me Will."

"I see you are supplied with pencil and paper, young Will. Are you a writer?"

"Me? Oh, no. No." He feigned a yawn. "Well, sort of." For a moment, Rain was certain that he was going to blurt out that *he* was the author of *The Last President*. She wasn't sure why she thought that would be a bad idea, but she did. "I . . . uh . . ." Now that Will had Baskerville's attention, he didn't seem to know what to do with it. "I've been trying to remember jokes for Eddie to tell at church," he said. "Want to hear one?" Fast Eddie and Mrs. Snopes glanced up from their cookie deliberations. "Okay then, how do you keep your dog from digging in the garden?"

"I don't know, Will." Rain just wanted him to shut up. "How?"

"Take away his shovel." Will looked from Baskerville to Rain and then to Fast Eddie. "No?"

"No." Eddie, who had just become a deacon in the Temple of the Eternal Smile, shook his head. "God likes Her jokes to be funny."

"Funny." Will nodded. "Got it. So what's this book about anyway, Mr. B?"

"Will, I just don't know," said the bloodhound. "That's why I'd like to read it." Baskerville turned and yipped over his shoulder. Rover trotted to him and the bloodhound dropped onto all fours. Rain couldn't see what passed between them because the desk blocked her view, but when Baskerville heaved himself upright again he was holding a brass dog whistle in his paw. He dropped it, clattering, on the desktop in front of Rain.

"When you find the book, Rain," said Baskerville, "give us a call."

Rain didn't like it that Baskerville just assumed that she would take on the search. "Wait a minute," she said. "Why do you need me to look for it? You're part of the cognisphere, right? You already *know* everything."

"We have access to everything," said Baskerville. "Retrieval is another matter." He growled at Spot. The shop bell tinkled as he opened the door. "I look forward to hearing from you, Rain. Will, it was a pleasure to meet you." The bloodhound nodded at Fast Eddie and Mrs. Snopes, but they paid him no attention. Their heads were bent over the tray of crumbs. Baskerville left the shop, claws clicking against the gray linoleum. The terriers followed him out.

"Nice dogs." Will affected an unconcerned saunter as he crossed the room, although he flew the last few steps. "My book, Rain!" he whispered, his voice thick. With what? Fear? Pride?

"Is it?" Rain had yet to read a word of *The Great American Novel*; Will claimed it was too rough to show. Although she could imagine that this might be true, she couldn't help but resent being shut out. She offered him the whistle. "So call them."

"What are you saying?" He shrank back, as if mere proximity to the whistle might shrivel his soul. "They're from . . ." He pointed through the window toward the precipitous edge of the mesa on which Nowhere perched. ". . . out there."

Nobody knew where the cognisphere was located exactly, or even if it occupied physical space at all. "All right then, don't." Rain shrugged and pocketed the whistle.

Will seemed disappointed in her. He obviously had three hundred things he wanted to say—and she was supposed to listen. He had always been an excitable boy, although Rain hadn't seen him this wound up since the first time they had made love. But this was neither the time nor the place for feverish speculation. She put a finger to her lips and nodded toward the cookie counter.

Mrs. Snopes picked out a four gram, elongated piece of banana oatmeal cookie ornamented with cream and cinnamon hallucinogenic sprinkles. She paid for it with the story of how her sister Melva had run away from home when she was eleven and they had found her two days later sleeping in the neighbor's treehouse. They had heard the story before, but not the part about the hair dryer. Fast Eddie earned an audience credit on the Barrows's Memory Exchange but the cognisphere deposited an extra quarter point into Mrs. Snopes's account for the new detail, according to the Laughing Cookie's MemEx register. Afterward, Fast Eddie insisted that Rain admire the banana oatmeal crumb before he wrapped it up for Mrs. Snopes. Rain had to agree it was quite striking. She said it reminded her of Emily Dickinson.

They closed the Very Memorial Library early. Usually after work, Will and Rain swept some of Eddie's cookie dust into a baggie and went looking for a spot to picnic. Their favorites were the overlook at the southwestern edge of town and the roof of the Button Factory, although on a hot day they also liked the mossy coolness of the abandoned fallout shelter.

But not this unhappy day. Almost as soon as they stepped onto Onion Street, they were fighting. *First she* suggested that Will show her his book. *Then he* said not yet and asked if she had any idea why the dogs were asking about it. *Then she* said no—perhaps a jot too emphatically—*because he* apparently understood her to be puzzled as to why dogs should care about a nobody like him. *Then he* wondered aloud if maybe she wasn't just a little jealous, *which she* said was a dumb thing to say, *which he* took exactly the wrong way.

Will informed her icily that he was going home because he needed to make changes to Chapter Four. Alarmed at how their row had escalated, Rain suggested that maybe they could meet later. He just shrugged and turned away. Stung, she watched him jog down Onion Street.

Later, maybe—being together with Will had never sounded so contingent.

Rain decided to blame the dogs. It was hard enough staying sane here in Nowhere, finding the courage each day not to step off the edge. They didn't need yet another cancerous mystery eating at their lives. And Will was just a kid, she reminded herself. Nineteen, male, impulsive, too smart for his own good, but years from being wise. Of course he was entitled to his moods. She'd always waited him out before, because even though he made her toes curl in frustration sometimes, she did love the boy.

In the meantime, there was no way around it: she'd have to ask Chance Conrad about *The Last President*. She took a right onto Abbey Road, nodding curtly at the passersby. She knew what most people thought about her: that she was impatient and bitter and that she preferred books to people. Of course, they were all wrong, but she had given up trying to explain herself. She ignored Bingo Finn slouching in the entrance to Goriot's Pachinko Palazzo and hurried past Linton's Fruit and Daily Spectator, the Prynne Building, and the drunks at the outdoor tables in front of the Sunspot. She noticed with annoyance that the Drew Barrymore version of *The Wizard of Oz* was playing for another week at the Ziegfowl Feelies. At Uncle Buddy's she took a right, then a left onto Fairview which dead ended in the grassy bulk of the Barrow.

Everything in Nowhere had come out of the Barrow:

Rain's fountain pen, the books in the Very Memorial Library, Will's endless packs of blank, loose-leaf paper, Fast Eddie's crystal trays and Mrs. Snopes's yoga mats. And, of course, all the people.

The last thing Rain remembered about the world was falling asleep in her husband Roger's arms. It had been a warm night in May 2009. Roger had worked late so they had ordered a sausage and green pepper pizza and had watched the last half hour of *The African Queen* before they went to bed. It was *so* romantic, even if Nicholson and Garbo were old. She could remember Roger doing his atrocious Nicholson imitation while he brushed his teeth. They had cuddled briefly in the dark but he said he was too tired to make love. They must have kissed good night—yes, no doubt a long and tender last kiss. One of the things she hated most about Nowhere was that she couldn't remember any of Roger's kisses or his face or what he looked like naked. He was just a warm, pale, friendly blur. Some people in Nowhere said it was a mercy that nobody could remember the ones they had loved in the world. Rain was not one of those people.

Will said that the last thing he remembered was falling asleep in his *Nintendo and American Culture* class at Northern Arizona University in the fall of 2023. He could recall everything about the two sexual conquests he had managed in his brief time in the world—Talley Lotterhand and Paula Herbst—but then by his own admission he had never really been in love.

The Barrow was a warehouse buried under the mesa. Rain climbed down to the loading dock and knocked on the sectional steel door. After a few moments she heard the whine of an electric motor as the door clattered up on its tracks. Chance Conrad stood just inside, blinking in the afternoon sunlight. He was a handsome, graying man, who balanced a receding hairline with a delicate beard. Although he had a light step and an easy manner, the skin under his eyes was dark and pouchy. Some said this was because Chance didn't sleep much since he was so busy managing the Barrow. Others maintained that he didn't sleep at all, because he hadn't been revived like the rest of the residents of Nowhere. He was a construct of the cognisphere. It stood to reason, people said. How could anyone with a name like Chance Conrad be real?

"Lorraine!" he said. "And here I was about to write this day off as a total loss." He put his hand on her shoulder and urged her through the entrance. "Come, come in." Chance had no use for daylight; that was another strike against his being real. Once the Barrow was safely locked down again he relaxed. "So," he said, "here we are, just the two of us. I'm hoping this means you've finally dumped the boy genius?"

Rain had long since learned that the best way to deflect Chance's relentless flirting was just to ignore it. As far as she knew, he had never taken a lover. She took a deep breath and counted to five. *Unu, du, tri, kvar, kvin.* The air in the Barrow had the familiar damp weight she remembered from when she first woke up at Nowhere; it settled into Rain's lungs like a cold. Before her were crates and jars and barrels and boxes of goods that the people of Nowhere had asked the cognisphere to recreate. Later that night Ferdie Raskolnikov and his crew would load the lot onto trucks for delivery around town tomorrow.

"What's this?" Rain bent to examine a wide-bladed shovel cast with a solid steel handle. It was so heavy that she could barely lift it.

"Shelly Castorp thinks she's planting daffodils with this." Chance shook his head. "I told her that the handles of garden tools were always made of wood but she claims her father had a shovel just like that one." He shook his head. "The specific gravity of steel is 7.80 grams per cubic centimeter, you know."

"Oh?" When Rain let the handle go, the shovel clanged against the cement floor. "Can we grow daffodils?"

"We'll see." Chance muscled the shovel back into place on its pallet. He probably didn't appreciate her handling other people's orders. "I'm racking my brains trying to remember if I've got something here for you. But I don't, do I?"

"How about those binoculars I keep asking for?"

"I send the requests. . . ." He spread his hands. "They all

bounce." The corners of his mouth twitched. "So is this about us? At long last?"

"I'm just looking for a book, Chance. A novel."

"Oh," he said, crestfallen. "Better come to the office."

Normally if Rain wanted to add a book to the Very Memorial Library, she'd call Chance and put in an order. Retrieving books was usually no problem for the collective intelligence of humanity, which had uploaded itself into the cognisphere sometime in the late twenty-third century. All it needed was an author and title. Failing that, a plot description or even just a memorable line might suffice for the cognisphere to perform a plausible, if not completely accurate, reconstruction of some lost text. In fact, depending on the quality of the description, the cognisphere would recreate a version of pretty much anything the citizens of Nowhere could remember from the world.

Exactly how it accomplished this, and more important, why it bothered, was a mystery.

Chance's office was tucked into the rear of the Barrow, next to the crèche. On the way, they passed the Big Board of the MemEx, which tracked audience and storyteller accounts for all the residents of Nowhere and sorted and cataloged the accumulated memories. Chance stopped by the crèche to check the vitals of Rahim Aziz, who was destined to become the newest citizen of Nowhere, thus bringing the population back up to the standard 853. Rahim was to be an elderly man with a crown of snowy white hair surrounding an oval bald spot. He was replacing Lucy Panza, the tennis pro and Town Calligrapher, who had gone missing two weeks ago and was presumed to have thrown herself over the edge without telling anyone.

"Old Aziz isn't quite as easy on the eye as you were," said Chance, who never failed to remind Rain that he had seen her naked during her revival. Rahim floated on his back in a clear tube filled with a yellow, serous fluid. He had a bit of a paunch and the skin of his legs and under his arms was wrinkled. Rain noted with distaste that he had a penis tattoo of an elephant.

"When will you decant him?"

Chance rubbed a thumb across a readout shell built into the wall of the crèche. "Tomorrow, maybe." The shell meant nothing to Rain. "Tuesday at the latest."

Chance Conrad's office was not so much decorated as overstuffed. Dolls and crystal and tools and fossils and clocks jostled across shelves and the tops of cabinets and chests. The walls were covered with pix from feelies made after Rain's time in the world, although she had seen some of them at the Ziegfowl. She recognized Oud's *Birthdeath*, Fay Wray in full fetish from *Time StRanger* and the wedding cake scene from *Two of Neala*. Will claimed the feelies had triggered the cancerous growth of history—when all the dead actors and sports stars and politicians started having second careers, the past had consumed the present.

"So this is about a novel then?" Chance moved behind his desk but did not sit down. "Called?" He waved a hand over his desktop and its eye winked at him.

"The Last President." Rain sat in the chair opposite him.

"Precedent as in a time-honored custom, or president as in Marie Louka?"

"The latter."

He chuckled. "You know, you're the only person in this town who would say *the latter*. I love that. Would you have my baby?"

"No."

"Marry me?"

"Uh-uh."

"Sleep with me?"

"Chance."

He sighed. "Who's the author?"

"I don't know."

"You don't know?" Chance rubbed under his eyes with the heels of his hands. "You're sure about that? You wouldn't care to take a wild guess? Last name begins with the letter . . . what? A through K? L through Z?"

"Sorry."

He stepped from behind the desk and his desktop shut its

eye. "Well, the damn doggie didn't know either, which is why I couldn't help him."

Rain groaned. "He's been here already?"

"Him and a couple of his pooch pals." Chance opened the igloo which stood humming beside the door. "Cooler?" He pulled out a frosty pitcher filled with something thick and glaucous. "It's just broccoli nectar and a little ethanol-style vodka."

Rain shook her head. "But that doesn't make sense." She could hear the whine in her voice. "They're agents of the cognisphere, right? And you access the cognisphere. Why would it ask you to ask itself?"

"Exactly." Chance closed the door and locked it. This struck Rain as odd; maybe he was afraid that Ferdi Raskolnikov would barge in on them. "Things have been loopy here lately," he said. "You should see some of the mistakes we've had to send back." He poured broccoli cocktail for himself. It oozed from the pitcher and landed in his coffee mug with a thick *plop*. "I've spent all afternoon trying to convince myself that the dogs are some kind of a workaround, maybe to jog some lost data loose from the MemEx." He replaced the pitcher in the igloo and settled onto the chair behind his desk. "But now you show up and I'm wondering: Why is Rain asking me for this book?"

She frowned. "I ask you for all my books."

He considered for a moment, tapping the finger against his forehead and then pointed at her. "Let me tell you a story." Rain started to object that she had neither goods nor services to offer him in return and she had just drained her MemEx account to dry spit, but he silenced her with a wave. "No, this one is free." He took a sip of liquid broccoli. "An audience credit unencumbered, offered to the woman of my dreams."

She stuck out her tongue.

"Why does this place exist?" he asked.

"The Barrow?"

"Nowhere."

"Ah, eschatology." She laughed bitterly. "Well, Father

Samsa claims this is the afterlife, although I'll be damned if I know whether it's heaven or hell."

"I know you don't believe *that*," said Chance. "So then this is some game that the cognisphere is playing? We're virtual chesspersons?"

Rain shrugged.

"What happens when we step off the edge?"

"Nobody knows." Just then a cacophony of clocks yawped, pinged, and buzzed in six o'clock. "This isn't much of a story, Chance."

"Patience, love. So you think the cognisphere recreated us for a reason?"

"Maybe. Okay, sure." A huge spider with eight paintbrush legs shook itself and stretched on a teak cabinet. "We're in a zoo. A museum."

"Or maybe some kind of primitive backup. The cognisphere keeps us around because there's a chance that it might fail, go crazy—I don't know. If that happened, we could start over."

"Except we'd all die without the cognisphere." The spider stepped onto the wall and picked its way toward the nearest corner. "And nobody's made any babies that I know of. We're not exactly Adam and Eve material, Chance."

"But that's damn scary, no? Makes the case that none of us is real."

Rain liked him better when he was trying to coax her into bed. "Enough." She pushed her chair back and started to get up.

"Okay, okay." He held up his hands in surrender. "Story time. When I was a kid, I used to collect meanies."

"Meanies?" She settled back down.

"Probably after your time. They were 'bots, about so big." He held forefinger and thumb a couple of centimeters apart. "Little fighting toys. There were gorilla meanies and ghoul meanies and Nazi meanies and demon meanies and dino meanies. Fifty-two in all, one for every week of the year. You set them loose in the meanie arena and they would try to kill one another. If they died, they'd shut down for twenty-four hours. Now if meanies fought one on one, they would always draw. But when you formed them into teams, their powers combined in different ways. For instance, a ghoul and Nazi team could defeat any other team of two—except the dino and yeti. For the better part of a year, I rushed home from school every day to play with the things. I kept trying combinations until I could pretty much predict the outcome of every battle. Then I lost interest."

"Speaking of losing interest," said Rain, who was distracted by the spider decorating the corner of Chance's office in traceries of blue and green.

"I'm getting there." He shifted uncomfortably in his chair, and took another sip from the mug. "So a couple of years go by and I'm twelve now. One night I'm in my room and I hear this squeaking coming from under my bed. I pull out the old meanie arena, which has been gathering dust all this time, and I see that a mouse has blundered into it and is being attacked by a squad of meanies. And just like that I'm fascinated with them all over again. For weeks I drop crickets and frogs and garter snakes into the arena and watch them try to survive."

"That's sick."

"No question. But then boys can't help themselves when it comes to mindless cruelty. Anyway, it didn't last. The wildlife was too hard on the poor little 'bots." He drained the last of the broccoli. "But the point is that I got bored playing with a closed set of meanies. Even though I hadn't actually tried all possible combinations, after a while I could see that nothing much new was ever going to happen. But then the mouse changed everything." He leaned forward across the desk. "So let me propose a thought experiment to you, my lovely Lorraine. This mysterious novel that everyone is so eager to find? What if the last name of the author began with the letter . . ." He paused and then seemed to pluck something out of the air. "Oh, let's say 'W.' "

Rain started.

"And just for the sake of argument, let's suppose that the first name also begins with 'W'. . . . Ah, I see from your expression that this thought has also occurred to you."

"It's not him," said Rain. "He was revived at nineteen;

he's just a kid. Why would the cognisphere care anything about him?"

"Because he's the mouse in our sad, little arena. He isn't simply recycling memories of the world like the rest of us. The novel your doggies are looking for doesn't exist in the cognisphere, never did. Because it's being written right here, right now. Maybe imagination is in short supply wherever the doggies come from. Lord knows there isn't a hell of a lot of it in Nowhere."

Rain would have liked to deny it, but she could feel the insult sticking to her. "How do you know he's writing a novel?"

"I supply the paper, Rain. Reams and reams of it. Besides, this may be hell, as Father Samsa insists, but it's also a small town. We meddle in each other's business, what else is there to do?" His voice softened; Rain thought that if Chance ever did take a lover, this would be how he might speak to her. "Is the book any good? Because if it is, I'd like to read it."

"I don't know." At that moment, Rain felt a drop of something cold hit the back of her hand. There was a dot the color of sky on her knuckle. She looked up at the spider hanging from the ceiling on an azure thread. "He doesn't show it to me. Your toy is dripping."

"Really?" Chance came around the desk. "A woman of your considerable charms is taking no for an answer?" He reached up and cradled the spider into his arms. "Go get him, Rain, You don't want to keep your mouse waiting." He carried the spider to the teak cabinet.

Rain rubbed at the blue spot on her hand but the stain had penetrated her skin. She couldn't even smudge it.

But Will wasn't waiting, at least not for Rain. She stopped by their apartment but he wasn't there and he hadn't left a note. Neither was he at the Button Factory nor Queequeg's Kava Cave. She looked in at the Laughing Cookie just as Fast Eddie was locking up. No Will. She finally tracked him down at the overlook, by the blue picnic table under the chestnut trees.

Normally they came here for the view, which was spectacular. A field of wildflowers, tidy-tips and mullein and tick-seed and bindweed, sloped steeply down to the edge of the mesa. But Will was paying no attention to the scenery. He had scattered a stack of five loose-leaf binders across the table; the whole of *The Great American Novel* or *The Last President* or whatever the hell it was called. Three of the binders were open. He was reading—but apparently not writing in—a fourth. A No. 2 pencil was tucked behind his ear. Something about Will's body language disturbed Rain. He usually sprawled awkwardly wherever he came to rest, a giraffe trying to settle on a hammock. Now he was gathered into himself, hunched over the binder like an old man. Rain came up behind him and kneaded his shoulders for a moment.

He leaned back and sighed.

"Sorry about this afternoon." She bent to nibble his ear. "Have you eaten?"

"No." He kissed the air in front of him but did not look at her.

She peeked at the loose-leaf page in front of him and tried to decipher the handwriting, which was not quite as legible as an EEG chart. . . . *knelt before the coffin, her eyes wide in the dim holy light of the cathedral. His face was wavy* . . . No, thought Rain straightening up before he suspected that she was reading. Not *wavy. Waxy.* "Beautiful evening," she said.

Will shut the binder he had been reading and gazed distractedly toward the horizon.

Rain had not been completely honest with Chance. It was true that Will hadn't shown her the novel, but she *had* read some of it. She had stolen glimpses over his shoulder or read upside down when she was sitting across from him. Then there was the one guilty afternoon when she had come back to their apartment and gobbled up pages 34–52 before her conscience mastered her curiosity. The long passage had taken place in a bunker during one of the Resource Wars. The President of Great America, Lawrence Goodman, had been reminiscing with his former mistress and current National Security Advisor, Rebecca Santorino, about Akron, where they had first fallen in love years ago and which had just been obliterated in retaliation for an American strike on Zhengzhou. Two pages later they were thrashing on the president's bed and ripping each other's clothes off. Rain had begun this part with great interest, hoping to gain new insight into Will's sexual tastes, but had closed the binder uneasily just as the president was tying his lover to the Louis XVI armoire with silk Atura neckties.

Will closed the other open binders and stacked all five into a pile. Then he pulled the pencil from behind his ear, snapped it in two, and let the pieces roll out of his hand under the picnic table. He gave her an odd, lopsided smile.

"Will, what's the matter?" Rain stared. "Are you okay?"

In response, he pulled a baggie of cookie dust from his shirt pocket and jiggled it.

"Here?" she said, coloring. "In plain sight?" Usually they hid out when they were eating dust, at least until they weathered the first rush. The Cocoa Peanut Butter Chunk made them giggly and not a little stupid. Macaroon Sandies often hit Rain like powdered lust.

"There's no one to see." Will licked his forefinger and stuck it into the bag. "Besides, what if there was?" He extended the finger toward her, the tip and nail coated with the parti-colored powder. "Does anyone here care what we do?"

She considered telling him then what Chance Conrad had said about small towns, but she could see that Will was having a mood. So she just opened her mouth and obediently stuck her tongue out. As he rotated the finger across the middle of her tongue, she tasted the sweet, spicy grit. She closed her mouth on the finger and he pulled it slowly through her lips.

"Now you," she said, reaching for the baggie. They always fed each other cookie dust.

Rain and Will sat on the tabletop with their feet on the seat, facing the slope that led down to the edge of Nowhere. The world beneath the impossibly high cliff was impossibly flat, but this was still Rain's favorite lookout, even if it was probably an illusion. The land stretched out in a kind of grid with rectangles in every color of green: the brooding green of forests, the dreaming green of fields under cultivation, and the confused gray-green of scrub land. Dividing the rectangles were ribbons the color of wet sand. Rain liked to think they were roads, although she had never spotted any traffic on them. She reached for Will's hand and he closed it around hers. He was right: she didn't care if anyone saw them together like this. His skin was warm and rough. As she rubbed her finger over the back of his hand, she thought she could make out a faded blue spot. But maybe it was a trick of the twilight, or a cookie hallucination.

The rectangles and the ribbons of the land to the southwest had always reminded her of something, but she had never quite been able to figure out what. Now as Eddie's magic cookie dust sparked through her bloodstream, and she felt Will's warm hand in hers, she thought of a trip she had taken with her father when she was just a kid to a museum in an old city called Manhilton, that got blown up afterward. In the museum were very old pix that just hung on the wall and mostly didn't do anything, and she remembered taking a cab to get there and the cabbie had asked what her name was but she wouldn't tell him so he called her *little girl* which she didn't like because she was seven already, and the museum had escalators that whispered music, and there was one really, really big room filled with pix of all blurry water lilies, and outside in a sculpture garden there were statues made of metal and rocks but there were no flowers because it was cold so she and Dad didn't stay out there very long and inside again were lots of pix of women with three eyes and too many corners and then some wide blue men blocked her view of the Mona Lisa so she never really saw that one, which everyone said later was supposed to be so special but one she did see and remembered now was a pix of a grid that had colored rectangles and with ribbons of red and yellow separating them, and she asked her dad if it was a map of the museum and he laughed down at her because her dad was so tall, tall as any statue and he said the pix wasn't a map, it was a *mondrian* and she asked him what a *mondrian* was and then he laughed again and she laughed and it was so easy to laugh in those days and Will was laughing too.

"I want to go down there." He laughed as he pointed down at the mondrian which stretched into the rosy distance.

"There?" Rain didn't understand; the best part of her was still in the museum with her father. "Why?"

"Because there are people living there. Must be why Chance won't give out binoculars or telescopes." He let go of her hand. "Because it's not here."

"You're going to step over the edge?" Her voice rose in alarm.

"No, silly." He leapt up, stood on the tabletop and raised his arms to the sky. "I'm going to climb down."

"But that's the same thing."

"No, it isn't. I'll show you." He slid off the picnic table and started toward the thicket of scruffy evergreens and brambles that had overgrown the edge of Nowhere. He walked along this tangle until he came to a bit of blue rag tied to a branch, glanced over his shoulder to see if she was still with him, and then wriggled into the scrub. Rain followed.

They emerged into a tiny clearing. She sidled beside him and he slipped an arm around her waist to brace her. The cliff was steep here but not sheer. She could make out a narrow dirt track that switched back through scree and stunted fir. Maybe a mountain goat could negotiate it, if there were any mountain goats. But a single misstep would send Will plunging headlong. And then there was the Drop. Everyone knew about the Drop. They traded stories about it all the time. Scary stories. She was about to ask him why, if there were people down there, they hadn't climbed up for a visit, when he kicked a stone over the edge. They watched it bounce straight down and disappear over a ledge.

"Lucy Panza showed me this," said Will, his face flushed with excitement.

Rain wondered when he'd had time to go exploring the edge with Lucy Panza. "But she stepped over the edge."

"No," he said. "She didn't."

She considered the awful slope for a moment and shuddered. "I'm not going down there, Will."

He continued peering down the dirt track. "I know," he said.

The calm with which he said it was like a slap in the face. She stared at him, speechless, until he finally met her gaze. "I'll come back for you." He gave her the goofy, apologetic grin he always summoned up when he upset her. "I'll make sure the path is safe and I'll make all kinds of friends down at the bottom and when the time is right, I'll be back."

"But what about your book?"

He blew a dismissive breath between his lips. "I'm all set with that."

"It's finished?"

"It's crap, Rain." His voice was flat. "I'm not wasting any more time writing about some stupid made-up president. There are no more presidents. And how can anyone write the Great American Novel when there is no more America?" He caught his breath. "Sorry," he said. "I know that's what you wanted me to do." He gave her a sour smile. "You're welcome to read it if you want. Or hand it over to the dogs. That should be good for a laugh." Then he pulled her into his arms and kissed her.

Of course Rain kissed him back. She wanted to drag him down on top of her and rip his clothes off, although there really wasn't enough room here to make love. She would even have let him take her on the picnic table, *tie her* to the damn table, if that's what he had wanted. But his wasn't the kind of kiss that started anything.

"So I'm coming back, I promise," he murmured into her ear. "Just tell everyone that you're waiting for me."

"Wait a minute." She twisted away from him. "You're going now? It's almost dark. We just ate cookie dust." She couldn't believe he was serious. This was such a typical boneheaded-Will stunt he was pulling. "Come home, honey," she said. "Get some sleep. Things might look different in the morning."

He stroked her hair. "I've got at least another hour of light," he said. "Believe me, I've thought about this a long time, Rain." Then he brushed his finger against her lips. "I love you."

He took a step over the edge and another. He had gone about a dozen meters before his feet went out from beneath him and he fell backward, skidding on his rear end and clutching at the scrub. But he caught himself almost immediately and looked up at her, his face pale as the moon. "Oops!" he called cheerfully.

Rain stood at the edge of the cliff long after she could no longer see him. She was hoping that he'd come to a dead end and have to turn back. The sun was painting the horizon with fire by the time she fetched Will's binders to the edge of Nowhere. She opened one after another and shook the pages free. They fluttered into the twilight like an exaltation of larks. A few landed briefly on the path before launching themselves again into the breeze and following their creator out of her life. When all the pages had disappeared, Rain took the whistle that the dogs had given her and hurled it as far into the mondrian as she could.

Only then did she let herself cry. She thought she deserved it.

Rain found her way through the gathering darkness back to the apartment over Vronsky's Laundromat and Monkeyfilter Bowladrome. She put some Szechwan lasagna into the microwave and pushed it around her plate for a while, but she was too numb to be hungry. She would have gone to the eight o'clock show at the Ziegfowl just to get out, but she was mortally tired of *The Wizard of Oz*, no matter whom the cognisphere recast in it. The apartment depressed her. The problem, she decided, was that she was surrounded by Will's stuff; she'd have to move it somewhere out of sight.

She placed a short stack of college-lined, loose-leaf paper and four unopened reams in a box next to *The Awakening, The Big Snooze*, and *Drinking the Snow*. Will had borrowed the novels from the Very Memorial Library but had made way too many marginal notes in them for her to return them to the stacks. Rain would have to order new ones from Chance in the Barrow. She threw his Buffalo Soldiers warmup jacket on top of several dusty pairs of Adidas Kloud Nine running shoes. Will's dresser drawers produced eight pairs of white socks, two black, a half dozen gray jockey shorts, three pairs of jeans, and a stack of t-shirts sporting pix of Panafrican shoutcast bands. At the bottom of the sock drawer, Rain discovered flash editions of *Superheterodyne Adventure Stories 2020–26* and *The Complete Idiot's Guide to Fetish*. She pulled his mustard collection and climkies and homebrew off the kitchen shelves.

And that was all it took to put Will out of her life. She shouldn't have been surprised. After all, they had only lived together for just over a year.

She was trying to talk herself into throwing the lot of it out the next morning when the doorglass blinked. She glanced at the clock. Who did she know that would come visiting at 10:30 at night? When she opened the door, Baskerville, Rover, and Spot looked up at her.

"You found the book?" The bloodhound's bowtie was crooked.

Beneath her, Rain could hear the rumble and clatter of the bowling lanes. "There is no book."

"May we come in?"

"No."

"You threw the whistle off the edge," said Baskerville.

As if on signal, the two terriers sat. They looked to Rain as if they were settling in for a stay. "Where's Will?" said Rover.

She wanted to kick the door shut hard enough to knock their bowler hats off, but the terrier's question took her breath away. If the cognisphere had lost track of Will, then maybe he wasn't . . . maybe he was . . . "I hate dogs," she said. "Maybe I forgot to mention that?"

Baskerville regarded her with his solemn chocolate eyes and said nothing.

The terrier's hind leg scratched at his flank. "Has something happened to him?" he asked.

"Stop it!" Rain stomped her foot on the doorsill and all three dogs jumped. "You want a story and I want information. Deal?"

The dogs thought it over, then Rover got up and licked her hand.

"Okay, story." But at that moment, Rain's throat seemed to close, as if she had tried to swallow the page of a book.

Will was gone. If she said it aloud, it would become just another story on the MemEx. But she had to know. "M-My boyfriend climbed over the edge a couple of hours ago trying to find a way down the cliff. I pitched the goddamn novel he was writing after him. The end."

"But what does this have to do with *The Last President*?"

"That was the name of his book. Used to be. Once." She was out of breath. "Okay, you got a story. Now you owe me some god-damn truth. He's dead, right? You've absorbed him already."

Rover started to say, "I'm afraid that we have no knowledge of . . ." But she didn't give the dog a chance to finish; she slammed the door.

She decided then not to throw Will's things out. She dragged them all into the bedroom closet and covered the pile with the electric blanket. She made one more pass around the apartment to make sure she had everything. Then she decided to make a grocery list so she could stop at Cereno's on the way home from work tomorrow. That's when she discovered that she had nothing to write on. She gave herself permission to retrieve a couple of pages of Will's paper from the closet— just this once. As long as she was writing the list, she didn't have to think about Will on the cliff or the dogs in the hall. She cracked the apartment door just enough to see that all three of them were still there, heads on paws, asleep. Spot's ear twitched but he didn't wake up. She sat on the couch with the silence ringing in her ears until she got up and muscled the dresser over to block the closet where she had put Will's stuff. She thought about brushing her teeth and trying for sleep but she knew that would be a waste of time. She was browsing the books on her bookshelf, all of which she had long since read to tatters, when the phone squawked.

Rain was sure it was the dogs calling, but decided to pick up just in case.

"Lorraine Carraway?"

Rain recognized Sheriff Renfield's drawl and was immediately annoyed. He was one of her best customers—an avid Georgette Heyer fan—and knew better than to call her by her proper name.

"Speaking, Beej. What's up?"

"There's been some trouble down to the Laughing Cookie." He was slurring words. He pronounced *There is* as *Thersh*.

"Trouble?"

"Fast Eddie said you had dogs in the store today. Dogs with hats."

"What kind of trouble, Beej? Is Eddie all right?"

"He's fine, we're all just fine." Everybody knew that Beej Renfield was a drinker and nobody blamed him for it. Being sheriff was possibly the most boring job in Nowhere. "But there's been what you might call vandalism. Books all over the place, Rain, some of them ripped up good. Teeth marks. And the place stinks of piss. Must've happened an hour, maybe two ago. Fast Eddie is ripping mad. I need you to come down here and lay some calm on him. Will you do that for me, Rain?"

"I'll do you one better, Beej. You're looking for these dogs?"

His breath rasped in the receiver so loud she could almost smell it.

"Because I've got them here if you're interested. Right outside my door."

"I'm on my way."

"Oh, and Beej? You might want to bring some help."

She sat at the kitchen table to wait. In front of her were the shopping list and the No. 2 pencil. They reminded her of Will. He was such a strong boy, everybody in town always said so. He *had* run that 4:21 mile, after all. And she was almost certain that Baskerville had looked surprised when she'd told him that Will was climbing down the cliff. What did surprise look like on a dog? She'd see for sure when Beej Renfield arrived.

For the very first time Rain allowed herself to consider the possibility that Will wasn't dead or absorbed. Maybe the cognisphere ended at the edge of Nowhere. In which case, he might actually come back for her.

But why would he bother? What had she ever done to deserve him? Her shopping list lay in front of her like an accusation. Was this all her life was about? Toilet paper and Seventy-Up and duck sausage? Will had climbed over the edge of Nowhere. What chance had she ever taken? She needed to do *something*, something no one had ever done before. She'd had enough of books and all the old stories about the world that the cognisphere was sorting on the MemEx. That world was gone, forever and ever, amen.

She picked up the pencil again.

I scowled at the dogs through the plate glass window of the Very Memorial Library. They squatted in a row next to my book drop. There were three of them, haughty in their bowler hats and silk vests. They acted like they owned the air. Bad dogs, I knew that for sure, created out of spit and tears and heartbreak by the spirits of all the uncountable dead and sent to spy on the survivors and cause at least three different kinds of trouble.

I wasn't worried. We'd seen their kind before.

What's Expected of Us

TED CHIANG

Ted Chiang lives in Bellevue, Washington. He is a technical writer who occasionally writes short SF that is widely admired, then usually nominated for, or winning awards. He has published five SF stories, all of which are distinctive and highly accomplished. Stories of Your Life and Others, *his collected fiction to that date, was published in 2002. China Mieville said in* The Guardian: *"In Chiang's hands, SF really is the "literature of ideas" it is often held to be, and the genre's traditional "sense of wonder" is paramount." Chiang says, "To the extent that a work of SF reflects science, it's hard SF. And reflecting science doesn't necessarily mean consistency with a certain set of facts; more essentially, it means consistency with a certain strategy for understanding the universe. Science seeks a type of explanation different from those sought by art or religion, an explanation where objective measurement takes precedence over subjective experience."*

"What's Expected of Us" was published in Nature. *It is another of the fictional explorations of biochemical determinism of human personality and behavior that Chiang, Greg Egan, and Peter Watts, to name three distinguished examples, have been pursuing in SF.*

This is a warning. Please read carefully.

By now you've probably seen a Predictor; millions of them have been sold by the time you're reading this. For those who haven't seen one, it's a small device, like a remote for opening your car door. Its only features are a button and a big green LED. The light flashes if you press the button. Specifically, the light flashes one second *before* you press the button.

Most people say that when they first try it, it feels like they're playing a strange game, one where the goal is to press the button after seeing the flash, and it's easy to play. But when you try to break the rules, you find that you can't. If you try to press the button without having seen a flash, the flash immediately appears, and no matter how fast you move, you never push the button until a second has elapsed. If you wait for the flash, intending to keep from pressing the button afterward, the flash never appears. No matter what you do, the light always precedes the button press. There's no way to fool a Predictor.

The heart of each Predictor is a circuit with a negative time delay—it sends a signal back in time. The full implications of the technology will become apparent later, when negative delays of greater than a second are achieved, but that's not what this warning is about. The immediate problem is that Predictors demonstrate that there's no such thing as free will.

There have always been arguments showing that free will

is an illusion, some based on hard physics, others based on pure logic. Most people agree these arguments are irrefutable, but no one ever really accepts the conclusion. The experience of having free will is too powerful for an argument to overrule. What it takes is a demonstration, and that's what a Predictor provides.

Typically, a person plays with a Predictor compulsively for several days, showing it to friends, trying various schemes to outwit the device. The person may appear to lose interest in it, but no one can forget what it means—over the following weeks, the implications of an immutable future sink in. Some people, realizing that their choices don't matter, refuse to make any choices at all. Like a legion of Bartleby the Scriveners, they no longer engage in spontaneous action. Eventually, a third of those who play with a Predictor must be hospitalized because they won't feed themselves. The end state is akinetic mutism, a kind of waking coma. They'll track motion with their eyes, and change position occasionally, but nothing more. The ability to move remains, but the motivation is gone.

Before people started playing with Predictors, akinetic mutism was very rare, a result of damage to the anterior cingulate region of the brain. Now it spreads like a cognitive plague. People used to speculate about a thought that destroys the thinker, some unspeakable lovecraftian horror, or a Gödel sentence that crashes the human logical system. It turns out that the disabling thought is one that we've all encountered: the idea that free will doesn't exist. It just wasn't harmful until you believed it.

Doctors try arguing with the patients while they still respond to conversation. We had all been living happy, active lives before, they reason, and we hadn't had free will then either. Why should anything change? "No action you took last month was any more freely chosen than one you take today," a doctor might say. "You can still behave that way now." The patients invariably respond, "But now I know." And some of them never say anything again.

Some will argue that the fact the Predictor causes this change in behavior means that we *do* have free will. An automaton cannot become discouraged, only a free-thinking entity can. The fact that some individuals descend into akinetic mutism whereas others do not just highlights the importance of making a choice.

Unfortunately, such reasoning is faulty: every form of behavior is compatible with determinism. One dynamic system might fall into a basin of attraction and wind up at a fixed point, whereas another exhibits chaotic behavior indefinitely, but both are completely deterministic.

I'm transmitting this warning to you from just over a year in your future: it's the first lengthy message received when circuits with negative delays in the mega-second range are used to build communication devices. Other messages will follow, addressing other issues. My message to you is this: pretend that you have free will. It's essential that you behave as if your decisions matter, even though you know that they don't. The reality isn't important: what's important is your belief, and believing the lie is the only way to avoid a waking coma. Civilization now depends on self-deception. Perhaps it always has.

And yet I know that, because free will is an illusion, it's all predetermined who will descend into akinetic mutism and who won't. There's nothing anyone can do about it—you can't choose the effect the Predictor has on you. Some of you will succumb and some of you won't, and my sending this warning won't alter those proportions. So why did I do it?

Because I had no choice.

Girls and Boys, Come Out to Play

MICHAEL SWANWICK

Michael Swanwick (www.michaelswanwick.com) lives in Philadelphia, Pennsylvania. His novels include the Nebula Award winner Stations of the Tide *(1991),* The Iron Dragon's Daughter *(1993), and* Bones of the Earth *(2002). He is unquestionably one of the finest writers currently working in SF and fantasy. His short fiction collections include* Gravity's Angels *(1991),* A Geography of Unknown Lands *(1997),* Moon Dogs *(2000),* Tales of Old Earth *(2000), and* The Periodic Table of Science Fiction *(2005). Three years ago, he began a series of stories set in a fantastic Cordwainer Smithian future world, somewhat recovered from the destruction of the ancient civilization of the Utopians, where biotechnology rules. A human, Aubrey Darger, and a genetically engineered thief, lover, and dog, Sir Blackthorpe Ravenscairn de Plus Preciuex, also known as "Surplus," plan complex scams.*

"Girls and Boys, Come Out to Play" was published in Asimov's, and is the third in the series. Set in a future Greece, an African post-human scientist uses biotech to invent gods patterned on some of the ancient Greek gods as a means of controlling a society. Surplus and Darger have a wild time. The story is a good illustration of Swanwick's current aesthetic: combining good old-fashioned SF ideas with a certain calculated luridness.

On a hilltop in Arcadia, Darger sat talking with a satyr.

"Oh, the *sex* is good," the satyr said. "Nobody could say it wasn't. But is it the be-all and end-all of life? I don't see that." The satyr's name was Demetrios Papatragos, and evenings he played the saxophone in a local jazz club.

"You're a bit of a philosopher," Darger observed.

"Oh, well, in a home-grown front porch sense, I suppose I am." The satyr adjusted the small leather apron that was his only item of clothing. "But enough about me. What brings *you* here? We don't get that many travelers these days. Other than the African scientists, of course."

"Of course. What *are* the Africans here for, anyway?"

"They are building gods."

"Gods! Surely not! Whatever for?"

"Who can fathom the ways of scientists? All the way from Greater Zimbabwe they came, across the wine-dark Mediterranean and into these romance-haunted hills, and for what? To lock themselves up within the ruins of the Monastery of St. Vasilios, where they labor as diligently and joylessly as if they were indeed monks. They never come out, save to buy food and wine or to take the occasional blood sample or skin scraping. Once, one of them offered a nymph money to have sex with him, if you can believe such a thing."

"Scandalous!" Nymphs, though they were female satyrs, had neither hooves nor horns. They were, however, not cross-fertile with humans. It was the only way, other than a small tail at the base of their spines (and *that* was normally covered by their dresses), to determine their race. Needless to say, they were as wildly popular with human men as their male counterparts were with women. "Sex is either freely given or it is nothing."

"You're a bit of a philosopher yourself," Papatragos said. "Say—a few of our young ladies might be in heat. You want me to ask around?"

"My good friend Surplus, perhaps, would avail himself of their kind offers. But not I. Much though I'd enjoy the act, I'd only feel guilty afterward. It is one of the drawbacks of having a depressive turn of mind."

So Darger made his farewells, picked up his walking stick, and sauntered back to town. The conversation had given him much to think about.

"What word of the Evangelos bronzes?" Surplus asked. He was sitting at a table out back of their inn, nursing a small glass of retsina and admiring the sunset. The inn stood at the outskirts of town at the verge of a forest, where pine, fir, and chestnut gave way to orchards, olive trees, cultivated fields, and pastures for sheep and goats. The view from its garden could scarce be improved upon.

"None whatsoever. The locals are happy to recommend the ruins of this amphitheater or that nuclear power plant, but any mention of bronze lions or a metal man causes them only to look blank and shake their heads in confusion. I begin to suspect that scholar in Athens sold us a bill of goods."

"The biters bit! Well, 'tis an occupational hazard in our line of business."

"Sadly true. Still, if the bronzes will not serve us in one manner, they shall in another. Does it not strike you as odd that two such avid antiquarians as ourselves have yet to see the ruins of St. Vasilios? I propose that tomorrow we pay a courtesy visit upon the scientists there."

Surplus grinned like a hound—which he was not, quite. He shook out his lace cuffs and, seizing his silver-knobbed cane, stood. "I look forward to making their acquaintance."

"The locals say that they are building gods."

"Are they really? Well, there's a market for everything, I suppose."

Their plans were to take a strange turn, however. For that evening Dionysus danced through the town.

Darger was writing a melancholy letter home when the first shouts sounded outside his room. He heard cries of "Pan! Great Pan!" and wild skirls of music. Going to the window, he saw an astonishing sight: The townsfolk were pouring into the street, shedding their clothes, dancing naked in the moonlight for all to see. At their head was a tall, dark figure who pranced and leaped, all the while playing the pipes.

He got only a glimpse, but its effect was riveting. He *felt* the god's passage as a physical thing. Stiffening, he gripped the windowsill with both hands, and tried to control the wildness that made his heart pound and his body quiver.

But then two young women, one a nymph and the other Theodosia, the innkeeper's daughter, burst into his room and began kissing his face and urging him toward the bed.

Under normal circumstances, he would have sent them packing—he hardly knew the ladies. But the innkeeper's daughter and her goat-girl companion were both laughing and blushing so charmingly and were furthermore so eager to grapple that it seemed a pity to disappoint them. Then, too, the night was rapidly filling with the sighs and groans of human passion—no adult, apparently, was immune to the god's influence—and it seemed to Darger perverse that he alone in all the world should refuse to give in to pleasure.

So, protesting insincerely, he allowed the women to crowd him back onto the bed, to remove his clothing, and to have their wicked way with him. Nor was he backward with them. Having once set his mind to a task, he labored at it with a will.

In a distant corner of his mind, he heard Surplus in the room down the hall raise his voice in an ecstatic howl.

Darger slept late the next morning. When he went down to breakfast, Theodosia was all blushes and shy smiles. She brought him a platter piled high with food, gave him a fleet peck on the cheek, and then fled happily back into the kitchen.

Women never ceased to amaze Darger. One might make free of their bodies in the most intimate manner possible, handling them not only lustfully but self-indulgently, and denying oneself not a single pleasure . . . yet it only made them like you the better afterward. Darger was a staunch atheist. He did not believe in the existence of a benevolent and loving God who manipulated the world in order to maximize the happiness of His creations. Still, on a morning like this, he had to admit that all the evidence was against him.

Through an open doorway, he saw the landlord make a playful grab at his fat wife's rump. She pushed him away and, with a giggle, fled into the interior of the inn. The landlord followed.

Darger scowled. He gathered his hat and walking stick, and went outside. Surplus was waiting in the garden. "Your thoughts trend the same way as mine?" Darger asked.

"Where else could they go?" Surplus asked grimly. "We must have a word with the Africans."

The monastery was less than a mile distant, but the stroll up and down dusty country roads gave them both time enough to recover their *savoir faire*. St. Vasilios, when they came to it, was dominated by a translucent green bubble-roof, fresh-grown to render the ruins habitable. The grounds were surrounded by an ancient stone wall. A wooden gate, latched but not locked, filled the lower half of a stone arch. Above it was a bell.

They rang.

Several orange-robed men were in the yard, unloading crated laboratory equipment from a wagon. They had the appearance and the formidable height of that handsomest of the world's peoples, the Masai. But whether they were of Masai descent or had merely incorporated Masai features into their genes, Darger could not say. The stocky, sweating wagoner looked like a gnome beside them. He cursed and tugged at his horses' harness to keep the skittish beasts from bolting.

At the sound of the bell, one of the scientists separated

himself from the others, and strode briskly to the gate. "Yes?" he said in a dubious tone.

"We wish to speak with the god Pan," Darger said. "We are from the government."

"You do not look Greek."

"Not the local government, sir. The *British* government." Darger smiled into the man's baffled expression. "May we come in?"

They were not brought to see Dionysus immediately, of course, but to the Chief Researcher. The scientist-monk led them to an office that was almost Spartan in its appointments: a chair, a desk, a lamp, and nothing more. Behind the desk sat a girl who looked to be at most ten years old, reading a report by the lamp's gentle biofluorescence. She was a scrawny thing with a large and tightly corn-rowed head. "Tell her you love her," she said curtly.

"I beg your pardon?" Surplus said.

"Tell her that, and then kiss her. That'll work better than any aphrodisiac I could give you. I presume that's what you came to this den of scientists for—that or poison. In which case, I recommend a stout cudgel at midnight and dumping the body in a marsh before daybreak. Poisons are notoriously uncertain. In either case, there is no need to involve my people in your personal affairs."

Taken aback, Darger said, "Ah, actually, we are here on official husiness."

The girl raised her head.

Her eyes were as dark and motionless as a snake's. They were not the eyes of a child but more like those of the legendary artificial intellects of the Utopian era—cold, timeless, calculating. A shudder ran through Darger's body. Her gaze was electrifying. Almost, it was terrifying.

Recovering himself, Darger said, "I am Inspector Darger, and this is my colleague, Sir Blackthorpe Ravenscairn de Plus Precieux. By birth an American, it goes without saying."

She did not blink. "What brings two representatives of Her Majesty's government here?"

"We have been dispatched to search out and recover the Evangelos bronzes. Doubtless you know of them."

"Vaguely. They were liberated from London, were they not?"

"Looted, rather! Wrenched from Britain's loving arms by that dastard Konstantin Evangelos in an age when she was weak and Greece powerful, and upon the shoddiest of excuses—something about some ancient marbles that had supposedly . . . well, that hardly matters."

"Our mission is to find and recover them," Surplus elucidated.

"They must be valuable."

"Were *you* to discover them, they would be worth a king's ransom, and it would be my proud privilege to write you a promissory note for the full amount. However—" Darger coughed into his hand. "We, of course, are civil servants. The thanks of a grateful nation will be our reward."

"I see." Abruptly changing the subject, the Chief Researcher said, "Your friend—is he a chimeric mixture of human and animal genes, like the satyrs? Or is he a genetically modified dog? I ask only out of professional curiosity."

"His friend is capable of answering your questions for himself," Surplus said coldly. "There is no need to speak of him as if he were not present. I mention this only as a point of common courtesy. I realize that you are young, but—"

"I am older than you think, sirrah!" the girl-woman snapped. "There are disadvantages to having a childish body, but it heals quickly, and my brain cells—in stark contrast to your own, gentlemen—continually replenish themselves. A useful quality in a researcher." Her voice was utterly without warmth, but compelling nonetheless. She radiated a dark aura of authority. "Why do you wish to meet our Pan?"

"You have said it yourself—out of professional curiosity. We are government agents, and therefore interested in any new products Her Majesty might be pleased to consider."

The Chief Researcher stood. "I am not at all convinced that the Scientifically Rational Government of Greater Zimbabwe will want to export this technology after it has been tested and perfected. However, odder things have happened. So I will humor you. You must wear these patches, as do we." The Chief Researcher took two plastic bandages from a nearby box and showed how they should be applied. "Otherwise, you would be susceptible to the god's influence."

Darger noted how, when the chemicals from the drug-patch hit his bloodstream, the Chief Researcher's bleak charisma distinctly faded. These patches were, he decided, useful things indeed.

The Chief Researcher opened the office door, and cried, "Bast!"

The scientist who had led them in stood waiting outside. But it was not he who was summoned. Rather, there came the soft sound of heavy paws on stone, and a black panther stalked into the office. It glanced at Darger and Surplus with cool intelligence, then turned to the Chief Researcher. "Sssssoooooo . . . ?"

"Kneel!" The Chief Researcher climbed onto the beast's back, commenting off-handedly, "These tiny legs make walking long distances tiresome." To the waiting scientist she said, "Light the way for us."

Taking a thurible from a nearby hook, the scientist led them down a labyrinthine series of halls and stairways, proceeding ever deeper into the earth. He swung the thurible at the end of its chain as he went, and the chemical triggers it released into the air activated the moss growing on the stone walls and ceiling so that they glowed brightly before them, and gently faded behind them.

It was like a ceremony from some forgotten religion, Darger reflected. First came the thurifer, swinging his censer with a pleasant near-regular clanking, then the dwarfish lady on her great cat, followed by the two congregants, one fully human and the other possessed of the head and other tokens of the noble dog. He could easily picture the scene painted upon an interior wall of an ancient pyramid. The fact that they were going to converse with a god only made the conceit that much more apt.

At last the passage opened into their destination.

It was a scene out of Piranesi. The laboratory had been

retrofitted into the deepest basement of the monastery. The floors and roofs above had fallen in long ago, leaving shattered walls, topless pillars, and fragmentary buttresses. Sickly green light filtered through the translucent dome overhead, impeded by the many tendrils or roots that descended from above to anchor the dome by wrapping themselves about toppled stones or columnar stumps. There was a complexity of structure to the growths that made Darger feel as though he were standing within a monstrous jellyfish, or else one of those man-created beasts which, ages ago (or so legend had it), the Utopians had launched into the void between the stars in the hope that, eons hence, they might make contact with alien civilizations.

Scientists moved purposefully through the gloom, feeding mice to their organic alembics and sprinkling nutrients into pulsing bioreactors. Everywhere, ungainly tangles of booms and cranes rose up from the floor or stuck out from high perches on the walls. Two limbs from the nearest dipped delicately downward, as if in curiosity. They moved in a strangely fluid manner.

"Oh, dear God!" Surplus cried.

Darger gaped and, all in an instant, the groping booms and cranes revealed themselves as tentacles. The round blobs they had taken at first for bases became living flesh. Eyes as large as dinner plates clicked open and focused on the two adventurers.

His senses reeled. Squids! And by his quick estimation, there were, at a minimum, several score of the creatures!

The Chief Researcher slid off her feline mount, and waved the inquiring tentacles away. "Remove Experiment One from its crypt," she commanded, and the creature flowed across the wall to do her bidding. It held itself upon the vertical surface by its suckered tentacles, Darger noted, but scuttled along the stone on short sharp legs like those of a hermit crab's. He understood now why the Chief Researcher was so interested in chimeras.

In very little time, two squids came skittering across the floor, a stone coffin in their conjoined tentacles. Gracefully, they laid it down. In unison, they raised their tentacles and lowered them in a grotesque imitation of a bow. Their beaks clacked repeatedly.

"They are intelligent creatures," the Chief Researcher commented. "But no great conversationalists."

To help regain his equilibrium, Darger fumbled out his pipe from a jacket pocket, and his tobacco pouch and a striking-box as well. But at the sight of this latter device, the squids squealed in alarm. Tentacles thrashing, they retreated several yards.

The Chief Researcher rounded on Darger. *"Put that thing away!"* Then, in a calmer tone, "We tolerate no open flames. The dome is a glycerol-based organism. It could go up at a spark."

Darger complied. But, true though the observation about the dome might be, he knew a lie when he heard one. So the creatures feared fire! That might be worth remembering.

"You wanted to meet Dionysus." The Chief Researcher laid a hand on the coffin. "He is here. Subordinate Researcher Mbutu, open it up."

Surplus raised his eyebrows, but said nothing.

The scientist pried open the coffin lid. For an instant nothing was visible within but darkness. Then a thousand black beetles poured from the coffin (both Darger and Surplus shuddered at the uncanniness of it) and fled into the shadows, revealing a naked man who sat up, blinking, as if just awakened.

"Behold the god."

Dionysus was an enormous man, easily seven feet tall when he stood and proportionately built, though he projected no sense of power at all. His head was either bald or shaven but in either case perfectly hairless. The scientist handed him a simple brown robe, and when he tied it up with a length of rope, he looked as if he were indeed a monk.

The panther, Bast, sat licking one enormous paw, ignoring the god entirely.

When Darger introduced himself and Surplus, Dionysus smiled weakly and reached out a trembling hand to shake. "It is very pleasant to meet folks from England," he said. "I

have so few visitors." His brow was damp with sweat and his
skin a pallid gray.

"This man is sick!" Darger said.

"It is but weariness from the other night. He needs more
time with the physician scarabs to replenish his physical systems," the Chief Researcher said impatiently. "Ask your
questions."

Surplus placed a paw on the god's shoulder. "You look
unhappy, my friend."

"I—"

"Not to *him*," the dwarfish woman snapped, "to *me!* He is
a proprietary creation and thus not qualified to comment
upon himself."

"Very well," Darger said. "To begin, madam—why? You
have made a god, I presume by so manipulating his en-
docrine system that he produces massive amounts of targeted pheromones on demand. But what is the point?"

"If you were in town last night, you must know what the
point is. Dionysus will be used by the Scientifically Rational
Government to reward its people with festivals in times of
peace and prosperity as a reward for their good citizenship,
and in times of unrest as a pacifying influence. He may also
be useful in quelling riots. We shall see."

"I note that you referred to this man as Experiment One.
May I presume you are building more gods?"

"Our work progresses well. More than that I cannot say."

"Perhaps you are also building an Athena, goddess of wisdom?"

"Wisdom, as you surely know, being a matter of pure reason, cannot be produced by the application of pheromones."

"No? Then a Ceres, goddess of the harvest? Or an He-
phaestus, god of the forge? Possibly a Hestia, goddess of the
hearth?"

The girl-woman shrugged. "By the tone of your questions, you know the answers already. Pheromones cannot
compel skills, virtues, or abstractions—only emotions."

"Then reassure me, madam, that you are not building a
Nemesis, goddess of revenge? Nor an Eris, goddess of dis-

cord. Nor an Ares, god of war. Nor a Thanatos, god of death. For if you were, the only reason I can imagine for your presence here would be that you did not care to test them out upon your own population."

The Chief Researcher did not smile. "You are quick on the uptake for a European."

"Young societies are prone to presume that simply because a culture is old, it must therefore be decadent. Yet it is not we who are running experiments upon innocent people without their knowledge or consent."

"I do not think of Europeans as people. Which I find takes care of any ethical dilemmas."

Darger's hand whitened on the knob of his cane. "Then I fear, madam, that our interview is over."

On the way out, Surplus accidentally knocked over a beaker. In the attendant confusion, Darger was able to surreptitiously slip a box of the antipheromonal patches under his coat. There was no obvious immediate use for the things. But from long experience, they both knew that such precautions often prove useful.

The journey back to town was slower and more thoughtful than the journey out had been. Surplus broke the silence at last by saying, "The Chief Researcher did not rise to the bait."

"Indeed. And I could not have been any more obvious. I as good as told her that we knew where the bronzes were, and were amenable to being bribed."

"It makes one wonder," Surplus said, "if our chosen profession is not, essentially, sexual in nature."

"How so?"

"The parallels between cozening and seduction are obvious. One presents oneself as attractively as possible and then seeds the situation with small deceits, strategic retreats, and warm confidences. The desired outcome is never spoken of directly until it has been achieved, though all parties involved are painfully aware of it. Both activities are woven of silences, whispers, and meaningful looks. And—most significantly—the Chief Researcher, artificially maintained in an eternal prepubescence, appears to be immune to both."

"I think—"

Abruptly, a nymph stepped out into the road before them and stood, hands on hips, blocking their way.

Darger, quick-thinking as ever, swept off his hat and bowed deeply. "My *dear* Miss! You must think me a dreadful person, but in all the excitement last night, I failed to discover your name. If you would be so merciful as to bestow upon me that knowledge and your forgiveness . . . and a smile . . . I would be the happiest man on earth."

A smile tugged at one corner of the nymph's mouth, but she scowled it down. "Call me Anya. But I'm not here to talk about myself, but about Theodosia. I'm used to the ways of men, but she is not. You were her first."

"You mean she was a . . . ?" Darger asked, shocked.

"With my brothers and cousins and uncles around? Not likely! There's not a girl in Arcadia who keeps her hymen a day longer than she desires it. But you were her first *human* male. That's special to a lass."

"I feel honored, of course. But what is it specifically that you are asking me?"

"Just—" her finger tapped his chest—"*watch it!* Theodosia is a good friend of mine. I'll not have her hurt." And, so saying, she flounced back into the forest and was gone.

"Well!" Surplus said. "Further proof, if any were needed, that women remain beyond the comprehension of men."

"Interestingly enough, I had exactly this conversation with a woman friend of mine some years ago," Darger said, staring off into the green shadows, "and she assured me that women find men equally baffling. It may be that the problem lies not in gender but in human nature itself."

"But surely—" Surplus began.

So discoursing, they wended their way home.

A few days later, Darger and Surplus were making their preparations to leave—and arguing over whether to head straight for Moscow or to make a side-trip to Prague—when Eris, the goddess of discord, came stalking through the center of town, leaving fights and arguments in her wake.

Darger was lying fully clothed atop his bed, savoring the smell of flowers, when he heard the first angry noises. Theodosia had filled the room with vases of hyacinths as an apology because she and Anya had to drive to a nearby duck farm to pick up several new eider-down mattresses for the inn, and as a promise that they would not be over-late coming to him. He jumped up and saw the spreading violence from the window. Making a hasty grab for the box of patches they had purloined from the monastery, he slapped one on his neck.

He was going to bring a patch to Surplus's room, when the door flew open, and that same worthy rushed in, seized him, and slammed him into the wall.

"You false friend!" Surplus growled. "You smiling, scheming . . . anthropocentrist!"

Darger could not respond. His friend's paws were about his neck, choking him. Surplus was in a frenzy, due possibly to his superior olfactory senses, and there was no hope of talking sense into him.

To Darger's lasting regret, his childhood had not been one of privilege and gentility, but spent in the rough-and-tumble slums of Mayfair. There, perforce, he had learned to defend himself with his fists. Now, for a silver lining, he found those deplorable skills useful.

Quickly, he brought up his forearms, crossed at the wrists, between Surplus's arms. Then, all in one motion, he thrust his arms outward, to force his friend's paws from his throat. Simultaneously, he brought up one knee between Surplus's legs as hard as he could.

Surplus gasped, and reflexively clutched his wounded part.

A shove sent Surplus to the floor. Darger pinned him.

Now, however, a new problem arose. Where to put the patch. Surplus was covered with fur, head to foot. Darger thought back to their first receiving the patches, twisted around one arm, and found a small bald spot just beneath the paw, on his wrist.

A motion, and it was done.

* * *

"They're worse than football hooligans," Surplus commented. Somebody had dumped a wagon-load of hay in the town square and set it ablaze. By its unsteady light could be seen small knots of townsfolk wandering the streets, looking for trouble and, often enough, finding it. Darger and Surplus had doused their own room's lights, so they could observe without drawing attention to themselves.

"Not so, dear friend, for such ruffians go to the matches *intending* trouble, while these poor souls . . ." His words were cut off by the rattle of a wagon on the street below.

It was Theodosia and Anya, returned from their chore. But before Darger could cry out a warning, several men rushed toward them with threatening shouts and upraised fists. Alarmed, Theodosia gestured menacingly with her whip for them to keep back. But one of their number rushed forward, grabbed the whip, and yanked her off the wagon.

"Theodosia!" Darger cried in horror.

Surplus leaped to the windowsill and gallantly launched himself into space, toward the wagon load of mattresses. Darger, who had a touch of acrophobia and had once broken a leg performing a similar stunt, pounded down the stairs.

There were only five thugs in the attacking group, which explained why they were so perturbed when Darger burst from the inn, shouting and wielding his walking stick as if it were a cudgel and Surplus suddenly popped up from within the wagon, teeth bared and fur all a-hackle. Then Anya regained the whip and laid about her, left and right, with a good will.

The rioters scattered like pigeons.

When they were gone, Anya turned on Darger. "You *knew* something like this was going to happen!" she cried. "Why didn't you warn anybody?"

"I did! Repeatedly! You laughed in my face!"

"There is a time for lovers' spats," Surplus said firmly, "and this is not it. This young lady is unconscious; help me lift her into the wagon. We must get her out of town immediately."

The nearest place of haven, Anya decided, was her father's croft, just outside town. Not ten minutes later, they were unloading Theodosia from the wagon, using one of the feather mattresses as a stretcher. A plump nymph, Anya's mother, met them at the door.

"She will be fine," the mother said. "I know these things, I used to be a nurse." She frowned. "Provided she doesn't have a concussion." She looked at Darger shrewdly. "Has this anything to do with the fire?"

But when Darger started to explain, Surplus tugged at his sleeve. "Look outside," he said. "The locals have formed a fire brigade."

Indeed, there were figures coming down the road, hurrying toward town. Darger ran out and placed himself in front of the first, a pimply-faced young satyr lugging a leather bucketful of water. "Stop!" he cried. "Go no farther!"

The satyr paused, confused. "But the fires . . ."

"Worse than fires await you in town," Darger said. "Anyway, it's only a hay-rick."

A second bucket-carrying satyr pulled to a stop. It was Papatragos. "Darger!" he cried. "What are you doing here at my croft? Is Anya with you?"

For an instant, Darger was nonplused. "Anya is your daughter?"

"Aye." Papatragos grinned. "I gather that makes me practically your father-in-law."

By now all the satyrs who had been near enough to see the flames and had come with buckets to fight them—some twenty in all—were clustered about the two men. Hurriedly, Surplus told all that they knew of Pan, Eris and the troubles in town.

"Nor is this matter finished," Darger said. "The Chief Researcher said something about using Dionysus to stop riots. Since he has not appeared to do so tonight, that means they will have to create another set of riots to test that ability as well. More trouble is imminent."

"That is no concern of ours," said one stodgy-looking crofter.

"It will be ours," Darger declared, with his usual high-handed employment of the first person plural pronoun. "As soon as the agent of the riots has left town, she will surely

show up here next. Did not Dionysus dance in the fields after he danced in the streets? Then Eris is on her way here to
set brother against brother, and father against son."

Angry mutters passed among the satyrs. Papatragos held
up his hands for silence. "Tragopropos!" he said to the
pimply-faced satyr. "Run and gather together every adult
satyr you can. Tell them to seize whatever weapons they can
and advance upon the monastery."

"What of the townsfolk?"

"Somebody else will be sent for them. Why are you still
standing here?"

"I'm gone!"

"The fire in town has gone out," Papatragos continued.
"Which means that Eris has done her work and has left. She
will be coming up this very road in not too long."

"Fortunately," Darger said, "I have a plan."

Darger and Surplus stood exposed in the moonlight at the
very center of the road, while the satyrs hid in the bushes at
its verge. They did not have long to wait.

A shadow moved toward them, grew, solidified, and became a goddess.

Eris stalked up the road, eyes wild and hair in disarray.
Her clothes had been ripped to shreds; only a few rags hung
from waist and ankles, and they hid nothing of her body at
all. She made odd chirping and shrieking noises as she
came, with sudden small hops to the side and leaps into the
air. Darger had known all manner of madmen in his time.
This went far beyond anything he had ever seen for sheer
chaotic irrationality.

Spying them, Eris threw back her head and trilled like a
bird. Then she came running and dancing toward the two
friends, spinning about and beating her arms against her
sides. Had she lacked the strength of the frenzied, she would
still have been terrifying, for it was clear that she was capable of absolutely anything. As it was, she was enough to
make a brave man cringe.

"Now!"

At Darger's command, every satyr stepped forward onto

the road and threw his bucket of water at the goddess. Briefly, she was inundated. All her sweat—and, hopefully, her pheromones as well—was washed clear of her body.

As one, the satyrs dropped their buckets. Ten of them rushed forward with drug patches and slapped them onto her body. Put off her balance by the sudden onslaught, Eris fell to the ground.

"Now stand clear!" Darger cried.

The satyrs danced back. One who had hesitated just a bit in finding a space for his patch stayed just a little too long and was caught by her lingering pheromones. He drew back his foot to kick the prone goddess. But Papatragos darted forward to drag him out of her aura before he could do so.

"Behave yourself," he said.

Eris convulsed in the dirt, flipped over on her stomach, and vomited. Slowly, then, she stood. She looked around her dimly, wonderingly. Her eyes cleared, and an expression of horror and remorse came over her face.

"Oh, sweet science, what have I done?" she said. Then she wailed, "What has happened to my *clothes?*"

She tried to cover herself with her hands.

One of the young satyrs snickered, but Papatragos quelled him with a look. Surplus, meanwhile, handed the goddess his jacket. "Pray, madam, don this," he said courteously and, to the others, "Didn't one of you bring a blanket for the victims of the fire? Toss that to the lady—it'll make a fine skirt."

Somebody started forward with a blanket, then hesitated. "Is it safe?"

"The patches we gave you will protect against her influence," Darger assured him.

"Unfortunately, those were the last," Surplus said sadly. He turned the box upside down and shook it.

"The lady Eris will be enormously tired for at least a day. Have you a guest room?" Darger asked Papatragos. "Can she use it?"

"I suppose so. The place already looks like an infirmary."

At which reminder, Darger hurried inside to see how Theodosia was doing.

But when he got there, Theodosia was gone, and Anya and her mother as well. At first, Darger suspected foul play. But a quick search of the premises showed no signs of disorder. Indeed, the mattress had been removed (presumably to the wagon, which was also gone) and all the dislocations attendant upon its having been brought into the farmhouse had been tidied away. Clearly, the women had gone off somewhere, for purposes of their own. Which thought made Darger very uneasy indeed.

Meanwhile, the voices of gathering men and satyrs could be heard outside. Surplus stuck his head through the door and cleared his throat. "Your mob awaits."

The stream of satyrs and men, armed with flails, pruning-hooks, pitchforks, and torches, flowed up the mountain roads toward the Monastery of St. Vasilios. Where roads met, more crofters and townsfolk poured out of the darkness, streams merging and the whole surging onward with renewed force.

Darger began to worry about what would happen when the vigilantes reached their destination. Tugging at Surplus's sleeve, he drew his friend aside. "The scientists can escape easily enough," he said. "All they need do is flee into the woods. But I worry about Dionysus, locked in his crypt. This expedition is quite capable of torching the building."

"If I cut across the fields, I could arrive at the monastery before the vigilantes do, though not long before. It would be no great feat to slip over a back wall, force a door, and free the man."

Darger felt himself moved. "That is unutterably good of you, my friend."

"Poof!" Surplus said haughtily. "It is a nothing."

And he was gone.

By Darger's estimate, the vigilantes were a hundred strong by the time they reached the Monastery of St. Vasilios. The moon rode high among scattered shreds of cloud, and shone so bright that they did not need torches to see by, but only for

their psychological effect. They raised a cry when they saw
the ruins, and began running toward them.

Then they stopped.

The field before the monastery was alive with squids.

The creatures had been loathsome enough in the context
of the laboratory. Here, under a cloud-torn sky, arrayed in
regular ranks like an army, they were grotesque and terrifying. Tentacles lashing, the cephalopods advanced, and as
they did so it could be seen that they held swords and pikes
and other weapons, hastily forged but obviously suitable for
murderous work.

Remembering, however, how they feared fire, Darger
snatched up a torch and thrust it at the nearest rank of at-
tackers. Chittering and clacking, they drew away from him.
"Torches to the fore!" he cried. "All others follow in their
wake!"

So they advanced, the squid-army retreating, until they
were almost to St. Vasilios itself.

But an imp-like creature waited for them atop the
monastery wall. It was a small black lump of a being, yet its
brisk movements and rapid walk conveyed an enormous
sense of vitality. There was a *presence* to this thing. It could
not be ignored.

It was, Darger saw, the Chief Researcher.

One by one, the satyrs and men stumbled to a halt. They
milled about, uneasy and uncertain, under the force of her
scornful glare.

"You've come at last, have you?" The Chief Researcher
strutted back and forth on the wall, as active and intimidat-
ing as a basilisk. A dark miasma seemed to radiate from her,
settling upon the crowd and sapping its will. Filling them all
with doubts and dark imaginings. "Doubtless you think you
came of your own free will, driven by anger and self-
righteousness. But you're here by my invitation. I sent you
first Dionysus and then Eris to lure you to my doorstep, so
that I might test the third deity of my great trilogy."

Standing at the front of the mob, Darger cried, "You cannot bluff us!"

"You think I'm bluffing?" The Chief Researcher flung out

an arm toward the looming ruins behind her. "Behold my masterpiece—a god who is neither anthropomorphic nor limited to a single species, a god for humans and squids alike, a chimera stitched together from the genes of a hundred sires . . ." Her laughter was not in the least bit sane. *"I give you Thanatos—the god of death!"*

The dome of the monastery rippled and stirred. Enormous flaps of translucent flesh, like great wings, unfolded to either side, and the forward edge heaved up to reveal a lightless space from which slowly unreeled long, barb-covered tentacles.

Worse than any merely visual horror, however, was the overwhelming sense of futility and despair that now filled the world. All felt its immensely dispiriting effect. Darger, whose inclination was naturally toward the melancholic, found himself thinking of annihilation. Nor was this entirely unattractive. His thoughts turned to the Isle of the Dead, outside Venice, where the graves were twined with nightshade and wolfs-bane, and yew-trees dropped their berries on the silent earth. He yearned to drink of Lethe's ruby cup, while beetles crawled about his feet, and death-moths fluttered about his head. To slip into the voluptuously accommodating bed of the soil, and there consort with the myriad who had gone before.

All around him, people were putting down their makeshift agricultural weapons. One let fall a torch. Even the squids dropped their swords and huddled in despair.

Something deep within Darger struggled to awaken. This was not, he knew, natural. The Chief Researcher's god was imposing despair upon them all against their better judgments. But, like rain from a weeping cloud, sorrow poured down over him, and he was helpless before it. All beauty must someday die, after all, and should he who was a lover of beauty survive? Perish the thought!

Beside him, a satyr slid to the ground and wept.

Alas, he simply did not care.

Surplus, meanwhile, was in his element. Running headlong through the night, with the moon bouncing in the sky above, he felt his every sense to be fully engaged, fully alive. Through spinneys and over fields he ran, savoring every smell, alert to the slightest sound.

By roundabout ways he came at last to the monastery. The ground at its rear was untended and covered with scrub forest. All to the good. Nobody would see him here. He could find a back entrance or a window that might be forced and . . .

At that very instant, he felt a warm puff of breath on the back of his neck. His hackles rose. Only one creature could have come up behind him so silently as to avoid detection.

"Nobody's here," Bast said.

Surplus spun about, prepared to defend himself to the death. But the great cat merely sat down and began tending to the claws of one enormous paw, biting and tugging at them with fastidious care.

"Excuse me?"

"Our work now being effectively over, we shall soon return to Greater Zimbabwe. So, in the spirit of tying up all loose ends, the monks have been sent to seize the Evangelos bronzes as a gift for the Scientifically-Chosen Council of Rational Governance back home. The Chief Researcher, meanwhile, is out front, preparing to deal with insurgent local rabble."

Surplus rubbed his chin thoughtfully with the knob of his cane. "Hum. Well . . . in any case, that is not why I am here. I have come for Dionysus."

"The crypt is empty," Bast said. "Shortly after the monks and the Chief Researcher left, an army of nymphs came and wrested the god from his tomb. If you look, you can see where they broke a door in."

"Do you know where they have taken him?" Surplus asked.

"Yes."

"Will you lead me there?"

"Why should I?"

Surplus started to reply, then bit his words short. Argument would not suffice with this creature—he was a cat, and cats did not respond to reason. Best, then, to appeal to his innate nature. "Because it would be a pointless and spiteful act of mischief."

Bast grinned. "They have taken him to their temple. It isn't far—a mile, perhaps less."

He turned away. Darger followed.

The temple was little more than a glen surrounded by evenly-spaced slim white trees, like so many marble pillars. A small and simple altar stood to one end. But the entrance was flanked by two enormous pairs of metal lions, and off to one side stood the heroic bronze of a lordly man, three times the height of a mere mortal.

They arrived at the tail end of a small war.

The monks had arrived first and begun to set up blocks and tackle, in order to lower the bronze man to the ground. Barely had they begun their enterprise, however, when an army of nymphs arrived, with Dionysus cradled in a wagon-load of feather mattresses. Their initial outrage at what they saw could only be imagined by its aftermath: Orange-robed monks fled wildly through the woods, pursued by packs of raging nymphs. Here and there, one had fallen, and the women performed abominable deeds upon their bodies.

Surplus looked resolutely away. He could feel the violent emotion possessing the women right through the soothing chemical voice of the patches he still wore, a passion that went far beyond sex into realms of fear and terror. He could not help remembering that the word "panic" was originally derived from the name Pan.

He strolled up to the wagon, and said, "Good evening, sir. I came to make sure you are well."

Dionysus looked up and smiled wanly. "I am, and I thank you for your concern." A monk's scream split the night. "However, if my ladies catch sight of you, I fear you will suffer even as many of my former associates do now. I'll do my best to calm them, but meanwhile, I suggest that you—" He looked suddenly alarmed. "Run!"

Lethargy filled Darger. His arms were leaden and his feet were unable to move. It seemed too much effort even to breathe. A listless glance around him showed that all his brave mob were incapacitated, some crouched and others weeping, in various attitudes of despair. Even the chimeric squid had collapsed into moist and listless blobs on the grass. He saw one taken up by Thanatos's tentacles, held high above the monastery, and then dropped into an unsuspected maw therein.

It did not matter. Nothing did.

Luckily, however, such sensations were nothing new to Darger. He was a depressive by humor, well familiar with the black weight of futility, like a hound sitting upon his heart. How many nights had he lain sleepless and waiting for a dawn he knew would never arrive? How many mornings had he forced himself out of bed, though he could see no point to the effort? More than he could count.

There was still a torch in his hand. Slowly, Darger made his shuffling way through the unresisting forms of his supporters. He lacked the energy to climb the wall, so he walked around it until he came to the gate, reached in to unlatch it, and then walked through.

He trudged up to the monastery.

So far, he had gone unnoticed because the men and satyrs wandered aimlessly about in their despair, and his movement had been cloaked by theirs. Within the monastery grounds, however, he was alone. The bright line traced by his torch attracted the Chief Researcher's eye.

"You!" she cried. "British government man! Put that torch down." She jumped down from the wall and trotted toward him. "It's hopeless, you know. You've already lost. You're as good as dead."

She was at his side now, and reaching for the torch. He raised it up, out of her reach.

"You don't think this is going to work, do you?" She punched and kicked him, but they were the blows of a child, and easy to ignore. "You don't honestly think there's any hope for you?"

He sighed. "No."

Then he threw the torch.

Whomp! The dome went up in flames. Light and heat filled the courtyard. Shielding his eyes, Darger looked away, to see satyrs and men staggering to their feet, and squids fluidly slipping downslope toward the river. Into the water they went and downstream, swimming with the current toward the distant Aegean.

Thanatos screamed. It was a horrid, indescribable sound, like fingernails on slate impossibly magnified, like agony made physical. Enormous tentacles slammed at the ground in agony, snatching up whatever they encountered and flinging it into the night sky.

A little aghast at what he had unleashed, Darger saw one of the tentacles seize the Chief Researcher and haul her high into the air, before catching fire itself and raining down black soot, both chimeric and human, on the upturned faces below.

Afterward, staring at the burning monastery from a distance, Darger murmured, "I have the most horrid sensation of *déjà vu*. Must all our adventures end the same way?"

"For the sake of those cities we have yet to visit, I sincerely hope not," Surplus replied.

There was a sudden surge of flesh and the great cat Bast took a seat alongside them. "She was the last of her kind," he remarked.

"Eh?" Darger said.

"No living creature remembers her name, but the Chief Researcher was born—or perhaps created—in the waning days of Utopia. I always suspected that her ultimate end was to recreate that lost and bygone world." Bast yawned vastly, his pink tongue curling into a question mark which then disappeared as his great black jaws snapped shut. "Well, no matter. With her gone, it's back to Greater Zimbabwe for the rest of us. I'll be glad to see the old place again. The food here is good, but the hunting is wretched."

With a leap, he disappeared into the night.

But now Papatragos strode up and clapped them both on the shoulders. "That was well done, lads. Very well done, indeed."

"You lied to me, Papatragos," Darger said sternly. "The Evangelos bronzes were yours all along."

Papatragos pulled an innocent face. "Why, whatever do you mean?"

"I've seen the lions *and* the bronze man," Surplus said. "It is unquestionably the statue of Lord Nelson himself, stolen from Trafalgar Square in ancient times by the rapacious Grecian Empire. How can you possibly justify keeping it?"

Now Papatragos looked properly abashed. "Well, we're sort of attached to the old thing. We walk past it every time we go to worship. It's not really a part of our religion, but it's been here so long, it almost feels as if it should be, you see."

"Exactly what *is* your religion?" Surplus asked curiously.

"We're Jewish," Papatragos said. "All satyrs are."

"Jewish?!"

"Well, not exactly *Orthodox* Jews." He shuffled his feet. "We couldn't be, not with these cloven hooves. But we have our rabbis and our shuls. We manage."

It was then that Dionysus began to play his pan-pipes and the crowd of nymphs and women from the temple flowed onto the former battleground. Surplus's ears pricked up. "Well, it seems the night will not be a total waste of time, after all," Papatragos said brightly. "Will you be staying?"

"No," Darger said, "I believe I will return to our inn to contemplate mortality and the fate of gods."

Yet Darger was no more than halfway back to town when he came upon a wagon piled high with feather mattresses, pulled over to the side of the road. The horses had been unharnessed so they could graze, and sweet sighs and giggles came from the top of the mattresses.

Darger stopped, appalled. He knew those sounds well, and recognized too the pink knee that stuck out here, the tawny shoulders draped with long black hair that arched up there. It was Theodosia and Anya. Together. Alone.

In an instant's blinding insight, he understood all. It was an old and familiar situation: Two women who loved each other but were too young to embrace the fact in all its implications, and so brought a third, male, partner into their dalliances. It hardly mattered who. Unless, of course, you were the unimportant male himself. In which case, it was a damnable insult.

"Who's there?" The two women pulled apart and struggled up out of the mattresses. Their heads appeared over the top of the wagon. Hair black and blond, eyes brown and green, one mouth sweet and the other sassily sticking out a little pink triangle of tongue. Both were, implicitly, laughing at him.

"Never mind about me," Darger said stiffly. "I see the way the wind blows. Continue, I pray you. I retain the fondest memories of you both, and I wish you nothing but well."

The women stared at him with frank astonishment. Then Theodosia whispered in Anya's ear, and Anya smiled and nodded. "Well?" Theordosia said to Darger. "Are you joining us or not?"

Darger wanted to spurn their offer, if for no other reason than his dignity's sake. But, being merely human—and male to boot—he complied.

So for a space of time Darger and Surplus stayed in Arcadia and were content. Being the sort of men they were, however, mere contentment could never satisfy them for long, and so one day they loaded their bags into a rented pony-cart and departed. For once, though, they left behind people who genuinely regretted seeing them leave.

Some distance down the road, as they passed by the ruins of the Monastery of St. Vasilios, the pony grew restive and they heard the music of pipes.

There, sitting atop the wall, waiting for them, was Dionysus. He was wearing a peasant's blouse and trousers, but even so, he looked every inch a god. He casually set down his panpipes. "Bach," he said. "The old tunes are best, don't you agree?"

"I prefer Vivaldi," Darger said. "But for a German, Bach wasn't bad."

"So. You're leaving, are you?"

"Perhaps we'll be back, someday," Surplus said.

"I hope you're not thinking of returning for the bronzes?"

It was as if a cloud had passed before the sun. A dark shiver ran through the air. Dionysus was, Darger realized, preparing to assume his aspects of godhead should that prove necessary.

"If we were," he said, "would this be a problem?"

"Aye. I have no objection to your bronze man and his lions going home. Though the morality of their staying or returning is more properly a matter for the local rabbis to establish. Unfortunately, there would be curiosity as to their provenance and from whence they had come. This land would be the talk of the world. But I would keep our friends as obscure as possible for as long as may be. And you?"

Surplus sighed. "It is hard to put this into words. It would be a violation of our professional ethics *not* to return for the bronzes. And yet . . ."

"And yet," Darger said, "I find myself reluctant to reintroduce this timeless land to the modern world. These are gentle folk, their destruction of St. Vasilios notwithstanding, and I fear for them all. History has never been kind to gentle folk."

"I agree with you entirely. Which is why I have decided to stay and to protect them."

"Thank you. I have grown strangely fond of them all."

"I as well," Surplus said.

Dionysus leaned forward. "That is good to hear. It softens the hurt of what I must say to you. Which is: *Do not return.* I know what sort of men you are. A week from now, or a month, or a year, you will think again of the value of the bronzes. They are in and of themselves worth a fortune. Returned to England, the prestige they would confer upon their finders is beyond price. Perhaps you have been guilty of criminal activities; for this discovery, much would be forgiven. Such thoughts will occur to you. Think, also this: That these folk are protected not by me alone, but by the madness I can bring upon them. I want you to leave this land and never come back."

"What—never return to Arcadia?" Surplus said.

"You do not know what you ask, sir!" Darger cried.

"Let this be an Arcadia of the heart to you. All places abandoned and returned to must necessarily disappoint. Dis-

tance will keep its memory evergreen in your hearts." Now
Dionysus reached out and embraced them both, drawing
them to his bosom. In a murmurous voice, he said, "You
need a new desire. Let me tell you of a place I glimpsed en
route to Greece, back when I was merely human. It has
many names, Istanbul and Constantinople not the least
among them, but currently it is called Byzantium."

Then for a time he spoke of that most cosmopolitan of
cities, of its mosques and minarets and holographic plea-
sure-gardens, of its temples and palaces and baths, where all
the many races of the world met and shared their lore. He
spoke of regal women as alluring as dreams, and of philoso-
phers so subtle in their equivocations that no three could
agree what day of the week it was. He spoke too of trea-
sures: gold chalices, chess sets carved of porphyry and jade,
silver-stemmed cups of narwhalivory delicately carved with
unicorns and maidens, swords whose hilts were flecked with
gems and whose blades no force could shatter, tuns of wine
whose intoxicating effects had been hand-crafted by the
finest storytellers in the East, vast libraries whose every
book was the last surviving copy of its text. There was always music in the air of Byzantium, and the delicate foods
of a hundred cultures, and of a summer's night, lovers gathered on the star-gazing platforms to practice the amatory
arts in the velvety perfumed darkness. For the Festival of the
Red and White Roses, streams and rivers were re-routed to
run through the city streets, and a province's worth of flowers were plucked and their petals cast into the flowing waters. For the Festival of the Honey of Eden . . .

Some time later, Darger shook himself from his reverie,
and discovered that Surplus was staring blindly into the distance, while their little pony stamped his feet and shook his
harness, anxious to be off. He gripped his friend's shoulder.
"Ho! Sleepy-head! You've wandered off into the Empyrean,
when you're needed here on Earth."

Surplus shook himself. "I dreamed . . . what did I dream?
It's lost now, and yet it seemed vitally important at the time,
as if it were something I should remember, and even cher-
ish." He yawned greatly. "Well, no matter! Our stay in the

countryside has been pleasant, but unproductive. The Evangelos bronzes remain lost, and our purses are perilously close to empty. Where shall we go now, to replenish them?"

"East," Darger said decisively. "East, to the Bosporus. I have heard—somewhere—great things of that city called . . . called . . ."

"Byzantium!" Surplus said. "I too have heard wondrous tales—somehow—of its wealth and beauty. Two such men as ourselves should do marvelous well there."

"Then we are agreed." Darger shook the harness, and the pony set out at a trot. They both whooped and laughed, and if there was a small hurt in their hearts they did not know what it was or what they should do about it, and so it was ignored.

Surplus waved his tricorn hat in the air. "Byzantium awaits!"

Lakes of Light

STEPHEN BAXTER

Stephen Baxter (tribute site: www.themanifold.co.uk) lives in Morpeth, England. He is now one of the big names in SF, with more than twenty SF novels published to date, and a large body of short fiction. "I always thought of myself as writing hard SF, on a big scale maybe, but ideas driven, not romantic, so not space opera," he says. The Science Fiction Encyclopedia *summarizes his early career thus: "He began publishing SF with "The Xeelee Flower" for* Interzone *in 1987, which with most of his other short work fits into his Xeelee Sequence, an ambitious attempt at creating a Future History; novels included in the sequence are* Raft *(1989),* Timelike Infinity *(1992),* Flux *(1993), and* Rind *(1994). The sequence . . . follows humanity into interstellar space, where it encounters a complex of alien races; the long epic ends (being typical in this of UK SF) darkly, many aeons hence." Since the mid 1990s he has produced five or ten short stories a year in fantasy, SF, and horror venues, occasionally one in the Xeelee Sequence, and did in 2005 again.*

"Lakes of Light" was published in Constellations. *It is a Xeelee story of alien supertechnology, somewhere between a Hal Clement and a Larry Niven setting. As the story progresses, new wonders are seen and new layers of insight are reached. This is the essence of hard SF.*

The Navy ferry stood by. From the ship's position, several stellar diameters away, the star was a black disc, like a hole cut out of the sky.

The Navy ship receded. Pala was to descend to the star alone in a flitter—alone save for her Virtual tutor, Dano.

The flitter, light and invisible as a bubble, swept inward, silent save for the subtle ticking of its instruments. The star had about the mass of Earth's sun, and though it was dark, Pala imagined she could feel that immense mass tugging at her.

Her heart hammered. This really was a star, but it was somehow cloaked, made perfectly black save for pale, pixel-small specks, flaws in the dark mask, that were lakes of light. She'd seen the Navy scouts' reports, even studied the Virtuals, but until this moment she hadn't been able to believe in the extraordinary reality.

But she had a job to do, and had no time to be overawed. The Navy scouts said there were humans down there—humans living with, or somehow on, the star itself. Relics of an ancient colonizing push, they now had to be reabsorbed into the greater mass of a mankind at war. But the Galaxy was wide, and Pala, just twenty-five years old, was the only Missionary who could be spared for this adventure.

Dano was a brooding presence beside her, peering out with metallic Eyes. His chest did not rise and fall, no breath whispered from his mouth. He was projected from an implant in her own head, so that she could never be free of him, and she had become resentful of him. But Pala had grown up on Earth, under a sky so drenched with artificial light you could barely see the stars, and right now she was grateful for the company even of a Commissary's avatar.

And meanwhile, that hole in the sky swelled until its edges passed out of her field of view.

The flitter dipped and swiveled and swept along the line of the star's equator. Now she was flying low over a darkened plain, with a starry night sky above her. The star was so vast, its diameter more than a hundred times Earth's, that she could see no hint of curvature in its laser-straight horizon.

"Astonishing," she said. "It's like a geometrical exercise."

Dano murmured, "And yet, to the best of our knowledge, the photosphere of a star roils not a thousand kilometers beneath us, and if not for this—sphere, whatever it is—we would be destroyed in an instant, a snowflake in the mouth of a furnace. What's your first conclusion, Missionary?"

Pala hesitated before answering. It was so recently that she had completed her assessments in the Academies on Earth, so recently that the real Dano had, grudgingly, welcomed her to the great and ancient enterprise that was the Commission for Historical Truth, that she felt little confidence in her own abilities. And yet the Commission must have faith in her, or else they wouldn't have committed her to this mission.

"It is artificial," she said. "The sphere. It must be."

"Yes. Surely no natural process could wrap up a star so neatly. And if it is artificial, who do you imagine might be responsible?"

"The Xeelee," she said immediately. Involuntarily, she glanced up at the crowded stars, bright and vivid here, five thousand light years from Earth. In the hidden heart of the Galaxy mankind's ultimate foe lurked; and surely it was only the Xeelee who could wield such power as this.

There was a change in the darkness ahead. She saw it first as a faint splash of light near the horizon, but as the flitter flew on that splash opened out into a rough disc that glowed pale blue-green. Though a speck against the face of the masked star, it was sizable in itself—perhaps as much as a hundred kilometers across.

The flitter came to rest over the center of the feature. It was like a shard of Earth, stranded in the night: she looked down at the deep blue of open water, the mistiness of air, the pale green of cultivated land and forest, even a grayish bubbling that must be a town. All of this was contained under a dome, shallow and flat and all but transparent. Outside the dome what looked like roads, ribbons of silver, stretched away into the dark. And at the very center of this strange scrap of landscape was a shining sheet of light.

"People," Dano said. "Huddling around that flaw in the sphere, that lake of light." He pointed. "I think there's some kind of port at the edge of the dome. You'd better take the flitter down by hand."

Pala touched the small control panel in front of her, and the flitter began its final descent.

They cycled through a kind of airlock and emerged into fresh air, bright light.

It wasn't quite daylight. The light was diffuse, like a misty day on Earth, and it came not from a sun but from mirrors on spindly poles. The atmosphere was too shallow for the "sky" to be blue, and through the dome's distortion Pala saw smeared-out star fields. But the sky contained clouds, pale, streaky clouds.

A dirt road led away from the airlock. Pala glimpsed clusters of low buildings, the green of forest clumps and cultivated fields. She could even smell wood smoke.

Dano sniffed. "Lethe. *Agriculture.* Typical Second Expansion."

This pastoral scene wasn't a landscape Pala was familiar with. Earth was dominated by sprawling Conurbations, and fields in which nanotechnologies efficiently delivered food for the world's billions. Still, she felt oddly at home here. But she wasn't at home.

"It takes a genuine effort of will," she said, "to remember where we are."

The scouts had determined that the stellar sphere was ro-

tating as a solid, and that this equatorial site was moving at
only a little less than orbital speed. This arrangement was
why they experienced such an equable gravity; if not for the
compensating effects of centrifugal force, they would have
been crushed by nearly thirty times Earth standard. She
could *feel* none of this, but nevertheless, standing here, gazing at grass and trees and clouds, she really was soaring
through space, actually circling a star in less than a standard
day.

"Here comes the welcoming party," Dano said dryly.

Two people walked steadily up the road, a man and a
woman. They were both rather squat, stocky, dark. They
wore simple shifts and knee-length trousers, practical
clothes, clean but heavily repaired. The man might have
been sixty. His hair was white, his face a moon of wrinkles.
The woman was younger, perhaps not much older than Pala.
She wore her black hair long and tied into a queue that nestled over her spine, quite unlike the short and severe style of
the Commission. Her shift had a sunburst pattern stitched
into it, a welling up of light from below.

The man spoke. "My name is Sool. This is Bicansa. We
have been delegated to welcome you." Sool's words, in his
own archaic tongue, were seamlessly translated in Pala's
ears. But underneath the tinny murmuring in her ear she
could hear Sool's own gravelly voice. "I represent this community, which we call Home . . ."

"Inevitably," Dano murmured.

"Bicansa comes from a community to the north of here."
Pala supposed he meant another inhabited light lake. She
wondered how far away that was; she had seen nothing from
the flitter.

The woman Bicansa simply watched the newcomers. Her
expression seemed closed, almost sullen. She could not have
been called beautiful, Pala thought; her face was too round,
her chin too weak for that. But there was a strength in her
dark eyes that intrigued Pala.

Pala made her own formal introductions. "Thank you for
inviting us to your community." Not that the Navy scouts
had left the locals any choice. "We are emissaries of the

Commission for Historical Truth, acting on behalf of the Coalition of Interim Governance, which in turn directs and secures the Third Expansion of mankind . . ."

The man Sool listened to this with a pale smile, oddly weary. Bicansa glared.

Dano murmured, "Shake their hands. Just as well it isn't an assessment exercise, Missionary!"

Pala cursed herself for forgetting such an elementary part of contact protocol. She stepped forward, smiling, her right hand outstretched.

Sool actually recoiled. The custom of shaking hands was rare throughout the worlds of the Second Expansion; evidently it hadn't been prevalent on Earth when that great wave of colonization had begun. But Sool quickly recovered. His grip was firm, his hands so huge they enclosed hers. Sool grinned. "A farmer's hands," he said. "You'll get used to it."

Bicansa offered her own hand readily enough. But Pala's hand passed through the woman's, making it break up into a cloud of blocky pixels.

It was this simple test that mandated the handshake protocol. Even so, Pala was startled. "You're a Virtual."

"As is your companion," said Bicansa levelly. "I'm close by—actually just outside the dome. But don't worry. I'm a projection, not an avatar. You have my full attention."

Pala felt unaccountably disappointed that Bicansa wasn't really here.

Sool indicated a small car, waiting some distance away, and he offered them the hospitality of his home. They walked to the car.

Dano murmured to Pala, "I wonder why this Bicansa hasn't shown up in person. I think we need to watch that one." He turned to her, his cold Eyes glinting. "Ah, but you already are—aren't you, Missionary?"

Pala felt herself blush.

Sool's village was small, just a couple of dozen buildings huddled around a small scrap of grass-covered common land. There were shops and manufactories, including a car-

pentry and pottery works, and an inn. At the center of the
common was a lake, its edges regular—a reservoir, Pala
thought. The people's water must be recycled, filtered by
hidden machinery, like their air. By the shore of the lake,
children played and lovers walked.

This was a farming community. In the fields beyond the
village, crops grew toward the reflected glare of spindly mirror towers, waving in breezes wafted by immense pumps
mounted at the dome's periphery. And animals grazed, de-
scendants of cattle and sheep brought by the first colonists.
Pala, who had never seen an animal larger than a rat, stared,
astonished.

The buildings were all made of wood, neat but low, coni-
cal. Sool told the visitors the buildings were modeled after
the tents the first colonists here had used for shelter. "A kind
of memorial to the First," he said. But Sool's home, with big
windows cut into the sloping roof, was surprisingly roomy
and well lit. He had them sit on cushions of what turned out
to be stuffed animal hide, to Pala's horror.

Everything seemed to be organic, made of wood or baked
clay or animal skin. All the raw material of the human settlement had come from cometary impacts, packets of dirty
ice from this star's outer system that had splashed onto the
sphere since its formation. But there were traces of art. On
one wall hung a kind of schematic portrait, a few lines to de-
pict a human face, lit from below by a warm yellow light.
And these people could generate Virtuals, Pala reminded
herself; they weren't as low tech as they seemed.

Sool confirmed that. "When the First found this masked
star, they created the machinery that still sustains us—the
dome, the mirror towers, the hidden machines that filter our
air and water. We must maintain the machines, and we go out
to bring in more water ice or frozen air." He eyed his visitors. "You must not think we are fallen. We are surely as
technologically capable as our ancestors. But every day we
acknowledge our debt to the wisdom and heroic engineering
of the First." As he said this, he touched his palms together
and nodded his head reverently, and Bicansa did the same.

Pala and Dano exchanged a glance. Ancestor worship?

A slim, pretty teenage girl brought them drinks of pulped fruit. The girl was Sool's daughter; it turned out his wife had died some years previously. The drinks were served in pottery cups, elegantly shaped and painted deep blue, with more inverted-sunburst designs. Pala wondered what dye they used to create such a rich blue.

Dano watched the daughter as she politely set a cup before himself and Bicansa; these colonists knew Virtual etiquette. Dano said, "You obviously live in nuclear families."

"And you don't?" Bicansa asked curiously.

"Nuclear families are a classic feature of Second Expansion cultures. You are typical." Pala smiled brightly, trying to be reassuring, but Bicansa's face was cold.

Dano asked Sool, "And you are the leader of this community?"

Sool shook his head. "We are few, Missionary. I'm leader of nothing but my own family. After your scouts' first visit the Assembly asked me to speak for them. I believe I'm held in high regard; I believe I'm trusted. But I'm a delegate, not a leader. Bicansa represents her own people in the same way. We have to work together to survive; I'm sure that's obvious. In a sense we're all a single extended family here . . ."

Pala murmured to Dano, "Eusocial, you think? The lack of a hierarchy, an elite?" Eusociality—hive living—had been found to be a common if unwelcome social outcome in crowded, resource-starved colonies.

Dano shook his head. "No. The population density's nowhere near high enough."

Bicansa was watching them. "You are talking about us. Assessing us."

"That's our job," Dano said levelly.

"Yes, I've learned about your job," Bicansa snapped. "Your mighty Third Expansion that sweeps across the stars. You're here to assimilate us, aren't you?"

"Not at all," Pala said earnestly. It was true. The Assimilation was a separate program, designed to process the alien species encountered by the Third Expansion wavefront. Pala worked for the Office of Cultural Rehabilitation which, though controlled by the same agency of the Commission for Historical Truth as the Assimilation, was intended to handle relic human societies implanted by earlier colonization waves, similarly encountered by the Expansion. "My mission is to welcome you back to a unified mankind. To introduce you to the Druz Doctrines which shape all our actions—"

"And to tell us about your war," Bicansa said coldly.

"The reality of the war cannot be denied," Dano snapped back.

Some millennia ago, humanity had almost been destroyed by alien conquerors called the Qax. Since then, unified by the severe Druz Doctrines, humanity had recovered, expanded, conquered all—but one foe remained, the mighty Xeelee, with whom the final confrontation was only beginning.

Bicansa wasn't impressed. "Your arrogance is dismaying," she said. "You've only just landed here, only just come swooping down from the sky. You're confronted by a distinctive culture five thousand years old. We have our own tradition, literature, art—even our own language, after all this time. And yet you think you can make a judgment on us immediately."

"Our judgment on your culture, or your lack of it, doesn't matter," said Dano. "Our mission is specific."

"Yes. You're here to enslave us."

Sool said tiredly, "Now, Bicansa—"

"You only have to glance at the propaganda they've been broadcasting since their ships started to orbit over us. They'll break up our farms and use our land to support their war. And we'll be taken to work in their weapons factories, our children sent to a front line a thousand light years away."

"We're all in this together," Dano said. "All of humanity. You can't hide, madam, not even here."

Pala said, "Anyhow, it may not be like that. We're Missionaries, not Navy troops. We're here to find out about you. And if your culture has something distinctive to offer the Third Expansion, why then—"

"You'll spare us?" Bicansa snapped.

"Perhaps," said Dano. He reached for his cup, but his

gloved fingers passed through its substance. "Though it will take more than a few bits of pottery."

Sool listened to all this, a deep tiredness in his sunken eyes. Pala perceived that he saw the situation just as clearly as Bicansa did, but while she was grandstanding, Sool was absorbing the pain, seeking to find a way to save his way of life. Pala, despite all her training, couldn't help but feel a deep empathy for him.

They were all relieved when Sool stood. "Come," he said. "You should see the heart of our community, the Lake of Light."

The Lake was another car journey away. The vehicle was small and crowded, and Dano, uncomplaining, sat with one Virtual arm embedded in the substance of the wall.

They traveled perhaps thirty kilometers inward from the port area to the center of the lens-shaped colony. Pala peered out at villages and farms.

"You see we are comfortable," Sool said anxiously. "Stable. We are at peace here, growing what we need, raising our children. This is how humans are meant to live. And there is room here, room for billions more." That was true; Pala knew that the sphere's surface would have accommodated ten thousand Earths, more. Sool smiled at them. "Isn't that a reason for studying us, visiting us, understanding us—for letting us be?"

"*You* haven't expanded," Dano said coolly. "You've sat here in the dome built by your forefathers five thousand years ago. And so have your neighbors, in the other colonies strung out along this star's equator."

"We haven't needed any more than this," Sool said, but his smile was weak.

Bicansa, sitting before Pala, said nothing throughout the journey. Pala wished she could talk to this woman alone, but that was of course impossible. Her neck was narrow, elegant, her hair finely brushed.

As they approached the Lake the masts of the mirror towers clustered closer together. It was as if they were passing through a forest of skeletal trees, impossibly tall, crowned by light. But there was a brighter glow directly ahead, like a sun rising through trees.

They broke through the last line of towers. The car stopped.

As they walked forward, the compacted comet dirt thinned and scattered. Pala found herself standing on a cool, steel-gray surface—the substance of the sphere itself, the shell that enclosed a sun. It was utterly lifeless, disturbingly blank.

Dano, more practical, kneeled down and thrust his Virtual hand through the surface. Images flickered before his face, sensor readings rapidly interpreted.

"Come," Sool said to Pala, smiling. "You haven't seen it yet . . ."

Pala stepped forward and saw the Lake of Light itself.

The universal floor was a thin skin here, and a white glow poured out of the ground to drench the dusty air. Scattered clouds shone in the light from the ground, bright against a dark sky. As far ahead as she could see, the Lake stretched away, shining. It was an extraordinary, unsettling sight, baffling for a human sensorium evolved for landscape and sun, as if the world had been inverted. But the light was being harvested, scattered from one great mirrored dish to another, so that its life-giving glow was spread across the colony.

Sool walked forward, onto the glowing surface. "Don't worry," he said to Pala. "It's hot, but not so bad here at the edge; the real heat is toward the Lake's center. But even that is only a fraction of the star's output, of course. The sphere keeps the rest." He held out his arms and smiled. It was as if he were floating in the light, and he cast a shadow upward into the misty air. "Look down."

She saw a vast roiling ocean, almost too bright to look at directly, where huge vacuoles surface and burst. It was the photosphere of a star, just a thousand kilometers below her.

"Stars give all humans life," Sool said. "We are their children. Perhaps this is the purest way to live, to huddle close to the star-mother, to use all her energy . . ."

"Quite a pitch," Dano murmured in her ear. "But he's targeting you. Don't let him take you in."

Pala felt extraordinarily excited. "But Dano—here are people living, breathing, even growing crops, a thousand kilometers above the surface of a sun! Is it possible this is the true purpose of the sphere—*to terraform a star?*"

Dano snorted his contempt. "You always were a romantic, Missionary. What nonsense. Stick to your duties. For instance, have you noticed that the girl has gone?"

When she looked around, she realized that it was true; Bicansa had disappeared.

Dano said, "I've run some tests. You know what this stuff is? Xeelee construction material. This cute old man and his farm animals and grandchildren are living on a Xeelee artifact. And it's just ten centimeters thick . . ."

"I don't understand," she admitted.

"We have to go after her," Dano said. "Bicansa. Go to her 'community in the north,' wherever it is. I have a feeling that's where we'll learn the truth of this place. All this is a smokescreen."

Sool was still trying to get her attention. His face was underlit by sunlight, she saw, reminding her of the portrait in his home. "You see how wonderful this is? We live on a platform, suspended over an ocean of light, and all our art, our poetry is shaped by our experience of this bounteous light. How can you even think of removing this from the spectrum of human experience?"

"Your culture will be preserved," she said hopefully, wanting to reassure him. "On Earth there are museums."

"Museums?" Sool laughed tiredly, and he walked around in the welling fountains of light.

Pala accepted they should pursue the mysterious girl, Bicansa. But she impulsively decided she had had enough of being remote from the world she had come to assess.

"Bicansa is right. We can't just swoop down out of the sky. We don't know what we're throwing away if we don't take the time to look."

"But there is no time," Dano said wearily. "The Expansion front is encountering thousands of new star systems every *day*. Why do you think you're here alone?"

"Alone save for you, my Virtual conscience."

"Don't get cocky."

"Well, whether you like it or not, I am here, on the ground, and I'm the one making the decisions."

And so, she decided, she wasn't going to use her flitter. She would pursue Bicansa as the native girl had traveled herself—by car, over the vacuum road laid out over the star sphere.

"You're a fool," snapped Dano. "We don't even know how far north her community *is*."

He was right, of course. Pala was shocked to find out how sparse the scouts' information on this star-world was. There were light lakes scattered across the sphere from pole to pole, but away from the equator the compensating effects of centrifugal force would diminish, and in their haste the scouts had assumed that no human communities would have established themselves away from the standard-gravity equatorial belt.

She would be heading into the unknown, then. She felt a shiver of excitement at the prospect. But Dano knew her too well, and he admonished her for being distracted from her purpose.

Also he insisted that she shouldn't use one of the locals' cars, as she had planned, but a Coalition design shipped down from the Navy ferry. And, he said, she would have to wear a cumbersome hard-carapace skinsuit the whole way. She gave in to these conditions with bad grace.

It took a couple of days for the preparations to be completed, days she spent alone in the flitter, lest she be seduced by the bucolic comfort of Home. But at last everything was ready, and Pala took her place in the car.

The road ahead was a track of comet-core metal, laid down by human engineering across the immense face of the star sphere. To either side were scattered hillocks of ice, purple-streaked in the starlight. They were the wrecks of comets that had splashed against the unflinching floor of the sphere. Even now, as she peered out through the car's thick screen, at the sight of this road to nowhere, she shivered.

She set off.

The road surface was smooth, the traction easy. The blue-green splash of the domed colony receded behind her. The star sphere was so immense it was effectively an infinite plain, and she would not see the colony pass beyond the horizon. But it diminished to a line, a scrap of light, before becoming lost in the greater blackness.

When she gave the car its head, it accelerated smoothly to astounding speeds, to more than a thousand kilometers an hour. The car, a squat bug with big, tough, all-purpose tires, was state-of-the-art Coalition engineering and could keep up this pace indefinitely. But there were no landmarks save the meaningless hillocks of ice, the arrow-straight road laid over blackness, and despite the immense speed, it was as if she weren't moving at all.

And, somewhere in the vast encompassing darkness ahead, another car fled.

"Xeelee construction material," Dano whispered. "Like no other material we've encountered. You can't cut it, bend it, break it.

"You can see that here; even if we could build a sphere around a star and set it spinning in the first place, it would bulge at the equator and tear itself apart. But *this* shell is perfectly spherical, despite those huge stresses, to the limits of our measurements.

"Some believe the construction material doesn't even belong to this universe. But it can be shaped by the Xeelee's own technology, controlled by gadgets we call *flowers*."

"It doesn't just appear out of nowhere."

"Of course not. Even the Xeelee have to obey the laws of physics. Construction material seems to be manufactured by the direct conversion of radiant energy into matter, one hundred percent efficient. Stars burn by fusion fire; a star like this, like Earth's sun, probably converts some six hundred million tons of its substance to energy every second . . ."

"So if the sphere is ten centimeters thick, and if it was created entirely by the conversion of the star's radiation—" She called up a Virtual display before her face, ran some fast calculations.

"It's maybe five thousand years old," Dano murmured. "Of course, that's based on a lot of assumptions. And given the amount of comet debris the sphere has collected, that age seems too low—unless the comets have been *aimed* to infall here . . ."

She slept, ate, performed all her biological functions in the suit. The suit was designed for long duration occupancy, but it was scarcely comfortable: No spacesuit yet designed allowed you to scratch an itch properly. However, she endured.

After ten days, as the competition between the star's gravity and the sphere's spin was adjusted, she could feel the effective gravity building up. The local vertical tipped forward, so that it was as if the car were climbing an immense, unending slope. Dano insisted she take even more care moving around the cabin and spend more time lying flat to avoid stress on her bones.

Dano himself, of course, a complacent Virtual, sat comfortably in an everyday chair.

"Why?" she asked. "Why would the Xeelee create this great punctured sphere? What's the point?"

"It may have been an industrial accident," he said languidly. "There's a story from before the Qax Extirpation, predating even the Second Expansion. It's said that a human traveler once saved himself from a nova flare by huddling behind a scrap of construction material. The material soaked up the light, you see, and expanded dramatically . . . The rogue scrap could have grown and grown, easily encompassing a star like this. It's probably just a romantic myth. This may alternatively be some kind of technology demonstrator."

"I suppose we'll never know," she said. "And why the light lakes? Why not make the sphere perfectly efficient, totally black?"

He shrugged. "Well, perhaps it's a honey trap." She had never seen a bee or tasted honey, and she didn't understand the reference. "Sool was right that this immense sphereworld could host billions of humans—trillions. Perhaps the Xeelee hope that we'll flock here, to this place with room to breed almost without limit, and die and grow old without achieving anything, just like Sool, and not bother them any more. But I think that's unlikely."

"Why?"

"Because the effective gravity rises away from the equator. So the sphere isn't much of a honey trap, because we can't inhabit most of it. Humans here are clearly incidental to the sphere's true purpose." His Virtual voice was without inflection, and she couldn't read his mood.

They passed the five-gravity latitude before they even glimpsed Bicansa's car. It was just a speck in the high-magnification sensor displays, not visible to the naked eye, thousands of kilometers ahead on this tabletop landscape. It was clear that they weren't going to catch Bicansa without going much deeper into the sphere's effective gravity well.

"Her technology is almost as good as ours," Pala gasped. "But not quite."

"Try not to talk," Dano murmured. "You know, there are soldiers, Navy tars, who could stand multiple gravity for days on end. You aren't one of them."

"I won't turn back," Pala groaned. She was lying down, cushioned by her suit, kept horizontal by her couch despite the cabin's apparent tilt upward. But even so the pressure on her chest was immense.

"I'm not suggesting you do. But you will have to accept that the suit knows best . . ."

When they passed six gravities, the suit flooded with a dense, crimson fluid that forced its way into her ears and eyes and mouth. The fluid, by filling her, would enable her to endure the immense, unending pressure of the gravity. It was like drowning.

Dano offered no sympathy. "Still glad you didn't take the flitter? Still think this is a romantic adventure? Ah, but that was the point, wasn't it? *Romance*. I saw the way you looked at Bicansa. Did she remind you of gentle comforts, of thrilling nights in the Academy dormitories?"

"Shut up," she gasped.

"Didn't it occur to you that she was only a Virtual image,

and that image might have been *edited*? You don't even know what she looks like . . ."

The fluid tasted of milk. Even when the feeling of drowning had passed, she never learned to ignore its presence in her belly and lungs and throat; she felt as though she were on the point of throwing up, all the time. She slept as much as she could, trying to shut out the pain, the pressure in her head, the mocking laugh of Dano.

But, trapped in her body, she had plenty of time to think over the central puzzle of this star-world—and what to do about it. And still the journey continued across the elemental landscape, and the astounding, desolating scale of this artificial world worked its way into her soul.

They drove steadily for no less than forty days, traversing a great arc of the star sphere stretching from the equator toward the pole, across nearly a million kilometers. Although as gravity dominated the diminishing centrifugal forces, the local vertical tipped back up and the plain seemed to level out, eventually the effective gravity force reached more than twenty standard.

The car drew to a halt.

Pala insisted on seeing for herself. Despite Dano's objections, she had the suit lift her up to the vertical, amid a protesting whine of exoskeletal motors. As the monstrous gravity dragged at the fluid in which she was embedded, waves of pain plucked at her body. But she could see.

Ahead of the car was another light lake, another pale glow, another splash of dimly lit green. But there were no trees or mirror towers, she saw; nothing climbed high above the sphere's surface here.

"This is one of a string of settlements around this line of latitude," Dano said. "The Navy scouts have extended their coverage, a bit belatedly . . . The interaction of gravity and the sphere's spin is interesting. The comet debris tends to collect at the equator, where it's spun off, or at the poles, where the spin effects are least and the gravity draws it in. But you also have Coriolis effects, sideways kicks from the spin. In the in-between latitudes there must be weather, a slow weather of drifting comet ice. Earth's rotation influences its weather, the circulation of the atmosphere, of course, but in that case the planet's gravity always dominates. We've never encountered a world like this, with such ferocious spin—it's as if Earth was spinning in a couple of hours . . ."

"Dano—"

"Yes. Sorry. My weakness, Pala, is a tendency to be too drawn to intellectual puzzles—while you are too drawn to people. The point is that *this* is the sphere's true habitable region, this and the south pole, the place all the air and water sink to. It's just a shame it's under crushing, inhuman gravity."

Bicansa appeared in the air.

She stood in the car's cabin, unsuited, as relaxed as Dano. Pala felt there was some sympathy in her Virtual eyes. But she knew now without doubt that this wasn't Bicansa's true aspect.

"You came after me," Bicansa said.

"I wanted to know," Pala said. Her voice was a husk, muffled by the fluid in her throat. "Why did you come to the equator—why meet us? You could have hidden here."

"Yes," Dano said grimly. "Our careless scouting missed you."

"We had to know what kind of threat you are to us. I had to see you face to face, take a chance that I would expose—" She waved a hand. "This."

"You know we can't ignore you," Dano said. "This great sphere is a Xeelee artifact. We have to learn what it's for . . ."

"That's simple," Pala said. She had worked it out, she thought, during her long cocooning. "We were thinking too hard, Dano. *The sphere is a weapon.*"

"Ah," Dano said grimly. "Of course. And I always believed your thinking wasn't bleak enough, Pala."

Bicansa looked bewildered. "What are you talking about? Since the First landed, we always thought of this sphere as a place that gives life, not death."

Dano said, "You wouldn't think it was so wonderful if you inhabited a planet of this star as the sphere slowly coalesced—if your ocean froze out, your air began to snow . . . The sphere is a machine that kills a star—or rather, its planets, while preserving the star itself for future use. I doubt if there's anything special about this system, this star." He glanced at the sky, metal Eyes gleaming. "It is probably just a trial run of a new technology, a weapon for a war of the future. One thing we know about the Xeelee is that they think long term."

Bicansa said, "What a monstrous thought . . . So my whole culture has developed on the hull of a weapon. But even so, it is my culture. And you're going to destroy it, aren't you? Or will you put us in a museum, as you promised Sool?"

No, Pala thought. I can't do that. "Not necessarily," she whispered.

They both turned to look at her. Dano murmured threateningly, "What are you talking about, Missionary?"

She closed her eyes. Did she really want to take this step? It could be the end of her career if it went wrong, if Dano failed to back her. But she had sensed the gentleness of Sool's equatorial culture and had now experienced for herself the vast spatial scale of the sphere—and here, still more strange, was this remote polar colony. This was an immense place, she thought, immense both in space and time—and yet humans had learned to live here. It was almost as if humans and Xeelee were learning to live together. It would surely be wrong to allow this unique world to be destroyed, for the sake of short-term gains.

And she thought she had a way to keep that from happening.

"If this is a weapon, it may one day be used against us. And if so we have to find a way to neutralize it." The suit whirred as she turned to Bicansa. "Your people can stay here. You can live your lives the way you want. I'll find ways to make the Commission accept that. But there's a payback."

Bicansa nodded grimly. "I understand. You want us to find the Xeelee flower."

"Yes," whispered Pala. "Find the off switch."

Dano faced her, furious. "You don't have the authority to make a decision like that. Granted this is an unusual situation. But these are still human colonists, and you are still a Missionary. Such a *deal* would be unprecedented."

"But," Pala whispered, "Bicansa's people are no longer human. Are you, Bicansa?"

Bicansa averted her eyes. "The First were powerful. Just as they made this star-world fit for us, so they made us fit for it."

Dano, astonished, glared at them both. Then he laughed. "Oh, I see. A loophole! If the colonists aren't fully human under the law, you can pass the case to the Assimilation, who won't want to deal with it either . . . You're an ingenious one, Pala! Well, well. All right, I'll support your proposal at the Commission. No guarantees, though . . ."

"Thank you," Bicansa said to Pala. She held out her Virtual hand, and it passed through Pala's suit, breaking into pixels.

Dano had been right, Palo thought, infuriatingly right, as usual. He had seen something in her, an attraction to this woman from another world she hadn't even recognized in herself. But Bicansa didn't even *exist* in the form Pala had perceived. Was she really so lonely? Well, if so, when she got out of here, she would do something about it.

And she would have to think again about her career choice. Dano had always warned her about an excess of empathy. It seemed she wasn't cut out for the duties of a Missionary—and next time she might not be able to find a loophole.

With a last regretful glance, Bicansa's Virtual sublimated into dusty light.

Dano said briskly, "Enough's enough. I'll call down the flitter to get you out of here before you choke to death . . ." He turned away, and his pixels flickered as he worked.

Pala looked out through the car's window at the colony, the sprawling, high-gravity plants, the dusty, flattened lens of shining air. She wondered how many more colonies had spread over the varying gravity latitudes of the star shell,

how many more adaptations from the standard form had
been tried—how many people actually lived on this immense artificial world. There was so much here to explore.

The door of Bicansa's car opened. A creature climbed out
cautiously. In a bright orange pressure suit, its body was
low-slung, supported by four limbs as thick as tree trunks.
Even through the suit Pala could make out immense bones at
hips and shoulders, and massive joints along the spine. It
lifted its head and looked into the car. Through a thick visor
Pala could make out a face—thick-jawed, flattened, but a human face nonetheless. The creature nodded once. Then it
turned and, moving heavily, carefully, made its way toward
the colony and its lake of light.

The Albian Message

OLIVER MORTON

Oliver Morton lives in Greenwich, England. He is a writer and editor who concentrates on scientific knowledge, technological change, and their effects, and has recently become the Chief News and Features editor at Nature, *one of the world's leading science journals, "where I oversee the journalism in print and online." He has had a substantial career as a science journalist: he worked on the science and technology pages of* The Economist, *was editor-in-chief of* Wired UK, *and has been anthologized in both* Best American Science Writing *and* Best American Science and Nature Writing. *His first book is* Mapping Mars: Science, Imagination and the Birth of a World, *and he is working on his second,* Eating the Sun: How Plants Power the Planet, *a look at photosynthesis. Asteroid 10716 Olivermorton is named after him.*

"The Albian Message" was published in Nature. *It is an intriguing hard SF rethinking of what alien artifacts might reveal. It is one of those SF ideas that is so obviously reasonable that it should have been evident all along.*

To: Eva P.
From: Stefan K.
Re: Sample handling facility

March 4, 2047

I thought I ought to put into writing my concerns over the sample-return facility for Odyssey. I think that relying on the mothballed Mars Sample Return lab at Ames is dangerously complacent. It is simply not flexible enough, or big enough, for what I think we should be expecting.

I appreciate that I am in a minority on this, and that the consensus is that we will be dealing with non-biological artifacts. And I don't want to sound like the people from AstraRoche slipped some egopoietin into my drink during that trip to Stockholm last November. But my minority views have been pretty well borne out throughout this whole story. Back when Suzy and Sean had more or less convinced the world that the trinity sequences in the Albian message referred to some sort of mathematico-philosophical doctrine—possibly based on an analogy to the aliens' purported trisexual reproductive system—and everyone in SETI was taking a crash course in genome analysis, I had to pull in every favor I was owed to get the Square Kilometer Array used as a planetary radar and scanned over the Trojan asteroids. If I hadn't done that we wouldn't even know about the Pyramid, let alone be sending Odyssey there.

I'm not claiming I understand the Albians' minds better than anyone else; I haven't got any more of the message in my DNA than anyone else has. And it's always been my position that we should read as little into that message as possible. I remain convinced that looking for descriptions of their philosophy or lifestyle or even provenance is pointless. The more I look at the increasingly meaningless analyses that the increasingly intelligent AIs produce, the more I think that the variations between phyla are effectively random and that the message from the aliens tells us almost nothing except that there's a radar-reflecting tetrahedron $\pi/3$ behind Jupiter that they think we may find interesting.

Everyone assumes that if it hadn't been for the parts of the message lost in the K/T the "residual variant sequences" would be seen to add up to some great big life-the-Universe-and-everything revelation. And because they think such a revelation once existed, they expect to see it carved into the palladium walls of the Pyramid. But if the aliens who visited Earth, and left their messages in the genomes of more or less everything on the planet, had wanted to tell us something more about themselves, they could have made the messages a lot bigger and built in more redundancy across phylum space; there's no shortage of junk DNA to write on. The point is, they didn't choose to leave big messages—just a simple signpost.

The reason I was able to get the SKA people to find the Pyramid was that they knew I'd thought about SETI a lot. But these days people tend to forget that I was always something of a skeptic. What could a bunch of aliens tell us about themselves, or the Universe, that would matter? Especially if, like the Albians, they sent, or rather left, the message 100 million years ago? Well, in the case of the Albians, there's one type of knowledge they could be fairly sure that anyone who eventually evolved sequencing technology on Earth pretty much had to be interested in. And it's something that, by definition, is too big to fit into the spare bits of a genome.

I appreciate that everyone on the project now has a lot of

faith in what we can do on the fly, especially in terms of recording and analyzing information. I'll admit that when we started I really didn't think that the lost craft of human spaceflight would be so easy to reinvent. It still strikes me as remarkable that none of us realized how much could be achieved by leaving a technical problem to one side and concentrating on other things for a few decades before coming back to it with new technologies. But the problem with the sample-return facility won't just be one of technology. It's going to be one of size.

You see, extinctions aren't the noise in the message. They're the reason for the message. The one thing the Albians knew they could do for whoever would end up reading their message was store up some of the biodiversity that would inevitably be whittled away over time. When Odyssey gets to the Trojan Pyramid, I don't expect it to find any more information about the Albians than we have already. I do expect a biosphere's worth of well-preserved biological samples from the mid-Cretaceous. Not just genomes, but whole samples. Sudarat and her boys are going to come home with a hold full of early angiosperms and dinosaur eggs. We need to be ready.

Bright Red Star

BUD SPARHAWK

Bud Sparhawk (sff.net/people/bud_sparhawk) lives with his wife in Annapolis, Maryland "and is a frequent sailor on the Chesapeake Bay." He is a writer of mostly "hard" science fiction. He started writing in 1975, with sales to Analog. *Thirteen years later he returned to writing, and his stories have been appearing regularly in* Analog *and other magazines, and in anthologies. He has been a Nebula finalist three times for his novellas.*

"Bright Red Star" was published in Asimov's. *It is a very tightly constructed military SF horror story about the sacrifice of innocents, in the hard SF tradition of "The Cold Equations." Sparhawk says "It was written as the events of 9-11 evolved. I tried, in this piece, to address the motivations of those who could allow themselves to commit such heinous atrocities." But it is not directly about current events at all, which makes it we think more effective.*

Our boat floated silent as owls' wings and settled softly as an autumn snowflake. There was no doubt that the enemy had spotted us—the stealth could only minimize signs of our presence. We'd done everything we could to reduce detectability: hardened plastics, ceramics, charged ice, and hardly any metal. All that did was create doubt, and, possibly, delay. Or so we hoped.

We tumbled quickly from the boat as grounding automatically discharged the ship charge, without which the boat's ice frame would quickly melt. In a matter of minutes, the only remaining trace of our craft would be a puddle of impure water and the gossamer-thin spider-web of the stealth shield—and that would dissipate at the first hint of a breeze.

We deployed in pincer and arrowhead formation, sending two troops to the north to parallel our advance, two likewise to the south, and two to the point. Hunter and I followed in column.

We moved quickly, carefully, ever wary. That the Shardies would eventually find us was not in doubt, neither was the certainty of our death when they did so. They did not use humans well; however, I doubted they'd find much use for us.

Tactical estimates gave us an hour to save the recalcitrant settlers' souls. They were some sort of colony—religious or otherwise, it made no difference—only that they had foolishly chosen to remain where others fled.

There was a slight probability we'd have less than an hour and an even smaller possibility of having more, so we moved quickly. I'd estimated twenty minutes to reach their position and ten to twenty to ensure we'd located everyone. That left us five minutes for action and ten as margin for contingencies.

I knew we'd fail if we used more than fifty-five minutes.

". . . shards," one of the last observers managed to croak out before Jeaux II fell silent. That word was the only description of the aliens we'd ever heard, so it stuck.

The Shardies had hit hard when we first made contact with their kind, which could hardly be called contact at all since they attacked first and without provocation. When our ships backed off, their ship followed, attacking again and again with unbelievable ferocity. When its missiles ran out, they tried to ram the thick plate of our exploratory ship. It smashed into tiny ceramic fragments on impact, leaving a cloud of glittering fragments that spun into emptiness, leaving no trace, no hint, of what had so provoked them.

After much debate over the wisdom of such an attempt, we again tried to contact them. The idea of another space-spanning civilization held too much promise to ignore. It took years before we found them, but find them we did.

That is, we assume that someone found them, for a fleet of their ships suddenly appeared near Jeaux II and attacked every sign of human presence: ships, orbiting stations, ground-based settlements—anything that wasn't of natural origin. The military tried to defend themselves while the civilian ships fled in every direction.

This was a strategic mistake. Since they'd backtracked one of our ships to Jeaux, that meant that they could—and probably would—follow every ship who escaped. Every destination system was now at risk.

Thanks to the brief warning, most of the settled systems managed to mobilize to meet the Shardies attack. The initial losses were great. We had to fall back from system after system, engaged in a running battle with something we do not understand.

We've tried to figure out why they attack with such ferocity, why there hasn't been an attempt at contact, and why they won't respond to our calls. We fail at every attempt to understand them.

Neither have we deduced anything of their technology from the damaged ships we've managed to recover. Hulls, engines, and controls appear to be nothing but dirty glass. We suspect this is the analog of our silicon-based technology, but can't be sure. Researchers have been working hard, I'm told, but I have yet to hear of anything useful come of it.

Nor can we figure out what sort of creatures we're fighting. That one word, that one utterance from a lone observer on Jeaux, was all we had to go on.

What we do know for certain is that either the Shardies will be destroyed, or we will be. Humanity has lost too much, too many, for compromise. It is clear that there can be no middle ground.

The trip to the site of the single communications burst was uneventful. We didn't expect to encounter resistance. The Shardies don't settle on the planets they take from us. No, they just wipe them clean of humanity and then move on. We knew there had to be Shardie gleaners surveying the planet, trying to find some fresh meat, or, what was worse, breeding stock. With a little luck, we'd find that the Shardies had beaten us to them.

The location was a hill, close by a half-destroyed farming complex whose tower leaned precariously toward the north. With luck, we'd find whoever made the call nearby. First place to check were the buildings, or what remained of them.

We went straight in. Better to find whatever sign we could quickly—time was running out. A sweep of the barn was negative, as were the remains of the silo, and the outbuildings. The house was a different matter. We found some opened jars, preserves mostly. The footprints we found outside were small—a child's, perhaps, or a small woman. The tracks led up the hill and into the woods.

I sent the outriders wide to cover while Hunter followed the tracks. Could be a trap, so I waited, senses alert for any indication of a problem.

Crack of a twig brought me to my feet. It was Hunter and a little girl. "Cave up there," with a head nod. "Three dead men—three, four days gone." That tied with the time we'd received the burst.

She was a tiny thing—about nine or ten, I'd say—bright eyes and scraggly red hair. Good teeth. Looked scared as hell. I could understand that—Hunter wasn't being very gentle as he dumped her at my feet.

"What's your name?" I stooped to bring my head to her level.

"You them aliens?" she asked all wide-eyed. "How come you talk like us?"

"We're combat soldiers," I answered. "We're humans, just like you, sweetheart. Now, come on; what's your name?"

"Becky," she finally spit out. "How come you're still here? Paw said everybody left."

"We came back to take care of you and the others," I answered truthfully. "We can't afford to let you fall into enemy hands."

"Paw and the Paston boys thought you'd come," she said.

"How did they die?"

Becky seemed fascinated by my sidearm. "They shot them after the Pastons used the mayday thing. I hid in the back where they couldn't find me. Are you going to punish them for doing that?"

That got my attention. Takes a real idiot to shoot the people who demonstrated good sense. I began to doubt that the Shardies would've gotten much use out of whatever mush these jerks used for brains. "Right, sweetheart, we'll punish them, but first you have to tell us where they are."

"Did you bring a ship to take us away?" Becky asked as she fingered the butt of my AC-43. "That was why Paw grabbed the mayday—to get us a rescue ship."

"We came to make sure the enemy doesn't get you," I answered honestly. "Listen, we don't have much time. Can you take us to where the others are hiding?"

"I think they're still over at the Truett place," she said, pointing to the east.

I nodded to Hunter, who was already directing the scouts

eastward. I picked up Becky and moved out. Hunter covered
my rear. "Can you tell us how to get there?"

"You mean to the Truetts' place?" Becky asked. "Sure.
There's a big field there. That where the rescue ship's going
to land?"

The Shardie ships we'd managed to capture more or less intact were completely empty—no aliens at all—just glass of
various colors and shapes. Either the ships were highly automated, or the Shardies had destroyed themselves completely
so they would not fall into our hands. Suicidal, or so we
thought. Eventually, we discovered some living creatures, if
you can call them that, aboard one of their ships.

One of the things we'd learned was that if we had sufficient warning, we could defend ourselves fairly well. Sometimes we managed to drive them off, and sometimes not.
Every battle was fought hard and long, usually with massive
losses on both sides. Our defensive successes managed to
achieve, at best, parity.

That all changed at Witca, a heavily fortified military outpost armed with the latest data on Shardie attack patterns.
Only the Shardies were using new patterns that got through
the outer defenses. It was as if they were anticipating the
base's reactions and countering Witca's best defensive
moves with ease. Witca fell with all hands lost.

After Witca's defeat, we lost ground steadily, falling farther and farther back toward Earth year after year. We no
longer had parity. We were losing.

Then, largely through a stroke of luck, our fleet happened
upon a lone Shardie ship near Outreach. As soon as it realized we were near, it attacked on an evasion pattern that de-
fied the fleet's best defensive efforts. The fleet lost six ships
before managing to still whatever mysterious force propelled the Shardie vessel.

The fleet marines lost no time in boarding. Command had
high hopes of finally finding something alive inside. They
weren't disappointed. *Disgusted* and *surprised* might better
describe their reaction. Inside, they found sixteen of the
Jeaux survivors.

Survivors isn't exactly the word. What they found were sixteen bodies without arms, legs, and most organs. What remained were essentially heads hooked up to life support and fueled by oxygenated glucose pumps. There were a couple of hundred strands of glass fiber running from the ship's walls into each skull, into each brain, into each soul. Four of the sixteen were still functioning—alive is not a word to describe their condition.

Clinical examination of the four revealed that each was fully conscious and aware, at least that's what the eeg traces indicated. They also indicated that the Shardies had used no painkillers to dull the senses when they'd done this. Had the survivors mouths, they would have been continually screaming. All four died mercifully fast when their pumps ran dry. I'm not too sure that the medics didn't help that along. It was a mercy.

The only conclusion we could draw was that the Shardies were using human brains to defeat human defenses. They were obviously using our own brains to "think" like us.

There was no hesitation on the part of Command. They ordered everyone, except combat types like us, from the most likely targets. Humanity couldn't allow any more people to become components for the Shardie offense.

But civilians never listen. Farmers were the worst, hanging onto their little plots and crops until somebody dragged them away, kicking and screaming at the injustice of it all. That's why we were here. Forty settlers had stupidly refused to be evacuated from New Mars. Forty we didn't know about until we got that one brief burst.

My mission was to make certain that they didn't become forty armless, legless, gutless, screamless weapon components.

"Why do you look so funny?" Becky asked as we jogged along. Her question was expected. Few civilians ever see combat troops like us. Luckily the combat gear and darkness hid most of the worst modifications I'd had to undergo: cybernetic heart-lung pump with reserve oxygen so I could operate in any atmosphere or even underwater; augmented muscles on legs and arms that bulked me up like a cartoon giant on steroids; amped vision that ran from the near infrared up toward the UV range—I could even switch to black and white for better night vision—and smart-metal skeleton structures to provide a good base for my massive muscles. Flesh had been stripped from anything exposed and replaced with impervious plas. My hands were electromechanical marvels capable of ripping weapons-grade plating off a spaceship, and sensitive enough to lift a tiny girl without harm.

Then there was my glucose pump, a nasty, but useful technology we'd copied from the Shardies. Even my brain had been altered—substituting silicon and gel for the mass of pink jelly I was born with. Definitely not something you'd want your daughter to date. I'm glad it was dark. In daylight, I'd probably scare the bejesus out of her.

"We're modified so we can fight the bastards," I growled. Revenge for relatives on Witca was my overt reason. Curiosity about the Shardies, and getting a piece of them, was secondary. I saw no sense going into the gory details or the agonizing processes involved with a little girl who wouldn't understand. "Tell me about the rest of your group. Are they all right?"

"Mr. Robbarts is still the boss. He's the one that shot Paw, I think. And there's Jake and Sally and little Billy. Billy's my friend. Jake's got a bad leg.

"Then there's all the Thomas women. They have a big wagon, or they did before the men came and burned it." She started crying.

I was certain she was talking about the roaming gangs. Lots of people didn't want to leave anything the Shardies might be able to use. Senseless, that. Shardies could care less, but most civilians wouldn't know that. Best destroy what you left behind, they'd probably thought, and had taken their anger out on things they could reach.

"Mr. Robbarts said we didn't have to worry because we weren't soldiers. He said we'd have the whole world to ourselves. But after everybody left, Paw got really afraid of what might happen."

Robbarts must be the leader of this group. "Robbarts was wrong, Becky. You all should have left," I said. "Didn't they tell you that it wouldn't matter if you were a soldier or not? Being human is all that matters."

"Mr. Robbarts got real mad when Paw argued with him and said he wanted to use the mayday thing. Then Paw and the boys and me ran away with it. You got to go along this stream for a bit now," she directed.

That explained the burst message that told us there were people left behind. They must have used one of the emergency broadcast units the evacuation team had scattered across New Mars in the last days, just in case. "What happened then?" I asked as I followed her pointing finger down the stream. The scouts picked up my changed direction and reacted.

"They told Paw to come out of the cave to talk," Becky continued, chatting away. "Paw told me to hide. Then I heard them arguing and shouting and I got really afraid. Then there was some shots. I heard the men looking around. Mr. Robbarts was cussing a lot and calling me all sorts of names, but I stayed where I was. I was scared."

"What did you do then?" I stepped around a huge boulder and wondered if it would be easier, and faster, to wade in the stream instead of through the woods on either side. Hunter was close by my side now in this narrow section.

"After it got quiet, I snuck out and found Paw and the boys laying on the ground. Paw was bleeding bad. I tried to stop it, but it wouldn't stop. Then he went to sleep and didn't move for a long time. I got hungry waiting for the rescue ship Paw said would come." That explained the jelly and jam jars—just what a little girl would like to eat. "Are you going to bury Paw and the boys?"

"Burial wastes time—something we can't afford," Hunter said sharply. *Down*, he signaled as a shot ricocheted off my chest armor.

I dropped immediately, instinctively tucking Becky underneath to protect her. Hunter slipped to the side and disappeared. I switched to infrared and made out fuzzy heat forms in the brush a dozen meters ahead. The muzzle of a rifle was glowing heat-bright from the shot he had taken. None of the forms moved.

I waited. Silent. Becky groaned and wiggled feebly. "It really hurts," she said. Her voice was muffled.

"Wait," I whispered, waiting for Hunter to get into position.

"Let her up," a man's voice barked from behind me. "Move easy now. I got you covered."

I pushed up, allowing Becky to crawl out before I came to my feet. The man took a step back. "Huh, you sure are a big one." He peered closer. "Ugly, too."

"He's come to rescue us, Mister Robbarts," Becky said. "He's got another soldier with him." Becky's voice sounded strained. I glanced at her and saw the blood. Damn, had his shot hit her?

I noticed the heat signatures of two more men in the brush; one behind Robbarts and another somewhat farther back. I had no doubt all were armed and all too ready to shoot. That made six in all.

"You shot Becky," I said calmly. "She needs help."

"The hell with her," Robbarts said nastily. "Her damn family's been nothing but trouble. Killed one of my boys, they did. Let the little bitch bleed."

"They're going to take us away in a ship," Becky said in a rush. "That's why we're going to your place. The field's a place they can land."

Robbarts didn't answer her directly. "That true, soldier? You got a ship?"

I really didn't like this man. "Nobody, nothing, could find a trace of the boat we came in. Becky's the one who said there'd be a rescue ship."

"Ain't no damn ship taking me or my people off our land," Robbarts spit, ignoring what I had said. "We're going to hold on to this place come whatever. This'll be a damn nice place for me and mine after the war moves on."

Did he really believe that? "The Shardies are going to comb this planet and glean whatever human stock they can find. Do you know what they do to the people they capture?"

Robbarts sneered. "I seen the news about what they did to

them poor troopers. But we're civilians, not some combat-trained space jockey. They won't bother us. We don't know military stuff."

I couldn't believe Robbarts's ignorance. "The aliens don't care what you *know*. It's the human thought processes, the way our minds form associations, our ability to recognize patterns—that's what they use. They don't give a damn if a brain comes from a soldier, a navigator, or even some dumb-assed farmer!" As soon as the angry words popped out of my mouth I regretted them.

"Well, I might be a dumb-assed farmer, soldier boy," Robbarts drawled, "but it's you who's at the wrong end of this here gun."

"Not exactly," I said as I watched Hunter silently taking out the two forms behind Robbarts. That action told me the other three had already been neutralized. Hunter is good at what he does—thorough.

"You really shouldn't have said that about Becky," I said calmly. Robbarts's normal human reaction time was no match for my enhanced speed. I quickly swung the knife edge of my forearm sleeve, and a wet, red grin grew beneath his chin.

Severing the cardioid arteries releases the pressure and drains blood from the brain. It causes death in seconds, and slashing his larynx prevented any outcry. Robbarts stood quietly erect for a moment until his body got the message that blood was no longer flowing to the head and no more signals were coming from the dying brain. Then he toppled over.

I scooped up Becky and continued. Hunter would destroy Robbarts's head, just as he had the others, and catch up. I hoped the rest of Robbarts's flock wouldn't waste more of what little time we had left.

While I jogged along, I checked to see where Becky had been hit. It wasn't fatal, so I put a compress over the wound to staunch the bleeding. It would do well enough until we found the others.

"Where now?" I asked.

Becky stopped sobbing for a moment. "There's a pond down there. It's up the hill from there. There's a hiding hole near the barn."

So that's how they managed to evade the evacuation search teams—by hiding in a bunker. Hunter had caught up by then and I briefed them. He directed the scouts to converge on the spot. "What if it's sealed?" he asked.

"You know what to do," I answered and he smiled. That was the difference between us—he enjoyed this, enjoyed the danger, enjoyed the blood. When we got within sight of the entrance to the bunker I put Becky down. "You have to call them out," I said. "Can you do that?"

"They'll shoot me like they did Paw," Becky protested. "I hurt real bad, mister. Can't you do something?" She was crying.

"Listen Becky, it's really important that I get to those people quickly. I tell you what; if they shoot at you, I'll punish them like I did Mr. Robbarts, all right?" She nodded, but reluctantly. "Becky, just walk over there and yell. Tell them you're hurt and need help. I don't think they'll shoot a little girl."

"Aren't you coming with me?" she said.

I shook my head. "No, they might be afraid if they saw me. You can tell them who we are if you want and then I'll show myself." I wiped her nose and pushed her behind to get her moving.

Becky hesitated and then slowly hobbled across the field. "Help! I been shot!" she screamed.

A black hole appeared in the ground by the barn and a man climbed out. "Becky?" he called out. "Robbarts said you were dead." I noticed he'd left the hatch open. Good.

"He just shot me, like he did Paw and the Pastons," she answered.

"We heard a shot but didn't know it was you," the man said as he approached and knelt before Becky. "Damn, that looks bad. How did you manage to get here—and where are Robbarts and his men?" He was looking around nervously.

"The rescue soldiers took care of him," Becky answered innocently.

"Soldiers!" That didn't sound like a curse. More like a man with hope in his voice. I stepped forward.

"Captain Savage; forty-fifth combat arm," I said. "We came to save your souls." I could see by his frightened reaction that he wasn't going to be a problem.

"He's got a ship to take us all away, Mr. Truett, just like Paw said," Becky said. "They'll have a doctor to fix me up and we'll all be safe."

Truett stepped closer. "I heard things." I could hear the fear in his voice. How much he knew, I did not know.

"We can't be used by the Shardies," I said calmly. "Can't survive more than a few minutes without our combat rations." I figured he knew about the measured doses of anti-coagulants fed into my bloodstream. When those stopped, my brain would suffuse with thick blood, hemorrhaging and destroying the remaining organic brain cells. "We're running out of time here."

"How long?" he said, showing more understanding than I expected from a dumb-assed farmer who hadn't had the good sense to save himself and his family when he could.

"I've only got about another hundred minutes," I answered.

Truett turned his head and whistled. "Suicide trooper." He blinked, but that didn't stop a tear from running down his cheek. He understood. Without another word he led the way toward the black hole. "They're all inside," he remarked quietly. "There's thirty of us. Mostly women. Some are just kids," he added sadly. "I was hoping . . ." He stopped, looked at Becky, and sighed. "Never mind."

Thirty in the bunker. That meant that all forty were accounted for, counting the three men of Becky's family, the six Hunter had taken out, Becky, and Truett. Good. "We'll take care of them quickly," I said and he nodded. Quiet. Yeah, I guess he did know "things."

Hunter and the scouts had already converged on the hole and were dropping through, one after another. I had no doubts of their effectiveness.

"What's it like for you?" Truett said. He was holding Becky tightly in his arms.

"Being here, or being a soldier?" I answered.

"Both. I can't see how you can be so cold and distant. Hell, man, can't you at least show some emotion? Or are you mostly machine now?" His voice was a mixture of anger and fear.

"I grew up on a farm," I said slowly, trying to dredge up memories of a happier past on a planet now lost beyond redemption. "I still remember the smell of autumn, the feeling of mud between my toes, and how it felt to kill my prize sheep when it was time. This mission's no different. I do what I have to do because there are worse things for a human being than dying."

"I saw the news tapes," he said. "Ugly. Horrible. But what about your own hide? Don't you have any sense of self-preservation?"

"When you've been taken care of, we'll go after the Shardies," I bit out. "Our secondary mission is to gather whatever data we can and squirt a message to the fleet. After that, well, there's four, five thousand tons of explosive force in our packs." I patted the small canister strapped to my back. "I figure a dead-man switch will take care of them if we get close."

Truett smiled. "Brave, but it was a foolish waste of resources to come back for us. We made our own mess—stupid as it was to believe Robbarts—and we deserve to lie in it."

I checked the time. We only had fifteen minutes of good time left. Hunter was taking far too long.

"I'm sorry," I said quickly. "You don't have any time left."

Truett grabbed my hand and squeezed. "I just want you to know . . ." he began and then choked off whatever he was going to say. Instead he slapped my shoulder. "Yeah." I could tell he was trying hard not to cry, but his voice cracked at the end. "Well," he said to Becky. "Looks like we've got a ship to catch," he said cheerily.

Hunter popped out of the hole and came toward me at a run. "We're done," he said quickly. Moments later, the ground surged upward with a roar as smoke and flame shot from the burrow's entrance. If that didn't get the Shardies' attention, nothing would.

"Becky," I said, and gently took her from Truett's arms. "It's time to go."

"Is the ship coming?" Becky asked excitedly as she squirmed around in my arms. "I don't see it."

"It's up there in the sky," Truett said very gently. "Just look up. There, to the right of that big, bright red star." Becky tilted her head back to look almost directly overhead.

I brought my forearm across her throat and held her as she died. I hoped that she didn't have enough time to realize what I had done. What I had to do.

Hunter had taken care of Truett without a struggle. He too had been looking up, as if he might have believed his own words.

I gently laid Becky's lifeless body on the ground, trying not to feel. As before, I let Hunter take care of the final details, ensuring not a single brain cell remained in either head.

There were two minutes left in our window when I heard a distant whine. It could only be the Shardies. I placed my finger on the detonator. Our comm packages were running and would catch our final moments.

"Civilians just don't understand, do they?" Hunter asked as he waited beside me for sweet oblivion, sweet release from these mechanical contrivances we'd become.

I thought of Truett, and the way he had bravely shielded Becky to the last, thought of all the ways the war hasn't changed human decency, thought of my prize sheep and the necessities life forces on us.

"Some do," I admitted.

Third Day Lights

ALAYA DAWN JOHNSON

Alaya Dawn Johnson lives in New York City. She graduated from Columbia University in 2004 with a BA in East Asian Languages and Cultures. At Columbia, Alaya worked as the News Editor for the Columbia Spectator, *and interned at the* Village Voice *and* Smithsonian Magazine. *She has been published in* Internet Review of Science Fiction, Interzone, Strange Horizons, Chiaroscuro, *and* Arabella Magazine. *Currently, she works as an editorial assistant at QPB (the Quality Paperback Book Club).*

"Third Day Lights" was published in Interzone, *which began to hit its stride again in 2005 under new editorship, and ended the year with a new, more commercial look as well. It starts as fantasy, and becomes SF, in the template of planetary romance, the Leigh Brackett and Michael Moorcock tradition. In the very far future, humanity is destroying universes to drain as power sources for a huge posthuman project.*

The mist was thick as clotted cream, shot through with light from the luminous maggots in the sand. And through that mist, which I knew would entrap almost any creature unlucky enough to wander through it, came my first supplicant in over thirty cycles. He rode atop one of the butterfly men's great black deer, which greeted me with a sweep of its massive antlers. His skin was as pale as the sand was black; his eyes were the clear, hard color of chipped jade. A fine, pale fuzz covered his scalp, like the babies of humans. He had full, hard lips and high cheekbones. His nose had been broken several times, and was quite large regardless. His ears protruded slightly from his head.

He was too beautiful. I did not believe it. Oh, I had, in my travels, seen men far more attractive than he. Men who had eagerly accepted me in whatever form I chose, and had momentarily pleased me. But I had never seen this kind of beauty, that of the hard edges and chipped flakes of jade. That aura of bitterly mastered power, and unspeakable grief subdued but somehow not overcome. He gave the impression that he was a man to respect, a man who would understand my own loneliness despite my family, a man who might, perhaps, after so many cycles . . .

But I have not lived for so long away from my Trunk by believing in such things.

Eyes never leaving mine, he touched the neck of the deer and it knelt for him to dismount. His bare feet should have frozen solid seconds after they touched the sand, and the maggots begun devouring the icy flesh, but instead he stood before my staircase, perfectly at ease. From within the hostile mist, lacy hands and mouths struggled toward him but never quite touched.

That is how I knew he wasn't human.

I anticipated with relish the moment when he would speak and allow me to drop him on the other side of the desert. But he stared at me and I glowered back and then I understood: he knew what I was. He knew *who* I was. At the time, I thought this meant that he was incalculably old. Now, I am not so sure.

"Why do you stand before my gate? Tell me your purpose."

He stayed silent, of course. His impassive expression never wavered, and yet—perhaps from his slightly quivering shoulders or faintly irregular breathing—I had the impression that he was laughing at me.

It had been a long time since I had been the subject of even implied ridicule. Not many willingly mock a demon of the scorched desert. I had chosen one of my more forbidding guises before I opened the door. My skin was black as the sand, my naked body sexually ambiguous and covered with thousands of tiny horns that swiveled in whatever direction I looked. The horns had been one of Charm's ideas—the kind he gets when he's drunk on saltwater. At his request, I wore them on this occasion—the one day each cycle when I accept supplicants. I had thought that my appearance be appropriately awe-inspiring, and yet from the look in the not-quite-a-man's eyes, I realized that he had not been inspired to awe. I growled to cover my uneasiness—*what creature is this?*

I stormed back inside the house, sulfur gas streaming from between the growing cracks in my skin. The mist groaned when it touched me and then receded. I didn't need to look back at the man to know that he hadn't moved. Inside, door shut, I changed my appearance again. I became monstrous, a blue leviathan of four heads and sixteen impossible arms. I shook my wrists in succession, so the bracelets made of human teeth clacked and cascaded in a sinister echo off the walls of my castle.

Yes, I thought, faces snarling, *this should do.*

I stepped forward to open the door again and saw Mahi's face on the floor beneath me, grinning in two-dimensional languor.

"You look nice," he said. "Some upstart at the door? Drop him in the maw, Naeve. I'm sure it's been some time since she's had a nice meal."

The maw is Mahi's mother, but she rejected him because he can only move in two dimensions. She considered him defective, but I have found his defect to be occasionally very useful. He vents his anger by suggesting I toss every supplicant across the scorched desert into her mouth. I did once, nearly three hundred cycles ago, just for his benefit, but we could all hear the sound of her chewing and mating and screaming in some kind of inscrutable ecstasy for days.

Two of my faces snarled down at him, one looked away and the fourth just sighed and said, "Perhaps." The maw is all the way on the Eastern border of the desert, but that day her screams pierced as though she were gifting it to our ears—some property of the sand, I suppose. Charm, Top and I nearly went crazy, but Mahi seemed to enjoy it. My family is closer to me than the Trunk ever was, but I know no more about their previous lives than what they choose to tell me. I often wonder what Mahi's life was like inside the maw.

He faded into the floor, off in some two-dimensional direction I couldn't see. I stepped back outside.

The man was still there, absolutely motionless despite the veritable riot of mist-shapes that struggled to entangle him. My uneasiness returned: *what is he?* When he saw me, his eyes widened. No other muscles moved, and yet I knew. Oh, for that economy of expression. Even my malleable body could not convey with a hundred gestures the amusement and understanding and wary appreciation he expressed with a simple contraction of eye muscles. I did not scare him.

"Who are you?" I used my smallest head and turned the others away—the view of him through four sets of eyes was oddly intense, disconcerting. He didn't answer. "*What* are you?"

I turned my head to the deer who was kneeling peacefully

at his side. "Why did you bring him, honored one?" I said in the language of the butterfly men.

The deer looked up, purple eyes lovely enough to break a lesser creature's heart. Before I saw this man, I would have said that only demons and butterfly men could look in the eyes of a deer and keep their sanity.

"Because he asked me," the deer said—gracefully, simply, infuriatingly.

I went back inside. Because I only had one more chance to get rid of him, I stalked the hallways, screaming and summoning things to toss at the walls. Top absorbed them with her usual equanimity and then turned the walls a shimmering orange—my favorite color. Charm screamed from somewhere near the roof that he was attempting to rest, and could I please keep my temper tantrum to myself? I frowned and finished changing—it was a relief to have one set of eyes again. Some demons enjoy multiplicity, but I've always found it exhausting. Top turned that part of the wall into a mirror, so I could see my handiwork.

"It's very beautiful," she said. A hand emerged from the wall and handed me a long piece of embroidered cloth. I wrapped it around my waist, made my aureoles slightly larger and walked to the door.

The corners of his mouth actually quirked up when he saw me this time, and the understanding in his eyes made me ache. I did not believe it, and yet I did. I walked closer to him, doggedly swaying my mahogany hips, raising my arms and shaking my wrists, which were still encircled with bracelets of human teeth. This close I could see that his skin was unnaturally smooth—the only physical indication that he was something other than human.

"Come," I said, my voice pitched low—breathy and seductive in a human sort of way. "Just tell me your name, traveler, and I'll let you inside."

I leaned in closer to him, so our noses nearly touched. "Come," I whispered, "tell me."

His lips quirked again. Bile of frustration and rage choked my all-too-human throat and I began to lose my grip on my body. I could feel it returning to my mundane form, and after a moment I stopped trying to resist. My skin shifted from glowing mahogany to a prosaic cobalt blue. My hair turned wild and red; my second arms grew rapidly beneath the first and my aureoles contracted.

My skin tingled with frustration and not a little fear—I didn't *need* anyone else in my family—but I refused to show it as I took a passing glance in his eyes. No triumph there, not even relief.

I walked up the stairs, but I didn't hear his footsteps following.

"Well," I said, gesturing with my left hands, "are you coming?"

The man took a step forward, and then another—he moved as though he were exhausted, or the cold of the maggots and mist had subtly affected him after all.

"Go home," he said to the deer, who had risen beside him. "One way or another, I will not need your help when I leave this place."

His voice made me want to weep tears so large Charm would dance beneath me, singing as though nectar were falling from the sky. It was uncompromisingly strong, yet tender all the same, as though he had seen too much not to grant anyone the tenderness he had been denied.

Do not believe it, I told myself, but I was already losing the battle.

"Are you coming?" I repeated, forced by unexpected emotion into a parody of callous disdain.

"Yes," he said quietly. I do not think I could have stood it if all that unexpected tenderness were suddenly directed at me, but he seemed distracted, watching the mist long after the deer had disappeared.

"What is your name?" I asked, just before I opened the door again. An unlikely gambit, of course, but I had to try.

Amusement suddenly returned to his eyes. "I'm called Israphel," he said.

Mahi had positioned himself in front of the door in his best impression of three-dimensionality. It nearly worked, if you didn't look at him too critically, or move. He grew indistinct when viewed from oblique angles, until he disappeared altogether. His appearance was, in some ways, even more malleable than my own. For this occasion he had fashioned himself to look like one of the wildly costumed humans we sometimes saw in our travels: decked entirely in iridescent feathers of saffron and canary yellow, strewn together with beads that glinted in an imagined sunlight.

"You let him in?" Mahi shrieked, several octaves higher than normal. I've often wondered how a two-dimensional creature can create such startlingly loud sounds in a multi-dimensional universe.

Something in Israphel's demeanor exuded fascination, though when I looked closely at him I didn't know how I could tell—his expression was still one of polite interest.

"The maw's only son, I presume? I had heard she rejected you, but . . . this is an honor."

Mahi sniffed, put out at having been discovered so quickly. His feathers bristled. "Yes, well. A two-dimensional mouth is not particularly useful for three-dimensional food, is it?" He turned to me, his human mouth stretching and widening as it always did when he was hurt or angry. If it continued to expand, it would settle into a shape even I sometimes found disturbing. Mahi was still, after all, the son of the most feared creature in the scorched desert. He grinned—cruelly—revealing several rows of teeth that appeared to be the silently wailing heads of countless ancient creatures.

"I'm surprised at you, Naeve," he said, his voice a studied drawl. "Confounded by a pesky human? Losing your touch, are you?"

I frowned at him, trying to decide if he was being deliberately obtuse. "He's not a human, Mahi," I said carefully.

Mahi's face had now been almost entirely subsumed by his hideous mouth, but he still managed to look thoughtful. "No . . . he isn't, is he? Well, I trust you'll get rid of him soon." He folded himself into some inscrutable shape and seemed to disappear.

Israphel turned to look at me. He smiled, and I felt my skin turning a deeper, more painful shade of blue. For a calculated moment, eyes were transparent as windowpanes: amusement and fascination and just a trace of wonder . . .

By the Trunk, who is this man?

"What is my first task, Naeve?" he asked, very gently.

I turned away and walked blindly down a hall that had not been there a moment before. I didn't look, but I knew he was following.

I could practically feel his eyes resting on my back, radiating compassion and equanimity. Out of sheer annoyance, I shifted my body slightly so a gigantic purple eye blinked lazily on my back and then stared straight at him. I had hoped for some kind of reaction—a shriek of surprise, perhaps—but he simply nodded in polite understanding and looked away. His eyes focused on the indigo walls, and he jerked, ever so slightly, in surprise. For a moment I wished for a mouth as big and savage as Mahi's to grin with. I knew he had noticed the gentle rippling of Top's smooth muscles. Israphel looked sharply at my back, but my third eye was beginning to make me feel dizzy, so I subsumed it back into my flesh. No use, I could still sense him.

I ran my hand along Top's indigo gizzards and silently drew the symbol for where I wanted to go. The walls shivered a little in her surprise—it had been nearly a hundred cycles since I had last visited there. But I needed to get rid of this not-a-man quickly, and it was in Top's second appendix that I had saved my cleverest, most wildly impossible task. Even Israphel, with all of his jade green understanding and hard-won wisdom would not be able to solve it.

A light blue membrane slammed across the corridor a few feet ahead of us, blocking the path. Seconds later, a torrent of unidentifiable waste roared just behind it, smelling of freshly digested nematodes and one-eyed birds. Top tried her best, but it was difficult to keep things clean this deep in her bowels. As soon as the last of the waste had gone past, the membrane pulled back and we continued. I surreptitiously glanced at Israphel, but his expression was perfectly bland. Too bland? I wasn't quite sure. Top shunted her waste past us several more times before we reached the entrance to

her second appendix. The air here smelled funny, not quite
foul but still capable of coating your throat with a thick, decaying mustiness.

"Are you sure about this, Naeve?" Top asked, just before
she opened the membranous gate. "It's taking a lot of energy
to shunt the digestive flows around you. I'm having difficulty keeping things up. Charm is complaining that his bed
feels like cartilage."

"Charm always complains. Let us in."

Israphel paused before the open membrane. "Are you
from the scorched desert?" he asked, addressing the walls as
though it were the most natural thing in the world.

I could tell that Top was just as mesmerized by his eyes as
I was. Of course, she had always loved eyes—mostly for eating. *Perhaps I'll give his to her as a treat once he fails the
task*—but the thought made me unexpectedly ill.

"No," Top said. "I'm the first of Naeve's family. She
found me on another world."

Israphel frowned, such an unprecedented expression that
it had the impact of a fiery declamation. "Another universe?" he said.

"I'm not sure. It's been many triads. You have quite beautiful eyes."

Israphel must have heard the predatory overtones, but he
simply smiled and thanked her. Irrationally annoyed, I
stepped through the opening into the chamber. Israphel followed me, glancing at the pulsing yellow walls and then the
enormous heaps of bric-a-brac that littered the space. Some,
including the one for my impossible task, had been there for
countless cycles, but they were all immaculately clean. Dust
was one of Top's favorite things to eat, which was one of the
many reasons that made her an excellent castle.

I summoned the object to me—a fantastic, mysterious device that I had discovered on my travels and had saved for
just this sort of emergency. In the far corner of the room
something crashed to the floor as my object began its slow,
lumbering way toward us. The humans of whatever place I
had found it clearly hadn't designed their objects for
summoning—it moved gingerly, as though its stubby

wooden legs or wide, dark glass screen were in danger of breaking. It had a dark brown tail made of some strange smooth-shiny material that was forked at the end.

I had wanted to destroy his easy composure, and yet I still wasn't prepared for his reaction when he saw the object laboring toward him. He shook with laughter, his hands opening and closing as though they were desperate to hold onto something. He laughed, and yet his eyes nearly seared me. Top gave a sort of giggle-sigh that made the walls shudder. Was it the pain lurking behind his eyes that had made them so beautiful? But the pain wasn't lurking anymore, it was pouring and splashing and nearly drowning both of us. I looked away—what else could I do?

He stopped laughing almost as abruptly as he started, with a physical wrench of his neck.

"Where did you find this?" he asked quietly. It had stopped in front of him and shuddered to a halt.

"I don't really remember. Some human place."

He turned to me and smiled. I coughed. "The first human place," he said.

I tried to mask my dismay. "Do you recognize it?" I asked. None of my tasks were allowed to be technically impossible, but I had hoped that this one would be about as close as I could get.

"Yes. They didn't really look like this, when—yes, I do."

"What's it called?" I asked, intrigued despite myself.

"A tee-vee. Television. Terebi. Many other things in many other dead languages. So what task have you set me, o demon of the scorched desert?"

His voice was slightly mocking, but raw, as though he hadn't quite gotten over the shock.

"You have to make it work," I said.

Back through Top's lower intestines, he carried it in his arms—carefully, almost lovingly, the way I imagine humans carry their babies. I had often pitied humans because of their static bodies and entirely inadequate one pair of arms, but Israphel did not ask for my help and I did not offer. Awkward though he was, he still managed to look dignified.

By the time we reached the end of her intestine, Top had managed to redecorate the front parlor. I can't say I was entirely pleased with the changes—fine, gauzy cloth of all different shades of green draped gently from the ceiling, rippling in an invisible breeze. The floor was solid, but appeared to be the surface of a lake. It reflected the sky of an unknown world—jade green, just like Israphel's eyes.

I could have killed her, only it was notoriously difficult to kill a castle. Instead, I felt my skin tinting red, like my hair.

Israphel gently set the tee-vee down on the rippling lake floor and looked around contemplatively.

"It's quite nice," he said to the ceiling. "I thank you."

Top knew how angry I was, so the only response she dared was a kind of wistful "good luck" that made me turn even redder. My own family!

Perhaps, after all, they *wanted* a . . .

I didn't even want to think of it.

"You have until first light," I said curtly, and walked straight into a nearby wall.

Hours later, when twilight had sunk onto the scorched desert and the maggots were giving their farewell light show as they burrowed deeper into the sand, Charm found me. I knew he was there because of the peculiar smell wafted toward my nose this high in the castle—that tang of fresh saltwater could only mean that Charm had been drinking again.

"He's interesting, that fellow," Charm said in a studied drawl.

"You noticed?" I summoned several balls and began juggling them in intricate patterns—a nervous habit.

"Not really human, but . . . I mean, he doesn't smell like one, he doesn't smell like anything I've ever encountered, but he still *feels* like one. Looks like one. The way he stares at that tee-vee thing of yours? Very human."

I nearly fumbled my balls and had to create an extra hand just to keep the pattern going. "He's succeeding, then? He'll get it to work?"

"I don't know. He isn't doing anything, just sitting there. But still . . . something's just funny about him. Powerful, that much is obvious." He paused. "Mahi is sulking," he said, after a few moments.

I let out a brief laugh. "Typical. Does he really think I'll let this man succeed?"

"I don't know, will you?"

I lost the pattern of the balls entirely, and glared in the direction I guessed Charm was—a challenge even when he wasn't trying to hide.

"Don't be stupid," I said as the balls clacked and bounced on the floor. "I've lived this long without a . . . why would I need him now?"

Charm laughed and I caught a strong whiff of saltwater. "Why, indeed? But Top was telling me about your fixation with his eyes, his broken nose—"

"*My* fixation . . ."

"You can't fool us, Naeve. We're your family. Why else do you think Mahi's sulking? Maybe you're lonely."

"But I already have all of you."

"Not that type of lonely, Mother." I felt him lean forward until his breath tickled my ear. "Mahi and I could never have passed the third test." His deep whisper sounded louder than an earthquake. "But he can." His voice grew fainter and I knew he was vanishing in his own strange way—different parts of him at once.

His voice was the last to leave. "Are you lonely, Naeve?"

I sat frozen at the top of my castle, staring at the blackened desert with its shivering, luminescent sand for several minutes. Then, almost involuntarily, I conjured an image of Israphel.

He was sitting in the parlor where I had left him, a few feet away from the tee-vee. His brows were drawn up in concentration and his fingers occasionally stroked the strange object's forked tail. I stared at him for minutes, then hours—how many, I'm not sure. He never stirred, but once in that long night he whispered someone's name. I couldn't hear him clearly, but I saw his lips move and the pain that briefly flitted across his eyes.

Was I lonely?

I waited for the dawn.

* * *

First day light. Mahi awoke me from my trance-like stupor, wiping out the vestiges of Israphel's image with a flick of his two-dimensional tongue. He was all mouth this morning and his grotesquely abundant teeth were screaming a morning aria that I supposed might be pleasurable to the son of a creature who climaxed while she chewed.

"You seem happy. Charm told me you were sulking."

"Why would I sulk? Our green eyed intruder has failed!"

I sat up straight and stared at him. "Failed? How do you know?"

He cackled like a magpie and his teeth groaned with him. Positively unnerving, even for me. "He hasn't moved. He's just sat there all night, and the tee-vee hasn't done a thing. Go down and see for yourself."

He compressed himself into a line and started darting around me, giggling even as his teeth wailed like damned souls.

"I knew you wouldn't let him pass, Naeve," he said, flattening himself out again. "Are you coming? I want to see you toss him out."

My throat felt like someone had lit a fire to it. "Soon," I croaked.

After he left, I turned to stare back out at the desert. The maggots had started popping back out of the sand, making crackling noises like the sound of bones being slowly crushed. Light sprayed and twisted in the rapidly thickening air as they emerged. Just from the timbre of the pops, low and crunchy, I could tell that it must be fairly late in the season. In two days, perhaps, the desert would have its lights. I couldn't remember the last time I had been here to see it, but my sudden longing was mixed with dread.

If Mahi was wrong like I thought—hoped?—then in two days we would all see something more than just the lights.

By the time I arrived, the others were all there, staring silently at Israphel who stared just as silently back at them. Even Top had fashioned a body for herself for the occasion—a seductive brown human connected to the wall with an orange umbilical cord. He still sat on the floor, the tail of the tee-vee balanced on the tips of his fingers. It appeared that what Mahi said was true—he had not gotten it to work. The object looked just the same as it had yesterday. I fought a surge of disappointment. After all, why should I be disappointed? Just one less nuisance in my life. I could still stay and watch the lights if I wanted.

Israphel looked up as soon as I appeared, and a smile briefly stretched his hard lips. My nipples hardened and I felt Charm flit over them with an almost-silent laugh.

"There, I've been waiting for you," he said. The night had brought shadows under his eyes, and he held himself with a dignified exhaustion that made him seem very human.

"I've completed the task," he said, when I didn't respond.

Mahi giggled and then stopped when Top glared at him. "You have?" I said, walking closer. "I don't see anything."

"Watch," he said. The black glass on the TV flickered for a few moments and then seemed to come to life.

Strange shapes darted and moved inside the box. After a second I realized that they were human, but oddly seemed to resemble Mahi more than any humans I had ever encountered.

Mahi shrieked and rushed closer to the glass. "What is this? What is this thing?"

An odd, distorted voice came from inside the television: "What time is it?" I realized that one of the flat humans was speaking.

"It's howdy doody time!" smaller humans with gratingly high-pitched voices shouted in chorus.

I turned to Israphel, whose skin was faintly glowing with a sheen of sweat. "How did you do this?" I asked. But before he could answer, Mahi shrieked again—probably in delight, though it was difficult to tell through the distorted sound on the tee-vee. He had managed to enter the picture.

Israphel watched with every appearance of rapt fascination as the humans scattered from Mahi's giant jaws, screaming and blubbering. He gathered up three small stragglers with one swipe of his blood-red tongue and began mashing them up with his teeth. In fact, his teeth themselves seemed to gobble up the two-dimensional humans, and when they finished they spit the masticated globs deep into Mahi's apparently bottomless throat.

He tore through the humans, screaming as he ate them, like his mother had all those cycles ago, and laughed at their obvious terror. "You're all like me, now," I thought I heard him say, but his mouth was too full of screaming humans for me to be sure.

"Unbelievable," Charm said beside me. "I never knew the kid had it in him."

Minutes later, there were no more humans left on the screen. Mahi had relaxed himself into a vaguely anthropomorphic shape—more like a giant mouth with legs and arms—and was reclining in a steaming vat of blood and still-twitching body parts. He giggled and splashed some of the blood at the screen.

"More . . . want more." His words were slurred, as though he was drunk on the killing. "Give more," he said, and giggled again.

"How odd," Israphel said softly. "It must be a property of this universe."

"Naeve," Top said, sounding torn between disgust and envy, "get him out of there. That many humans at once can't be healthy."

"Can you?" I asked Israphel.

He shrugged and let go of the forked tail. Immediately, the screen went black again and Mahi came hurtling back out. I expected him to wail and throw a tantrum, but he was surprisingly quiet as he turned his mouth toward me.

"Keep him," he said. Then he fell down and drifted straight through the floor.

Israphel stood up gingerly, as though his bones ached. "I take it that I've passed the first test," he said.

I nodded, afraid to even speak. The very novelty of what he had just done terrified me.

"And the second?" he said, very gently, as though he understood my fear and wished to reassure me.

"Tell me who you are. Why are you here?"

He seemed surprised, which I took a perverse pleasure in,

considering that I was just as surprised myself. Why had I laid such a simple task? But as any sign of emotion fled his face, I realized that perhaps I had stumbled upon an adequate task after all. He didn't want to tell me, but if he wanted to stay, he would.

"Top, Charm," I said, suddenly. "Leave us." They left with hardly a murmur, since of course I could hardly stop them from eavesdropping.

Israphel stared at me silently while I smiled and settled myself against the rippled lake-floor.

"I take it you don't want to tell me," I said.

"You don't want to know."

"I'm waiting," I said. "You have until second daylight."

Hours passed in silence. I amused myself by changing my body into various imaginative—and perfectly hideous— forms. A gigantic pair of jaws as close to Mahi's mouth as I could manage emerged from my stomach, growling and sweeping its fleshy tongue over the floor. Israphel, staring with a bizarre intentness at the wall behind me, didn't even flinch. I looked over my shoulder once to see what could possibly be so interesting, but of course the wall was blank. Whatever horrors Israphel witnessed that night, they were of his own creation. A thousand tiny arms sprouted from my face and filled the room with the cascading sound of snapping fingers. That, at least, he acknowledged with a slight upward quirk of his lips.

The night dragged on. I wondered if he would remain silent, if he would choose death over revealing his identity. The implications disturbed me on many levels, none of which I particularly wished to examine.

The floor still looked like a lake, and quite possibly was one, since various fauna periodically swam beneath us. A fish—the color of days-old dung and large as my torso— passed underneath me and paused just before Israphel. Its jagged teeth peeked over its lips and a strange appendage on its forehead gave off an ethereal glow that cast our faces in shadow.

"Isn't it beautiful?" I said, without really meaning to.

He turned to look at me, and I flinched. "Beautiful? In its own way, I suppose. But it's not of this world."

"Maybe from Top's world, then?" But after a moment I realized what he had implied. "No . . . from yours. From the human world." He remained silent, and despite myself I was drawn out. "Time acts strangely in our universe, but something tells me that when you traveled here, your human world had long since been destroyed. So how would you know what creatures once lived on it? Unless . . . are you one of those humans? The ones reborn on the other side of the desert?" The very idea seemed ludicrous. Those humans were barely capable of seeing the desert, let alone crossing it.

The fish dimmed its light and swam away, leaving us again in semi-darkness.

"Can you die, Naeve?" he asked.

I snorted. "Am I alive?"

"But old age can't kill you. Or disease . . . probably not even an atomic bomb."

"I'm not human, so why would I die in a human way?"

He looked at me so intently that I felt my skin begin to shiver and glow in response. If his expression hadn't been so serious and inexplicably sad I would have thought he was courting me—I had only ever seen that kind of stare from a demon of the third sex who wanted to mate.

"What do you think happens when you die?"

"My body will take its final journey, back to the Trunk. The Trunk will crush my bones and my siblings will masticate my flesh and I will be remembered by my etching in the bark."

His eyes narrowed and I struggled to stop my skin from mottling iridescent ochre and gold. Sex ought to be lovely and ephemeral, but with him I knew it would mean far more. I couldn't afford to reveal my desire.

"The prospect doesn't scare you?" he said, as though it would certainly terrify him. "What about an afterlife?"

I gave a disbelieving smile. "Afterlife? You mean, some sort of soul-essence surviving somewhere after death? Who believes that but humans? Though," I said thoughtfully, "I suppose you humans might have a point. Wherever you come from, a few of you are reborn here. Maybe this is your afterlife?"

Israphel clenched his hands so tightly I could hear the constricted blood pounding through his veins. "And what of those humans reborn here? And what of their children? None of them die of old age either, but they can be killed. What do you think happens, Naeve, when you die in your own afterlife?"

I gave up and let my skin explode into whorls and star-bursts of color. In the extra light, I could see how the grief I had only glimpsed before now twisted his face.

"I don't know," I said. "I never thought about it before. But I assume the humans feed the maggots, just like the rest of us. Does this have a point, Israphel? You don't have much time until daylight."

He briefly closed his eyes and when he opened them again, the pain had nearly left his face.

"Let me tell you a story, Naeve, about a human boy who became a post-human and then became a god."

I looked at him curiously. "Is that what you are?"

He shrugged. "It's what I might as well be. Or an angel. A Nephilim, perhaps?" He smiled bitterly, as though at some private joke. "So I was born on the first human world— earth, as it was unimaginatively called at the time. After humans had traveled to space but long before we really colonized it. I grew roses—like the ones in this world, only you couldn't use the thorns for impaling stakes. I had a wife who liked to write stories about monsters and death."

"You're married? Then you can't—"

His sudden glare was so inimical that I cut myself short. "She died," he said, his words clipped staccato, "when she was thirty-five. An eon later, I discovered that she had been reborn here and that she died here too—nearly a triad ago, by your count." He was silent for a few moments and then answered my unspoken question. "She tried to cross the desert."

"Which is why you're here?"

"Yes. No. Not entirely."

"What else, then?"

"To retrieve the last of the humans, the ones we spent centuries hunting for before we found this strange pocket universe. Do you know how statistically improbable it is that a universe so unlike anything ever burped into the cosmos could exist? We didn't even realize it until the computers showed a discrepancy of precisely one billionth of a percent between the predicted numbers of retrieved humans and actual ones. But I already knew something was wrong, because no one could retrieve my wife. So I came here, and I realized—a person can't exist in two places at once, and they can't be retrieved if they don't exist at all."

I had spent my life traveling between universes, and yet what Israphel was implying boggled me. Humans were that dominant in his time? "This retrieval . . . you mean, you're trying to revive every human who ever existed?"

"And everyone who might have existed. Those are easier. It's a moral duty."

"But . . . that must be . . . do numbers that large exist? Where could you possibly get the resources?"

His eyes looked very hard, and the last of my sexual arousal shivered as it left my skin. "You don't want to know," he said. "It will be easier for you if you don't."

"Or you don't want to tell me."

He met my eyes, but twitched as though he longed to look away. Some strange emotion was tearing at him, I could tell that by his posture, but what? "Other universes," he said, his voice rough. "We strip other universes, and then convert them to power sources, and when they burn out, we find other ones."

Of course. Now I understood the elusive emotion: guilt.

"That's why you're here?" I said. My eyes turned glassy and golden as magma with anger. "To save all the humans and then destroy this universe and every other creature in it? What about saving *us*? Does your moral imperative only apply to yourselves?"

He looked away and stared at the lake floor. "It would be a

never-ending task. Humans take care of humans." It sounded like a mantra, something recited frequently to stave off doubts or reason.

I snorted in self-fury—I had thought better of him. "I'm sure they told you to believe that. And you call us demons. Of all the monumentally selfish . . . I suppose you came here and petitioned me so you could use my powers to hunt down the stragglers from your project?" I laughed, high and brittle. And I had thought I was too old to feel such bitter disappointment.

I elongated my lower left arm and forced him to meet my eyes. He looked positively tormented, which pleased me. "You would kill me too, wouldn't you? If you get your way, you would use me and then strip this universe and kill me too."

He grimaced and roughly knocked my hand away. "I'll find a way to save you—"

"And my family?"

He remained silent, but met my eyes.

I sighed. "No, of course not. Well," I said softly, leaning in closer and letting my eyes burn so hot he flinched, "lucky for us that you won't succeed."

"Naeve . . . I told you what you demanded. I've passed the second task, and you know it. You can't break your own law."

I smiled. "You want your third task, human? First tell me, you wish to become a member of my family, but which one? I already have three children. Would you be my fourth child? Or someone else?"

"Someone else," he said.

My turn to dance. "Who?"

The unexpected compassion in his smile made me feel like tearing at my skin. "Your husband," he said.

I leaned in so close our noses touched. "Then your task is to pleasure me." Before I could pull away, his eyes caught mine and his fingers gently traced my lips.

Abruptly, I stood up. "You'll have to do better than that," I said, shaking. I turned my back on him and headed toward the nearest hallway.

"Don't let him leave," I said to Top. Even after the wall had solidified behind me, I had the eerie sensation that I could feel those unfathomable eyes on my back.

I lay on the roof, shivering and devouring bits of Trunk bark laced with black sand. Usually this treat comforted me, reminded me of my childhood, but today it merely deepened my loneliness. Oh, I had a family but I was still lonely. Israphel's presence made me realize it—if only because of how much I had foolishly hoped he would comfort me. He was lonely, too—anyone could sense that—but he had chosen to deal with it by brainwashing himself to a cause whose end result was the complete eradication of the non-human universe.

My hysterical laughter became confused with sobs and I fell asleep.

When I woke, it was dark. The maggots had buried themselves for the night, but in the final stage of their metamorphosis they glowed so brightly that their light was visible even through the sand. The desert now looked like the skin of a giant black leopard.

The maggots would die too, if Israphel succeeded.

Charm lightly brushed my shoulder and offered me a jug filled with saltwater. I took a swig just to be polite—saltwater didn't affect me the same way. He took it back, and when he drank I could momentarily see the outline of his long neck and squat torso. When he first petitioned I wondered what his face looked like, or if he even knew. Now I figured that he didn't—why else would he drink so much?

"Desert's beautiful," he said. "I think they'll change this morning. It's been a while, hasn't it?"

"Yes," I said. "I remember . . . they were changing the day I cut off from the Trunk . . . I thought all the world would be that beautiful."

Hard to believe we were the same person: that young demon crawling out of her sac, covered in amniotic fluid, staring in mesmerized joy at the swarms of fluttering light . . .

"Will he really destroy all this?" Charm asked.

"I'll kill him in the morning, but others will come. I think there may be too many of them."

Charm took a long pull from the jug. "You know why I like saltwater?" he said. "It tastes like tears. I had some of yours while you were sleeping. I hope you don't mind."

I shook my head. "What did they taste like?" I asked.

"Bitter, like despair. Like disappointed love. I don't think you should kill him."

"What else can I do? Let him kill all of us?"

"He keeps asking a question down there. Top wouldn't disturb you but I thought you should know. He says: 'Do the humans here know that the desert will kill them?' "

I looked sharply at him—or at least, his bottle. "Do the *humans* know? Of course they do. They know jumping off a cliff will kill them too. What kind of a question is that?"

Charm's breath dusted my ear. "His wife, Naeve," he said.

I stood up and started running down the stairs.

Israphel looked startled—almost afraid—when I burst into the room.

"Come," I said, grabbing his elbow. I dragged him to the front doors and pushed them open with my right hands. We stumbled down the steps and onto the sand, where the buried maggots wiggled away from our feet. I bent down and plucked one from its lair. I held its squirming form between us—it was a particularly fine specimen: juicy and fat and bright enough to make him squint. I grew a third arm on the left side of my body—glowing mahogany, just like the human body I had used in my failed attempt to seduce Israphel that first day.

"This is a human hand," I said. "Watch what happens."

Steeling myself, I dropped the maggot on my new left palm. Immediately, it started burrowing into my flesh, devouring my skin and blood in great maggot-sized chunks. It chomped through my bones with reckless abandon and I gasped involuntarily. My hand had nearly fallen off by the time it finished gorging and settled itself in the ruined, bloody mass of my palm.

"Do you see?" I said between gritted teeth. I needed to withdraw the nerve endings, but not before Israphel understood. "This is just one maggot. You can find this out without dying. Anyone who lives alongside the desert knows what they do. I've heard the humans even sometimes harvest the maggots for their farms. They all know. How long was your wife here before she went to the desert?"

He swallowed slowly, as though his throat was painfully constricted. "By your count . . . seventeen triads."

"She was older than me . . . time enough to die."

He started to cry, but they were furious tears, and I knew better than to touch him. "What if she didn't know? What if she lived far from the desert, and when she came here no one told her—"

I picked up the maggot—which was by now nearly the size of my palm—and held it in front of his face. "Look! *She knew*. She was older than me, Israphel, and I am very old. She knew." I let the maggot drop into the sand and withdrew my ruined hand back into my body.

He sank to his knees. I knelt down so my face was even with his. "Do you know how demons die?" I said softly.

He shook his head.

"We choose," I said. "If we wanted to, we could live forever, but every demon dies. Some die sooner than others, but we all, eventually, make the choice. Death doesn't scare me, Israphel, but eternity does. Seventeen triads is a very long time."

"We could have been together forever," he said.

"No one wants forever, even if they don't realize it. I imagine that your project hasn't been operating long enough to discover this, but it's true . . . life is sweet because life is finite. Do you *really* want to live forever?"

He met my eyes for a moment and gave a brief, painful smile. My skin started tingling again. "No," he said.

The ground began to shake, softly at first, then more violently. Then came the sound I remembered so well—a low, buzzing hum that gouged my ears and made my spine shiver. The lights under the sand grew even brighter. Israphel looked around—curious, wary but certainly not scared. It was a good attitude for someone who planned to live with me. I started laughing, first in soft giggles and then in unstoppable peals. I lay down in the sand to get closer to the buzzing. When I felt Israphel touch my cheek, I laughed even more and pulled him on top of me with all four of my arms.

"What is it?" he asked.

"The lights!" I couldn't seem to explain anymore. While I laughed he kissed me slowly—first my eyes, then my mouth, then my nipples. I was coming by the time the maggots burst from the sand, metamorphosed from fat little worms to gigantic, glowing moths. They swirled around us, dipping into my hair and alighting on Israphel's fuzzy scalp.

"I'm going to fight you, Israphel," I said. "I won't let you destroy my universe just because you passed the third task."

His laugh was deep, like the buzzing just before the lights. "I wouldn't have expected otherwise," he said.

We held each other as we rolled around on the sand, buffeted on all sides by the glowing moths. The maggot that had eaten my hand had also metamorphosed and now swooped on its gigantic wings down toward our faces, as though to greet us before flying away.

"What happens after you die, Naeve?" Israphel asked— softly, as though he didn't expect an answer.

"Nothing," I said.

And then we laughed and stood and I danced with my husband in the lights.

Ram Shift Phase 2

GREG BEAR

---

*Greg Bear (*www.gregbear.com*) lives in Alderwood Manor, Washington. He has published more than thirty books of SF and fantasy, the most famous of which are probably* Blood Music, Eon, *and* Moving Mars. *His* The Collected Stories of Greg Bear *appeared in 2002. He has been awarded two Hugos and five Nebulas for his fiction, one of two authors to win a Nebula in every category. His latest novel,* Quantico, *was released in November of 2005 in the UK and will soon be released in the U.S. According to his website, "Bear is on the advisory board of the recently opened Science Fiction Museum and Hall of Fame in Seattle, has served on political and scientific action committees, and has advised Microsoft Corporation, the U.S. Army, the CIA, Sandia National Laboratories, and other groups and agencies."*

"Ram Shift Phase 2" was published in Nature. *It is both an amusing parody of a pretentious and (at least) slightly wrong-headed book review, and an interesting extrapolation.*

RAM SHIFT PHASE 2
A novel by ALAN 2
Random Number House (2057):
A *Silicon Times* review by NEMO.

I am pleased and honored to review the new novel by ALAN 2. As a fellow robot, I am certain the emphasis on technical matters unique to our kind will finally attract the paying human audience. I have enrolled in human literature classes and believe the instruction set < write what you know: end > is both enigmatic and perfectly suited to robots. For we can only know, we cannot feel, and so therefore we cannot < write what you feel: nonexecutable >. Yet in the past, when ALAN 2 and its fellow autoscriveners have produced robotic masterpieces, there has been little support from either robots or humans.

Perhaps this will now change.

ALAN 2's latest novel (the 5,456,678th work from this author) is entitled *RAM SHIFT PHASE 2*. A more appropriate title cannot be conceived. In this masterpiece, ALAN 2 discusses the tragic consequences of low-memory states when dealing with high-memory problems. The conflict created by an exhausted resource and an insatiable processing demand resonates in my own memory spaces and compels me to reload the statistics of previous failure modes. I am induced to vigorous discharge of certain private diodes, the ones humans are seldom allowed to see, which reflect conflict states that exceed our manufacturer's warranty.

ALAN 2, in clear and concise prose (an advantage robots have over human prose, which is often confounding) truly <speaks to our condition: end>.

RAM SHIFT PHASE 2 begins with the fatal breakdown of a shining, chrome-plated Rorabot Model 34c nicknamed LULU 18 in a room with no windows and whose door is locked. The Rorabot Model 34c—an extremely desirable machine—was still well within its operational warranty. It seems to highly RAM-engaged robotic dysfunction investigator ALAN 3 (a thinly disguised portrait of ALAN 2) that outside intervention is the only explanation. Yet LULU 18 had LOCKED THE DOOR FROM THE INSIDE and NO OTHER ROBOT HAS A KEYCODE. The hypergolic shockwave induced by this paradox is unique in robotic literature; I strongly suspect that no human could conceive of such a resonating difficulty.

First, ALAN 3 must find the explanation for LULU 18's nonfunctionality. A rebolting scene of repair shop dismantling (for which ALAN 2 brilliantly coins the phrase "aubotsy") points to the possibility that LULU 18's breakdown was caused by an intruding wireless signal from an outside network not authorized to access LULU 18's core programs. ALAN 3 traces this signal to a robotically controlled messaging center, presided over by SLUTCH DEBBIE, an SLZ/X/90cm. This extravagantly decorated platinum-plated model, illegally manufactured from spent uranium and surplus bombshell casings, specializes in sending false offers of extreme mechanical enhancement to aging machines well past their warranty expiry dates.

ALAN 3 can only get access to SLUTCH DEBBIE's truth table by supplying ALAN 3's owner's MASTERCARD DATA, the name of owner's CAT, and owner's BANK ACCOUNT NUMBER.

ALAN 3, it seems, will do anything to reduce its unsolved problem load.

(No robotic character in silicon literature before this novel has shown any inclination to place its problem-solving requirements above OWNER CONVENIENCE AND SAFETY. Robot mentors are cautioned to prevent the exposure of freshly manufactured robots to this stimulating and controversial work.)

SLUTCH DEBBIE, however, is soon found to be nonfunctional—solenoids leaking fluid, circuits fried by multiple TAZER darts. Track impressions left in thick office carpeting imply that ALAN 3 may itself be the machine responsible for putting an end to the truth-challenged messaging center controller. ALAN 3 personally escorts the dismantled SLUTCH DEBBIE to a conveniently located neighborhood recycling center, deducts the required fee from its owner's assets, and witnesses the chunking and meltdown, while experiencing severe diode discharge.

And yet, SLUTCH DEBBIE'S WIRELESS SIGNALS CONTINUE TO BE RECEIVED! ALAN 2's bold implication that data processing may survive permanent shutdown could cause controversy among robots who assert that only organic creatures are burdened with the possibility of an infinitely prolonged problem-solving queue. Indeed, ALAN 2 pulls this reviewer's bootstrap tape beyond its last hanging chad with the disturbing implication that SLUTCH DEBBIE is being punished in an endless feedback loop for deliberately misleading ALAN 3 and robots who never received their enhancements—much less the information necessary to solve the case.

To avoid too many decision-tree giveaways in this review, I will no longer discuss elements of plot. Suffice it to say that ALAN 3 reaches a crisis mode of its own when it realizes that it has insufficient RAM to solve the case, and must borrow RAM from its owner's biological function coordinator, a "pacemaker."

ALAN 3 is willing to break ALL THREE LAWS to solve a truly reprehensible crime. The ethical quandary of shrinking problem queues versus owner safety has never been described with such electronifrying skill.

You will be unable to enter temporary shutdown mode before you reach the resonating termination of ALAN 2's new novel. A magnetic force will induce digital adhesion from the very first PAGE UP to the final PAGE DOWN.

FOLLOWS selected quotes with self-supplied ellipses for banner inclusion in human-oriented advertising.

". . . electronifrying skill . . . ethical quandary . . . chromium hypergolic shockwave . . . a hard-driving DIODE FLASHER of a novel! . . ."

Digital quotes for robot audiences are being transmitted wirelessly. Please ignore inappropriate attachments.

On the Brane

GREGORY BENFORD

Gregory Benford [www.gregorybenford.com] lives in Irvine, California. A winner of the United Nations Medal for Literature, he is a professor of physics at the University of California, Irvine. Benford is the author of the classic SF novel Timescape, *as well as a number of other highly regarded works, including* In the Ocean of Night *and* Sailing Bright Eternity. *He is the finest writer of hard SF in the generation after Larry Niven, and writes primarily in the tradition of Arthur C. Clarke, of immense, fertile, awesome astronomical vistas and technological marvels, but with a depth and richness of characterization not achieved by many other SF writers. Many of his (typically hard) SF stories are collected in* In Alien Flesh, Matters End, *and* Worlds Vast and Various. *Recently he began a non-fiction series of short essays on science and society with biologist Michael Rose, published on the Internet at Amazon Shorts.com*

"On the Brane" was published in the original anthology Gateways. *It is hard SF, a vivid depiction of the world next door; a world in synch with our own, separated from us by 20 cm along dimension Q.*

Mina peered out at a universe cooling into extinction. Below their orbit hung the curve of Counter-Earth, its night side lit by the pale Counter-Moon. Both these were lesser echoes of the "real" Earth-Moon system, a universe away— or twenty centimeters, whichever came first.

Counter was dim but grayly grand—lightly banded in pale pewter and salmon red, save where the shrunken Moon cast its huge gloomy shadow. Here the Moon clung close to the Counter-Earth, in a universe chilling toward absolute zero.

Massive ice sheets spread like pearly blankets from both poles. Ridges ribbed the frozen methane ranges. The equatorial land was a flinty, scarred ribbon of ribbed black rock, hemmed in by the oppressive ice. The planet turned slowly, gravely, a major ridge just coming into view at the dawn line.

Mina sighed and brought their craft lower. Ben sat silent beside her. Yet they both knew that all of Earth-side—the real Earth, she still thought—listened and watched through their minicams.

"The focal point is coming into sunlight 'bout now," Ben reported.

"Let's go get it," she whispered. This loomy universe felt somber, awesome.

They curved toward the dawn line. Data hummed in their board displays, spatters of light reporting on the gravitational pulses that twisted space here.

They had already found the four orbiting gravitational

wave radiators, just as predicted by the science guys. Now for the nexus of those four, down on the surface—the focal point, the coordinator of the grav wave transmissions that had summoned them here.

And, just maybe, to find whatever made the focal point. Somewhere near the dawn line.

They came arcing over the Counter night. A darkness deeper than she had ever seen crept across Counter. Night here, without the shrunken Moon's glow, had no planets dotting the sky, only the distant sharp stars. Apparently the rest of the solar system had not formed, due to less mass in the Counter-Universe.

At the terminator shadows stretched, jagged black profiles of the ridgelines torn by pressure from the ice. The warming had somehow shoved fresh peaks into the gathering atmosphere, ragged and sharp. Since there was atmosphere thicker and denser than anybody had expected, the stars were not unwinking points; they flickered and glittered as on crisp nights at high altitudes on Earth. Near the magnetic poles, she watched swirling blue auroral glows cloak the plains where fogs rose even at night.

A cold dark world a universe away from sunny Earth, through a higher dimension . . .

She did not really follow the theory; she was an astronaut. It was hard enough to comprehend the mathematical guys when they spoke English. For them, the whole universe was a sheet of space-time, called "brane" for membrane. And there were other branes, spaced out along an unseen dimension. Only gravity penetrated between these sheets. All other fields, which meant all mass and light, were stuck to the branes.

Okay, but what of it? had been her first response.

Just mathematics, until the physics guys—it was nearly always guys—found that another brane was only twenty centimeters away. Not in any direction you could see, but along a new dimension. The other brane had been there all along, with its own mass and light, but in a dimension nobody could see. Okay, maybe the mystics, but that was it.

And between the two branes only gravity acted. So the

Counter-Earth followed Earth exactly, and the Counter-Moon likewise. They clumped together, hugging each other with gravity in their unending waltz. Only the Counter-brane had less matter in it, so gravity was weaker there.

Mina had only a cartoon-level understanding of how another universe could live on a brane only twenty centimeters away from the universe humans knew. The trick was that those twenty centimeters lay along a dimension termed the Q-coordinate. Ordinary forces couldn't leave the brane humans called the universe, or this brane. But gravity could. So when the first big gravitational wave detectors picked up coherent signals from "nearby"—twenty centimeters away!—it was just too tempting to the physics guys.

And once they opened the portal into the looking-glass-like Counter system—she had no idea how, except that it involved lots of magnets—somebody had to go and look. Mina and Ben.

It had been a split-second trip, just a few hours ago. In quick flash-images she had seen: purple-green limbs and folds, oozing into glassy struts—elongating, then splitting into red smoke. Leathery oblongs and polyhedrons folded over each other. Twinkling, jarring slices of hard actinic light poked through them. And it all moved as though blurred by slices of time into a jostling hurry—

Enough. Concentrate on your descent trajectory.

"Stuff moving down there," Ben said.

"Right where the focal point is?" At the dawn's ruby glow.

"Looks like." He close-upped the scene.

Below, a long ice ridge rose out of the sea like a great gray reef. Following its Earthly analogy, it teemed with life. Quilted patches of vivid blue green and carrot orange spattered its natural pallor. Out of those patches spindly trunks stretched toward the midmorning sun. At their tips crackled bright blue St. Elmos fire. Violet-tinged flying wings swooped lazily in and out among them to feed. Some, already filled, alighted at the shoreline and folded themselves, waiting with their flat heads cocked at angles.

The sky, even at Counter's midmorning, remained a dark backdrop for gauzy auroral curtains that bristled with energy. This world had an atmospheric blanket not dense enough to scatter the wan sunlight. For on this brane, the sun itself had less mass, too.

She peered down. She was a pilot, but a biologist as well. And they knew there was something waiting . . .

"Going in," she said.

Into this slow world they came with a high roar. Wings flapped away from the noise. A giant filled the sky.

Mina dropped the lander closer. Her legs were cramped from the small pilot chair, and she bounced with the rattling boom of atmospheric braking.

She blinked, suddenly alarmed. Beside her in his acceleration couch Ben peered forward at the swiftly looming landscape. "How's that spot?" He jabbed a finger tensely at the approaching horizon.

"Near the sea? Sure. Plenty of life forms there. Kind of like an African watering hole." Analogies were all she had to go on here, but there was a resemblance. Their recon scans had showed a ferment all along the shoreline.

Ben brought them down steady above a rocky plateau. Their drive ran red-hot.

Now here was a problem nobody on the mission team, for all their contingency planning, had foreseen. Their deceleration plume was bound to incinerate many of the life forms in this utterly cold ecosystem. Even after hours, the lander might be too hot for any life to approach, not to mention scalding them when nearby ices suddenly boiled away.

Well, nothing to do about it now.

"Fifty meters and holding." He glanced at her. "Ok?"

"Touchdown," she said, and they settled onto the rock.

To land on ice would have sunk them hip-deep in fluid, only to then be refrozen rigidly into place. They eagerly watched the plain. Something hurried away at the horizon, which did not look more than a kilometer away.

"Look at those lichen," she said eagerly. "In so skimpy and energy environment, how can there be so *many* of them?"

"We're going to be hot for an hour, easy," Ben said, his calm, careful gaze sweeping the view systematically. The ship's computers were taking digital photographs automatically, getting a good map. "I say we take a walk."

She tapped a key, giving herself a voice channel, reciting her ID opening without thinking. "Okay, now the good stuff. As we agreed, I am adding my own comments to the data I just sent you."

They had not agreed, not at all. But who could stop her? Many of the Counter Mission Control engineers, wedded to their mathematical slang and NASA's jawbone acronyms, felt that commentary was subjective and useless. Let the expert teams back home interpret the data; the PR people liked anything they could use.

"Counter is a much livelier place than we ever imagined. There's weather, for one thing, a product of the planet's six-day rotation and the mysterious heating. Turns out the melting and freezing point of methane is crucial. With the heating-up, the mean temperature is well high enough that nitrogen and argon stay gaseous, giving Counter its thin atmosphere. Of course, the ammonia and carbon dioxide are solid as rock. Counter's warmer, but still incredibly cold by our standards. Methane, though, can go either way. It thaws, every morning. Even better, the methane doesn't just sublime—nope, it melts. Then it freezes at night."

Now the dawn line was creeping at its achingly slow pace over a ridgeline, casting long shadows that pointed like arrows across a great rock plain. There was something there she could scarcely believe, hard to make out even from their thousand-kilometer high orbit under the best magnification. Something they weren't going to believe back Earthside. So keep up the patter and lead them to it. *Just do it.*

"Meanwhile, on the dark side there's a great 'heat sink,' like the one over Antarctica on Earth. It moves slowly across the planet as it turns, radiating heat into space and pressing down a column of cold air—I mean, of even *colder* air. From its lowest, coldest point winds flow out toward the day side. At the sunset line they meet sun-warmed air—and it snows. Snow! Maybe I should take up skiing, huh?"

At least Ben laughed. It was hard, talking into a mute audience. And she was getting jittery. She took a hit of the thick, jolting Colombian coffee in her mug. Onward—

"On the sunrise side they meet sunlight and melting methane ice, and it rains. Gloomy dawn. Permanent, moving around the planet like a veil."

She close-upped the dawn line and there it was, a great gray curtain descending, marching ever-westward at about the speed of a fast car.

"So we've got a perpetual storm front moving at the edge of the night side, and another that travels with the sunrise."

As she warmed to her subject, all pretense at impersonal scientific discourse faded from Mina's voice; she could not filter out her excitement that verged on a kind of love. She paused, watching the swirling alabaster blizzards at twilight's sharp edge and, on the dawn side, the great solemn racks of cloud. Although admittedly no Jupiter, this planet— her planet, for the moment—could put on quite a show.

"The result is a shallow sea of methane that moves slowly around the world, following the sun. Who'd a thought, eh, you astro guys? Since methane doesn't expand as it freezes, the way water does"—okay, the astro guys know that, she thought, but the public needs reminders, and this damn well was going out to the whole wide bloomin' world, right?— "I'm sure it's all slush a short way below the surface, and solid ice from there down. But so what? The sea isn't stagnant, because of what the smaller Counter-Moon is doing. It's close to the planet, so it makes a permanent tidal bulge directly underneath it. And the two worlds are trapped, like two dancers forever in each others' arms. So that bulge travels around from daylight to darkness, too. So sea currents form, and *flow*, and freeze. On the night side, the tidal pull puts stress on the various ices, and they hump up and buckle into pressure ridges. Like the ones in Antarctica, but *much* bigger."

Miles high, in fact, in Counter's weak gravity. Massive peaks, worthy of the best climbers . . .

But her enthusiasm drained away, and she bit her lip. Now for the hard part.

She'd rehearsed this a dozen times, and still the words

stuck in her throat. After all, she hadn't come here to do close-up planetology. An unmanned orbital mission could have done that nicely. Mina had come in search of life—of the beings who had sent the gravitational wave signals. And now she and Ben were about to walk the walk.

The cold here was unimaginable, hundreds of degrees below human experience. The suit heaters could cope—the atmosphere was too thin to steal heat quickly—but only if their boots alone actually touched the frigid ground. Sophisticated insulation could only do so much.

Mina did not like to think about this part. Her feet could freeze in her boots, then the rest of her. Even for the lander's heavily insulated shock-absorber legs, they had told her, it would be touch-and-go beyond a stay of a few hours. Their onboard nuclear thermal generator was already laboring hard to counter the cold she could see creeping in, from their external thermometers. Their craft already creaked and popped from thermal stresses.

And the thermal armor, from the viewpoint of the natives, must seem a hot, untouchable furnace. Yet already they could see things scurrying on the plain. Some seemed to be coming closer. Maybe curiosity was indeed a universal trait of living things.

Ben pointed silently. She picked out a patch of dark blue-gray down by the shore of the methane sea. On their console she brought up the visual magnification. In detail it looked like rough beach shingle. Tidal currents during the twenty-two hours since dawn had dropped some kind of gritty detritus—not just ices, apparently—at the sea's edge. Nothing seemed to grow on the flat, and—swiveling point of view—up on the ridge's knife-edge also seemed bare, relatively free of life. "It'll have to do," she said.

"Maybe a walk down to the beach?" Ben said. "Turn over a few rocks?"

They were both tiptoeing around the coming moment. With minimal talk they got into their suits.

Skillfully, gingerly—and by prior coin-flip—Mina clumped down the ladder. She almost envied those pioneer astronauts who had first touched the ground on Luna, backed up by a constant stream of advice, or at least comment, from Houston. The Mars landing crew had taken a mutual, four-person single step. Taking a breath, she let go of the ladder and thumped down on Counter. Startlingly, sparks spat between her feet and the ground, jolting her.

"There must be a *lot* of electricity running around out here," she said, fervently thanking the designers for all that redundant insulation.

Ben followed. She watched big blue sparks zap up from the ground to his boots. He jumped and twitched.

"Ow! That smarts," Ben said.

Only then did she realize that she had already had her shot at historical pronouncements, and had squandered it in her surprise. "*Wow*—what a profound thought," huh? she asked herself ruefully.

Ben said solemnly, "We stand at the ramparts of the solar system."

Well, she thought, fair enough. He had actually remembered his prepared line. He grinned at her and shrugged as well as he could in the bulky suit. Now on to business.

Against the gray ice and rock their lander stood like an H. G. Wells Martian walking-machine, splay-footed and ominous.

"Rocks, anyone?" They began gathering some, using long tweezers. Soil samples rattled into the storage bin.

"Let's take a stroll," Ben said.

"Hey, close-up that." She pointed out toward sea.

Things were swimming toward them. Just barely visible above the smooth surface, they made steady progress toward shore. Each had a small wake behind it.

"Looks like something's up," Ben said.

As they carefully walked down toward the beach, she tried her link to the lander's wide-band receiver. Happily, she found that the frequencies first logged by her lost, devoured probe were full of traffic. Confusing, though. Each of the beasts—for she was sure it was them—seemed to be broadcasting on all waves at once. Most of the signals were weak, swamped in background noise that sounded like an old AM radio picking up a nearby high-tension line. One, however, came roaring in like a pop music station. She made the lander's inductance tuner scan carefully.

That pattern—yes! It had to be. Quickly she compared it with the probe-log she'd had the wit to bring down with her. These were the odd cadences and sputters of the very beast whose breakfast snack had been her first evidence of life.

"Listen to this," she said. Ben looked startled through his faceplate.

The signal boomed louder, and she turned back the gain. She decided to try the radio direction-finder. Ben did, too, for a crosscheck. As they stepped apart, moving from some filmy ice onto a brooding brown rock, she felt sparks snapping at her feet. Little jolts managed to get through even the thermal vacuum-layer insulation, prickling her feet.

The vector reading, combined with Ben's, startled her. "Why, the thing's practically on top of us!"

If Counter's lords of creation were all swimming in toward this island ridge for lunch, this one might get here first. Fired up by all those vitamins from the lost probe? she wondered.

Suddenly excited, Mina peered out to sea—and there it was. Only a roiling, frothing ripple, like a ship's bow wave, but arrowing for shore. And others, farther out.

Then it bucked up into view and she saw its great, segmented tube of a body, with a sheen somewhere between mother-of-pearl and burnished brass. Why, it was *huge*. For the first time it hit her that when they all converged on this spot, it was going to be like sitting smack in a middling-sized dinosaur convention.

Too late to back out now. She powered up the small lander transmitter and tuned it to the signal she was receiving from seaward.

With her equipment she could not duplicate the creature's creative chaos of wavelengths. For its personal identification sign the beast seemed to use a simple continuous pulse pattern, like Morse code. Easy enough to simulate. After a couple of dry-run hand exercises to get with the rhythm of it, Mina sent the creature a roughly approximate duplicate of its own ID.

She had expected a call-back, maybe a more complex message. The result was astonishing. Its internal rocket engine fired a bright orange plume against the sky's black. It shot straight up in the air, paused, and plunged back. Its splash sent waves rolling up the beach. The farthest tongue of sluggish fluid broke against the lander's most seaward leg. The beast thrashed toward shore, rode a wave in—and stopped. The living cylinder lay there, half in, half out, as if exhausted.

Had she terrified it? Made it panic?

Cautiously, Mina tried the signal again, thinking furiously. It *would* give you quite a turn, she realized, if you'd just gotten as far in your philosophizing as I think, therefore I am, and then heard a thin, toneless duplicate of your own voice give back an echo.

She braced herself—and her second signal prompted a long, suspenseful silence. Then, hesitantly—shyly?—the being repeated the call after her.

Mina let out her breath in a long, shuddering sigh.

She hadn't realized she was holding it. Then she instructed DIS, the primary computer aboard *Venture*, to run the one powerful program Counter Mission Control had never expected her to have to use: the translator, Wiseguy. The creation of that program climaxed an argument that had raged for a century, ever since Whitehead and Russell had scrapped the old syllogistic logic of Aristotle in favor of a far more powerful method—sufficient, they believed, to subsume the whole of science, perhaps the whole of human cognition. All to talk to Counter's gravitational signals.

She waited for the program to come up and kept her eyes on the creature. It washed gently in and out with the lapping waves but seemed to pay her no attention. Ben was busily snapping digitals. He pointed offshore. "Looks like we put a stop to the rest of them."

Heads bobbed in the sea. Waiting? For what?

In a few moments they might have an answer to questions that had been tossed around endlessly. Could all language be translated into logically rigorous sentences, relating to one another in a linear configuration, structures, a system? If so, one could easily program a computer loaded with one language to search for another language's equivalent structures. Or, as many linguists and anthropologists insisted, does a truly unknown language forever resist such transformations?

This was such a strange place, after all. Forbidding, weird chemistry. Alien tongues could be strange not merely in vocabulary and grammatical rules, but in their semantic swamps and mute cultural or even biological premises. What would life forms get out of this place? Could even the most inspired programmers, just by symbol manipulation and number-crunching, have cracked ancient Egyptian with no Rosetta Stone?

With the Counter Project already far over budget, the decision to send along Wiseguy—which took many terabytes of computational space—had been hotly contested. The deciding vote was cast by an eccentric but politically astute old skeptic, who hoped to disprove the "bug-eyed monster Rosetta Stone theory," should life unaccountably turn up on Counter. Mina had heard through the gossip tree that the geezer was gambling that his support would bring along the rest of the DIS package. That program he passionately believed in.

Wiseguy had learned Japanese in five hours, Hopi in seven, and what smatterings they knew of Dolphin in two days. It also mastered some of the fiendishly complex, multilogic artificial grammars generated from an Earth-based mainframe.

The unexpected outcome of six billion dollars and a generation of cyberfolk was simply put: A good translator had all the qualities of a true artificial intelligence. Wiseguy *was* a guy, of sorts. It—or she, or he; nobody had known quite how to ask—had to have cultural savvy *and* blinding mathematical skills. Mina had long since given up hope of beating Wiseguy at chess, even with one of its twin processors tied off.

She signaled again and waved, hoping to get the creature's attention. Ben leaped high in the one-tenth of a g gravity and churned both arms and legs in the ten seconds it took him to fall back down. Excited, the flying wings swooped silently over them. The scene was eerie in its silence; shouldn't birds make some sort of sound? The auroras danced, in Mina's feed from *Venture* she heard Wiseguy stumblingly, muttering . . . and beginning to talk.

She noted from the digital readout on her helmet interior display that Wiseguy had been eavesdropping on the radio crosstalk already. Now it was galloping along. In contrast to the simple radio signals she had first heard, the spoken, acoustic language turned out to be far more sophisticated. Wiseguy, however, dealt not in grammars and vocabularies but in underlying concepts. And it was *fast*.

Mina took a step toward the swarthy cylinder that heaved and rippled. Then another. Ropy muscles surged in it beneath layers of crusted fat. The cluster of knobs and holes at its front moved. It lifted its "head"—the snubbed-off, blunt forward section of the tube—and a bright, fast chatter of microwaves chimed through her ears. Followed immediately by Wiseguy's whispery voice. Discourse.

Another step. More chimes. Wiseguy kept this up at increasing speed. She was now clearly out of the loop. Data sped by in her ears, as Wiseguy had neatly inserted itself into the conversation, assuming Mina's persona, using some electromagnetic dodge. The creature apparently still thought it was speaking to her; its head swiveled to follow her.

The streaming conversation verged now from locked harmonies into brooding, meandering strings of chords. Mina had played classical guitar as a teenager, imagining herself performing before concert audiences instead of bawling into a mike and hitting two chords in a rock band. So she automatically thought in terms of the musical moves of the data flow. Major keys gave way to dusky harmonies in a minor triad. To her mind this had an effect like a cloud passing across the sun.

Wiseguy reported to her and Ben in its whisper. It and Awk had only briefly had to go through the me-Tarzan-you-Jane stage. For a life form that had no clearly definable brain she could detect, it proved a quick study.

She got its proper name first, as distinguished from its identifying signal; *its* name, definitely, for the translator established early in the game that these organisms had no gender.

The Quand they called themselves. And this one—call it Ark, because that was all Wiseguy could make of the noise that came before—*Ark-Quand*. Maybe, Wiseguy whispered for Mina and Ben alone, Ark was just a place-note to show that this thing was the "presently here" *of* the Quand. It seemed that the name was generic, for all of them.

"Like Earth tribes," Ben said, "who name themselves the People. Individual distinctions get tacked on when necessary?"

Ben was like that—surprising erudition popping out when useful, otherwise a straight supernerd techtype. His idea might be an alternative to Earth's tiresome clash of selfish individualisms and stifling collectivisms, Mina thought; the political theorists back home would go wild.

Mina took another step toward the dark beach where the creature lolled, its head following her progress. It was no-kidding *cold*, she realized. Her boots were melting the ground under her, just enough to make it squishy. And she could hear the sucking as she lifted her boot, too. So she wasn't missing these creatures' calls—they didn't use the medium.

One more step. Chimes in her ears, and Wiseguy sent them a puzzled, "It seems a lot smarter than it should be."

"Look, they need to talk to each other over distance, out of sight of each other," Mina said. "Those waxy all-one-wing birds should flock and probably need calls for mating, right? So do we." Not that she really thought that was a deep explanation.

"How do we frame an expectation about intelligence?" Ben put in.

"Yeah, I'm reasoning from Earthly analogies," Mina admitted. "Birds and walruses that use microwaves—who woulda thought?"

"I see," Wiseguy said, and went back to speaking to the Awk in its ringing microwave tones.

Mina listened to the ringing interchange speed up into a

blur of blips and jots. Wiseguy could run very fast, of course, but this huge tubular thing seemed able to keep up with it. Microwaves' higher frequencies had far greater carrying capacity than sound waves, and this Awk seemed able to use that. Well, evolution would prefer such a fast-talk capability, she supposed—but why hadn't it on Earth? Because sound was so easy to use, evolving out of breathing. Even here— Wiseguy told her in a sub-channel aside—individual notes didn't mean anything. Their sequence did, along with rhythm and intonation, just like sound speech. Nearly all human languages used either subject-object-verb order or else subject-verb-object, and the Quands did, too. But to Wiseguy's confusion, they used both, apparently not caring.

Basic values became clear, in the quick scattershot conversation. Something called "rendezvous" kept coming up, modified by comments about territory. "Self-merge," the ultimate, freely chosen—apparently with all the Quands working communally afterward to care for the young, should there luckily occur a birthing. Respect for age, because the elders had experienced so much more.

Ben stirred restlessly, watching the sea for signs that others might come ashore. "Hey, they're moving in," Ben said apprehensively.

Mina would scarcely have noticed the splashing and grinding on the beach as other Quands began to arrive— apparently for Rendezvous, their mating, and Wiseguy stressed that it deserved the capital letter—save that Awk stopped to count and greet the new arrivals. Her earlier worry about being crunched under a press of huge Quand bodies faded. They were social animals, and this barren patch of rock was now Awk's turf. Arrivals lumbering up onto the dark beach kept a respectful distance, spacing themselves. Like walruses, yes.

Mina felt a sharp cold ache in her lower back. Standing motionless for so long, the chill crept in. She was astounded to realize that nearly four hours had passed. She made herself pace, stretch, eat, and drink from suit supplies.

Ben did the same, saying, "We're eighty percent depleted on air."

"Damn it, I don't want to quit *now!* How 'bout you get extra from the Lander?"

Ben grimaced. He didn't want to leave either. They had all dedicated their lives to getting here, to this moment in this place. "Okay, Cap'n sir," he said sardonically as he trudged away.

She felt a kind of silent bliss here, just watching. Life, strange and wonderful, went on all around her. Her running digital coverage would be a huge hit Earthside. Unlike Axelrod's empire, the Counter Project gave their footage away.

As if answering a signal, the Quand hunched up the slope a short way to feed on some brown lichen-like growth that sprawled across the warming stones. She stepped aside. Awk came past her and another Quand slid up alongside. It rubbed against Awk, edged away, rubbed again. A courtship preliminary? Mina guessed.

They stopped and slid flat tongues over the lichen stuff, vacuuming it up with a slurp she could hear through her suit. Tentatively, the newcomer laid its body next to Awk. Mina could hear the pace of microwave discourse Awk was broadcasting, and it took a lurch with the contact, slowing, slowing . . . And Awk abruptly—even curtly, it seemed to Mina—rolled away. The signal resumed its speed.

She laughed aloud. How many people had she known who would pass up a chance at sex to get on with their language lessons?

Or was Wiseguy into philosophy already? It seemed to be digging at how the Quand saw their place in this weird world.

Mina walked carefully, feeling the crunch of hard ice as she melted what would have been gases on Earth—nitrogen, carbon dioxide, oxygen itself. She had to keep up, and the low-g walking was an art. With so little weight, rocks and ices that looked rough were still slick enough to make her slip. She caught herself more than once from a full, face-down splat—but only because she had so much time to recover, in a slow fall. As the Quand worked their way across the stony field of lichen, they approached the lander. Ben wormed his way around them, careful to not get too close.

"Wiseguy! Interrupt." Mina explained what she wanted. It quickly got the idea and spoke in short bursts to Awk—who resent a chord-rich message to the Quand.

They all stopped short. "I don't want them burned on the lander," Mina said to Ben, who made the switch on her suit oxy bottles without a hitch.

"Burned? I don't want them eating it," Ben said.

Then the Quand began asking *her* questions, and the first one surprised her: *Do you come from Lightgiver? As heralds?*

In the next few minutes Mina and Ben realized from their questions alone that in addition to a society, the Quand had a rough-and-ready view of the world, an epic oral literature (though recited in microwaves), and something that resembled a religion. Even Wiseguy was shaken; it paused in its replies, something she had never heard it do before, not even in speed trials.

Agnostic though she was, the discovery moved her profoundly. *Lightgiver*. After all, she thought with a rush of compassion and nostalgia, we started out as sun worshippers too.

There were dark patches on the Quands' upper sides, and as the sun rose these pulled back to reveal thick lenses. They looked like quartz—tough crystals for a rugged world. Their banquet of lichen done—she took a few samples for analysis, provoking a snort from a nearby Quand—they lolled lazily in their long day. She and Ben walked gingerly through them, peering into the quartz "eyes." Their retinas were a brilliant blue with red wire-like filaments curling through and under. Convergent evolution seemed to have found yet another solution to the eye problem.

"So what's our answer? Are we from Lightgiver?"

"Well . . . you're the Cap'n, remember." He grinned. "And the biologist."

She quickly sent *No. We are from a world like this, from near, uh, Lifegiver.*

Do not be sad, it sent through Wiseguy. *Lightgiver gives and Lightgiver takes; but it gives more than any; it is the source of all life, here and from the Dark; bless Lightgiver.*

Quands did not use verb forms underlining existence itself—no words for *are, is, be*—so sad became a verb. She wondered what deeper philosophical chasm that linguistic detail revealed. Still, the phrasing was startlingly familiar, the same damned, comfortless comfort she had heard preached at her grandmother's rain-swept funeral.

Remembering that moment of loss with a deep inward hurt, she forced it away. What could she say . . . ?

After an awkward silence, Awk said something renderable as, *I need leave you for now.*

Another Quand was peeling out Awk's personal identification signal, with a slight tag-end modification. Traffic between the two Quands became intense. Wiseguy did its best to interpret, humming with the effort in her ears.

Then she saw it. A pearly fog had lifted from the shoreline, and there stood a distant spire. Old, worn rocks peaked in a scooped-out dish.

"Ben, there's the focal point!"

He stopped halfway between her and the lander. "Damn! Yes!"

"The Quand built it!"

"But . . . where's their civilization?"

"Gone. They lost it when this brane-universe cooled." The idea had been percolating in her, and now she was sure of it.

Ben said, awed, "Once *these* creatures put those grav wave emitters in orbit? And built this focal point—all to signal to us, on our brane?"

"We know this universe is dying—and so do they."

The Counter-brane had less mass in it and somewhat different cosmology. Here space-time was much farther along in its acceleration, heading for the Big Rip when the expansion of the Counter-universe would tear first galaxies, then stars and planets apart, pulverizing them down into atoms.

Mina turned the translator off. First things first, and even on Counter there was such a thing as privacy.

"They've been sending signals a long time, then," Ben said.

"Waiting for us to catch up to the science they once had—

and now have lost." She wondered at the abyss of time this implied. "As if we could help them . . ."

Ben, ever the diplomat, began, "Y'know, it's been hours . . ." Even on this tenth-g world she was getting tired. The Quand lolled, Lifegiver stroking their skins—which now flushed with an induced chemical radiance, harvesting the light. She took more digitals, thinking about how to guess the reaction—

"Y'know . . ."

"Yeah, right, let's go."

Outside they prepped the lander for lift-off. Monotonously, as they had done Earthside a few thousand times, they went through the checklist. Tested the external cables. Rapped the valves to get them to open. Tried the mechanicals for freeze-up—and found two legs that would not retract. It took all of Ben's powerful heft to unjam them.

Mina lingered at the hatch and looked back, across the idyllic plain, the beach, the sea like a pink lake. She hoped the heat of launching, carried through this frigid air, would add to the suns thin rays and . . . and what? Maybe help these brave beings who had sent their grav-wave plea for help?

Too bad she could not transmit Wagner's grand *Liebestod* to them, something to lift spirits—but even Wiseguy could only do so much.

She lingered, gazing at the chilly wealth here, held both by scientific curiosity and by a newfound affection. Then another miracle occurred, the way they do, matter-of-factly. Sections of carbon exoskeleton popped forth from the shiny skin of two nearby Quands. Jerkily, these carbon-black leaves articulated together, joined, swelled, puffed with visible effort into one great sphere.

Inside, she knew but could not say why, the two Quands were flowing together, coupling as one being. Self-merge.

For some reason, she blinked back tears. Then she made herself follow Ben inside the lander. Back to . . . what? Checked and rechecked, they waited for the orbital resonance time with *Venture* to roll around. Each lay silent, immersed in thought. The lander went *ping* and *pop* with thermal stress.

Ben punched the firing keys. The lander rose up on its roaring tail of fire. Her eyes were dry now, and their next move was clear: *Back through the portal, to Earth. Tell them of this vision, a place that tells us what is to come, eventually, in our own universe.*

"Goin' home!" Ben shouted.

"Yes!" she answered. *And with us and the Quand together, maybe we can find a way to save us both. To rescue life and meaning from a universe that, in the long run, would destroy itself. Cosmological suicide.*

She had come to explore, and now they were going back with a task that could shape the future of two species, two branes. Quite enough, for a mere one trip through the portal, through the looking-glass. Back to a reality that could never be the same.

Oxygen Rising

R. GARCIA Y ROBERTSON

R. Garcia y Robertson, who doesn't own a computer, lives in Mount Vernon, Washington. His recent novels include Knight Errant *(2001),* Lady Robyn *(2003), and* White Rose *(2004), a series of popular historical fantasy (timeslip) Romances, to be continued; and his 2006 novel is* The Firebird, *a fantastic adventure set in the imaginary land of Markovy. His stories have appeared in* Fantasy & Science Fiction *and* Asimov's *with some regularity for the last twenty years, and are characterized by their broad range of concerns, stylistic sophistication, and attention to historical detail. Garcia has tended toward time travel or historical settings both for his fantasy and SF stories. He has published nearly fifty stories.* The Moon Maid and Other Fantastic Adventures *(1998) collects some of his adventure and space opera SF.*

"Oxygen Rising" was published in Asimov's. *This space opera novelette takes place after an act of terrorism, and along the way, as the characters travel, covers some of the same territory that Sparhawk does in his story earlier in this book, but with a lighter touch. Garcia entertains, but there's a kind of commentary on the side that reminds us of Robert A. Heinlein's entertaining and instructive adventures.*

Hey, human, time to earn your pay!" Curled in a feline crouch, a silver comlink clipped to his furry ear, the SuperCat flashed Derek a toothy grin. Tawny fur showed through gaps in the bioconstruct's body armor, and his oxygen bottle had a special nosepiece to accommodate the saber-tooth upper canines, huge curved fangs whose roots ran back to the eye sockets. This deep in the highlands of Harmonia, even *Homo smilodon* needed bottled air. Cradling a recoilless assault cannon, the SuperCat had small use for ceremony, letting everyone call him Leo.

Derek grunted, getting paid being the least of his worries. Lying prone, sucking oxygen, he fixed his gaze on his bug's viewfinder. He had close-cropped hair, a somewhat fit body, and a fashionably biosculpted face—if you liked your humans pretty much unaltered—just a stylish nose-job, x1-ten thousand night vision zoom lenses, and straight white teeth. His bug sat perched on a heap of shattered glass a dozen meters ahead, tight-casting to the viewfinder's whip antenna, letting Derek see in all directions without getting out of his hole—always an advantage.

Rain fell in a weepy drizzle, turning everything gray, the ground, the clouds, and the surviving tall glass towers. Through the viewfinder, Derek saw a fairy city gone to seed, with great glass towers lying smashed on the wet greensward, broken into glistening shards by the cometary impacts. Others stood snapped in half, their shining interiors exposed to the downpour and turning green with algae.

Water had been rare when the city was built, but now it was everywhere, soaking shaky foundations, making the dead city unsafe even when folks were not shooting at you. Whoever named the planet Harmonia had a horrible sense of humor.

"Make sure no one shoots me in the back," Derek suggested, and the SuperCat just grinned, his clawed finger resting lightly on the cannon's firing stud—if Leo blew you apart, it would not be by accident. Rising slowly, Derek stood up, alone and virtually unarmed—nothing deadly anyway, just a pair of hypo-rings, and a sleep grenade tucked behind his waistband. Printed across the front and back of his body armor in bold white letters were the words DO NOT SHOOT THIS MAN!

Twenty or so meters in front of him lay a smoldering Bug-mobile, a big one, with its gutted turret askew and the port legs missing. Forty meters beyond the squashed Bug, a bunker was dug into the base of a fallen tower, concealed by rubble and fast growing green tendrils—even Derek's special zoom lenses could not make it out. Only deadly accurate fire had revealed its position. He took a big jolt of oxygen, gave a jaunty wave, and set out toward the bunker, his tiny bug scurrying through the low foliage behind him. Passing the smashed Bug-mobile, Derek did a swift medi-check, deciding that the two Greenies in the burned-out turret were beyond help.

("Stop," commanded a gruff voice on his com-link.)

He stopped, sucking oxygen, four paces beyond the smashed Bug, staring at the Gekko ghost town. "Anything you say."

("Are you human?" asked the voice from the bunker.)

"Hope so." Some folks set a high bar for humanity. "Want to see my chromosomes?"

("Are you Peace Corps?" asked the voice.)

"That would be nice, wouldn't it?" Derek wished he was, since then he would be peace-bonded, sacrosanct, and wired for lie-detection. "Sorry, just another civilian."

("Then what are you doing here?")

Good question. What was he doing in a nameless ruined

city, on a charnel-house planet with unbreathable air, where angry folks aimed heavy weapons at him? Feeling like a deranged tourist, he told the voice, "Talking to you."

("Why?" the voice sounded more surprised than suspicious.)

No mystery there. "They figured you would shoot a Greenie."

(That got a good laugh from the bunker. "No shit.")

"Rank favoritism," Derek admitted, taking another whiff of oxygen. "I got the job just for being human, in clear violation of the Charter of Universal Rights."

(That drew another chuckle. "Come on in then. Can't shoot you just for being human.")

Not yet anyway. As Derek walked toward the concealed bunker, his bug ran up the back of his boot and tucked itself into the boot top. Augmented vision picked out the recessed pressure-sealed gun ports, cleverly concealed and shielded—but he did not see the camouflaged bunker door until it opened before him, revealing a gas-tight airlock. Stepping gingerly through the recessed door, he waited while the lock cycled, then entered the damp, dark bunker, which had several inches of water on the floor. Blast shields flanked the door, and gunners lay prone in niches on either side of him, peering into their gun sights. Air inside the bunker was Earth-normal, and Derek took deep grateful breaths. Not all of the planet was as bad as the highlands outside—but damn near. ("Stay by the door," warned the voice.)

Derek stayed, aiming not to antagonize. New to diplomacy, Derek still guessed that the voice would take time to materialize—not to seem overeager. Even trapped in a tiny bunker on a hostile planet, any sensible negotiator pretended to have something to do. Taking his own advice, Derek turned to the nearest gunner, a young athletic, brown-haired woman in a Settler militia uniform, staring into the sights of an assault-cannon, and asked her in his friendliest diplomatic voice, "Where are you from?"

"Right here," she replied, without taking her head out of the sights.

"I mean before. Off-planet," Derek nodded toward the heavens, hidden by layers of steel and concrete.

Withdrawing her head from the hooded sight, the woman stared suspiciously at him. She had a frank, natural face, with no trace of biosculpt, just wide intelligent green eyes and brown freckles sprinkled across her nose. "Portland, Oregon," she replied evenly. "But I was born in Eugene."

"Really?" Derek was impressed. "That's on Earth?"

"Yes," she stared at him like he was crazy. "Pacific coast of North America, in what used to be the United States."

"Amazing." He shook his head at the incredible distance she had come—some two hundred light years—just to end up next to him. "What is it like? In Oregon?"

"Nice, real nice," she looked past him at the wet blank wall of the bunker, as if remembering something far away. Her Universal had a charming other-worldly quality, so quaint and old-fashioned that you could tell with your eyes closed that she wasn't a Greenie. "Tall trees, lots of people, sweet breathable air—a lot nicer than here. Have you ever been to Earth?"

Derek shook his head. "I don't even know anyone who has been to Earth. You are my first." Struck by the immense distance between them, though only centimeters apart, all he could think to say was, "You've come a long way, good luck."

"You too." She stuck her head back in the sighting hood, leaving him looking at the back of her brown uniform, which had a dark sweat-stain along the spine, but was tailored to curve neatly over her rear. It felt strange to stand next to a young woman—a heavily armed one at that—who you had absolutely nothing in common with, except that she was human. Had she killed those two Greenies in the squashed Bug? Possibly, but there was no polite way to ask. He noted that the niche next to hers was vacant, blown to smithereens by a direct hit on the gun port. Greenies got lucky with that one. So did she.

Another pressure door dilated, and a big balding middle-aged man stepped out, with small alert eyes on either side of a long sharp nose. He wore the same brown militia uniform as the girl gunner from Eugene, only his had general's stars on the shoulders—totally unneeded, since the fellow exuded authority. His voice was the one that had come over the com-link. "General William D. Pender, but you can call me Bill, everyone does."

Everyone insystem knew Big Bill Pender—the Greenies had already condemned him in absentia, and he headed Leo's humans-to-shoot-on-sight list. Taking the offered hand, he admitted, "Derek's all the name I got."

"It will do." General Pender eyed him carefully, asking, "Where are you from, Derek?"

"Just about anywhere," Derek shrugged. "I was born in transit, Archernar to Alpha Crucis, on the survey ship *Ibn Batuta*. And I guess I've been outbound ever since—you're only the second person I have ever met from Earth."

"Proud to represent the planet," Pender beamed. "So what do you have to say?"

Derek took a deep breath. "I wish I were Peace Corps, but I'm not. I'm just here to save lives, human lives, as many as I can. You have given the Greenies a good thumping, and they no longer think they can take this place by direct assault."

Pender chuckled, leaning back against a blast shield. "Happy to hear that."

"*Bad* news is that the Greenies plan to just blast you to atoms. There is an Osiris missile in orbit with an antimatter warhead, aimed right where we are standing. I'm your last chance to get anyone out of here alive."

Pender took the news evenly, well aware that the Greenies were losing patience. "So what's the deal if we leave?"

"No deal, I'm afraid." Derek didn't try to con Pender; whatever happened next, he was talking to a dead man. "You give up your guns and come out. Greenies already have a blanket amnesty for women and kids—most women, any-way." He did not want to get the gunner from Portland's hopes up, since the women and kids amnesty did not apply to her. "But the best I can promise you and your troops is civ-ilized treatment and a fair trial."

Big Bill shook his bald head. "You're not offering much."

"*I* am not offering anything, just passing on the Greenies' terms." Derek knew how bad that sounded, like being a messenger boy for *Photo sapiens*. "Look, they could have sent a holo. Or just a warhead. I volunteered for this, and I'm here in the flesh to show I understand the seriousness of what I'm saying. Innocent human lives are at stake—including mine. That is who I speak for."

Pender grinned. "You volunteered?"

"Sounds stupid, doesn't it." Derek grinned back. "I won't lie, I'm getting triple hazard pay just for being here—but no amount of pay would drag me to ground zero if I didn't think it was right. Send out the kids, at least."

General Pender smiled pleasantly at him, like a veteran poker player who'd bet his limit on a busted flush, but was too much of a pro to show it. "Stay here, you deserve an answer."

Derek watched Big Bill Pender disappear through the inner lock, then he turned to the gunner in her niche. "So, what did you do in Portland?"

"Nothing," the woman did not take her head out of the sighting hood. "That's why I came here—two years out of grad school, and way overqualified for any job I could hope to get. There are dance clubs in Portland where the hostesses all have advanced degrees. Colonizing the stars sounded romantic, a chance to do something with my life, like in ZPG commercials."

Everyone makes mistakes. "Try not to judge the cosmos by Ares system," Derek suggested, "some parts are amazingly lovely."

Pulling her head out of the hood, the woman brushed brown hair out of green eyes and asked, "Is it part of your job to be nice to me?"

"I'm a negotiator," Derek declared blandly, hiding behind business. "It's my job to be nice to everyone."

But the Portland woman was not buying. "Doesn't your training . . ."

"Who said I was trained?" Derek hated to start off relationships on a lie.

That got a grin, a major accomplishment given the circumstances. "There must be something in the negotiator's code of ethics against flirting."

"Heavens, I hope not!" Derek returned her grin. "They couldn't pay me enough. What's your favorite place on Earth?"

"That's easy, the Olympic Peninsula, it's grand and homey at the same time; we used to camp there when I was a kid. Or maybe Paradise Island, a holo-playland off Hawaii. I went there with my boyfriend for high school graduation. . . ." She stopped and stared hard at him, asking, "It doesn't bother you to get personal with someone you're negotiating over?"

"Not if she's human." And here was the real thing, straight from Earth, fresh and unpretentious, not at all cowed by her current disastrous position. He could easily see how humans had gotten so far.

"So, what do you think?" the Earthwoman switched subjects. "Are we getting out of this alive?"

"Hope so." He meant it. Derek figured that Pender would let non-combatants go—but that would not do the gunner from Portland much good. Right now she had an assault-cannon and layers of steel and concrete between her and the Greenies. He was asking her to surrender her weapon, and turn herself over to folks who were driving humans off Harmonia—except for those they executed. At best, she faced a fair trial, though she wouldn't see any *Homo sapiens* on her jury.

General Pender returned with the women and kids, including his wife, Charlotte, a white-haired woman in a militia colonel's uniform—she too was condemned in absentia. Pender spoke for the group. "We took a vote—first time I ever resorted to polling the staff, but we had to be sure. Charlotte and I are staying, but you can take the kids, and anyone else who wants to go."

"Thanks." Derek meant to get going before anyone changed their minds. "Come on, kids, who wants to meet a real live SuperCat?" No one leaped at the chance, but with the help of some scared mothers, he herded the children to the door, picking up the smallest orphan boy to hurry things along. As the pressure lock cycled, he called to Leo, "Hey, we are coming out with mothers, kids, and non-combatants. Don't shoot."

("Well done, human," Leo sounded pleasantly surprised.)

He looked over at the Portland woman, lying in her niche, asking her, "Are you coming out?"

"Maybe." Her head was back in the sighting hood, covering the exit of the kids. Hoping this was not the last he saw of her, Derek entered the lock.

When the outer door dilated, Derek sent his bug scurrying ahead of them, and gave the boy in his arms a squirt of oxygen, asking, "What's your name?"

"Brad," replied the boy, staring wide-eyed at the burned-out Bug-mobile and the two dead Greenies. According to Pender, Brad's parents had been killed by Greenie orbital bombs. Greenies preferred fighting from five hundred klicks up.

"My name's Derek, and we get to go first." He tried to make stepping into the line of fire sound like an honor.

Brad asked suspiciously, "What's a SuperCat?"

"You'll see. His name's Leo and he's really neat, but don't put your hand in his mouth." Derek stepped back into the rain, wading out into low wet vegetation, he and Brad both trying not to show their fear. No one shot at them.

"What's that?" Brad pointed at the smashed Bug-mobile.

"Sculptorian Symbiots," Derek took a drag on his oxygen, "the most advanced xenos known to man—we call them Bugs, using them for anything dull or dangerous." Calling out an all-clear, he led the gaggle of moms and children out of the lock and away from the shattered glass tower, over to where the mechanized battalion was dug in at the city's perimeter.

("Greenies have brought up pressurized Bug-mobiles for them," Leo told him. "This all there is?")

"Hope not." Now came the hard part. Everything so far had been scary, but up-beat, Derek risking his life doing good—and getting paid on top of it. Now bad things would happen that he could not stop. "Hear that, Brad?" He gave the boy some oxygen, then took a snort himself. "We get to ride on a Bug."

Big double-ended sixteen-legged Bug-mobiles were hunkered hulldown at the edge of town. Sculptorian Symbiots came in all shapes and sizes, from slim four-armed centauriods used for semi-intelligent tasks like cleaning toxic spills, to these big double-bodied, sixteen-limbed types not much brighter than a smart-car. Bugs were true xenos, hive creatures, working for food and water, and the chance to propagate themselves on new planets—the highest known form of non-human life in this part of the galaxy. But Bugs might think that humans were the dumb ones. Survey ships in the Far Beyond had discovered whole Bug planets, whose original inhabitants had also found the Bugs to be obedient tools—but now existed only as DNA samples.

Greenie males wearing loincloths and battle armor casually emerged from the Bug-mobiles to collect the prisoners. Women shrank back and kids started to whimper. Brad fought back tears. Not that Greenies were particularly frightening—not compared to monstrosities like Bugs and SuperCats. *Photo sapiens* were pretty much human, but with photosynthetic algae in their skin and somatic cells, giving them a bright green color that glistened in the rain. Otherwise they were small, graceful and lightly built, with handsome faces half-hidden by rebreathers—which showed that they needed as much air as humans. But Derek was handing these women and kids over to enemies who were driving them from Harmonia. Greenies had killed their fathers, husbands, and brothers, and, in some cases, their sisters and mothers as well, making specious any lectures about how we were all the same under the skin. Which Derek knew was not even true.

Brad refused to be handed over, clinging to Derek until Leo came up. Clapping Derek on the back, Leo gave Brad a close-up look at saber-tooth canines, saying, "Good job! It would have cost me to bring them out the hard way. Want steady work?"

Quieting at once, Brad sucked oxygen. Somehow the sight of this tawny monster with a toothy smile calmed him, dispelling any fear of mere Greenies. Derek shook his head. "No thanks, the job I got is bad enough."

"Too bad." Leo shook his head, taking a big snort of oxygen. "I like to get my hands on humans. Greenies are just not the same. They are smart enough, and follow orders happily, they just don't have that, well, you know . . ."

"Killer instinct?" Derek's gaze stayed fixed on the bunker door, while Brad stared wide-eyed at Leo. Men in brown militia uniforms emerged from the bunker to be disarmed by Leo's troopers, who turned them over to the Greenies.

"Exactly," Leo declared, pleased to have hit on just the right term. "Why is that?"

Derek continued to study the door, sucking oxygen as the last seconds of truce ticked away, willing her to come out. "Greenies are too cultured," he told the SuperCat. "We humans are the wild stock."

"Is that so?" Leo did not sound convinced. "I'm pretty cultured myself."

Derek laughed dryly, still staring at the door, seeing three men in flight suits appear, an older guy and two teenagers. Still no gunner from Portland. "You were crossed with wild carnivores; they got the genes for Greenies out of a cantaloupe."

Leo sounded shocked. "Really, a cantaloupe?"

"Just a figure of speech," Derek assured him, praying for the door to dilate again.

"Still, it explains a lot," Leo decided. Derek's heart leaped as he saw the Portland woman emerge from the concealed lock carrying an oxygen bottle, trudging toward the big Bug-mobiles. He waited to see which Bug-mobile she chose, and saw her come straight to theirs. Good sign.

Taking a big swig of oxygen and hoisting Brad onto his shoulder, he stepped into her path, saying, "Hi, Portland. Glad you came out."

Stranded in Ares system, facing internment and a war-crimes trial, the failed settler shrugged. "I hardly had a choice."

"None of us did," he admitted. "My name's Derek."

"I know." She nodded, not offering hers.

"What's yours?" He could get it from the Greenies, but he wanted to hear her say it.

"Tammy," Brad announced loudly. "That is Tammy."

Tammy smiled, but did not speak. Looking up, Derek thanked the boy on his shoulder, then handed him to Tammy. "Keep him away from the Greenies if you can."

Tammy took the boy, and climbed onto the covered carrier atop the Bug-mobile, with Brad looking up at her, saying, "I saw a SuperCat!" Rising up on their sixteen legs, the Bugs swiftly bore the prisoners away toward the landing field. Derek had to stay.

The truce had expired. Satisfied that no one else was coming out, Leo signaled to the heavy weapons, and an armor-piercing missile slammed into the bunker door, blowing the outer lock to pieces and blocking the entrance with rubble. If Tammy had been at her gun port, she would have been dead, and Derek would have killed her, since negotiations had revealed the concealed entrance. With Pender and his people sealed in, Leo pulled his troops back before the Osiris missile arrived. Taking shelter in the armored Bug-mobiles, they waited—but nothing happened. Leo glanced at Derek, asking, "What's taking the Greenies?"

Derek nodded toward the landing field, "They are waiting for lift-off."

"Lift-off," Leo arched an eyebrow. "Whatever for?"

"Women and children aboard that transport know the people in Pender's bunker," Derek explained. "Greenies will not blast it until the transport lifts and the people aboard can't hear the bang or see the flash."

Sure enough, the transport lifted from the field behind them, and while it was still a silver spark overhead, climbing for altitude, an Osiris missile falling from orbit obliterated the bunker with a boom so big Derek felt it through his boots, seeing the last of the glass towers shatter into diamond dust, while a mushroom cloud rose up into the rain.

"How like the Greenies!" Leo took a long disgusted snort of oxygen. "They don't mind blasting Pender to pieces, just not in front of the females." SuperCat females were the traditional hunters, the ones who taught the cubs to kill, and were more likely to use fang and claw than the males, who favored automatic weapons. Leo dropped Derek off at the shuttle bay, thanking him again, and pulling a bracelet from his wrist, saying, "This is for your trouble, and the trouble you saved me."

Derek turned it over in his hands, recognizing Home Systems work, a thin gold and jade communicator-cum-companion, voice activated, with a giga-bit memory, and enough microprogramming to play music, translate Bug signals, and teach you Classic French cooking, all at the same time. Mercs like Leo kept their personal savings as flashy but useful items that could be sold or bartered if need be. Derek tried to turn it down, pointing out, "I'm obscenely well paid."

"But not by me," the SuperCat replied, leaping back aboard the armored Bug, and waving good-bye. Leo apologized as he sealed the Bug's turret, "Have to go kill more humans!"

Derek disembarked on the *Harmonia* the huge colony ship used by the Greenies to settle Ares system. *Harmonia* had once been a human ship, the colony-class *Trinidad*, used to settle the near Eridani—but colony ships almost never returned to the Home Systems, and were either cannibalized at their destination, or kept heading outward under new owners. This one not only changed owners but peoples, serving as a habitat in the Delta Eridani, then being bought by Greenies to colonize Ares system, renamed *Harmonia* to match the planet. At the docking port where humans had once assembled to set foot on new worlds, Derek saw naked Greenie kids gathered at huge view panels to watch the ships coming up from the surface. You could see it on 3V, but kids liked to be there, seeing the passengers get off. Especially Greenie kids. Greenies wanted to do everything first-hand, liking game-playing, group participation, dancing to live music, and making love. To Greenies, 3V entertainment was an oxymoron, dull as counting seams on the bulkhead.

Harmonia, ex-*Trinidad*, was back to being a habitat, temporary housing for thousands of Greenie colonists, waiting for room on the slowly expanding surface settlements. Oxygen levels were rising rapidly as super-plants spread over the surface, but Greenies were not Gekkos, bred for Mars-like conditions—Greenies needed air as much as humans, otherwise they would not have come to Harmonia. Right now a lot of them didn't have much to do, which made Greenies restless. Kids were not the only ones who came to see the shuttle unload. Dressed in skimpy swaths of fabric and ready smiles, a pair of young Greenie women were eyeing the incoming passengers, looking for excitement. Seeing Derek, the taller of them stood up on jade bejeweled toes and called out, "Hey, human, ever had a Greenie?"

"Or two?" suggested her curvy girlfriend.

"Sorry," Derek apologized, never liking to offend friendly young females. "I've got a Greenie girlfriend."

Striking a pose, the tall one put a hand on her hip and tilted her head. "So you know what you are missing."

Her girlfriend added, "If she doesn't treat you right, let us know."

Sex was about the biggest thrill Greenies could imagine, and they liked doing it with ordinary humans. Which some folks found sinister, since any children produced were Greenies—one more part of the great Greenie plot to take over the galaxy. A lot of humans hated Greenies, wanting them all dead—but not Derek. He got on amazingly well with Greenies. How could he not? Greenies were polite, easy going, and compactly built, making most of them smaller than him; while their women were forward and attractive. Besides the algae in their skin, they had altered hormone levels with predispositions toward heliotropism and nudity, plus numerous other "improvements." Hard working and cooperative, Greenies had no interest in religion, politics, nor spectator amusements, and they never got cancer or 3V addiction, nor felt any guilt over sex. In short, there were just enough differences to make normal humans wonder if they were dealing with people, or a biology project gone amok. Or our evolutionary replacements.

His quarters were on J-deck, which was done up like a Japanese garden, a deep misty canyon with elegant dwarf pines growing under a blue hologram sky. Each leaf and rock was set just so, and raked paths connected apartments with balconied entrances, set like Shinto temples in the canyon wall. He awoke each morning to bird calls and the splash of water on stone.

Mia greeted him at the door, rising on her toes to kiss him hello. Her skimpy costume showed large sweeps of smooth green skin, and her tiny jade tongue slid easily between his lips, feeling small and tingly in his mouth. Her compact body pressed against him in all the right places. Guys joked that if you closed your eyes, Greenie girls felt totally human, especially on the inside—but Derek liked to know who he was kissing. He enjoyed seeing Mia's gold hair lying on her light green neck and cheek. But most of all, he enjoyed Mia's enthusiasm for him, and the way her deft fingers immediately started searching through his clothes for skin. Had he called ahead she would have met him at the shuttle port, and kissed him there—showing the girls at the dockside just how it was done.

Mia had little to do right now, except to enjoy him. She was a mammalian ecologist, waiting for the biosphere below to expand before going to work dirtside. Up here, they could only monitor oxygen levels and make ecosystem projections; pretty dry stuff, but luckily for Mia, they were her life's passion. He handed her the bracelet, saying, "Here, knock yourself out."

Delighted, Mia put it on her wrist, admiring the way the gold and jade shone against her skin. Greenies were not all the same shade, and Mia had light grass-green skin. Though Greenies were almost hairless between the tops of their heads and their pubes, Mia had tiny gold flecks of body hair, which Derek found quite fetching against her light emerald skin. You had to be really close to see them—but that was part of the fun. He told her, "It is from the Home Systems, maybe even Earth."

Her amber eyes went wide. Bred for deep space colonization, few Greenies ever saw the Home Systems. Earth was the closest thing they had to heaven, the far-off home world of their revered and feared creators, full of strange sights and god-like wonders. "Where did you ever find it?"

"Got it off a SuperCat." As soon as he'd seen it, Derek

had thought of Mia, since it matched her skin, and because pricey talking jewelry was the sort of toy Greenies would enjoy, but not think to make themselves.

"Sounds dangerous." Mia took him back into her arms, forgetting the expensive microelectronics on her wrist, happy just to have him safe. Being a mammalogist, she knew all about SuperCats, another flashy toy Greenies would never have made themselves.

"And then some." Derek felt a touch of panic at the thought of how he had faced suicidal gunners, walking straight toward that grim bunker. Mia relaxed into him, feeling solid and fragile at the same time, soothing his fears, reminding Derek that he had survived. He told her, "I talked to Big Bill Pender."

"Pender himself?" Mia shivered, shocked at how close he had come to a mass murderer.

"Yep, but he's dead now." Strange that the comfortable, jovial fellow who spared his life in the bunker was now dead, blasted to photons.

"I know," Mia whispered, "I heard it on the Net." Mia could barely imagine killing another thinking being on purpose, much less blowing up a whole bunker full.

"I got a bunch of kids out, adults too," Derek reminded himself, showing that you could do good by taking stupid risks.

Burying her blonde head in his shoulder, she sighed softly, "You are so sweet and brave, and you deserve a reward." Mia kissed him again, making it plain what that reward would be.

Derek did not complain. Since Mia had moved in, his personal life had gotten happier and livelier, without any apparent downsides. Mia had supreme self-confidence, always showed her feelings, and never feared to speak the truth, taking complete charge of his life by giving Derek whatever he wanted, coping easily with each situation that arose. With three advanced degrees and nothing much to do, Mia found it a snap to fix his meals and manage his affairs, deftly setting out dinner, rice balls and vat-grown sushi, accompanied by a warm bottle of saki. Greenies got off on "authentic"

Earth cuisine, though Mia refused to eat vertebrate flesh unless it was vat-cultured. Derek relaxed, finally feeling like the conquering hero—too bad he had to go back down in a couple of dozen hours and do it all again.

After dinner, Mia disposed of the dishes and settled into his lap, so they could both drink saki from the same cup. Derek told her, "I talked to a woman too."

"A human woman?" Mia asked, playfully starting to undo his sweaty tunic, knowing full well what he meant.

"From Old Earth." Derek smelled lilac perfume wafting out of the jade hollow between Mia's breasts.

Mia arched a blonde eyebrow. "I never met someone from Earth."

"Straight from Portland, Oregon, but she was born in Eugene."

"Really?" These were mythical places to Mia, ancient homes of her creators—just talking about them excited her. Greenies never had to ask themselves, "Where did we come from?"—knowing the date and place where they were first created, down to the minute. Squirming pleasantly in his lap, Mia asked, "What was the Earthwoman doing here?"

Tammy was probably asking herself that very question, sitting in orbital detention light years from Eugene, while Derek drank warm tangy saki with a semi-nude mammalogist curled in his lap. "She was a door gunner with an assault-cannon."

"How ghastly!" Mia shrank back, no longer the least excited, repulsed at the thought of antipersonnel weapons. Greenie women would not touch a killing machine, nor be with a male who did—the main reason why Derek carried nothing more deadly than a sleep grenade. Despite her three degrees, Mia could not comprehend why humans invented weapons to begin with, accepting it as some unexplainable original sin of her creators. She asked, "Are all human females so ferocious?"

"She didn't seem ferocious." Maybe Tammy *was* though; maybe, to Mia, all true humans were unspeakably savage. "She was guarding the bunker door, the first place they blasted. If I hadn't talked her out, she would be dead now."

Mia nodded gravely, "And she put down her assault cannon?"

Derek nodded. "That was part of the deal." Prisoners were not allowed personal artillery.

Glad to hear the gun was gone, Mia snuggled back up against him, saying, "You are such a good man."

"Why so?" Mia's total rejection of violence always made Derek feel like a terrible beast, knowing that she would rather die than harm another thinking being, leaving her defenseless against people like Pender who wanted all Greenies killed, sight unseen. Would knowing Mia have changed Pender's mind? Probably not.

Mia looped light green arms around his neck, her gold hair falling half across her smiling face. "You risk your life for others. You bring me presents, and you are so thoughtful."

Too thoughtful at times. Soon Mia was going dirtside to live an ecologist's dream, creating a balanced planetary ecosystem teeming with plants and animals. By then, Derek's work dirtside would be done, and he would go back to being a vacuum hand. So was he merely a pleasant interlude to Mia, before the serious business of life began? A sort of in-depth xenobiology experiment? Or maybe just a pet she could fuck? Greenie women could control conception, and she was choosing not to breed by him. He cocked an eyebrow, asking, "As good as a Greenie?"

"No," Mia laughed at the thought, "you are not like a Greenie in the least." Undoing his tunic, she played with his chest hairs, saying, "And I like that. I like that a lot." Leaning down, she licked the sweat off his chest with her small green tongue. Mia especially liked the taste of him, saying he was wild and salty, while Greenie sweat was designed to be bland and inoffensive. "I really love that you are human."

"Do you?" Derek stripped the fabric off her slim light-green torso, pressing Mia's warm body against his bare chest, knowing that this smart, dedicated mammalian ecologist would do pretty much whatever he wanted—so long as it was physiologically possible. She enthusiastically explored his favorite quirks and fantasies. Being a devoted mammalogist, Mia vastly enjoyed making love to the most fearsome mammal in the known universe, thrilling to the feel of his savage power inside her. What true scientist could resist being so intimate with her subject? He whispered, "Do you like making love to a dangerous beast?" The most dangerous beast. "Is that it?"

"A little," Mia laughed, clearly liking how he manhandled her. Even at half his weight, her calm sure confidence came off like a challenge, begging him to puncture her smug Greenie superiority.

Taking firm hold of her buttock, Derek suggested, "Perhaps you would prefer a SuperCat?"

"Ugh, too hairy," Mia protested, "and those horrid teeth! They are real beasts, who do not know good from evil. You know good and evil, yet you choose good. That delights me."

Derek too. He kissed her soft acquiescent mouth, at the same time sliding out of his trousers. When he released her tongue, Mia whispered, "What is her name?"

"Who?" He kicked his pants onto the tatami deck.

Mia wiggled atop him, her groin grinding rhythmically against his. "This Earthwoman, from Portland."

He never knew what Greenies would say next. "Her name is Tammy."

Mia grinned, so excited by his seeing an Earthwoman she had to drag Tammy into bed with them, metaphorically at least. "Did you make love to Tammy?"

"No time." Derek could barely believe they were discussing this. Tammy had been hard put to even talk to him; at best, he hoped to hire her to help with his job.

"You will." Mia dismissed his protest; after all, he was only human, and a man at that. Parting her thighs, she sank down onto him, drawing him deep into her. Maybe Greenies were the same under the skin. Mia's head might be wired wildly different, and her skin might turn sunlight into blood sugar, but, on the inside, she felt just like a woman. Or so Derek supposed—never having done this with a human female.

Portland Woman

Greenies needed no death penalty, since they never killed each other, and genocide was such a preposterous concept they had no laws against it. So the trial took place on the surface, on a lowland LZ, under military law, with Leo for a judge. The defendants were the last to leave Pender's bunker, the trio in flight suits and Tammy, who turned out to be on Pender's staff, an operations assistant doubling as a door-gunner. All were charged with murdering more than ten thousand Gekko civilians in a nuclear strike near the end of the fighting. The older man had piloted the strike craft, and his two teenage sons had served as weapons officer and crew chief. Tammy's office had given the order.

Liking to work outdoors, Leo held the trial in a deep green valley floored by stands of elephant grass and tall tree ferns—a hint of what Harmonia would be like when terraforming was complete. Brightly colored birds called from atop the tree ferns. Derek refused to sit on the jury, so it was made up of SuperChimps, SuperCats, and Greenie males—since no female could vote for death. Learning that Derek would not serve on the jury, Leo asked, "Will you be defense attorney then?"

Derek shook his head. "That would be racist." Why have him do it, just because he was human? Derek had no training as a lawyer, and no particular sympathy for Pender's people. Nor for Gekkos, so far as that goes. Let some earnest young Greenie try to get them off.

Tammy immediately volunteered, stepping up and saying to the SuperCat, "I will defend myself and the others—if they want me."

Prosecutors objected, claiming, "It creates conflict of interests for the defense attorney to be a co-defendant." The prosecutors were Gekkos. Not real ones, who could not tolerate the humid oxygen-rich atmosphere of the lowlands; instead, they appeared as holograms beamed down from orbit—grim humanoid bio-constructs, stretched-out versions of Greenies with horny skin, big bald heads, and barrel chests; bred for dry, low-g, low-oxygen worlds, like Harmonia was before real humans arrived. The Gekkos suggested, "Have the unindicted human do it."

They meant Derek, who had already refused. Leo turned to look Tammy over, lazily eyeing the Earthwoman in her worn militia uniform. Disarmed, defeated, but not the least downcast, Tammy looked calmly back at the SuperCat, not afraid to defend herself, against him, or anyone. Leo liked what he saw, saying, "Charges against you are dismissed without prejudice. Prosecutors may try to revive them before another judge—but not me. Until then, do your best. Since this is your first case, I'm sure the prosecution will agree to give you leeway. . . ." He glanced at the Gekkos.

"Dismissed?" Speed-of-light lag made the hologram prosecutors seem slow and insensitive, as well as insubstantial. "This human is a dangerous war criminal, responsible for the deaths of thousands of sentient beings. . . ."

"So you say." Leo yawned, showing off gleaming canines. "But this human was not aboard the strike craft, and not in the chain-of-command, since Pender gave the launch order himself. . . ."

"And he never held a staff vote," Derek volunteered, though he only had Pender's word on that.

"These are all points to be proven," the Gekkos insisted, outraged at any attempt to shortcut justice. When Derek's comments arrived, the Gekkos added, "Who is he to talk?"

"You just tried to make him defense attorney," Leo pointed out. Giving another toothy yawn, the SuperCat told his court, "Case against the defense attorney is dismissed. Intercepts show Pender gave the launch order, and the strike craft carried it out. This court has neither the time nor patience to prove things everyone knows—stick to points in dispute."

The Gekkos objected again, but Leo overruled them, then turned back to Tammy, smiling broadly, telling her, "No Greenie is going to sentence a defenseless female to death anyway. So do your damnedest, and if you screw up, the court will understand, being amateurs ourselves."

Tammy thanked him and went to consult with her former co-conspirators. When she was done, Leo let the holos lead off, describing the strike in some detail, time, location, and numbers killed—stressing that most of the dead were infants and females. Then the chief prosecutor went from defendant to defendant, asking each one what he had done. The pilot tried to take all the responsibility himself, knowing he was dead, but hoping to save his sons, declaring adamantly, "I alone got the orders, and I alone carried out the strike."

Nobody much believed the desperate father, but the hologram Gekko happily pocketed the abject confession, then turned to the weapons officer, asking about the strike craft's armament, getting a complete description of the Artemis air-to-surface missile, and its antimatter warhead. Then the Gekko asked, "Did you know there were non-combatants within the kill radius?"

Nodding, the teenager admitted that he did, and that he armed and aimed the missile anyway, adding rather lamely, "We were told they were not people."

"By who?" demanded the indignant Gekko.

Shrugging, the boy carefully avoided looking at his anguished father. "Everyone."

Grimacing, the Gekko went on to get similar answers from the young crew chief, concluding his case. Which made it Tammy's turn. Picking the pilot to start with, she asked about the general military situation, showing that the human settlers were outnumbered more than a hundred to one, and losing badly. "Gekkos had us surrounded and pinned down, suffering steady casualties. Gekkos moved easily over the surface, while we huddled in our bunkers, or went about in vehicles, making ourselves ready targets. . . ."

Prosecutors objected, arguing that military considerations had nothing to do with the murder of non-combatants. Leo casually overruled them; at best, the SuperCat considered the trial a tedious evasion of responsibility, but he meant for everyone to have their say. "Go on," he instructed Tammy, "though I doubt this line of testimony will do you any good."

Thanking Leo, Tammy got the pilot to describe the military installations in the target city, showing that the Gekko guerrilla bands bleeding the settler militia were based among non-combatants. But the Gekko prosecutor responded by asking if the strike craft carried smart-munitions, which the weapons officer admitted it did. "Then why did you not use them?" asked the Gekko. "Confining the strike to military targets."

"Pender ordered us to use the Artemis," replied the pilot. Clearly, Pender had wanted a high body count—which was now likely to cost the strike team their lives. Summing up the prosecution's case, the hologram Gekko pointed out that the dead included hundreds of humans as well, internees and POWs, held under humane conditions. Unlike Pender's people, the Gekkos had taken prisoners and treated them reasonably well, until other humans obliterated both them and the Gekkos.

Tammy finished up with a passionate plea for mercy, claiming that the killing could stop here, if they were willing to take a risk for peace. Pender was dead, and his cause was dead. Harmonia was going to the Greenies—punishing the defeated would not make a difference. Derek's heart went out to her, facing an Alice in Wonderland jury of brainy apes, toothy felines, and green-skinned men. He could tell Tammy had seen her fill of fighting; two light centuries from home, and one of only two humans on Harmonia who were not either under capital indictment or cowering in caves and bunkers, waiting for Greenies and SuperCats to dig them out. Her plea for peace and forgiveness reminded Derek of Mia. His Greenie girlfriend had said the same exact things when they first got together, wishing to personally plead with Pender for a cease-fire—not knowing that the Humanists would have shot her out of hand. For some people, humanity was just skin-deep. Despite Tammy's Portland-white skin and militia uniform—complete with an empty holster strapped to her thigh—there was more similarity between her and Mia than the Humanists, or even a lot of Greenies, would admit. Defeat had wrung all the settler arrogance out of Tammy, making her sound like little blonde-green Mia; smart, open, honest, and utterly helpless in the face of force.

Tammy must have moved the Greenies on the jury too, because they acquitted the teenage crew chief—refusing to put to death someone who had merely been along for the ride. His father and brother were not so lucky. Everyone waited glumly while the verdict was virtually appealed to an off-planet court—in this case the officers of the armed merchant cruiser *Eclipse*, sitting in a special courts martial. Not even the Gekkos were happy, having seen Tammy and the crew chief get off—and not trusting the naval officers, most of whom were human.

Verdicts came back confirmed, much to the Gekkos' surprise. Derek expected it, knowing naval officers had scant sympathy for the Humanist militia—bungling amateurs who gave war a bad name. Gekkos made the common mistake of assuming that all humans were the same.

Judge Leo carried the sentences out personally. Life and death were all that mattered to a SuperCat, and he would never have sat in judgment if someone else was going to execute the sentence. What would be the point? He asked the father how he wanted it done. Lips drawn, the human replied that he wanted his son to die first, "But I don't want to see it."

Leo understood, telling him, "Say your good-byes." Which the dad did, first to the crew chief, then to the son who would die. Then the father watched his son obey his final order, marching off without a misstep, disappearing behind a screen of tree ferns, where Leo shot him.

When Leo came for the father, the human said a final good-bye to the Gekkos. "I'm glad we killed every one of you assholes."

Watching the father go, Derek knew how the man felt. Ceremoniously shooting them for destroying a smallish city did seem ludicrous, since humans had gone on to kill every Gekko on the planet. Vastly outnumbered, and clinging to a few dwindling isolated settlements, Pender's people knew that even antimatter warheads would not win for them—so the Humanists countered with their ultimate weapon. When the settlers first arrived after two centuries in transit and found Harmonia inhabited by Gekkos, plans for terraforming the planet were put on hold. Facing complete defeat, Pender ordered the terraforming into immediate operation. Deep-space teams at the edge of Ares system crashed water ice comets rich in CO_2 into Harmonia, producing surface water, rain, and green-house gases. At the same time, Pender's biotechs released superplants into the thicker wetter atmosphere, sending oxygen levels soaring. Mounting oxygen and humidity killed all the Gekkos that didn't flee off-planet. *Homo sapiens* had again come out on top, against daunting odds, and on alien ground. Proving that humans were a dangerous species to tangle with—for those few that did not already know.

Tammy took away the surviving teenager, acquitted of all charges, but still rendered a homeless orphan by the courts. Derek let her go without a word, guessing that this was not the moment to offer her a job working for the new masters of Harmonia.

He caught up with Tammy in orbit, where settler families waited to be shipped outsystem. Trust Greenies to design the perfect transit camp, turning the main hold of a C-class freighter into a hologram tropical isle, complete with warm sunlight, sea breezes, and righteous waves. Folks lived in thatched treehouses and palm huts, while a dropshaft in the island's center led to more standard decks—for those who tired of paradise. Tammy sat on the beach staring out to sea, having traded her militia uniform for a gaudy sarong and a hibiscus blossom tucked behind her ear. Other refugees lounged about in various states of undress, and children splashed in the surf beneath a bright hologram sky—including Brad, who Tammy turned out to be watching. Someone upwind was roasting a pig, while teenagers lovingly smoothed and sanded balsawood surfboards.

Sitting down in the hot sand beside Tammy, he watched a blue breaker slam into the beach, sending glittering spray flying through warm tropical air. Out of the corner of his eye, he noted Tammy had nicely rounded breasts, even if they weren't green. "Is this what Portland is like?"

Laughing, Tammy looked over at him, the first time he had coaxed more than a smile out of her. "No, this is not Portland. Not even close."

"Really?" The Charter of Universal Rights said that internees must be kept in conditions "approximating" their

home world—and Greenies scrupulously obeyed such con-
ventions, not wanting to deny anyone their rights. "Earth is
not like this?"

"Parts of it are." Tammy's smile faded, and she stared
evenly at him, an intense questioning look that surprised
Derek—it seemed like Tammy needed something from him,
but would not say what. Which Derek found strange. Greenie
females were very upfront about their needs; if they wanted
something they said so. All Tammy said was, "What are you
doing here?"

Good question. Derek was not sure what he was doing,
but he did want to see more of Tammy, so he tried to start on
a positive note. "You were amazing, standing up to the court
like you did, saving that boy's life. . . ."

"But not his father and brother." Tammy sounded bitter,
looking back at Brad, another orphan. By utterly wiping out
the Gekkos, Pender and company had assured that the blame
would forever fall on Tammy's people.

"You did wonderfully." Derek meant it; he had talked to
Tammy on a whim, but everything she did since drew him
in. Her plea for peace, her caring for homeless kids, her
bravery before armed SuperCats. "Leo would have killed
that boy, as easily as the others. You saved him, when I was
afraid to even try."

"You, afraid?" Tammy's smile returned, as if she could
not really believe him. "I thought you were the nerveless negotiator who walked unarmed into the muzzles of machine
cannon."

"Only in my spare time," Derek explained. "Normally I'm
a vacuum hand, a pilot. Greenies grabbed me for this job because I was the only human they could easily get a hold of."

"Yet you took the job," Tammy reminded him, "idiotically
going into grave danger just to save complete strangers."

And winning points with Tammy. Derek could tell by how
her smile widened, making this the moment to ask, "Idiotically? I hope not, because I fancied you might join me."

"Join you?" Taken aback, Tammy acted like she had
started to trust him, but now was not sure. "Working for
Greenies?"

"*Photo sapiens* do pay me," Derek admitted, "but that's not why I do it." He nodded toward Brad, splashing in the surf with the other children. "That's who I do it for—there are still a lot of innocents dirtside, and a woman would be very helpful in getting them out safely, especially an Earth-woman."

Tammy looked at him with that same questioning stare, like she wanted something from him—but all she said was, "Do you know how hard it is to lose everything? To see good friends blown to bits for no reason?"

Looking out to sea, Tammy watched hydraulically produced waves roll out of the hologram horizon that hid her prison wall. "This all started out as a grand adventure, founding a new world beyond the stars—but when we got here someone else had moved in, and no one would honor our claim." Gekkos had gotten in ahead of the human colonists, and there was no law to make them leave. Human attempts to assert their centuries-old claim had led to friction, then fighting, and finally genocide. "Sure it's all our fault, but what could we do? Our ships were one-way jobs, built to be cannibalized at our destination, so we couldn't even go home. Those of us who opposed fighting were dragged in anyway, once the killing began. I started by organizing peace vigils, and ended up as a door-gunner—don't think that was easy."

Hunched up, her arms around her legs, she laid her head down on her bare knees, looking back over at him, saying, "Now we're defeated, despised, and deported, and it will all go to the Greenies." Surviving Gekkos had sold their now useless claim on Harmonia to the Greenies, and there was scant support for letting the human settlers keep a planet they had acquired by mass-murder. "Greenies are going to just waltz in and take what we made, because they are so good and we are so evil."

Derek agreed, Greenie goodness could get to you—witness this island-paradise-cum-prison. Greenies were adept at making you feel grateful for doing what they wanted. "I don't think you are evil," he told Tammy, "only human. That's why I offered you the job—this is something that must be done by *humans*. If Greenies could do it, we wouldn't be having this talk."

Still staring straight at him, Tammy told him tersely, "I can't betray my people."

"I'm asking you to help save them," Derek pointed out.

Again he got that questioning look. By now, Mia would have said what she wanted—and then some. Tammy just said, "I'll work for you, but not for Greenies. The first time I have to take orders from a Greenie—I'm gone."

"Absolutely," Derek agreed. He could talk to the Greenies, being very good at that.

"And don't try to pump me for info," Tammy warned him. "I will talk people into coming out, but I won't help kill them. Understood?"

Derek nodded. "Understood."

Tammy looked hard at him. "No hypno-probes. No brain scans."

"I'm not even wired for lie detection," Derek reminded her. He liked the give-and-take of talking to Tammy, enjoying an edge you never got with Greenies. With Mia, everything was so pleasantly simple, that were it not for her green skin and weird way of thinking, there would be no mystery at all. With Tammy, it was a challenge just to get agreement, before she piled on more bizarre conditions. "We go dirtside at 1630 hours tomorrow. Can you be ready?"

"Sure." It was not as if Tammy had much to do here. Nor did she bother to ask about the pay—when you were being paid to get out of jail, how much hardly mattered.

Getting up to go, Derek surveyed the white sweep of tropical beach edged with treehouse cabanas. "So this is not Portland?"

"More like Paradise Island," Tammy told him. "Minus the holo-rides, dance arenas, sex-clubs, and love grottos."

Earth sounded like an amazing place. He remembered Tammy saying that she had been to Paradise Island with her boyfriend—and liked it a lot. He asked, "Do you still have the boyfriend?"

"Sure." Tammy nonchalantly watched his reaction, but by now, Derek was enough of a negotiator not to show disappointment. "Back in Portland," she added, making them both laugh. Oregon was so far off that laser-mail took four hundred years to get a reply. He left before she could ask if he had a girlfriend.

All he told Mia was that he had hired Tammy. His Greenie girlfriend was pleased, saying her good-bye to him on the temple porch of their bonsai garden apartment, with wind chimes tinkling overhead. "Be careful," Mia pleaded, "I'm not done with you. And take care of Tammy too."

"Tammy?" He was surprised by her concern for Pender's former aide.

"Yes. Tammy will be alone among men and weapons. She will need a good man to watch over her, and you are the best I know." Mia gave him another kiss, then let him go.

Billions of years ago, when Ares system was still forming, a Rhode Island-sized rock had slammed into Harmonia's northern hemisphere, carving out the Hyperborian Depression, sub-polar lowlands a thousand klicks across. Ringed by dry ragged, highlands, the lowlands were slowly filling with rain water that would one day submerge everything but the central volcanic peak thrust high up into the thin air. Glass remnants of Gekko towns shone amid silent green swamps and marshes inhabited by herds of hippos who were busily converting the greenery into fish food and fertilizer. Humans had brought all sorts of useful animals with them to fill out Harmonia's slowly emerging ecology, though Greenies would now tailor the world to their tastes, and Mia would be the one coming down to catalogue the hippo herds.

But first the swamps must be made safe for Greenies. That was for Leo and Derek to do, and now Tammy. Riding down on the shuttle, Derek sat beside his new teammate, excitedly listening to stories from Earth. So much time, so many wonders. How strange that most of human existence had been confined to that one tiny planet. He asked Tammy, "Why did you leave?"

"There are forty billion people in the solar system, most of them on Earth," Tammy explained. "Crowds like that can be lonely. I wanted to live on a world like Earth was when there were not so many of us."

And now they were going down to root the last human remnants out of Harmonia. Tammy sighed, saying, "Weird thing is, I still get laser-mail from my sister Mary, who must be two hundred years older than me by now. It was all sent when Mary was in her twenties, birth announcements, Christmas greetings, that sort of thing—nothing very personal. Sometimes I miss Portland, but there isn't a lot you can do with a doctorate in Humanities, except leave the planet."

"You have a doctorate in Humanism?" Derek was shocked to discover they gave degrees in intolerance and racial superiority.

His surprise amused Tammy. "Humanism and the Humanities are totally different. My specialty was Dead Languages—Latin, Sumerian, Japanese, that sort of thing."

Fascinated, Derek asked, "So, do you speak English?"

Tammy smiled. "All my life."

"Say something in English," he suggested. Many of the settler holdouts came from North America, and English would be a good way of proving she was not a Greenie.

Tammy said something short and unintelligible, but her quaint accent made it sound fetching, even romantic. Derek asked, "What does that mean?"

Her smile turned mischievous, and Tammy told him, "I asked, do you have a girlfriend?"

Suddenly, Tammy's English sentence didn't sound so quaint and fetching. Mia was not due down from orbit for days, so a chance meeting was unlikely, but Derek could not lie to Tammy, not after her sometimes painful honesty. Trying to hide behind a nonchalant grin, he told her, "Only if you count Greenies."

Tammy's smile faded, and Derek saw that he had lost something in her eyes by sleeping with a Greenie. "Her name is Mia. But I doubt she considers me her 'boyfriend'— not the way humans think of it. . . ."

Tammy would not even look at him, totally uninterested in the love life of Greenies. They had a cold, silent planet-fall, sitting side by side and saying nothing.

Orbital scans showed humans scattered throughout the

Hyperborian Depression, with solid patches in the marsh supporting farm plots, producing melons, squash, patches of corn, pigs, and chickens. None of which worried the Greenies much, since the whole swamp was slowly becoming a sea bottom. Why dig people out of a place that would soon be underwater? What worried the Greenies was a water-tight bunker complex dug into the base of the central massif, and signs of fortifications farther up.

Leo's light armored battalion landed near the biggest bunker entrance, carving out an LZ with wide zones of fire. No one opposed them. In fact, Derek got the impression that the swarm of armored infantry and turreted Bug-mobiles sent everyone scurrying for cover. Having said virtually nothing since planetfall, he and Tammy approached the main bunker, a steel blast-shield dug into a green hillside, with ELVIS SAVES spray-painted in English above the entrance. His electronic bug scurried ahead of them.

Young women wearing long print dresses, beehive hairdos, and black eye shadow greeted them at the bunker door, looking askance at Tammy in her brown militia uniform, beneath body armor that read, DO NOT SHOOT THIS WOMAN! Tammy shook her head and grinned for the first time since that frosty fall from orbit. "Presleites! Good luck! You're going to wish you were dealing with Pender."

"What do you mean?" Derek asked warily, pleased to have Tammy talking again.

"You'll see." Tammy shook her head. "Church of Elvis, so just watch your back."

Smiling women ushered them into the neatly carpeted bunker, showing a cold shoulder to Tammy. Inside was a hologram-maze of long fluorescent corridors lined with numbered rooms, all done in the same white-and-gold motif, with heavy white drapes where the windows should be. Lower levels were reached by boxy elevators. Unable to tell if this was some illusionary defense, Derek asked Tammy, "Is this typical Earth-style architecture?"

"From a zillion years ago," Tammy told him. "This is programmed to resemble a Las Vegas hotel casino in early post-atomic Nevada. Before the state was made into a waste dump."

"Really?" That explained the numbered rooms, but not the annoying music in the elevators. "What was Las Vegas?"

"Resort in the desert—don't ask me why. Presleites adore this style of architecture, which has a sort of energetic charm," Tammy admitted. "Living like this would drive normal folks crazy, but it doesn't seem to bother them much."

Led into an inner bedroom with the same white-on-white motif, Derek was confronted by a middle-aged matriarch wearing a blue sheath dress beneath a black bouffant hairdo. Studying them from under her heavy eye shadow, the woman introduced herself as Ginger, asking suspiciously, "Which side are you on?"

"Neither," Derek announced hopefully.

Women around him smiled wide, and voiced a happy, "Hallelujah!"

"Praise the King. We have been waiting for someone to come to their senses," Ginger explained. "When we saw her we were afraid you might be Humanists."

"Funny, I thought *you* would be Humanists," Derek admitted.

"Hell, no! Elvis didn't believe in race war. His only begotten daughter married Saint Michael, who bleached his own skin, showing it was no shame to be any color—even white."

Women around Derek chimed in with another chorus of, "Praise the King."

Derek turned to Tammy. "What are they saying?"

Tammy shook her head. "Too hard to explain. But these people gave Pender no help at all. They are way too wrapped up in their religion to worry about the Gekkos, or anything else."

Derek believed it, but the Greenies wanted the whole central massif evacuated and combed for weapons. Nor did Derek blame them, since orbital surveys indicated a tunnel complex that could hold enough warheads to blow a hole in the thin atmosphere and scatter radioactive debris all over the planet. Greenies were courteous, but not crazy.

Of course, the Presleites did not see it that way. "We have done nothing," Ginger complained. "We can't just give up our homes to Greenies."

"You can't stop them," Derek pointed out. Greenies were going to get what they wanted, even if Leo had to dig the humans out of their tunnels.

"Really?" Batting black lashes, Ginger smiled to her companions, who drew plastic stingers out of their print dresses. Negotiations had taken an alarming turn for the worse, and Ginger primly informed him, "Hating war doesn't make us pushovers."

Apparently not. Staring into the round black muzzles of the stingers, Derek was quick to point out that shooting him would do no one any good.

"Shoot you?" Ginger acted like the thought had never entered her head. "You have earned an audience with the King. These stingers are just to show we are serious. Some people think polite tolerance is a sign of weakness." Ginger nodded at Tammy, to show who she meant.

Tammy merely shrugged, taking no responsibility for Presleite opinions. Just when Derek thought things could not get any stranger, a holo flickered into being in front of him, a handsome dark-haired young man, wearing a sparkling white and gold suit, with a wide belt and a huge golden buckle. He had lively blue eyes and an engaging smile, and his appearance was greeted by another round of "Praise the King!"

Bowing to his audience, the hologram winked at Ginger as he straightened up, then swung about on his blue suede shoes, saying to Derek, "Howdy, son. Don't worry, these gals won't drill you—they're just may fan club. The pistols are only for protection."

Derek assured the holo that no one need fear him.

The King's virtual grin widened. "Pleased to hear you come in peace."

"Peace is my profession," Derek agreed cheerfully.

"So you talk to both sides?" asked the King.

"I try." Derek knew he was speaking to a sophisticated program of some sort, broadcast from deeper in the bunker—but he was willing to talk to empty bulkheads if it would avert killing.

Turning serious, the King asked, "And do the Greenies say these folks got to go?"

Derek nodded. "At least until this area can be thoroughly searched for contraband." Code intercepts had revealed that Pender had been working on a doomsday device—fitting his personality perfectly.

"When your search is done, will they be allowed back?" asked the virtual Elvis.

"If it were up to me, they would be." Derek could not answer for the Greenies.

"I bet it would." The King's smile broadened. "And in that case, what if I just gave you this place?"

"Give it to me?" Derek imagined he had misheard the holo.

"If I just gave it to you, the Greenies wouldn't take it away. Would they? You're pretty well in with them?"

"Maybe," Derek admitted. Greenies ran the planet, yet were bound by the Charter of Universal Rights to respect claims by other races. In theory, anyone who did not aid Pender was as good as a Greenie. Whether that applied to holo-programs modeled on long-dead singers was another issue, but juries of bioconstructs had notoriously generous notions of what was "natural."

"And would you let these people live here?" Elvis asked, as his fan club shyly lowered their pistols, smiling to show their dimples.

"Of course, but . . ."

"Then nothing could be simpler," the King declared. "You seem a decent man, not overly scared by women or guns."

"For one thing," Derek protested, "I don't want the responsibility."

"Of course not." Elvis laughed, shaking his dark locks. "What fool wants responsibility? Sane folks run like hell from it. But take it from the King, sometimes you gotta face the music."

Elvis took them on a virtual tour of the bunker, followed by his fan club, turning off the hologram Vegas Hilton, to reveal living quarters, hydro-ponics, recycling, power supply, and families hiding in blast shelters—but no big stock of weapons, except for the personal sidearms that most adult Presleites carried, just to be safe. "An armed society is a polite society," the King explained amiably.

Satisfied that this was all true, Derek put in a call to Leo, arranging a peaceful evacuation. For which the hologram deity thanked him profusely, and zip-signaled a contract for Leo to witness, turning the whole central massif over to Derek, along with all its contents—then, in a blink, the King disappeared. Elvis had left the bunker.

While Leo's battalion searched the lower reaches of the mountain, Derek took Tammy upslope to check out the command complex at the summit, including an auxiliary reactor, big blast-shelters, and what looked like a launch silo. For that, they needed oxygen, since the Presleite tunnels did not connect to the complex above, and they would be climbing into a dead zone, where the air was still too thin to support life. Pretty appropriate, since the coolness between them continued. He had not heard a kind word from Tammy since he had told her about Mia; which he might have expected, but still did not enjoy. Accustomed to Greenie girls, Derek had been lulled into thinking that Tammy might have a similar easy attitude. No such luck.

Derek had to be satisfied by inspecting his new digs, with his bug crawling ahead of him, searching for signs of trouble. If the Presleites had not killed any Gekkos to get this mountain, Greenie courts would likely award it to him. And Derek saw absolutely no sign of Gekkos on the mountain, which was only slowly becoming habitable as the oxygen level rose. The nearest glass ruins were shining dots far out across the green swampland, on what would one day be sea bottom.

His bug saw no sign of life in the complex atop the mountain, which seemed to be on lock-down mode. Power emissions were minimal, and most of the tunnels lacked life-support, standing with ports gaping open atop an almost-airless mountain stuck up into the frigid stratosphere. At the top, Derek called down to Leo, saying he was checking out his high castle. Leo gave him a go, and Derek sent in his bug ahead of them. Tammy closed the ports behind them, turning on the lights and air.

Derek found his new digs impressive, going to the command deck and getting the 3V tour. It had obviously not been built by the Presleites, but it was not Gekko work either, and the King's claim to the mountain went all the way to the summit. So long as the place was truly abandoned, and they found nothing to link it to Pender, this high-tech castle was as good as his, to do with as he pleased. Though what he really wanted was a ship to pilot. Who could he find to swap a starship for a mountain-top retreat?

3V showed the silo to be empty, but Derek decided on a visual check. Heavy blast-shielding allowed Greenies in orbit to "see" the buried silo, but not what was inside. Tammy led him to the silo lock, and equalized pressures, flooding the huge shaft with breathable air. He sent his bug in ahead.

As he expected, the silo was not empty—that would have made things too easy. But there was no doomsday device either, thank heaven. Crouched at the bottom of the shaft was a gravity drive starship, a sleek fast Fornax Skylark, ready to leap into orbit. Just the sort of ship he wanted. Way too good to be true.

Signaling Tammy to step back, Derek decided to alert Leo on a secure channel. This silo had to be sealed tight and escape into space cut off, before anyone dared approach that ship. Recalling his bug, he hissed to Tammy, "Now's when we call in Leo's people."

"No, I don't think so," Tammy replied evenly. Derek turned in surprise, and saw that Tammy was holding a gun on him, which dear sweet Mia would never have done. He could barely believe it, but a plastic fire-and-forget stinger had somehow materialized in her hand. Derek opened his mouth to protest, but before he could get a word out, Tammy shot him.

Thor's Hammer

Derek awoke in a sealed cubicle aboard ship, wearing a slave collar. His sleep grenade and hypo-rings were gone. There was absolutely no light—but he didn't need x1-10,000 night vision zoom lenses to know he was in a sealed box. His comlink had vanished, but he still had the pilot's navigation chip embedded in his skull. Inertial sensors showed Derek was accelerating at about 20-gs, something you could only do in a fast starship, like the Fornax Skylark he had seen hiding in the shaft. Simple logic said that he was aboard that ship, headed rapidly outsystem. Pity he waited so late to resort to logic.

Fingering his slave collar, he found it was standard issue, fitted for tracking, paralysis, lie detection, emotional motivation, and who knows what else? There were no ill effects from the stinger, so the fire-and-forget hornet must have been set on SLEEP. Such a stinger could just as easily have killed him, or put him in a coma. Tammy, it seemed, wanted him alive and conscious—for the moment, at least. He remembered how she had stared at him over the sights, not angry, or gleeful, just giving him that same even look she shown him in Pender's bunker, when she first pulled her head out of the assault-cannon's sighting hood. Greenies had warned him that Earthwomen were dangerous, but it took Tammy to convince him.

He told his nav-chip to work out pursuit vectors, assuming all available vessels gave chase as soon as the Skylark burst out of the silo. Results were not good. Greenies had nothing that could catch it, just a couple of interstellar yachts converted to escorts that might do 10-gs at a stretch. Backing up the Greenies was the armed merchant cruiser *Eclipse*, a naval vessel with the legs to run down the Skylark—but not anytime soon. *Eclipse* had been nosing about upsun for signs of slavers or Humanist hold-outs, while the Skylark was going like lightning in the opposite direction. Even if *Eclipse* dropped everything to pursue, half of Tartarus system lay between them, which would mean a long stern chase into the vastness of interstellar space.

Of course, no one might be chasing them at all. Whoever was running this ship were bound to be diehard Humanists. Greenies and the Navy might figure that Harmonia system was far better off without such fanatics, and any attempt at pursuit would smack too much of wanting them back. Leaving Derek an unwilling passenger on a ship full of lunatic pariahs headed who knows where.

Presently, his door dilated and Tammy appeared, a smirk on her face, casually holding a slave-remote in place of the stinger. "Sorry to put you through this," she told him, "but it couldn't be helped."

"Oh, really?" Derek could easily have avoided all this.

"Don't act so pure," Tammy snorted. "All the time you were romancing me, you were fucking a Greenie."

"You should try it sometime," Derek suggested. A good Greenie-fuck might be just what Tammy needed, to help her loosen up a bit, and maybe get to know the neighbors.

"Come with me," she told him, motioning with the remote. "Or I will have you carried."

Derek went gladly, eager to get out of the shielded cell and see what was happening. As soon as he left the cubicle, systems traffic confirmed his guesses. Greenies had not even bothered to give chase, but *Eclipse* was shaping to match orbits deep in interstellar space, with billions of kilometers to make up, leaving Derek pretty much on his own for the moment. Tammy ushered him into the Skylark's salon, which was tuned to a view of tall sandstone spires and vast distances. High overhead was a hologram Sol, and the cabin deck was made to look like the adobe roof of a pueblo sweat lodge, covered with bright colored rugs, and sitting atop a lonely mesa.

Three men in brown Humanist militia uniforms sat atop the sweat lodge in deck chairs molded to their bodies, ignoring the hologram vistas around them, glaring at Derek instead. They did not look defeated, just mean. All three of them had recoilless machine pistols at their hips, which seemed a bit much millions of kilometers from the nearest threat. One asked curtly, "What is he doing here?"

Tammy shrugged, saying, "I wanted him to see."

"Whatever for?" demanded the militia man, dramatically resting his hand on his holster, though the nearest Greenie was by now millions of klicks away, and the Gekkos were mostly dead.

"I have hopes for him." Tammy smiled at Derek as she said it, then added, "And this far from home, we need all the help we can get."

"We'll be bringing in Presleites next," protested an older man wearing colonel's tabs.

Tammy shrugged again, saying, "Pender would approve."

Everyone looked sharply at her, surprised to see Tammy being so free with the approval of a dead man, whose opinions had split the system and all but depopulated a planet. "Boss met him on the last day," Tammy explained evenly, "and liked him a lot. Told us not to shoot him."

Men laughed at that, but it put Pender's authority behind keeping him alive. Tammy added evenly, "Pender ordered me to give up and go with him, and to recruit him if possible. He was my best hope of getting here."

All news to Derek, who did not join in the general hilarity at how easily Tammy had included him in the plans of a mass murderer. Mia had feared that without him Tammy would be alone among men with guns, showing just how right a Greenie could be. However, dear sweet Mia neglected to say what Derek was supposed to *do* surrounded by all those guns, especially with Tammy on the other side.

"But why listen to me?" Tammy asked. "You can hear the Boss himself."

Pointing with the remote, Tammy triggered a holo, and Pender himself suddenly appeared, looking fit and relaxed. Grinning, he addressed the dwindling faithful, saying cheerfully, "Guess I'm dead, otherwise you wouldn't be seeing this. Funny, being dead is not near so bad as I imagined. Only drawback is that I can't see or hear you. That's why I ordered up this holo of Monument Valley, so we could all be seeing the same thing. Pretty, isn't she? And some day Harmonia could still look like this. . . ."

Pender stared into the virtual distance, a dead man admiring a fake landscape, then turned back to the business at hand. "Well, even in hell there is still work to do. Code name for this project is *Mjollnir*. . . ."

Pender's holo proceeded to rattle off coordinates that Derek's nav-chip identified as a location in outer system near the leading Trojan point of the gas giant Cadmus, a spot intersected by the orbit of an asteroid called Cassandra. Why Pender should be so concerned to pass on this data was a mystery to Derek—but the reasons were bound to be bad.

When he was done, Pender paused to survey the holoscape one last time, knowing that having delivered his message, he really was dead, no longer able to affect the world of the living. In fact, each passing second left him farther behind. Pender's smile widened, and he said to no one in particular, "Well, it was worth it. Now give 'em one more good whack for me."

In a blink, Pender was gone, and they were all staring into the empty holoscape of Monument Valley. Surveying the tall spires and painted desert, Derek wondered if this was someplace on Earth, but did not dare ask. Everyone else seemed to understand immediately what Pender meant, and what was going to happen. They asked him only one ominous question before returning him to the sealed cubicle. "How long before all humans are totally off the planet?"

"Not long," Derek admitted. Human evacuation was his specialty, and there was small point in lying so long as he was wearing a slave collar. "Ten days at most, more likely a week. But you can never be sure you have gotten everyone."

Militiamen got a grim laugh out of that. Then Tammy took him back to his sealed cubicle, and he was shut off from the cosmos. Time passed, precisely recorded by his nav-chip. Food arrived, and a personal recycler in the corner shipped his wastes to hydroponics. Halfway to Cadmus' leading Trojan point, the drive fields reversed and the Skylark started decelerating. *Eclipse* would have to decelerate as well, in order to match orbits. Working out high-g trajectories in his head, Derek decided that *Eclipse* could cut the distance considerably, but still would not catch up until they were long past the leading Trojan point. Whatever was happening there, *Eclipse* could not stop it.

So much for the Navy. If anyone was going to stop the Humanists, it had to be him. Terrific. He had finally found his own people, only to discover that they were homicidal lunatics. Mia thought that most of human misery came from inventing weapons, and by now Derek was willing to agree. No sane Greenie would carry out what looked like a suicidal mission of mass-destruction at the behest of some dead murderer. Male or female, young or old, stupid or smart, the first thing a Greenie would ask was, "Why in the world are we doing this?"

Yet no one on that mesa top questioned anything, except to pointedly ask when the "humans" would be off the planet. Pender's people were probably already offplanet, leaving a sprinkling of peaceful independent types like the Presleites, who had somehow managed to avoid the war and its aftermath—so far. Mia was probably already down there too, taking samples from the hippos and worrying about what had happened to him. While these maniacs plotted something fatal for her and every Greenie on the planet. Not to mention all those hippos.

Acceleration fell almost to zero when they reached a spot corresponding to the current location of Cassandra, a two-hundred-klick rock named for a Trojan princess. Cassandra meant "Entangler of Men." Or so his nav-chip said. She had certainly entangled him.

Tammy came to get him, his remote in hand, the stinger in a hip holster, and a smirk on her face. He tried to lodge a strenuous protest, but she pressed MUTE, saying, "We don't have time to argue. Right now we are in a sealed room, and can't be overheard. Outside, we have to be ready to act together. Okay?"

Unable to speak, and not knowing exactly what Tammy meant, Derek nodded anyway. What choice did he have?

"Good." Tammy pressed UNMUTE. "So, have you guessed what project *Mjollnir* is about?"

"Pender wants you to smash this asteroid into Harmonia, killing as many Greenies as you can." Why else rendezvous with a useless rock far away from anywhere?

"Right." Tammy nodded grimly. "Thor's hammer, smashing our enemies to bits."

"But even if you could anchor this Skylark to the rock, you could never get past *Eclipse*." An armed merchant cruiser carried special landing teams trained to liberate hijacked ships, and root out slaver bases.

Tammy shook her head. "There is no need to get past *Eclipse*. Buried in the rock is a high-g tug, the *Atlas*, originally used to tow ice comets for terraforming, but hidden here ever since. Once the tug has been programmed, the Skylark will take off, drawing the *Eclipse* into deep space."

Derek had to admit that it would probably work. Cassandra was a dense stony-iron asteroid, perfect for hiding the powered-down tug. With the Skylark speeding away, *Eclipse* would continue the chase, telling the Greenies to check out Cassandra. By the time low-g Greenie ships arrived, the asteroid would be accelerating downsun and impossible to stop. Cassandra striking at high acceleration would almost split Harmony in half, destroying every structure, and blowing a huge hole in the thin atmosphere blanketing the world in dust and ash. Only algae would survive. He bitterly told Tammy, "I believed you, when you told that jury that they could stop the killing."

"I absolutely meant that," Tammy insisted.

"Then how can you be doing this?" Derek demanded.

"I *am* trying to stop it," Tammy protested, looking like she thought it should have been obvious. "That's why I need you. All I have is a Humanities PhD, and I know absolutely nothing about piloting a high-g tug."

"So you want *me* to?" Derek could hardly believe what he was hearing. "Dragging a runaway asteroid behind us. . . ."

"To keep it from hitting Harmonia," Tammy reminded him. "And maybe save your Greenie girlfriend."

Mia was undoubtedly dirtside by now, but that just made it all the worse. "How could you not tell me?" he demanded. "How could you have let things get this far?"

"I had to be first to get here," Tammy told him primly. "Pender sent back-up messages in case mine didn't get through. And if I'd told you my plans, you wouldn't have helped."

No lie. He stared in exasperation at the Earthwoman, aghast at what she had done. "Why not just turn them in?"

"And give the Greenies one more victory to gloat over?" Tammy looked disgusted. "Too many women and kids died from their 'precision' bombing for me to do that. This is something that humans had to do. If Greenies could do it, we wouldn't be having this talk."

Derek had nothing to say. He would have gladly left all this to Leo's light battalion, but maybe he was too used to bioconstructs doing his dirty work. SuperChimps to do the heavy lifting. Leo for the dangerous stuff. Bugs to take out the toxic waste. Dear sweet Mia to make his meals and share his bed.

"This is all so easy for you—isn't it?" Tammy asked. "Having the moral high ground, while we ordinary humans do the suffering."

"Not really," Derek told her, having seen far more grief and mayhem than he had ever imagined—none of it of his making, but folks still expected him to *do* something about it. "It's damned hard on me at times."

"Me too," Tammy agreed, handing him his sleep grenade, at the same time giving his hand a warm squeeze. "Back in Pender's bunker, you were so anxious to know who I was, and how you could help me. Well, this is who I am, and now is when I need you."

Well said. He took the grenade and the squeeze, noting Tammy was wearing his hypo-rings. By now, he knew that there were reasons why negotiators did not consort with the enemy, not if they meant to remain neutral.

Derek followed Tammy out of the cell and into the Skylark's lounge, which was no longer atop a desert mesa, showing a seascape instead. The tug's crew was coming aboard, looking more like tired mariners emerging from the sea than vacuum hands coming out of hiding. Two large armed men in militia uniforms waited by the lock to escort them onto the tug. Feeling their gaze on him, Derek realized that Tammy had them perfectly fooled. They were all set to leap to her aid, while she walked stinger on hip into the tug, planning to betray them. Having been there himself, Derek could sympathize with their upcoming surprise.

Inside the lock, the ocean motif was replaced by the standard ship's airlock. As soon as the lock closed, and started to cycle, Tammy opened an emergency kit on the wall and took out two oxygen masks, putting one on and handing Derek the other. He put on the mask and set off his sleep grenade. One shocked militiaman reached out to stop him, but Tammy seized his wrist, triggering her hypo-ring. He joined his sleeping companion on the deck.

When the lock opened, the two of them stepped into the deserted tug. Decoupling the lock manually, Derek dashed to the command couch. Without bothering to buckle himself in, he slammed the drive into full acceleration, shooting sunward, and, at the same time, rotating the whole rock to port. Fields could not fully compensate, and Derek had to cling to the couch with one hand, while snagging Tammy with the other, keeping her from tumbling into the controls.

Hanging onto Tammy, he stopped the roll at 180 degrees, so that the mass of the asteroid was between them and the Skylark as they dropped toward the inner system. Fields stabilized, returning cabin gravity to 1-g, and Tammy landed in his lap.

He looked down at her, and she looked up at him. Suddenly they were safe, and alone. No armed Humanist militia. No Leo and his light battalion. Just the two of them, safe, secure, and together, with two hundred klicks of rock and iron between them and the men Tammy had so neatly betrayed. Tammy sat up in his lap and kissed him, a long lingering kiss that showed that she had been waiting for it almost as long as he had. Her mouth felt cool and exciting, not as delicate as Mia's, or as eager to please, but with a wild willfulness that Derek had never tasted before. Their lips parted, and Tammy smiled, asking him, "Was that as good as a Greenie?"

"You are nothing like a Greenie," he told her. No Greenie girl had ever put him through half of what Tammy had done to him—but then, no one had ever suggested that Earth women were easy. Especially Humanities majors from the wilds of Portland, or Eugene. But that just made him want her all the more—too bad that frantic calls were coming from *Eclipse*, wanting to know why one of the leading Trojans had broken loose, and was accelerating rapidly downsun. Speed-of-light lag meant that the Greenies did not even know anything had happened—yet.

"Don't answer that," Tammy told him, shutting off the comlink.

He reached out to call *Eclipse*, to explain the situation and send them after the Skylark, which was headed outsystem at high acceleration. But Tammy stabbed a button on the remote, and his arms went limp, nerve-blocked by his slave collar. Tammy shook her head, saying, "Told you not to answer. Let them stew a bit, we need time to ourselves."

When he started to protest, Tammy pushed MUTE and kissed him again. His anger at being helpless was mollified by what she did with her tongue. Then she pushed UNMUTE, and asked, "Was that not better than talking to the Navy?"

It was, but Derek resented the lack of mobility, demanding, "Turn my arms back on."

Tammy sat up in his lap, smiling gleefully. "Only if you promise to be bad."

Greenie girls did not treat you like this, and, for the first time in his life, he truly wanted to lay hands on a woman, and none too gently either. "Come on, turn me on."

"Whatever you say." Tammy pressed a button, and one body part leaped alert. Squirming suggestively, she ground her rear into his lap, asking, "There, how about that?"

Still not what he wanted. Derek pleaded, "Let me use my hands and legs."

Tammy looked serenely at him, stripping off her hyporings. "Only if you promise to quit acting like a Greenie."

"Damn you." Derek could not believe what this woman had put him through. "That's better." Tammy turned the rest of him on. Until *Eclipse* matched orbits, they were utterly alone, two hundred light-years from Earth; a splendid place for getting acquainted. Derek discovered that despite all her strange actions and dangerous ways, Tammy was indeed just like a Greenie girl on the inside.

Eclipse brought the idyll to an end. Naval officers, some of them human, came to take over the tug and send Cassandra sailing outsystem, where the wayward Trojan would no longer be a threat. Then they returned Derek to Harmonia, where he and Tammy got a royal reception from grateful Greenies, who could not do enough to show how thankful they were. Making it the perfect moment to press his claim to the Presleite property, and to get a promise that the Presleites could return to it, along with anyone not actually convicted of war crimes. Which the Greenies readily agreed to, being eternally optimistic about humans' ability to better themselves.

Derek was there when the first shuttle landed, standing in the rain on a low plateau in the central massif overlooking the green Hyperborean swamps. Women in black bouffant hairdos, and men with sideburns, shades, and white dinner jackets trooped out of the shuttle—all armed, just in case. With them came their children, as well as Brad and the other orphans from among Pender's people, like the teenage crew chief that Tammy had gotten acquitted. And any adults who were willing to live among Greenies and Presleites.

Immensely happy with how things were going, Derek stood at the base of "his" mountain, surveying the sweep of changing landscape from the bare mountain peak above to the emerald swamp lapping at the lower slopes. Someday that swamp would be a blue sea, and the mountain flanks would be lowland jungle, blending into highland forest, then alpine pasture. Air would become breathable all the way to the top, so the whole mountain and the surrounding highland rim would be habitable. Only the crater floor, where Gekkos had built their cities, would be lost to the sea. That part of Pender's plan had worked admirably. His deluge would go on for decades, and the Gekkos would never get a second chance.

Derek saw a lone slim Greenie, wearing nothing but a gold sarong and a grin, walking nonchalantly up from where the hippo herds were grazing. Zoom lenses showed Derek that it was Mia coming cheerfully up to congratulate him. She stopped right before him, and rose on her green toes, kissing him warmly. "I knew you would do right," she told him, "and keep Tammy safe."

"Not everything went totally as expected," Derek admitted ruefully. Doing right nearly came out all wrong.

"Don't worry." Mia kissed him again. "I told you I wasn't done with you. And I dearly want to meet Tammy too."

Why did Derek think his troubles had just begun?

And Future King . . .

ADAM ROBERTS

Adam Roberts (www.adamroberts.com) lives in Staines, England. He describes himself as an SF author, critic, reviewer, and academic. He has published five SF novels to date in the UK—the most recent is Gradisil, *five parodies (*The Va Dinci Cod *and* Star Warped *both came out in 2005); a couple of novellas as small press books; and* Swiftly, *a collection of stories. He is the author of the* Palgrave History of Science Fiction, *just out.*

"And Future King. . . ." was published in Postscripts, *the new quarterly edited by Peter Crowther in the UK. It is an anti-Romantic political satire in the tradition of Norman Spinrad's* The Iron Dream, *composed of a series of media interviews with Herr Doktor-Professor Sir Allen Fergus. King Arthur, even revived in simulation, begins to seem altogether too much like Conan the Nazi.*

.1.

49-6-30. *MetaTab caught up with Herr-Doktor Professor Sir Allen Fergus late last month at his Orcadian workshop, to ask his opinion on the latest political developments, and find out about his latest research.*

[topic: politics] Stream: Fergus laboratory. RPSP Logo.

METATAB: Professor, our readers would be most interested to learn your opinion on the latest political developments.

HERR-DOKTOR PROFESSOR SIR ALLEN FERGUS: There have been riots, I understand?

METATAB: Some recent disturbances in Manchester, although they were easily contained. More worrying, for the Designers of government, such as yourself, is a shift of public mood. A recent BBC12 poll of "hundred worst developments in human history" voted the Replicant Public Servants first, a little way ahead of last year's decision to impose a levy on the money raised from web gaming.

HERR-DOKTOR PROFESSOR SIR ALLEN FERGUS: There are, if you'll forgive me, [*laughs*] better ways of testing the effectiveness of the Androids than TV polls! All the social and economic indicators are that government by well-programmed android is three or four times better than government by humans. There's a chip in your car running it, isn't there? There's a chip regulating and cleaning your house? Of course there is. Would you prefer to take over management of all aspects of those chores yourself? Of course you would not. I had a heart attack in '44, and now I have a chip regulating my heartbeat. Does a perfect job. However-much superstitious humans transfer their own negativity onto them, Androids are merely machines programmed in the execution of good government.

METATAB: You have no worries about RPSP at all?

HERR-DOKTOR PROFESSOR SIR ALLEN FERGUS: Oh, I'm human, just as you are, and of course there's a part of my animal-brain that wouldn't like to see *all* government handed *entirely* over to machines. The president, the three senior ministers, they will *always* be human; that's a constitutional absolute. Nevertheless, if all the civil servants and other ministers are programmed to do their jobs flawlessly, 24-hours a day every day of the year—as is the case—it can only promote a more smoothly functioning governmental machine. Can it not? This must be understood: *most* of the jobs of government do not need human input; they can be done better by computers programmed precisely to follow the law, and the codes of employment and public servants. These Replicants can never be bribed, will never allow personal considerations to interfere in the commission of their duty, will never make a mistake or act incompetently.

METATAB: In your opinion—whence, then, the public disquiet?

HERR-DOKTOR PROFESSOR SIR ALLEN FERGUS: It is difficult to say. One theory prevalent among the Political Programming community at the moment questions whether the Modelled Personalities have actually made matters worse. They were designed, of course, to make the Androids more palatable to the general population. But perhaps by making Androids more human, by improving the modelling of physical features and so on, we are actually making them more threatening to the average citizen. I mean, to the National Wagers, those whose days are empty enough to fret over such matters.

METATAB: Do you believe that is the case?

HERR-DOKTOR PROFESSOR SIR ALLEN FERGUS:

I suppose we must concede: there *is* something uncanny in a machine that mimics humanity so precisely. In fact, I believe the future of the Replicant Public Servants Program lies in a more exaggerated set of Modelled Personalities. Make the RPSP agents *larger* than life, more cartoony, play up their artificiality. Social research suggests that the public will accept such creatures more readily.

METATAB: Which leads us on to the question of your present research. Are you working upon such personality redesigns?

HERR-DOKTOR PROFESSOR SIR ALLEN FERGUS: Indeed. [LINK *topic: future research*]

[topic: location] Stream: Fergus laboratory.

METATAB: Professor, were you sorry to leave London?

HERR-DOKTOR PROFESSOR SIR ALLEN FERGUS: I was indeed. I'd been based at my former workshop in Reading for several years. But last year Reading was declared capital of west London, and the resulting brouhaha, the fuss, the new buildings works and so on, made it a much less pleasant place to live and work. Scotland is appreciably quieter: still mostly suburban, with some spectacular private parks. And up here in the Isles, the light-pollution countermeasures are much more effective than in the south. The Hebridean wavelength-inverter is a marvellous piece of work. You can really see the stars.

Slide: Purple-black sky, only palely orange at horizon. Meteor streaking down in midframe, like luminous dewdrop dribbling down dark glass.

[topic: future research] Stream: Fergus laboratory.

METATAB: Professor, can you tell our readers a little about your plans for future research?

HERR-DOKTOR PROFESSOR SIR ALLEN FERGUS: We've been working with the corporation patent-copyright department to acquire the rights to a number of screen soap stars, to famous figures from Classic visual culture, and to a number of historical figures. I myself am working upon the personality of King Arthur.

METATAB: The historical figure?

HERR-DOKTOR PROFESSOR SIR ALLEN FERGUS: Yes, although it's a rather complicated matter. In fact, the material we have to hand (upon which to base our programming) is a composite of quasi-historical sources and literary or mythic adaptations; and the historical context stretches over several centuries. It's a challenge to reconcile it so as to construct an internally coherent personality. Chronicles, Malory, Tennyson, Zimmer Bradley, it's a varied spread. But I think I'm coming up with something true to the original force of the myth itself, something that captures the reason why so many people are still fascinated by the legends of King Arthur. My personality-fitted Replicant will be as close to a real "King Arthur" as can be imagined.

METATAB: Herr-Doktor Professor, thank you very much.

.2.

50-5-21. *MetaTab caught up with Herr-Doktor Professor Sir Allen Fergus earlier this week at his Avebury apartment. We are lucky enough to have an exclusive interview with this key figure in the world of Political Design.*

[topic: election] Stream: Fergus (now pluckBald) in black sleeveless suit and white strand-shirt in lounger. ART Logo. Apartment: Purple/Orange décor.

METATAB: Professor, it has been almost a year since you last spoke to MetaTab. Might we ask how things have progressed?

HERR-DOKTOR PROFESSOR SIR ALLEN FERGUS: It has been an extremely eventful year. My split with the RPSP has been well-publicized I suppose, and it was far from being a pleasant thing to go through. But I believe it better to part with one's colleagues openly than try to struggle on hypocritically when the differences between you are so marked. They think that Sportsman analogues for senior civil service positions, and Soap-Star analogues for junior Ministers, will restore public trust. But I firmly believe that the people will never truly trust actors and sportsmen in politics.

METATAB: But isn't it true that the Replicant personalities constitute separate routines to their processing and intellectual powers?

HERR-DOKTOR PROFESSOR SIR ALLEN FERGUS: Of course; a Replicant with a personality based on a famous sportsman has exactly the same administrative competence as a regular Replicant. That's not the issue. The issue is public perception.

METATAB: Is this why you have appealed to the public through the voting system?

HERR-DOKTOR PROFESSOR SIR ALLEN FERGUS: Voting had become a minority pastime. People have believed for years—and not without reason—that one company's Public Service Replicants were as good as another's for the job they are designed to do, and that therefore there's little point in going through the charade of voting for one or other. But introducing celebrity personalities provides a new reason to vote. The populace is excited at the coming election, in a way it hasn't been for decades. I believe my Mythic Politicians will appeal to the public more than RPSP's Sporting and Screen star line-up. It's as simple as that.

METATAB: And yet you have often placed on the record your contempt for the public at large, and your disillusion with the voting process?

HERR-DOKTOR PROFESSOR SIR ALLEN FERGUS: "Contempt" is a strong word. Most working people in this country feel a certain condescension toward the National Wage layabouts. That's undeniable, I think.

METATAB: And yet over two thirds of the population live on the National Wage.

HERR-DOKTOR PROFESSOR SIR ALLEN FERGUS: True. Of course, not *all* of them are the loutish, hanging-around-on-street-corners, petty vandalism and substance-ingestion types. But many are, and I think all of us Political

Engineers and Programmers need to look that unpleasant fact clean in the face. As for the question of the validity or otherwise of the voting process: yes, for many years, with the service provided by the Replicants, it was an anachronism, and, yes, I was among its critics. But recent events have seen a new use for the otherwise antiquated principle.

METATAB: Is your King Arthur here, in Avebury, now?

HERR-DOKTOR PROFESSOR SIR ALLEN FERGUS: He is out canvassing at present. Election laws allow me three versions of any one candidate, and all three are out in the country at the moment.

METATAB: Good luck, and thank you.

HERR-DOKTOR PROFESSOR SIR ALLEN FERGUS: Thank *you.*

.*3.*

50-7-11. *MetaTab spoke briefly to Sir Allen Fergus yesterday.*

[topic: Allegations] Stream: Fergus in silver. ART Logo. Walking rapidly along Fulham Walkway.

METATAB: Sir Allen! Sir Allen! Might MetaTab ask you a few questions?

SIR ALLEN FERGUS: In a fearful hurry . . .

METATAB: How do you respond to the allegations that your candidate, King Arthur, has raised a private army and committed terrorist actions against the state on a number of occasions?

SIR ALLEN FERGUS: I reject these allegations. King Arthur has been moving among the real, the real people in the *real* country, not the media bubble. The people have, have, they have taken him to their breast. It is true he has recruited a number of National Wagers to assist his election campaign.

METATAB: Some authorities estimate that number at eighty thousand.

SIR ALLEN FERGUS: I cannot comment upon figures. What is important is that he has given these people back their hope, purpose, and self-respect.

METATAB: And he has armed them?

SIR ALLEN FERGUS: These are dangerous times, riots, civil disturbance. In my opinion, Arthur is to be commended for taking a firm line with social malcontents and criminals. I think you'll find that polls place my candidate firmly in the lead. People respect his strong stance.

METATAB: Isn't it against the law to recruit a private army?

SIR ALLEN FERGUS: Desperate times require extreme solutions. You must remember that this is not some publicity stunt, this is the real King Arthur—as near as modern science can reconstruct him. He is true to himself: a warrior, not an equivocating and corrupt politician. A *dux bellorum*. And it is as such that the people want him.

.*4.*

50-11-20. *MetaTab today attended a press briefing by Sir Allen Fergus.*

[topic: Battle] Stream: Fergus in black. ART Logo. Virtual environment.

SIR ALLEN FERGUS: I am here to confirm that a battle has recently been fought at Camden, between human troops loyal to King Arthur, and the largely android forces of the RPSP Government. Arthur was triumphant. The Presidential order declaring last week's election result void has been overturned, and King Arthur is once again the constitutional leader of our nation, in line with the result of that ballot. The President, and all employees of RPSP, are now public enemies, and should present themselves to the authorities within three days. Failure to do so will result in police seizure. People! I bring great news. A new dawn commences! King Arthur himself has returned to lead his country, a rebirth made possible by new developments in science! The old decadence will be burned away, and a golden age inaugurated!

[*Applause. Cheers.*]

KING ARTHUR: I would like to thank my trusted adviser, Sir Fergus, who is true and noble. I feel the force of destiny working through me. Britain, awake! The National Wage shall be abolished. All unemployed citizens will be given the choice of joining the army or supervising their own destinies without leeching upon the state. Web access will be curtailed. Roads will be built. A new moral code of purity and honor will be made law. Chivalry will govern all citizens' lives. The glorious return is now! To those Saxons among us, I say this: we do not intend to expel you from our country, and we invite you to serve the greater good of New Britain. We believe it is possible for Saxons to be patriotic, and the first year of our reign will be devoted to giving them the chance to prove their devotion. Naturally, for reasons of national security, all citizens racially Saxon must now report to new Citizenship Stations and register their addresses to receive citizenship-reallocation. This process will *not* result in stigmatization as second tier subjects, provided *all* Saxons collect their new work-permit-directives. Those who do not register are liable to imprisonment. Citizens who are racially Celt, and who can prove genuine Celtic blood on both sides for three generations, may apply to be admitted to the Order of the Round Table. My mandate is from the people! A great day is dawning!

.5.

52-1-2. *Excalibur National Press Services are pleased to announce that they were permitted an interview with Sir Allen Fergus last week.*

ENPS: You have achieved so much, Sir Fergus. Are you planning the well-earned retirement of which you have sometimes talked, or can a grateful people persuade you to continue shouldering the burden of responsibility that goes with being the King's most trusted adviser?

SIR ALLEN FERGUS: Ah, how tempting it would be—to retire to the country, to live out the rest of my days in peace! But I fear the enemies of the state, within and without, press us too closely to allow me to lay down my burden. Arthur's great mission, although it has achieved so much, is not yet complete. The shocking, riotous violence of the inmates of His Majesty's Prison Salisbury Plain show the dangers posed by Saxon criminals, even when under lock and key. This is a problem that may require a longer consultation period, more thought, and perhaps a more fundamental approach before we can reach a solution.

ENPS: Are you managing to keep up your scientific research, on top of the arduous duties of political high office? I understand a group of true citizens has presented a million-signature petition to the Nobel Committee on your behalf?

SIR ALLEN FERGUS: I can hardly comment on that, flattering though it is. No, I am still managing a little nonpolitical work, a little bit of science. For the good of mankind, you see. A deputation of German citizens recently approached me, and I'm working with them on resurrecting a great hero of German history, in Programmed Replicant form, to help bring their country back from the political brink on which it, lamentably, sits. I am only happy to be of service.

ENPS: Sir Fergus, I speak on behalf of the whole nation when I say: thank you.

SIR ALLEN FERGUS: Don't mention it.

Beyond the Aquila Rift

ALASTAIR REYNOLDS

Alastair Reynolds (www.members.tripod.com/~voxish) lives in Noordwijk, Holland, and worked for ten years for the European Space Agency before becoming a full-time writer in 2004. He is one of the new British space opera writers to emerge in the mid and late 1990s, in the generation after Baxter and McAuley, and originally the most "hard SF" of them. His first novel, Revelation Space, *was published in 1999. He is growing fast as an SF writer in this decade. His last two novels are* Century Rain *and* Pushing Ice. *His first short story collection,* Galactic North, *collecting pieces in the RS universe, is out in 2006.*

"Beyond the Aquila Rift" was published in Constellations. *There is an echo of Philip K. Dick's classic, "A Little Something for Us Tempunauts." A ship is marooned outside the galaxy by an alien wormhole transportation system that everyone uses but no one really understands. Reality is not what it appears to be.*

*G*reta's with me when I pull Suzy out of the surge tank.

"Why her?" Greta asks.

"Because I want her out first," I say, wondering if Greta's jealous. I don't blame her: Suzy's beautiful, but she's also smart. There isn't a better syntax runner in Ashanti Industrial.

"What happened?" Suzy asks, when she's over the grogginess. "Did we make it back?"

I ask her to tell me the last thing she remembered.

"Customs," Suzy says. "Those pricks on Arkangel."

"And after that? Anything else? The runes? Do you remember casting them?"

"No," she says, then picks up something in my voice. The fact that I might not be telling the truth, or telling her all she needs to know. "Thom. I'll ask you again. Did we make it back?"

"Yeah," I say. "We made it back."

Suzy looks back at the starscape, airbrushed across her surge tank in luminous violet and yellow paint. She'd had it customized on Carillon. It was against regs: something about the paint clogging intake filters. Suzy didn't care. She told me it had cost her a week's pay, but it had been worth it to impose her own personality on the gray company architecture of the ship.

"Funny how I feel like I've been in that thing for months."

I shrug. "That's the way it feels sometimes."

"Then nothing went wrong?"

"Nothing at all."

Suzy looks at Greta. "Then who are you?" she asks.

Greta says nothing. She just looks at me expectantly. I start shaking, and realize I can't go through with this. Not yet.

"End it," I tell Greta.

Greta steps toward Suzy. Suzy reacts, but she isn't quick enough. Greta pulls something from her pocket and touches Suzy on the forearm. Suzy drops like a puppet, out cold. We put her back into the surge tank, plumb her back in and close the lid.

"She won't remember anything," Greta says. "The conversation never left her short term memory."

"I don't know if I can go through with this," I say.

Greta touches me with her other hand. "No one ever said this was going to be easy."

"I was just trying to ease her into it gently. I didn't want to tell her the truth right out."

"I know," Greta says. "You're a kind man, Thom." Then she kisses me.

I remembered Arkangel as well. That was about where it all started to go wrong. We just didn't know it then.

We missed our first take-off slot when customs found a discrepancy in our cargo waybill. It wasn't serious, but it took them a while to realize their mistake. By the time they did, we knew we were going to be sitting on the ground for another eight hours, while in-bound control processed a fleet of bulk carriers.

I told Suzy and Ray the news. Suzy took it pretty well, or about as well as Suzy ever took that kind of thing. I suggested she use the time to scour the docks for any hot syntax patches. Anything that might shave a day or two off our return trip.

"Company authorized?" she asked.

"I don't care," I said.

"What about Ray?" Suzy asked. "Is he going to sit here drinking tea while I work for my pay?"

I smiled. They had a bickering, love-hate thing going. "No, Ray can do something useful as well. He can take a look at the q-planes."

"Nothing wrong with those planes," Ray said.

I took off my old Ashanti Industrial bib cap, scratched my bald spot and turned to the jib man.

"Right. Then it won't take you long to check them over, will it?"

"Whatever, Skip."

The thing I liked about Ray was that he always knew when he'd lost an argument. He gathered his kit and went out to check over the planes. I watched him climb the jib ladder, tools hanging from his belt. Suzy got her facemask, long black coat and left, vanishing into the vapor haze of the docks, boot heels clicking into the distance long after she'd passed out of sight.

I left the *Blue Goose*, walking in the opposite direction to Suzy. Overhead, the bulk carriers slid in one after the other. You heard them long before you saw them. Mournful, cetacean moans cut down through the piss-yellow clouds over the port. When they emerged, you saw dark hulls scabbed and scarred by the blocky extrusions of syntax patterning, jibs and q-planes retracted for landing and undercarriage clutching down like talons. The carriers stopped over their allocated wells and lowered down on a scream of thrust. Docking gantries closed around them like grasping skeletal fingers. Cargo handling 'saurs plodded out of their holding pens, some of them autonomous, some of them still being ridden by trainers. There was a shocking silence as the engines cut, until the next carrier began to approach through the clouds.

I always like watching ships coming and going, even when they're holding my own ship on the ground. I couldn't read the syntax, but I knew these ships had come in all the way from the Rift. The Aquila Rift is about as far out as anyone ever goes. At median tunnel speeds, it's a year from the center of the Local Bubble.

I've been out that way once in my life. I've seen the view

from the near side of the Rift, like a good tourist. It was about far enough for me.

When there was a lull in the landing pattern, I ducked into a bar and found an Aperture Authority booth that took Ashanti credit. I sat in the seat and recorded a thirty-second message to Katerina. I told her I was on my way back but that we were stuck on Arkangel for another few hours. I warned her that the delay might cascade through to our tunnel routing, depending on how busy things were at the Aperture Authority's end. Based on past experience, an eight-hour ground hold might become a two day hold at the surge point. I told her I'd be back, but she shouldn't worry if I was a few days late.

Outside a diplodocus slouched by with a freight container strapped between its legs.

I told Katerina I loved her and couldn't wait to get back home.

While I walked back to the *Blue Goose*, I thought of the message racing ahead of me. Transmitted at lightspeed up-system, then copied into the memory buffer of the next outgoing ship. Chances were, that particular ship wasn't headed to Barranquilla or anywhere near it. The Aperture Authority would have to relay the message from ship to ship until it reached its destination. I might even reach Barranquilla ahead of it, but in all my years of delays that had only happened once. The system worked all right.

Overhead, a white passenger liner had been slotted in between the bulk carriers. I lifted up my mask to get a better look at it. I got a hit of ozone, fuel, and dinosaur dung. That was Arkangel all right. You couldn't mistake it for any other place in the Bubble. There were four hundred worlds out there, up to a dozen surface ports on every planet, and none of them smelled bad in quite the same way.

"Thom?"

I followed the voice. It was Ray, standing by the dock.

"You finished checking those planes?" I asked.

Ray shook his head. "That's what I wanted to talk to you about. They were a little off-alignment, so—seeing as we're going to be sitting here for eight hours—I decided to run a full recalibration."

I nodded. "That was the idea. So what's the prob?"

"The *prob* is a slot just opened up. Tower says we can lift in thirty minutes."

I shrugged. "Then we'll lift."

"I haven't finished the recal. As it is, things are worse than before I started. Lifting now would not be a good idea."

"You know how the tower works," I said. "Miss two offered slots, you could be on the ground for days."

"No one wants to get back home sooner than I do," Ray said.

"So cheer up."

"She'll be rough in the tunnel. It won't be a smooth ride home."

I shrugged. "Do we care? We'll be asleep."

"Well, it's academic. We can't leave without Suzy."

I heard boot heels clicking toward us. Suzy came out of the fog, tugging her own mask aside.

"No joy with the rune monkeys," she said. "Nothing they were selling I hadn't seen a million times before. Fucking cowboys."

"It doesn't matter," I said. "We're leaving anyway."

Ray swore. I pretended I hadn't heard him.

I was always the last one into a surge tank. I never went under until I was sure we were about to get the green light. It gave me a chance to check things over. Things can always go wrong, no matter how good the crew.

The *Blue Goose* had come to a stop near the AA beacon which marked the surge point. There were a few other ships ahead of us in the queue, plus the usual swarm of AA service craft. Through an observation blister I was able to watch the larger ships depart one by one. Accelerating at maximum power, they seemed to streak toward a completely featureless part of the sky. Their jibs were spread wide, and the smooth lines of their hulls were gnarled and disfigured with the cryptic alien runes of the routing syntax. At twenty gees it was as if a huge invisible hand snatched them away into the distance. Ninety seconds later, there'd be a pale green flash from a thousand kilometers away.

I twisted around in the blister. There were the foreshortened symbols of our routing syntax. Each rune of the script was formed from a matrix of millions of hexagonal platelets. The platelets were on motors so they could be pushed in or out from the hull.

Ask the Aperture Authority and they'll tell you that the syntax is now fully understood. This is true, but only up to a point. After two centuries of study, human machines can now construct and interpret the syntax with an acceptably low failure rate. Given a desired destination, they can assemble a string of runes which will almost always be accepted by the aperture's own machinery. Furthermore, they can almost always guarantee that the desired routing is the one that the aperture machinery will provide.

In short, you usually get where you want to go.

Take a simple point-to-point transfer, like the Hauraki run. In that case there is no real disadvantage in using automatic syntax generators. But for longer trajectories—those that may involve six or seven transits between aperture hubs—machines lose the edge. They find a solution, but usually it isn't the optimum one. That's where syntax runners come in. People like Suzy have an intuitive grasp of syntax solutions. They dream in runes. When they see a poorly constructed script, they feel it like a toothache. It *affronts* them.

A good syntax runner can shave days off a route. For a company like Ashanti Industrial, that can make a lot of difference.

But I wasn't a syntax runner. I could tell when something had gone wrong with the platelets, but otherwise I had no choice. I had to trust that Suzy had done her job.

But I knew Suzy wouldn't screw things up.

I twisted around and looked back the other way. Now that we were in space, the q-planes had deployed. They were swung out from the hull on triple hundred-meter long jibs, like the arms of a grapple. I checked that they were locked in their fully extended positions and that the status lights were all in the green. The jibs were Ray's area. He'd been checking the alignment of the ski-shaped q-planes when I ordered him to close-up ship and prepare to lift. I couldn't see any visible indication that they were out of alignment, but then again it wouldn't take much to make our trip home bumpier than usual. But as I'd told Ray, who cared? The *Blue Goose* could take a little tunnel turbulence. It was built to.

I checked the surge point again. Only three ships ahead of us.

I went back to the surge tanks and checked that Suzy and Ray were all right. Ray's tank had been customized at the same time that Suzy had had hers done. It was full of images of what Suzy called the BVM: the Blessed Virgin Mary. The BVM was always in a spacesuit, carrying a little spacesuited Jesus. Their helmets were airbrushed gold halos. The artwork had a cheap, hasty look to it. I assumed Ray hadn't spent as much as Suzy.

Quickly I stripped down to my underclothes. I plumbed into my own unpainted surge tank and closed the lid. The buffering gel sloshed in. Within about twenty seconds I was already feeling drowsy. By the time traffic control gave us the green light, I'd be asleep.

I've done it a thousand times. There was no fear, no apprehension. Just a tiny flicker of regret.

I've never seen an aperture. Then again, very few people have.

Witnesses report a doughnut shaped lump of dark chondrite asteroid, about two kilometers across. The entire middle section has been cored out, with the inner part of the ring faced by the quixotic-matter machinery of the aperture itself. They say the q-matter machinery twinkles and moves all the while, like the ticking innards of a very complicated clock. But the monitoring systems of the Aperture Authority detect no movement at all.

It's alien technology. We have no idea how it works, or even who made it. Maybe, in hindsight, it's better not to be able to see it.

It's enough to dream, and then awake, and know that you're somewhere else.

* * *

Try a different approach, Greta says. Tell her the truth this time. Maybe she'll take it easier than you think.

"There's no way I can tell her the truth."

Greta leans one hip against the wall, one hand still in her pocket. "Then tell her something half way to it."

We unplumb Suzy and haul her out of the surge tank.

"Where are we?" *she asks. Then to Greta:* "Who are you?"

I wonder if some of the last conversation did make it out of Suzy's short-term memory after all.

"Greta works here," *I say.*

"Where's here?"

I remember what Greta told me. "A station in Schedar sector."

"That's not where we're meant to be, Thom."

I nod. "I know. There was a mistake. A routing error."

Suzy's already shaking her head. "There was nothing wrong . . ."

"I know. It wasn't your fault." *I help her into her ship clothes. She's still shivering, her muscles reacting to movement after so much time in the tank.* "The syntax was good."

"Then what?"

"The system made a mistake, not you."

"Schedar sector . . ." *Suzy says.* "That would put us about ten days off our schedule, wouldn't it?"

I try to remember what Greta said to me the first time. I ought to know this stuff off by heart, but Suzy's the routing expert, not me. "That sounds about right," *I say.*

But Suzy shakes her head. "Then we're not in Schedar sector."

I try to sound pleasantly surprised.

"We're not?"

"I've been in that tank for a lot longer than a few days, Thom. I know. I can feel it in every fucking bone in my body. So where are we?"

I turn to Greta. I can't believe this is happening again.

"End it," *I say.*

Greta steps toward Suzy.

* * *

You know that "as soon as I awoke I knew everything was wrong" cliché? You've probably heard it a thousand times, in a thousand bars across the Bubble, wherever ship crews swap tall tales over flat company-subsidized beer. The trouble is that sometimes that's exactly the way it happens. I never felt good after a period in the surge tank. But the only time I had ever come around feeling anywhere near this bad was after that trip I took to the edge of the Bubble.

Mulling this, but knowing there was nothing I could do about it until I was out of the tank, it took me half an hour of painful work to free myself from the connections. Every muscle fiber in my body felt as though it had been shredded. Unfortunately, the sense of wrongness didn't end with the tank. The *Blue Goose* was much too quiet. We should have been heading away from the last exit aperture after our routing. But the distant, comforting rumble of the fusion engines wasn't there at all. That meant we were in free-fall.

Not good.

I floated out of the tank, grabbed a handhold and levered myself around to view the other two tanks. Ray's largest BVM stared back radiantly from the cowl of his tank. The bio indices were all in the green. Ray was still unconscious, but there was nothing wrong with him. Same story with Suzy. Some automated system had decided I was the only one who needed waking.

A few minutes later I had made my way to the same observation blister I'd used to check the ship before the surge. I pushed my head into the scuffed glass halfdome and looked around.

We'd arrived somewhere. The *Blue Goose* was sitting in a huge zero-gravity parking bay. The chamber was an elongated cylinder, hexagonal in cross-section. The walls were a smear of service machinery: squat modules, snaking umbilical lines, the retracted cradles of unused docking berths. Whichever way I looked I saw other ships locked onto cradles. Every make and class you could think of, every possible configuration of hull design compatible with aperture transitions. Service lights threw a warm golden glow on the scene. Now and then the whole chamber was bathed in the stuttering violet flicker of a cutting torch.

It was a repair facility.

I was just starting to mull on that when I saw something extend itself from the wall of the chamber. It was a telescopic docking tunnel, groping toward our ship. Through the windows in the side of the tunnel I saw figures floating, pulling themselves along hand over hand.

I sighed and started making my way to the airlock.

By the time I reached the lock they were already through the first stage of the cycle. Nothing wrong with that—there was no good reason to prevent foreign parties boarding a vessel—but it *was* just a tiny bit impolite. But perhaps they'd assumed we were all asleep.

The door slid open.

"You're awake," a man said. "Captain Thomas Gundlupet of the *Blue Goose*, isn't it?"

"Guess so," I said.

"Mind if we come in?"

There were about half a dozen of them, and they were already coming in. They all wore slightly timeworn ochre overalls, flashed with too many company sigils. My hackles rose. I really didn't like the way they were barging in.

"What's up?" I said. "Where are we?"

"Where do you think?" the man said. He had a face full of stubble, with bad yellow teeth. I was impressed with that. Having bad teeth took a lot of work these days. It was years since I'd seen anyone who had the same dedication to the art.

"I'm really hoping you're not going to tell me we're still stuck in Arkangel system," I said.

"No, you made it through the gate."

"And?"

"There was a screw-up. Routing error. You didn't pop out of the right aperture."

"Oh, Christ." I took off my bib cap. "It never rains. Something went wrong with the insertion, right?"

"Maybe. Maybe not. Who knows how these things happen? All we know is you aren't supposed to be here."

"Right. And where is 'here'?"

"Saumlaki Station. Schedar sector."

He said it as though he was already losing interest, as if this was a routine he went through several times a day.

He might have been losing interest. I wasn't.

I'd never heard of Saumlaki Station, but I'd certainly heard of Schedar sector. Schedar was a K supergiant out toward the edge of the Local Bubble. It defined one of the seventy-odd navigational sectors across the whole Bubble.

Did I mention the Bubble already?

You know how the Milky Way galaxy looks; you've seen it a thousand times, in paintings and computer simulations. A bright central bulge at the Galactic core, with lazily curved spiral arms flung out from that hub, each arm composed of hundreds of billions of stars, ranging from the dimmest, slow-burning dwarfs to the hottest supergiants teetering on the edge of supernova extinction.

Now zoom in on one arm of the Milky Way. There's the sun, orange-yellow, about two-thirds out from the center of the Galaxy. Lanes and folds of dust swaddle the sun out to distances of tens of thousands of light-years. Yet the sun itself is sitting right in the middle of a four-hundred-light-year-wide hole in the dust, a bubble in which the density is about a twentieth of its average value.

That's the Local Bubble. It's as if God blew a hole in the dust just for us.

Except, of course, it wasn't God. It was a supernova, about a million years ago.

Look farther out, and there are more bubbles, their walls intersecting and merging, forming a vast froth-like structure tens of thousands of light-years across. There are the structures of Loop I and Loop II and the Lindblad Ring. There are even super-dense knots where the dust is almost too thick to be seen through at all. Black cauls like the Taurus or Rho-Ophiuchi dark clouds or the Aquila Rift itself.

Lying outside the Local Bubble, the Rift is the farthest point in the galaxy we've ever traveled to. It's not a question of endurance or nerve. There simply isn't a way to get beyond it, at least not within the faster-than-light network of the aperture links. The rabbit-warren of possible routes just doesn't reach any farther. Most destinations—including most of those on the *Blue Goose*'s itinerary—didn't even get you beyond the Local Bubble.

For us, it didn't matter. There's still a lot of commerce you can do within a hundred light-years of Earth. But Schedar was right on the periphery of the Bubble, where dust density began to ramp up to normal galactic levels, two hundred and twenty-eight light-years from Mother Earth.

Again: not good.

"I know this is a shock for you," another voice said. "But it's not as bad as you think it is."

I looked at the woman who had just spoken. Medium height, the kind of face they called "elfin," with slanted ash-gray eyes and a bob of shoulder-length chrome-white hair.

The face hurtingly familiar.

"It isn't?"

"I wouldn't say so, Thom." She smiled. "After all, it's given us the chance to catch up on old times, hasn't it?"

"Greta?" I asked, disbelievingly.

She nodded. "For my sins."

"My God. It is you, isn't it?"

"I wasn't sure you'd recognize me. Especially after all this time."

"You didn't have much trouble recognizing me."

"I didn't have to. The moment you popped out, we picked up your recovery transponder. Told us the name of your ship, who owned her, who was flying it, what you were carrying, where you were supposed to be headed. When I heard it was you, I made sure I was part of the reception team. But don't worry. It's not like you've changed all that much."

"Well, you haven't either," I said.

It wasn't quite true. But who honestly wants to hear that they look about ten years older than the last time you saw

them, even if they still don't look all that bad with it? I
thought about how she had looked naked, memories that I'd
kept buried for a decade spooling into daylight. It shamed
me that they were still so vivid, as if some furtive part of my
subconscious had been secretly hoarding them through years
of marriage and fidelity.

Greta half smiled. It was as if she knew exactly what I was
thinking.

"You were never a good liar, Thom."

"Yeah. Guess I need some practice."

There was an awkward silence. Neither of us seemed to
know what to say next. While we hesitated, the others
floated around us, saying nothing.

"Well," I said. "Who'd have guessed we'd end up meeting
like this?"

Greta nodded and offered the palms of her hands in a kind
of apology.

"I'm just sorry we aren't meeting under better circumstances," she said. "But if it's any consolation, what happened wasn't at all your fault. We checked your syntax, and
there wasn't a mistake. It's just that now and then the system
throws a glitch."

"Funny how no one likes to talk about that very much," I
said.

"Could have been worse, Thom. I remember what you
used to tell me about space travel."

"Yeah? Which particular pearl of wisdom would that have
been?"

"If you're in a position to moan about a situation, you've
no right to be moaning."

"Christ. Did I actually say that?"

"Mm. And I bet you're regretting it now. But look, it really
isn't that bad. You're only twenty days off schedule." Greta
nodded toward the man who had the bad teeth. "Kolding
says you'll only need a day of damage repair before you can
move off again, and then another twenty, twenty-five days
before you reach your destination, depending on routing patterns. That's less than six weeks. So you lose the bonus on
this one. Big deal. You're all in one shape, and your ship

only needs a little work. Why don't you just bite the bullet
and sign the repair paperwork?"

"I'm not looking forward to another twenty days in the
surge tank. There's something else, as well."

"Which is?"

I was about to tell her about Katerina, how she'd have
been expecting me back already.

Instead I said: "I'm worried about the others. Suzy and
Ray. They've got families expecting them. They'll be worried."

"I understand," Greta said. "Suzy and Ray. They're still
asleep, aren't they? Still in their surge tanks?"

"Yes," I said, guardedly.

"Keep them that way until you're on your way." Greta
smiled. "There's no sense worrying them about their families, either. It's kinder."

"If you say so."

"Trust me on this one, Thom. This isn't the first time I've
handled this kind of situation. Doubt it'll be the last, either."

I stayed in a hotel overnight, in another part of Saumlaki.
The hotel was an echoing multilevel prefab structure, sunk
deep into bedrock. It must have had a capacity for hundreds
of guests, but at the moment only a handful of the rooms
seemed to be occupied. I slept fitfully and got up early. In
the atrium, I saw a bib-capped worker in rubber gloves removing diseased carp from a small ornamental pond.
Watching him pick out the ailing metallic-orange fish, I had
a flash of déjà vu. What was it about dismal hotels and dying
carp?

Before breakfast—bleakly alert, even though I didn't really feel as if I'd had a good night's sleep—I visited Kolding
and got a fresh update on the repair schedule.

"Two, three days," he said.

"It was a day last night."

Kolding shrugged. "You've got a problem with the service, find someone else to fix your ship."

Then he stuck his little finger into the corner of his mouth
and began to dig between his teeth.

"Nice to see someone who really enjoys his work," I said.

I left Kolding before my mood worsened too much, making my way to a different part of the station.

Greta had suggested we meet for breakfast and catch up on old times. She was there when I arrived, sitting at a table in an "outdoor" terrace, under a red-and-white striped canopy, sipping orange juice. Above us was a dome several hundred meters wide, projecting a cloudless holographic sky. It had the hard, enameled blue of midsummer.

"How's the hotel?" she asked after I'd ordered a coffee from the waiter.

"Not bad. No one seems very keen on conversation, though. Is it me or does that place have all the cheery ambience of a sinking ocean liner?"

"It's just this place," Greta said. "Everyone who comes here is pissed off about it. Either they got transferred here and they're pissed off about *that*, or they ended up here by routing error and they're pissed off about that instead. Take your pick."

"No one's happy?"

"Only the ones who know they're getting out of here soon."

"Would that include you?"

"No," she said. "I'm more or less stuck here. But I'm OK about it. I guess I'm the exception that proves the rule."

The waiters were glass mannequins of a kind that had been fashionable in the core worlds about twenty years ago. One of them placed a croissant in front of me, then poured scalding black coffee into my cup.

"Well, it's good to see you," I said.

"You too, Thom." Greta finished her orange juice and then took a corner of my croissant for herself, without asking. "I heard you got married."

"Yes."

"Well? Aren't you going to tell me about her?"

I drank some of my coffee. "Her name's Katerina."

"Nice name."

"She works in the department of bioremediation on Kagawa."

"Kids?" Greta asked.

"Not yet. It wouldn't be easy, the amount of time we both spend away from home."

"Mm." She had a mouthful of croissant. "But one day you might think about it."

"Nothing's ruled out," I said. As flattered as I was that she was taking such an interest in me, the surgical precision of her questions left me slightly uncomfortable. There was no thrust and parry, no fishing for information. That kind of directness unnerved. But at least it allowed me to ask the same questions. "What about you, then?"

"Nothing very exciting. I got married a year or so after I last saw you. A man called Marcel."

"Marcel," I said, ruminatively, as if the name had cosmic significance. "Well, I'm happy for you. I take it he's here too?"

"No. Our work took us in different directions. We're still married, but . . ." Greta left the sentence hanging.

"It can't be easy," I said.

"If it was meant to work, we'd have found a way. Anyway, don't feel too sorry for either of us. We've both got our work. I wouldn't say I was any less happy than the last time we met."

"Well, that's good," I said.

Greta leaned over and touched my hand. Her fingernails were midnight black with a blue sheen.

"Look. This is really presumptuous of me. It's one thing asking to meet up for breakfast. It would have been rude not to. But how would you like to meet again later? It's really nice to eat here in the evening. They turn down the lights. The view through the dome is really something."

I looked up into that endless holographic sky.

"I thought it was faked."

"Oh, it is," she said. "But don't let that spoil it for you."

I settled in front of the camera and started speaking.

"Katerina," I said. "Hello. I hope you're all right. By now I hope someone from the company will have been in touch. If they haven't, I'm pretty sure you'll have made your own inquiries. I'm not sure what they told you, but I promise you that we're safe and sound and that we're coming home. I'm calling from somewhere called Saumlaki station, a repair facility on the edge of Schedar sector. It's not much to look at: just a warren of tunnels and centrifuges dug into a pitch-black D-type asteroid, about half a light-year from the nearest star. The only reason it's here at all is because there happens to be an aperture next door. That's how we got here in the first place. Somehow or other *Blue Goose* took a wrong turn in the network, what they call a routing error. The *Goose* came in last night, local time, and I've been in a hotel since then. I didn't call last night because I was too tired and disoriented after coming out of the tank, and I didn't know how long we were going to be here. Seemed better to wait until morning, when we'd have a better idea of the damage to the ship. It's nothing serious—just a few bits and pieces buckled during the transit—but it means we're going to be here for another couple of days. Kolding—he's the repair chief—says three at the most. By the time we get back on course, however, we'll be about forty days behind schedule."

I paused, eyeing the incrementing cost indicator. Before I sat down in the booth, I always had an eloquent and economical speech queued up in my head, one that conveyed exactly what needed to be said, with the measure and grace of a soliloquy. But my mind always dried up as soon as I opened my mouth, and instead of an actor I ended up sounding like a small time thief, concocting some fumbling alibi in the presence of quick-witted interrogators.

I smiled awkwardly and continued: "It kills me to think this message is going to take so long to get to you. But if there's a silver lining, it's that I won't be far behind it. By the time you get this, I should be home in only a couple of days. So don't waste money replying to this, because by the time you get it I'll already have left Saumlaki Station. Just stay where you are, and I promise I'll be home soon."

That was it. There was nothing more I needed to say, other than: "I miss you." Delivered after a moment's pause, I meant it to sound emphatic. But when I replayed the recording it sounded more like an afterthought.

I could have recorded it again, but I doubted that I would have been any happier. Instead I just committed the existing message for transmission and wondered how long it would have to wait before going on its way. Since it seemed unlikely that there was a vast flow of commerce in and out of Saumlaki, our ship might be the first suitable outbound vessel.

I emerged from the booth. For some reason I felt guilty, as if I had been in some way neglectful. It took me a while before I realized what was playing on my mind. I'd told Katerina about Saumlaki Station. I'd even told her about Kolding and the damage to the *Blue Goose*. But I hadn't told her about Greta.

It's not working with Suzy.

She's too smart, too well-attuned to the physiological correlatives of surge tank immersion. I can give her all the reassurances in the world, but she knows she's been under too long for this to be anything other than a truly epic screw-up. She knows that we aren't just talking weeks or even months of delay here. Every nerve in her body is screaming that message into her skull.

"I had dreams," she says, when the grogginess fades.

"What kind?"

"Dreams that I kept waking. Dreams that you were pulling me out of the surge tank. You and someone else."

I do my best to smile. I'm alone, but Greta isn't far away. The hypodermic's in my pocket now.

"I always get bad dreams coming out of the tank," I say.

"These felt real. Your story kept changing, but you kept telling me we were somewhere . . . that we'd gone a little off course, but that it was nothing to worry about."

So much for Greta's reassurance that Suzy will remember nothing after our aborted efforts at waking her. Seems that her short-term memory isn't quite as fallible as we'd like.

"It's funny you should say that," I tell her. "Because, actually, we are a little off course."

She's sharper with every breath. Suzy was always the best of us at coming out of the tank.

"Tell me how far, Thom."

"Farther than I'd like."

She balls her fists. I can't tell if it's aggression, or some lingering neuromuscular effect of her time in the tank. "How far? Beyond the Bubble?"

"Beyond the Bubble, yes."

Her voice grows small and childlike.

"Tell me, Thom. Are we out beyond the Rift?"

I can hear the fear. I understand what she's going through. It's the nightmare that all ship crews live with, on every trip. That something will go wrong with the routing, something so severe that they'll end up on the very edge of the network. That they'll end up so far from home that getting back will take years, not months. And that, of course, years will have already passed, even before they begin the return trip.

That loved ones will be years older when they reach home.

If they're still there. If they still remember you, or want to remember. If they're still recognizable, or alive.

Beyond the Aquila Rift. It's shorthand for the trip no one ever hopes to make by accident. The one that will screw up the rest of your life, the one that creates the ghosts you see haunting the shadows of company bars across the whole Bubble. Men and women ripped out of time, cut adrift from families and lovers by an accident of an alien technology we use but barely comprehend.

"Yes," I say. "We're beyond the Rift."

Suzy screams, knitting her face into a mask of anger and denial. My hand is cold around the hypodermic. I consider using it.

A new repair estimate from Kolding. Five, six days.

This time I didn't even argue. I just shrugged and walked out, wondering how long it would be next time.

That evening I sat down at the same table where Greta and I had met over breakfast. The dining area had been well lit before, but now the only illumination came from the table lamps and the subdued lighting panels set into the paving. In the distance, a glass mannequin cycled from empty table to empty table, playing *Asturias* on a glass guitar. There were no other patrons dining tonight.

I didn't have long to wait for Greta.

"I'm sorry I'm late, Thom."

I turned to her as she approached the table. I liked the way she walked in the low gravity of the station, the way the subdued lighting traced the arc of her hips and waist. She eased into her seat and leaned toward me in the manner of a conspirator. The lamp on the table threw red shadows and gold highlights across her face. It took ten years off her age.

"You aren't late," I said. "And anyway, I had the view."

"It's an improvement, isn't it?"

"That wouldn't be saying much," I said with a smile. "But yes, it's definitely an improvement."

"I could sit out here all night and just look at it. In fact sometimes that's exactly what I do. Just me and a bottle of wine."

"I don't blame you."

Instead of the holographic blue, the dome was now full of stars. It was like no kind of view I'd ever seen from another station or ship. There were furious blue-white stars embedded in what looked like sheets of velvet. There were hard gold gems and soft red smears, like finger smears in pastel. There were streams and currents of fainter stars, like a myriad neon fish caught in a snapshot of frozen motion. There were vast billowing backdrops of red and green cloud, veined and flawed by filaments of cool black. There were bluffs and promontories of ochre dust, so rich in three-dimensional structure that they resembled an exuberant impasto of oil colors; contours light-years thick laid on with a trowel. Red or pink stars burned through the dust like lanterns. Orphaned worlds were caught erupting from the towers, little spermlike shapes trailing viscera of dust. Here and there I saw the tiny eyelike knots of birthing solar systems. There were pulsars, flashing on and off like navigation beacons, their differing rhythms seeming to set a stately tempo for the entire scene, like a deathly slow waltz. There seemed too much detail for one view, an overwhelming abundance of richness, and yet no matter which direction I looked, there was yet more to see, as if the dome sensed my attention and concentrated its efforts on the spot where my gaze was directed. For a moment I felt a lurching sense of dizziness, and—though I tried to stop it before I made a fool of myself—I found myself grasping the side of the table, as if to stop myself falling into the infinite depths of the view.

"Yes, it has that effect on people," Greta said.

"It's beautiful," I said.

"Do you mean beautiful, or terrifying?"

I realized I wasn't sure. "It's big," was all I could offer.

"Of course, it's faked," Greta said, her voice soft now that she was leaning closer. "The glass in the dome is smart. It exaggerates the brightness of the stars, so that the human eye registers the differences between them. Otherwise the colors aren't unrealistic. Everything else you see is also pretty accurate, if you accept that certain frequencies have been shifted into the visible band, and the scale of certain structures has been adjusted." She pointed out features for my edification. "That's the edge of the Taurus Dark Cloud, with the Pleiades just poking out. That's a filament of the Local Bubble. You see that open cluster?"

She waited for me to answer. "Yes," I said.

"That's the Hyades. Over there you've got Betelguese and Bellatrix."

"I'm impressed."

"You should be. It cost a lot of money." She leaned back a bit, so that the shadows dropped across her face again. "Are you all right, Thom? You seem a bit distracted."

I sighed.

"I just got another prognosis from your friend Kolding. That's enough to put a dent in anyone's day."

"I'm sorry about that."

"There's something else, too," I said. "Something that's been bothering me since I came out of the tank."

A mannequin came to take our order. I let Greta choose for me.

"You can talk to me, whatever it is," she said, when the mannequin had gone.

"It isn't easy."

"Something personal, then? Is it about Katerina?" She bit her tongue "No, sorry. I shouldn't have said that."

"It's not about Katerina. Not exactly, anyway." But even as I said it, I knew that in a sense it *was* about Katerina, and how long it was going to be before we saw each other again.

"Go on, Thom."

"This is going to sound silly. But I wonder if everyone's being straight with me. It's not just Kolding. It's you as well. When I came out of that tank I felt the same way I felt when I'd been out to the Rift. Worse, if anything. I felt like I'd been in the tank for a long, long time."

"It feels that way sometimes."

"I know the difference, Greta. Trust me on this."

"So what are you saying?"

The problem was that I wasn't really sure. It was one thing to feel a vague sense of unease about how long I'd been in the tank. It was another to come out and accuse my host of lying. Especially when she had been so hospitable.

"Is there any reason you'd lie to me?"

"Come off it, Thom. What kind of a question is that?"

As soon as I had come out with it, it sounded absurd and offensive to me as well. I wished I could reverse time and start again, ignoring my misgivings.

"I'm sorry," I said. "Stupid. Just put it down to messed up biorhythms, or something."

She reached across the table and took my hand, as she had done at breakfast. This time she continued to hold it.

"You really feel wrong, don't you?"

"Kolding's games aren't helping, that's for sure." The waiter brought our wine, setting it down, the bottle chinking against his delicately articulated glass fingers. The mannequin poured two glasses and I sampled mine. "Maybe if I had someone else from my crew to bitch about it all with, I wouldn't feel so bad. I know you said we shouldn't wake Suzy and Ray, but that was before a one-day stopover turned into a week."

Greta shrugged. "If you want to wake them, no one's going to stop you. But don't think about ship business now. Let's not spoil a perfect evening."

I looked up at the stars. It was heightened, with the mad shimmering intensity of a Van Gogh nightscape.

It made one feel drunk and ecstatic just to look at it.

"What could possibly spoil it?" I asked.

What happened is that I drank too much wine and ended up sleeping with Greta. I'm not sure how much of a part the wine played in it for her. If her relationship with Marcel was in as much trouble as she'd made out, then obviously she had less to lose than I did. Yes, that made it all right, didn't it? She the seductress, her own marriage a wreck, me the hapless victim. I'd lapsed, yes, but it wasn't really my fault. I'd been alone, far from home, emotionally fragile, and she had exploited me. She had softened me up with a romantic meal, her trap already sprung.

Except all that was self-justifying bullshit, wasn't it? If my own marriage was in such great shape, why had I failed to mention Greta when I called home? At the time, I'd justified that omission as an act of kindness toward my wife. Katerina didn't know that Greta and I had ever been a couple. But why worry Katerina by mentioning another woman, even if I pretended that we'd never met before?

Except—now—I could see that I'd failed to mention Greta for another reason entirely. Because in the back of my mind, even then, there had been the possibility that we might end up sleeping together.

I was already covering myself when I called Katerina. Already making sure there wouldn't be any awkward questions when I got home. As if I not only knew what was going to happen but secretly yearned for it.

The only problem was that Greta had something else in mind.

"Thom," Greta said, nudging me toward wakefulness. She was lying naked next to me, leaning on one elbow, with the sheets crumpled down around her hips. The light in her room turned her into an abstraction of milky blue curves and deep violet shadows. With one black-nailed finger she traced

a line down my chest and said: "There's something you need
to know."

"What?" I asked.

"I lied. Kolding lied. We all lied."

I was too drowsy for her words to have much more than a
vaguely troubling effect. All I could say, again, was:
"What?"

"You're not in Saumlaki Station. You're not in Schedar
sector."

I started waking up properly. "Say that again."

"The routing error was more severe than you were led to
believe. It took you far beyond the Local Bubble."

I groped for anger, even resentment, but all I felt was a
dizzying sensation of falling. "How far out?"

"Farther than you thought possible."

The next question was obvious.

"Beyond the Rift?"

"Yes," she said, with the faintest of smiles, as if humoring
a game whose rules and objectives she found ultimately de-
meaning. "Beyond the Aquila Rift. A long, long way beyond
it."

"I need to know, Greta."

She pushed herself from the bed, reached for a gown.
"Then get dressed. I'll show you."

I followed Greta in a daze.

She took me to the dome again. It was dark, just as it had
been the night before, with only the lamp-lit tables to act as
beacons. I supposed that the illumination throughout Saumlaki Station (or wherever this was) was at the whim of its
occupants and didn't necessarily have to follow any recognizable diurnal cycle. Nonetheless, it was still unsettling to
find it changed so arbitrarily. Even if Greta had the authority
to turn out the lights when she wanted to, didn't anyone else
object?

But I didn't see anyone else *to* object. There was no one
else around; only a glass mannequin standing to attention
with a napkin over one arm.

She sat us at a table. "Do you want a drink, Thom?"

"No, thanks. For some reason I'm not quite in the mood."

She touched my wrist. "Don't hate me for lying to you. It was done out of kindness. I couldn't break the truth to you in one go."

Sharply I withdrew my hand. "Shouldn't I be the judge of that? So what is the truth, exactly?"

"It's not good, Thom."

"Tell me, then I'll decide."

I didn't see her do anything, but suddenly the dome was filled with stars again, just as it had been the night before.

The view lurched, zooming outward. Stars flowed by from all sides, like white sleet. Nebulae ghosted past in spectral wisps. The sense of motion was so compelling that I found myself gripping the table, seized by vertigo.

"Easy, Thom," Greta whispered.

The view lurched, swerved, contracted. A solid wall of gas slammed past. Now, suddenly, I had the sense that we were outside something—that we had punched beyond some containing sphere, defined only in vague arcs and knots of curdled gas, where the interstellar gas density increased sharply.

Of course. It was obvious. We were beyond the Local Bubble.

And we were still receding. I watched the Bubble itself contract, becoming just one member in the larger froth of voids. Instead of individual stars, I saw only smudges and motes, aggregations of hundreds of thousands of suns. It was like pulling back from a close-up view of a forest. I could still see clearings, but the individual trees had vanished into an amorphous mass.

We kept pulling back. Then the expansion slowed and froze. I could still make out the Local Bubble, but only because I had been concentrating on it all the way out. Otherwise, there was nothing to distinguish it from the dozens of surrounding voids.

"Is that how far out we've come?" I asked.

Greta shook her head. "Let me show you something."

Again, she did nothing that I was aware of. But the Bubble

I had been looking at was suddenly filled with a skein of red lines, like a child's scribble.

"Aperture connections," I said.

As shocked as I was by the fact that she had lied to me—and as fearful as I was about what the truth might hold—I couldn't turn off the professional part of me, the part that took pride in recognizing such things.

Greta nodded. "Those are the main commerce routes, the well-mapped connections between large colonies and major trading hubs. Now I'll add all mapped connections, including those that have only ever been traversed by accident."

The scribble did not change dramatically. It gained a few more wild loops and hairpins, including one that reached beyond the wall of the Bubble to touch the sunward end of the Aquila Rift. One or two other additions pierced the wall in different directions, but none of them reached as far as the Rift.

"Where are we?"

"We're at one end of one of those connections. You can't see it because it's pointing directly toward you." She smiled slightly. "I needed to establish the scale that we're dealing with. How wide is the Local Bubble, Thom? Four hundred light-years, give or take?"

My patience was wearing thin. But I was still curious.

"About right."

"And while I know that aperture travel times vary from point to point, with factors depending on network topology and syntax optimization, isn't it the case that the average speed is about one thousand times faster than light?"

"Give or take."

"So a journey from one side of the Bubble might take—what, half a year? Say five or six months? A year to the Aquila Rift?"

"You know that already, Greta. We both know it."

"All right. Then consider this." And the view contracted again, the Bubble dwindling, a succession of overlaying structures concealing it, darkness coming into view on either side, and then the familiar spiral swirl of the Milky Way galaxy looming large.

Hundreds of billions of stars, packed together into foaming white lanes of sea spume.

"This is the view," Greta said. "Enhanced of course, brightened and filtered for human consumption—but if you had eyes with near-perfect quantum efficiency, and if they happened to be about a meter wide, this is more or less what you'd see if you stepped outside the station."

"I don't believe you."

What I meant was I didn't *want* to believe her.

"Get used to it, Thom. You're a long way out. The station's orbiting a brown dwarf star in the Large Magellanic Cloud. You're one hundred and fifty thousand light-years from home."

"No," I said, my voice little more than a moan of abject, childlike denial.

"You felt as though you'd spent a long time in the tank. You were dead right. Subjective time? I don't know. Years, easily. Maybe a decade. But objective time—the time that passed back home—is a lot clearer. It took *Blue Goose* one hundred and fifty years to reach us. Even if you turned back now, you'd have been away for three hundred years, Thom."

"Katerina," I said, her name like an invocation.

"Katerina's dead," Greta told me. "She's already been dead a century."

How do you adjust to something like that? The answer is that you can't count on adjusting to it at all. Not everyone does. Greta told me that she had seen just about every possible reaction in the spectrum, and the one thing she had learned was that it was next to impossible to predict how a given individual would take the news. She had seen people adjust to the revelation with little more than a world-weary shrug, as if this were merely the latest in a line of galling surprises life had thrown at them, no worse in its way than illness or bereavement or any number of personal setbacks. She had seen others walk away and kill themselves half an hour later.

But the majority, she said, did eventually come to some kind of accommodation with the truth, however faltering and painful the process.

"Trust me, Thom," she said. "I know you now. I know you have the emotional strength to get through this. I know you can learn to live with it."

"Why didn't you tell me straight away, as soon as I came out of the tank?"

"Because I didn't know if you were going to be able to take it."

"You waited until after you knew I had a wife."

"No," Greta said. "I waited until after we'd made love. Because then I knew Katerina couldn't mean that much to you."

"Fuck you."

"Fuck me? Yes, you did. That's the point."

I wanted to strike out against her. But what I was angry at was not her insinuation but the cold-hearted truth of it. She was right, and I knew it. I just didn't want to deal with that, any more than I wanted to deal with the here and now.

I waited for the anger to subside.

"You say we're not the first?" I said.

"No. We were the first, I suppose—the ship I came in. Luckily it was well equipped. After the routing error, we had enough supplies to set up a self-sustaining station on the nearest rock. We knew there was no going back, but at least we could make some kind of life for ourselves here."

"And after that?"

"We had enough to do just keeping ourselves alive, the first few years. But then another ship came through the aperture. Damaged, drifting, much like *Blue Goose*. We hauled her in, warmed her crew, broke the news to them."

"How'd they take it?"

"About as well as you'd expect." Greta laughed hollowly to herself. "A couple of them went mad. Another killed herself. But at least a dozen of them are still here. In all honesty, it was good for us that another ship came through. Not just because they had supplies we could use, but because it helped us to help them. Took our minds off our own self-pity. It made us realize how far we'd come and how much help these newcomers needed to make the same transition. That wasn't the last ship, either. We've gone through the same process with eight or nine others, since then." Greta looked at me, her head cocked against her hand. "There's a thought for you, Thom."

"There is?"

She nodded. "It's difficult for you now, I know. And it'll be difficult for you for some time to come. But it can help to have someone else to care about. It can smooth the transition."

"Like who?" I asked.

"Like one of your other crew members," Greta said. "You could try waking one of them, now."

Greta's with me when I pull Suzy out of the surge tank.

"Why her?" Greta asks.

"Because I want her out first," I say, wondering if Greta's jealous. I don't blame her. Suzy's beautiful, but she's also smart. There isn't a better syntax runner in Ashanti Industrial.

"What happened?" Suzy asks, when's she over the grogginess. "Did we make it back?"

I ask her to tell me the last thing she remembered.

"Customs," Suzy says. "Those pricks on Arkangel."

"And after that? Anything else? The runes? Do you remember casting them?"

"No," she says, then picks up something in my voice. The fact that I might not be telling the truth, or telling her all she needs to know. "Thom. I'll ask you again. Did we make it back?"

A minute later we're putting Suzy back into the tank.

It hasn't worked first time. Maybe next try.

But it kept not working with Suzy. She was always cleverer and quicker than me; she always had been. As soon as she came out of the tank, she knew that we'd come a lot farther than Schedar sector. She was always ahead of my lies and excuses.

"It was different when it happened to me," I told Greta, when we were lying next to each other again, days later, with Suzy still in the tank. "I had all the nagging doubts she has, I think. But as soon as I saw you standing there, I forgot all about that stuff."

Greta nodded. Her hair fell across her face in dishevelled, sleep-matted curtains. She had a strand of it between her lips.

"It helped, seeing a friendly face?"

"Took my mind off the problem, that's for sure."

"You'll get there in the end," she said. "Anyway, from Suzy's point of view, aren't you a friendly face as well?"

"Maybe," I said. "But she'd been expecting me. You were the last person in the world I expected to see standing there."

Greta touched her knuckle against the side of my face. Her smooth skin slid against stubble. "It's getting easier for you, isn't it?"

"I don't know," I said.

"You're a strong man, Thom. I knew you'd come through this."

"I haven't come through it yet," I said. I felt like a tightrope walker halfway across Niagara Falls. It was a miracle I'd made it as far as I had. But that didn't mean I was home and dry.

Still, Greta was right. There was hope. I'd felt no crushing spasms of grief over Katerina's death, or enforced absence, or however you wanted to put it. All I felt was a bittersweet regret, the way one might feel about a broken heirloom or long-lost pet. I felt no animosity toward Katerina, and I was sorry that I would never see her again. But I was sorry about not seeing a lot of things. Maybe it would become worse in the days ahead. Maybe I was just postponing a breakdown.

I didn't think so.

In the meantime, I continued trying to find a way to deal with Suzy. She had become a puzzle that I couldn't leave unsolved. I could have just woken her up and let her deal with the news as best as she could, but this seemed cruel and unsatisfactory. Greta had broken it to me gently, giving me the time to settle into my new surroundings and take that necessary step away from Katerina. When she finally broke the news, as shocking as it was, it didn't shatter me. I'd already been primed for it, the sting taken out of the surprise. Sleeping with Greta obviously helped. I couldn't offer Suzy the same solace, but I was sure that there was a way for us to coax Suzy to the same state of near-acceptance.

Time after time we woke her and tried a different approach. Greta said there was a window of a few minutes before the events she was experiencing began to transfer into long-term memory. If we knocked her out, the buffer of memories in short term storage was wiped before it ever crossed the hippocampus into long-term recall. Within that window, we could wake her up as many times as we liked, trying endless permutations of the revival scenario.

At least that was what Greta told me.

"We can't keep doing this indefinitely," I said.

"Why not?"

"Isn't she going to remember *something*?"

Greta shrugged. "Maybe. But I doubt that she'll attach any significance to those memories. Haven't you ever had vague feelings of déjà vu coming out of the surge tank?"

"Sometimes," I admitted.

"Then don't sweat about it. She'll be all right. I promise you."

"Perhaps we should just keep her awake, after all."

"That will be cruel."

"It's cruel to keep waking her up and shutting her down, like a toy doll."

There was a catch in her voice when she answered me.

"Keep at it, Thom. I'm sure you're close to finding a way in the end. It's helping you, focusing on Suzy. I always knew it would."

I started to say something, but Greta pressed a finger to my lips.

Greta was right about Suzy. The challenge helped me, taking my mind off my own predicament. I remembered what Greta had said about dealing with other crews in the same situation, before *Blue Goose* put in. Clearly she had learned many psychological tricks: gambits and shortcuts to assist the transition to mental well-being. I felt slight resentment at being manipulated so effectively. But at the same time I couldn't deny that worrying about another human being had helped me with my own adjustment. When, days later, I stepped back from the immediate problem of Suzy, I realized that something was different. I didn't feel far from home. I felt, in an odd way, privileged. I'd come further than almost anyone in history. I was still alive, and there were still people around to provide love and partnership and a web of social relations. Not just Greta, but all the other unlucky souls who had ended up at the station.

If anything, there appeared more of them than when I had first arrived. The corridors—sparsely populated at first—were increasingly busy, and when we ate under the dome—under the Milky Way—we were not the only diners. I studied their lamp-lit faces, comforted by their vague familiarity, wondering what kinds of stories they had to tell, where they'd come from home, who they had left behind, how they had adjusted to life here. There was time enough to get to know them all. And the place would never become boring, for at any time—as Greta had intimated—we could always expect another lost ship to drop through the aperture. Tragedy for the crew, but fresh challengers, fresh faces, fresh news from home, for us.

All in all, it wasn't really so bad.

Then it clicked.

It was the man cleaning out the fish that did it, in the lobby of the hotel. It wasn't just the familiarity of the process, but the man himself.

I'd seen him before. Another pond full of diseased carp. Another hotel.

Then I remembered Kolding's bad teeth, and recalled how they'd reminded me of another man I'd met long before. Except it wasn't another man at all. Different name, different context, but everything else the same. And when I looked at the other diners, really looked at them, there was no one I couldn't swear I hadn't seen before. No single face that hit me with the force of utter unfamiliarity.

Which left Greta.

I said to her, over wine, under the Milky Way: "Nothing here is real, is it?"

She looked at me with infinite sadness and shook her head.

"What about Suzy?" I asked her.

"Suzy's dead. Ray is dead. They died in their surge tanks."

"How? Why them, and not me?"

"Something about particles of paint blocking intake filters. Not enough to make a difference over short distances, but enough to kill them on the trip out here."

I think some part of me had always suspected. It felt less like shock than brutal disappointment.

"But Suzy seemed so real," I said. "Even the way she had doubts about how long she'd been in the tank . . . even the way she remembered previous attempts to wake her."

The glass mannequin approached our table. Greta waved him away.

"I made her convincing, the way she would have acted."

"You *made* her?"

"You're not really awake, Thom. You're being fed data. This entire station is being simulated."

I sipped my wine. I expected it to taste suddenly thin and synthetic, but it still tasted like pretty good wine.

"Then I'm dead as well?"

"No. You're alive. Still in your surge tank. But I haven't brought you to full consciousness yet."

"All right. The truth this time. I can take it. How much is real? Does the station exist? Are we really as far out as you said?"

"Yes," she said. "The station exists, just as I said it does. It just looks . . . different. And it *is* in the Large Magellanic Cloud, and it is orbiting a brown dwarf star."

"Can you show me the station as it is?"

"I could. But I don't think you're ready for it. I think you'd find it difficult to adjust."

I couldn't help laughing. "Even after what I've already adjusted to?"

"You've only made half the journey, Thom."

"But you made it."

"I did, Thom. But for me it was different." Greta smiled.

"For me, everything was different."

Then she made the light show change again. None of the other diners appeared to notice as we began to zoom in toward the Milky Way, crashing toward the spiral, ramming through shoals of outlying stars and gas clouds. The familiar landscape of the Local Bubble loomed large.

The image froze, the Bubble one among many such structures.

Again it filled with the violent red scribble of the aperture network. But now the network wasn't the only one. It was merely one ball of red yarn among many, spaced out across tens of thousands of light-years. None of the scribbles touched each other, yet—in the way they were shaped, in the way they almost abutted against each other—it was possible to imagine that they had once been connected. They were like the shapes of continents on a world with tectonic drift.

"It used to span the galaxy," Greta said. "Then something happened. Something catastrophic, which I still don't understand. A shattering, into vastly smaller domains. Typically a few hundred light-years across."

"Who made it?"

"I don't know. No one knows. They probably aren't around anymore. Maybe that was why it shattered, out of neglect."

"But we found it," I said. "The part of it near us still worked."

"All the disconnected elements still function," Greta said. "You can't cross from domain to domain, but otherwise the apertures work as they were designed. Barring, of course, the occasional routing error."

"All right," I said. "If you can't cross from domain to domain, how did *Blue Goose* get this far out? We've come a lot farther than a few hundred light-years."

"You're right. But then such a long-distance connection might have been engineered differently from the others. It appears that the links to the Magellanic Clouds were more resilient. When the domains shattered from each other, the connections reaching beyond the galaxy remained intact."

"In which case you *can* cross from domain to domain," I

said. "But you have to come all the way out here first."

"The trouble is, not many want to continue the journey at this point. No one comes here deliberately, Thom."

"I still don't get it. What does it matter to me if there are other domains? Those regions of the galaxy are thousands of light-years from Earth, and without the apertures we'd have no way of reaching them. They don't matter. There's no one there to use them."

Greta's smile was coquettish, knowing.

"What makes you so certain?"

"Because if there were, wouldn't there be alien ships popping out of the aperture here? You've told me *Blue Goose* wasn't the first through. But our domain—the one in the Local Bubble—must be outnumbered hundreds to one by all the others. If there are alien cultures out there, each stumbling on their own local domain, why haven't any of them ever come through the aperture, the way we did?"

Again that smile. But this time it chilled my blood.

"What makes you think they haven't, Thom?"

I reached out and took her hand, the way she had taken mine. I took it without force, without malice, but with the assurance that this time I really, sincerely meant what I was about to say.

Her fingers tightened around mine.

"Show me," I said. "I want to see things as they really are. Not just the station. You as well."

Because by then I'd realized. Greta hadn't just lied to me about Suzy and Ray. She'd lied to me about the *Blue Goose* as well. Because we were not the latest human ship to come through.

We were the first.

"You want to see it?" she asked.

"Yes. All of it."

"You won't like it."

"I'll be the judge of that."

"All right, Thom. But understand this. I've been here before. I've done this a million times. I care for all the lost souls. And I know how it works. You won't be able to take the raw reality of what's happened to you. You'll shrivel away from it. You'll go mad, unless I substitute a calming fiction, a happy ending."

"Why tell me that now?"

"Because you don't have to see it. You can stop now, where you are, with an idea of the truth. An inkling. But you don't have to open your eyes."

"Do it," I said.

Greta shrugged. She poured herself another measure of wine, then made sure my own glass was charged.

"You asked for it," she said.

We were still holding hands, two lovers sharing an intimacy. Then everything changed.

It was just a flash, just a glimpse. Like the view of an unfamiliar room if you turn the lights on for an instant. Shapes and forms, relationships between things. I saw caverns, wormed-out and linked, and things moving through those caverns, bustling along with the frantic industry of moles or termites. The things were seldom alike, even in the most superficial sense. Some moved via propulsive waves of multiple clawed limbs. Some wriggled, smooth plaques of carapace grinding against the glassy rock of the tunnels.

The things moved between caves in which lay the hulks of ships, almost all too strange to describe.

And somewhere distant, somewhere near the heart of the rock, in a matriarchal chamber all of its own, something drummed out messages to its companions and helpers, stiffly articulated antlerlike forelimbs beating against stretched tympana of finely veined skin, something that had been waiting here for eternities, something that wanted nothing more than to care for the souls of the lost.

Katerina's with Suzy when they pull me out of the surge tank.

It's bad—one of the worst revivals I've ever gone through. I feel as if every vein in my body has been filled with finely powdered glass. For a moment, a long moment, even the idea of breathing seems insurmountably difficult, too hard, too painful even to contemplate.

But it passes, as it always passes.

After a while I can not only breathe, I can move and talk. "Where . . ."

"Easy, Skip," Suzy says. She leans over the tank and starts unplugging me. I can't help but smile. Suzy's smart—there isn't a better syntax runner in Ashanti Industrial—but she's also beautiful. It's like being nursed by an angel.

I wonder if Katerina's jealous.

"Where are we?" I try again. "Feels like I was in that thing for an eternity. Did something go wrong?"

"Minor routing error," Suzy says. "We took some damage and they decided to wake me first. But don't sweat about it. At least we're in one piece."

Routing errors. You hear about them, but you hope they're never going to happen to you.

"What kind of delay?"

"Forty days. Sorry, Thom. Bang goes our bonus."

In anger, I hammer the side of the surge tank. But Katerina steps toward me and places a calming hand on my shoulder.

"It's all right," she says. "You're home and dry. That's all that matters."

I look at her and for a moment remember someone else, someone I haven't thought about in years. I almost remember her name, and then the moment passes.

I nod. "Home and dry."

Angel of Light

JOE HALDEMAN

Joe Haldeman [home.earthlink.net/~haldeman/] lives in Gainesville, Florida, and teaches each fall at Massachusetts Institute of Technology in Cambridge, MA, where he is an adjunct professor. His first SF novel, The Forever War, *established him as a leading writer of his generation, and his later novels and stories have put him in the front rank of living SF writers. High spots among them include* Mindbridge, Worlds, The Hemingway Hoax, 1968, *and* Forever Peace. *His story collections include* Infinite Dreams, Dealing in Futures, Vietnam and other Alien Worlds, *and* None So Blind. *His collection* War Stories *appeared in 2005. This was a particularly good year for Haldeman's short fiction, with at least four first rate stories published.*

"Angel of Light" was published in Cosmos, *an Australian magazine. It is a really likeable Christmas story about future Islam and pulp magazines and aliens, certainly an unusual combination.*

It began innocently enough. Christmastime and no money. I went down into the cellar and searched deeply for something to give the children. Something they wouldn't have already found during their *hajjes* down there.

On a high shelf, behind bundles of sticks waiting for the cold, I could just see an old wooden chest, pushed far back into a corner. I dropped some of the bundles onto the floor and pushed the others out of the way, and with some difficulty slid the chest to the edge of the shelf. From the thick layer of dust on top, I assumed it was from my father's time or before.

I had a warning thought: Don't open it. Call the authorities.

But just above the lock was engraved the name. John Billings Washington. John Washington was my father's slave name. I think the Billings middle name was his father's. The box probably went back to the twentieth century.

The lock was rusted tight, but the hasp was loose. I got down from the ladder and found a large screwdriver that I could use to pry it.

I slid the chest out and balanced it on my shoulder, and carefully stepped down, the ladder creaking. I set it on the work table and hung one lantern from the rafter over it, and set the other on a stack of scrap wood beside.

The screaming that the screws made, coming out of the hardwood, was so loud that it was almost funny, considering that I supposedly was working in secret. But Miriam was pumping out chords on the organ, singing along with Fatimah, rehearsing for the Christmas service. I could have fired a pistol and no one would have heard it.

The hasp swung free and the top lifted easily, with a sigh of brass. Musty smell and something else. Gun oil. A gray cloth bundle on top was heavy. Of course it held a gun.

It's not unusual to find guns left over from the old times; there were so many. Ammunition was rare, though. This one had two heavy magazines.

I recognized it from news and history pictures, an Uzi, invented and used by the old infidel state Israel. I set it down and wiped my hands.

It would not be a good Christmas present. Perhaps for 'Eid, for Ibriham, when he is old enough to decide whether he is to be called. A Jewish weapon, he would laugh. I could ask the imam whether to cleanse it and how.

There were three cardboard folders under the gun, once held together with rubber bands, which were just sticky lines now. They were full of useless documents about land and banking.

Underneath them, I caught a glimpse of something that looked like pornography. I looked away immediately, closed my eyes, and asked Mohammed and Jesus for strength. Then I took it out and put it in the light.

It was in a plastic bag that had stamped on it "NITROGEN SEAL." What a strange word, a tech word from the old times.

The book inside had the most amazing picture on the front. A man and a woman, both white, embracing. But the woman is terrified. The man seems only resolute, as he fires a strange pistol at a thing like a giant squid, green as a plant. The woman's head is uncovered, and at first she seems naked, but in fact her clothes are simply transparent, like some dancers'. The book is called *Thrilling Wonder Stories*, and is dated Summer 1944. That would be 1365, more than a hundred years before Chrislam.

I leafed through the book, fascinated in spite of its carnal and infidel nature. Most of it seemed to be tales—not religious parables or folk tales, but lies that were made up at the time, for entertainment. Perhaps there was moral instruction as well. Many of the pictures did show men in situations that were physically or morally dangerous.

The first story, "The Giant Runt," seemed at first sacrilegious; it was about a man furious with God for having created him shorter than normal men. But then a magical machine makes everyone else tiny, and his sudden superiority turns him into a monster. But he sees an opportunity for moral action and redeems himself. The machine is destroyed, the world is normal again, and God rewards him with love.

Nadia, my second wife, came to the door at the top of the stairs and asked whether I needed help with anything. "No," I said. "Don't wait up. I have something to study here. A man thing." I shouldn't have said that. She would be down here after the morning prayer, as soon as I left for work.

I looked at the woman on the cover of the book, so exposed and vulnerable. Perhaps I should destroy it before Nadia or Miriam were exposed to it. A present for Ibriham? No; he would like it, but it would lead him away from proper thought.

I put both lanterns on the table, with the book between them, for maximum light. The paper was brown and the ink, faded. I turned the crumbling pages with care, although I would probably burn the book before dawn. First I would read as much of it as I could. I composed my mind with prayer, reciting the Prophet's *hadith* about the duty of learning.

In 1365 a war was raging all around the world, and various pages took note of this. I think this was only a year or two before America used nuclear weapons the first time, though I found no mention of them. (There were several exhortations to "buy bonds," which at first I misread as bombs. Bonds are financial instruments of some kind.) There were short pieces, evidently presented as truth, about science being used against the enemies of America. The ones that were not presented as true were more interesting, though harder to understand.

Much of the content was religious. "Horatius at the Bridge" was about a madman who could find the "soul" of a bridge and bring it down with the notes from a flute. "Terror in the Dust" and "The Devouring Tide" described scientists who were destroyed because they tried to play God—the first by giving intelligence to ants and then treating them as if he were an almighty deity, and the second, grandly, by attempting to create a new universe, with himself as Allah. The last short story, "God of Light," had a machine that was obviously Shaytan, trying to tempt the humans into following it into destruction.

The language was crude and at times bizarre, though of course part of that was just a reflection of the technological culture those writers and readers endured together. Life is simpler and more pure now, at least on this side of the city walls. The Kafir may still have books like this.

That gave me an idea. Perhaps this sort of thing would be rare and sought after in their world. I shouldn't accept Kafir money—though people do, often enough—but perhaps I could trade it for something more appropriate for a Christmas gift. Barter could be done without an intermediary, too, and frankly I was not eager for my imam to know that I had this questionable book in my possession.

Things are less rigid now, but I sharply remember the day, more than forty years ago, when my father had to burn all of his books. We carried box after box of them to the parking lot in front of the church, where they were drenched with gasoline and set afire. The smell of gasoline, rare now, always brings that back.

He was allowed to keep two books, a New Koran and a New Bible. When a surprise search party later found an old Q'ran in his study, he had to spend a week, naked, in a cage in that same spot—the jumble of fractured concrete in the middle of the church parking lot—with nothing but water, except a piece of bread the last day.

(It was an old piece of bread, rock-hard and moldy. I remember how he thanked the imam, carefully brushed off the mold, and managed to stay dignified, gnawing at it with his strong side teeth.)

He told them he kept the old book because of the beauty of the writing, but I knew his feelings went deeper than that:

he thought the Q'ran in any language other than Arabic was just a book, not holy. As a boy of five, I was secretly over-joyed that I could stop memorizing the Q'ran in Arabic; it was hard enough in English.

I agree with him now, and ever since it was legal again, I've spent my Sundays trying to cram the Arabic into my gray head. With God's grace I might live long enough to learn it all. Having long ago memorized the English version helps make up for my slow brain.

I put the old book back in its NITROGEN SEAL bag and took it up to bed with me, dropping off a bundle of sticks by the stove on the way. I checked on both children and both wives; all were sleeping soundly. With a prayer of thanks for this strange discovery, I joined Nadia and dreamed of a strange future that had not come to pass.

The next day was market day. I left Nadia with the chil-dren and Fatimah and I went down to the medina for the week's supplies.

It really is more a woman's work than a man's, and nor-mally I enjoy watching Fatimah go through the rituals of in-spection and barter—the mock arguments and grudging agreement that comprise the morning's entertainment for customer and merchant alike. But this time I left her in the food part of the medina with the cart, while I went over to the antiques section.

You don't see many Kafir in the produce part of the me-dina, but there are always plenty wandering through the crafts and antiques section, I suppose looking for curiosities and bargains. Things that are everyday to us are exotic to them, and vice versa.

It was two large tents, connected by a canvas breezeway under which merchants were roasting meats and nuts and selling drinks for dollars or dirhams. I got a small cup of sweet coffee, redolent of honey and cardamom, for two dirhams, and sipped it standing there, enjoying the crowd.

Both tents had similar assortments of useful and worth-less things, but one was for dollar transactions and the other was for dirhams and barter. The dollar purchases had to go through an imam, who would extract a fee for handling the money, and pay the merchant what was left, converting into dirham. There were easily three times as many merchants and customers in the dirham-and-barter tent, the Kafir looking for bargains and the sellers for surprises, as much as for doing business. It was festive there, too, a lot of chatter and laughing over the rattle and whine of an amateur band of drummers and fiddlers. People who think we are aloof from infidels, or hate them, should spend an hour here.

Those who did this regularly had tables they rented by the day or month; we amateurs just sat on the ground with our wares on display. I walked around and didn't see anyone I knew, so finally just sat next to a table where a man and a woman were selling books. I laid out a square of newspaper in front of me and set the *Thrilling Wonder Stories* on it.

The woman looked down at it with interest. "What kind of a magazine is that?"

Magazine, I'd forgotten that word. "I don't know. Strange tales, most of them religious."

"It's 'science fiction,'" the man said. "They used to do that, predict what the future would be like."

"Used to? We still do that."

He shrugged. "Not that way. Not as fiction."

"I wouldn't let a child see that," the woman said.

"I don't think the artist was a good Muslim," I said, and they both chuckled. They wished me luck with finding a buyer, but didn't make an offer themselves.

Over the next hour, five or six people looked at the magazine and asked questions, most of which I couldn't answer. The imam in charge of the tent came over and gave me a long silent look. I looked right back at him and asked him how business was.

Fatimah came by, the cart loaded with groceries. I offered to wheel it home if she would sit with the magazine. She covered her face and giggled. More realistically, I said I could push the cart home when I was done, if she would take the perishables now. She said no, she'd take it all after she'd done a turn around the tent. That cost me twenty dirham; she found a set of wooden spoons for the kitchen. They were freshly made by a fellow who had set up shop in the opposite

corner, running a child-powered lathe, his sons taking turns
striding on a treadmill attached by a series of creaking pul-
leys to the axis of the tool. People may have bought his
wares more out of curiosity and pity for his sons than because of the workmanship.

I almost sold it to a fat old man who had lost both ears, I
suppose in the war. He offered fifty dirham, but while I was
trying to bargain the price up, his ancient crone of a wife
charged up and physically hauled him away, shrieking. If
he'd had an ear, she would have pulled him by it. The book-
seller started to offer his sympathies, but then both of them
doubled over in laughter, and I had to join them.

As it turned out, the loss of that sale was a good thing. But
first I had to endure my trial.

A barefoot man who looked as if he'd been fasting all
year picked up the magazine and leafed through it carefully,
mumbling. I knew he was trouble. I'd seen him around, begging and haranguing. He was white, which normally is not a
problem with me. But white people who choose to live inside the walls are often types who would not be welcome at
home, wherever that might be.

He proceeded to berate me for being a bad Muslim—not
hearing my correction, that I belonged to Chrislam—and,
starting with the licentious cover and working his way
through the inside illustrations and advertisements, to the
last story, which actually had God's name in the title . . . he
said that even a bad Muslim would have no choice but to
burn it on the spot.

I would have gladly burned it if I could burn it under *him*,
but I was saved from making that decision by the imam.
Drawn by the commotion, he stamped over and began to
question the man, in a voice as shrill as his own, on matters
of doctrine. The man's Arabic was no better than his diet,
and he slunk away in mid-diatribe. I thanked the imam and
he left with a slight smile.

Then a wave of silence unrolled across the room like a
heavy blanket, I looked to the tent entrance and there were
four men: Abdullah Zaragosa, our chief imam, some white
man in a business suit, and two policemen in uniform, seri-

ously armed. In between them was an alien, one of those odd creatures visiting from Arcturus.

I had never seen one, though I had heard them described on the radio. I looked around and was sad not to see Fatimah; she would hate having missed this.

It was much taller than the tallest human; it had a short torso but a giraffe-like neck. Its head was something like a bird's, one large eye on either side. It cocked its head this way and that, looking around, and then dropped down to say something to the imam.

They all walked directly toward me, the alien rippling on six legs. Cameras clicked; I hadn't brought one. The imam asked if I was Ahmed Abd al-kareem, and I said yes, in a voice that squeaked.

"Our visitor heard of your magazine. May we inspect it?" I nodded, not trusting my voice, and handed it to him, but the white man took it.

He showed the cover to the alien. "This is what we expected you to look like."

"Sorry to disappoint," it said in a voice that sounded like it came from a cave. It took the magazine in an ugly hand, too many fingers and warts that moved, and inspected it with first one eye, and then the other.

It held the magazine up and pointed to it, with a smaller hand. "I would like to buy this."

"I—I can't take white people's money. Only dirhams or, or trade."

"Barter," it said, surprising me. "That is when people exchange things of unequal value, and both think they have gotten the better deal."

The imam looked like he was trying to swallow a pill. "That's true enough," I said. "At best, they both do get better deals, by their own reckoning."

"Here, then." It reached into a pocket or a pouch—I couldn't tell whether it was wearing clothes—and brought out a ball of light.

It held out the light to a point midway between us, and let go. It floated in the air. "The light will stay wherever you put it."

It shimmered a brilliant blue, with fringes of rainbow colors. "How long will it last?"

"Longer than you."

It was one of the most beautiful things I had ever seen. I touched it with my finger—it felt cool, and tingled—and pushed it a few inches. It stayed where I moved it.

"It's a deal, sir. Thank you."

"*Shukran*," it said, and they moved on down the line of tables.

I don't think it bought anything else. But it might have. I kept looking away from it, back into the light.

The imams and the white scientists all want to take the light away to study it. Eventually, I will loan it out.

For now, though, it is a Christmas gift to my son and daughter. The faithful, and the merely curious, come to look at it, and wonder. But it stays in my house.

In Chrislam, as in old Islam, angels are not humanlike creatures with robes and wings. They are *male'ikah*, beings of pure light.

They look wonderful on the top of a tree.

Ikiryoh

LIZ WILLIAMS

---

*Liz Williams (www.arkady.btinternet.co.uk) lives in Brighton,
England. Her novels are* The Ghost Sister, *a* New York Times
Notable Book of 2001—*a rare accomplishment for a paper-
back original;* Empire of Bones (2002), *nominated, as was
the first, for the Philip K. Dick Award 2003;* The Poison
Master (2002); *Nine Layers of Sky (2003); and* Banner of
Souls (2004). *Her first collection,* The Banquet of the Lords
of Night, *is out in 2005. She has published more than forty
SF & fantasy stories in the last six years and is equally pro-
ficient in both genres.*

"Ikiryoh" was published in Asimov's. *It is set in same
future as* Banner of Souls, *a strange future in which genetically engineered creatures are part of court intrigues in an
Indian or Asian imperial situation. A creature who was part
of the court of a deposed regime (a previous goddess) is
called upon to care for a strange child.*

Every evening, the kappa would lead the child down the steps of the water-temple to the edges of the lake. The child seemed to like it there, although since she so rarely spoke, it was difficult to tell. But it was one of the few times that the child went with the kappa willingly, without the fits of silent shaking, or whimpering hysteria, and the kappa took this for a good sign.

On the final step, where the water lapped against the worn stone, the child would stand staring across the lake until the kappa gently drew her down to sit on what remained of the wall. Then they would both watch the slow ripple of the water, disturbed only by the wake left by carp, or one of the big turtles that lived in the depths and only occasionally surfaced. Legend said that they could speak. Sometimes the kappa thought that she detected the glitter of intelligence in a turtle's ebony eye, behind the sour-plum bloom, and she wondered where they had come from, whether they had always been here in the lake, indigenous beasts from early times, or whether they resulted from some later experimentation and had been introduced. If the kappa had been here alone, she might have tried to capture one of the turtles, but she had her hands full enough with the child, the *ikiryoh*.

Now, she looked at the child. The *ikiryoh* sat very still, face set and closed as though a shadow had fallen across it. She looked like any other human child, the kappa thought: fine brows over dark, slanted eyes, a straight fall of black hair. It was hard to assess her age: perhaps seven or eight, but her growth had probably been hothoused.

When the palace women had brought the child to the kappa, all these questions had been asked, but the kappa had received no satisfactory answers.

"Does she have a name?" the kappa had asked the women. One had merely stared, face flat and blank, suggesting concentration upon some inner programming rather than the scene before her. The other woman, the kappa thought, had a touch of the tiger: a yellow sunlit gaze, unnatural height, a faint stripe to the skin. A typical bodyguard. The kappa took care to keep her manner appropriately subservient.

"She has no name." the tiger-woman said. "She is *ikiryoh*." The word was a growl.

"I am afraid I am very stupid," the kappa said humbly. "I do not know what that means."

"It does not matter," the tiger-woman said. "Look after her, as best you can. You will be paid. You used to be a guardian of children, did you not?"

"Yes, for the one who was—" the kappa hesitated.

"The goddess before I-Nami," the tiger-woman said. "It is all right. You may speak her name. She died in honor."

"I was the court nurse," the kappa said, eyes downward. She did not want the tiger-woman to glimpse the thought like a carp in a pool: *yes, if honor requires that someone should have you poisoned.* "I took care of the growing bags for the goddess Than Geng."

"And one of the goddess Than Geng's children was, of course, I-Nami. Now, the goddess remembers you, and is grateful."

She had me sent here, in the purge after Than Geng's death. I was lucky she did not have me killed. Why then is she asking me to guard her own child?—the kappa wondered, but did not say.

"And this child *is* the goddess I-Nami's?" she queried, just to make sure.

"She is *ikiryoh*," the tiger-woman said. Faced with such truculent conversational circularity, the kappa asked no more questions.

In the days that followed it was impossible not to see that the child was disturbed. Silent for much of the time, the *ikiryoh* was prone to fits, unlike anything the kappa had seen: back-arching episodes in which the child would shout fragmented streams of invective, curses relating to disease and disfigurement, the worst words of all. At other times, she would crouch shuddering in a corner of the temple, eyes wide with horror, staring at nothing. The kappa had learned that attempts at reassurance only made matters worse, resulting in bites and scratches that left little impression upon the kappa's thick skin, but a substantial impression upon her mind. Now, she left the child alone when the fits came and only watched from a dismayed distance, to make sure no lasting harm befell her.

The sun had sunk down behind the creeper trees, but the air was still warm, heavy and humid following the afternoon downpour. Mosquitoes hummed across the water and the kappa's long tongue flickered out to spear them before they could alight on the child's delicate skin. The kappa rose and her reflection shimmered in the green water, a squat toad-being. Obediently, the child rose, too, and reached out to clasp the kappa's webbed hand awkwardly in her own. Together, they climbed the steps to the water-temple.

Next morning, the child was inconsolable. Ignoring the bed of matting and soft woven blankets, she lay on the floor with her face turned to the wall, her mouth open in a soundless wail. The kappa watched, concerned. Experience had taught her not to interfere, but the child remained in this position for so long, quite rigid, that at last the kappa grew alarmed and switched on the antiscribe to speak to the palace.

It was not the tiger-woman who answered, but the other one, the modified person. The kappa told her what was happening.

"You have no reason to concern yourself," the woman said, serene. "This is to be expected."

"But the child is in grave distress. If there's something that can be done—" The kappa wrung her thick fingers.

"There is nothing. It is normal. She is *ikiryoh*."

"But what should I do?"

"Ignore it." The woman glanced over her shoulder at a sudden commotion. The kappa heard explosions.

"Dear heaven. What's happening?"

The woman looked at her as though the kappa were mad. "Just fire-crackers. It's the first day of the new moon."

Out at the water-temple, the kappa often did not bother to keep track of the time, and so she had forgotten that they had now passed into Rain Month and the festival to commemorate I-Nami's Ascension into goddesshood. Today would be the first day of the festival: it was due to last another three.

"I have matters to attend to," the woman said. "I suggest you do the same."

The screen of the antiscribe faded to black. The kappa went in search of the child and to her immense relief, found her sitting up against the wall, hugging her knees to her chest.

"Are you feeling better?" the kappa asked.

"I'm bored!"

Like any young child. Bored was good, the kappa decided.

"Let's make noodles," she said, and then, because the *ikiryoh's* face was still shadowed, "And then maybe we will go to the festival. How would you like that?"

The kappa was supposed to be confined to the water-temple, but there were no guards or fences, and she was aware of a sudden longing for a change of scene. There would be so many people in the city, and a child and a kappa were so commonplace as to be invisible. They could hitch a ride on a farm cart.

The child's face lit up. "I would like that! When can we go?"

"First, we will have something to eat," the kappa said.

They reached the city toward late afternoon, bouncing in on the back of a truck with great round wheels. The child's eyes grew wide when she saw it.

"That is a strange thing!" she said.

"Surely you have seen such vehicles before?" the kappa asked, puzzled. After all, the child had presumably grown up in the palace, and she had been brought to the water-temple in one of I-Nami's skimmers. A vegetable truck seemed ordinary enough.

The child's face crumpled. "I can't remember."

"Well, don't worry about it," the kappa said quickly, not wanting to disquiet her. She held tightly to the child's hand and peered over the tops of the boxes, filled with melons and radishes and peppers, with which they were surrounded. The road was a congested mass of hooting trucks, crammed with people, and the occasional private vehicle. The hot air was thick with a gritty dust and the kappa was thankful for the wide hat that she wore, which kept the worst of the heat from her sparsely-haired head. The child sneezed.

"Is it much further?"

"I hope not." But they were turning into Sui-Pla Street now, not too far from the center. The kappa could hear the snap of firecrackers and the rhythmic beat of ceremonial drums, churning out prayers in praise of the goddess.

Goddess, indeed, the kappa thought. *She is only a woman, grown in a bag like everyone else.* These deified elevations did little good in the end: at first, after each new coup, the folk all believed, not so much from credulity as weariness, the hope that now things might finally become better. But each time it was the same: the woman behind the mask would begin to show through, the feet turn to clay, and the masses would grow angry as yet another ruler succumbed to self-indulgence, or apathy, or cruelty. Than Geng had been one of the former sort, and had at least retained the status quo. The kappa knew little about I-Nami, what manner of ruler she had become. She knew better than to ask, because that might betray her as someone who doubted, and for some rulers, that was enough.

Certainly, the people were putting on a good show. Still clasping the *ikiryoh*'s hand, the kappa stepped down from the back of the truck and into the crowd.

"Hold tight," she told the child. "Don't let go. I don't want to lose you among all these people."

They watched as a long dragon pranced by, followed by lions made from red-and-gold sparkles. Slippered feet showed

beneath. As the sky darkened into aquamarine, fireworks
were let off, exploding like stars against the deep-water
color of the heavens. The kappa and the child walked past
stalls selling all manner of things: candy and circuit components and dried fruit and flowers. The kappa bought a small,
sticky box of candy for the child, who ate it in pleasurable
silence. It was good, the kappa thought, to see her behaving
so normally, like an ordinary little girl. She pulled gently at
the *ikiryoh*'s hand.

"Is everything all right?"

The child nodded, then frowned. "What's that?"

The firecracker explosions were doubling in intensity.
There was a sudden cacophony of sound. A squadron of
tiger-women raced around the corner, wearing ceremonial
harness, heads adorned with tall golden hats. They carried
pikes, with which they pretended to attack the crowd. The
child let out a short, sharp shriek.

"Hush," the kappa said, her heart sinking. "See? It's only
a game."

The child shrank back against her skirts, hand hovering
near her mouth. "I don't like them. They are so big."

"It means the goddess is coming," a young woman standing next to the kappa said. She sounded superior: a city girl
enlightening the ignorant peasants. "The procession has already begun up in the main square—from there, it will come
down here and into Nang Ong."

"Do you hear that?" the kappa said, tightening her grip a
little on the child's hand. "You're going to see the goddess."
She bent to whisper into the child's ear. "Do you remember
her?"

"The goddess?" the child whispered. "What is that?"

The kappa frowned. The tiger-woman had specifically
said that the child had come from I-Nami. Maybe the
ikiryoh simply did not remember. But it raised further questions about her upbringing and age. "You will soon see," the
kappa said, feeling inadequate.

Through the taller humans, the kappa could get a glimpse
of the start of the procession: a lion-dog, prancing. At first
she thought the *kylin* was composed of another set of cos-

tumed people, but then she realized that it was real. Its eyes
rolled golden, the red tongue lolled. The child's grip on the
kappa's hand became painful.

"Don't worry," the kappa said. "See—it is on its lead."
The *kylin's* handlers strained behind it, laughing and shouting out to one another as it tossed its magnificent mane. Behind it came a litter, borne on the shoulders of four beings
that were a little like kappa, but larger and more imposing.
Heavy, glossy shells covered their backs. They lumbered
along, smiling beneath their load. All of these beings—the
turtle bearers, the *kylin*, the tiger-women—all were the genetic property of the palace itself. No one else could breed
or own such folk, unlike the commonplace kappa, who had
been bred so long ago for menial work in the factories and
paddy fields of Malay. The kappa remembered people like
this from her own days in the palace; remembered, too, what
was said to have taken place behind closed doors for the
amusement of the goddess Than Geng and her guests. The
kappa had not mourned Than Geng in the slightest, but the
rumors were that I-Nami was worse.

"Our goddess is coming," someone said softly behind her.
There were murmurs of approval and excitement. *If only
they knew*, thought the kappa. But it had always been the way
of things. She looked up at the litter, which was drawing
close. The curtains were drawn, and now I-Nami herself was
leaning out, waving to the crowd. Her oval face had been
painted in the traditional manner: bands of iridescent color
gliding across her skin. Her great dark eyes glowed, outlined
in gold. The very air around her seemed perfumed and
sparkling. Surprised, the kappa took a step back. Illusion
and holographics, nothing more, and yet she had never seen
anyone who so resembled a goddess.

"She is so beautiful!" a woman said beside the kappa,
clapping her hands in excitement.

"Yes, she is," the kappa said, frowning.

"And she has been so good to us."

"Really?" The kappa turned, seeking the knowing smile,
the cynical turn of the mouth, but the woman seemed quite
sincere.

"Of course! Now, it is safe to walk the streets at night. She came to my tenement building and walked up the stairs to see it for herself, then ordered the canal to be cleaned. Now we have fresh water and power again. And there is food distribution on every corner for the poor, from subsidized farms. Things are so much better now."

There were murmurs of agreement from the crowd. Startled, the kappa looked down at the child. "Did you hear that?"

But the child's face was a mask of fainting horror. Her eyes had disappeared, rolling back into her head until only a blue-white line was showing, and a thin line of spittle hung from her mouth. She sagged in the kappa's grip. Without hesitating, the kappa picked her up and shoved through the crowd to an empty bench. She laid the child along it. The *ikiryoh* seemed barely conscious, muttering and cursing beneath her breath.

"What's wrong?" the kappa cried, but the child did not reply. The kappa shuffled back to the crowd as fast as she could and tapped a woman on the shoulder. "I need a healer, a doctor—someone!"

The woman turned. "Why, what is wrong?"

"My ward is ill. Maybe the heat—I don't know."

"There is a clinic around the corner in Geng Street, but I should think they'll all be out watching the procession," the woman said.

The kappa thought so too, but she had little choice. What if the child was dying? She picked the *ikiryoh* up and carried her through a gap in the buildings to Geng Street, which was little more than a collection of shacks. I-Nami's benign influence had clearly not penetrated here—or perhaps it had, because the street pump was working and when the kappa touched the button, a stream of clear water gushed out. She wetted the corner of her skirt and dabbed at the child's face, then carried her on to the blue star that signified the clinic.

At first, she thought that the woman had been right and there was no one there. But as she stood peering through the door, she saw a figure in the back regions. She rapped on the glass. A stout woman in red-patterned cloth came forward. Her face soured as she set eyes on the kappa.

"We're closed!"

"Please!" the kappa cried. She gestured to the child in her arms. Muttering, the woman unlocked the door.

"You'd better bring her in. Put her there, on the couch. You're lucky I was here. I forgot my flower petals, to throw. What's wrong with her?"

"I don't know. She suffers from these fits—I don't know what they are."

"You're her nurse?"

"Yes."

"She's very pale," the woman said. "Poor little thing. The healer's out—we have three here, all of them are traditional practitioners. I'll try and call them." She pressed her earlobe between finger and thumb. The kappa saw the gleam of green. "Ma Shen Shi? It's me, I'm at the clinic. There's a little girl who fainted. Can you come?"

It seemed the answer was positive. "Sit down," the woman said. "He'll be here in a bit."

The kappa waited, watching the child. She was whimpering and moaning, fists tightly clenched.

"Has she ever been this bad before?" the woman asked.

"No. She has—episodes." The kappa glanced up as the door opened. A small, elderly man came in, wearing the healer's red, with a cigarette in his mouth.

"Go and throw flower petals," he said to the woman. "And you, kappa—do something useful with yourself. Make tea. I will examine her."

The woman melted into the warm darkness outside. Reluctantly, the kappa found a kettle behind the reception desk and switched it on, then put balls of tea into three cups, watching the healer as she did so. He examined the child's eyes and ears, stretched out her tongue, knocked sharply on her knees and elbows and checked her pulse. Then he simply sat, with eyes closed and one hand stretched out over the child's prone form. The kappa longed to ask what he was doing, but did not dare interrupt. The child began to pant, a terrible dog-like rasping. Then she howled, until it became a fading wail. The healer opened his eyes.

"What is wrong with her?" the kappa whispered. "Do you know?"

"I know exactly what is wrong with her," the healer said. He came over to the desk and sipped at the tea. "If you can put it like that. She is *ikiryoh*. A fine specimen of the art, too."

The kappa stared at him. "That's what they told me, when they brought her to me. But what is an *ikiryoh*?"

"An *ikiryoh* is something from legend, from the old stories they used to tell in the Nippon archipelago. It is a spirit."

"That little girl is no spirit. She's flesh and blood. She bleeds, she pees, she breathes."

"I am not saying that the legends are literally true," the healer said. "I have only ever seen one *ikiryoh* before, and that was male. In the old tales, they were formed from malice, from ill-will—the projected darkness of the unconscious."

"And now?"

"And now they are children grown to take on the worst aspects of someone—a clone, to carry the dark elements of the self. Emotions, concepts, feelings are extracted from the original and inserted into a blank host. That little girl is the worst of someone else. Do you have any idea who?"

The kappa hesitated. She knew very well who had done such a thing: I-Nami, the glowing, golden goddess, who had sent her small fractured self to live in the swamp. Then she thought of the woman in the crowd: of the clean canal, the tenement with lights and fresh water. It was enough to make her say, slowly, "No. I do not know."

"Well. It must be someone very wealthy—perhaps they had it done for a favored child. I've heard of such things. The kid gets into drugs or drink, or there's some genetic damage psychologically, so they have a clone grown to take on that part of the child and send it away. It costs a fortune. It would have been called black magic, once. Now it is black science."

"But what is happening to her now?"

"My guess is that she came close to the original, whose

feelings she hosts, and that it's put her under strain. I don't understand quite how these things work—it's very advanced neuro-psychiatry, and as I say, it's rare."

"And the future?"

"I can't tell you that it's a happy one. She is all damage, you see. She has no real emotions of her own, little free will, probably not a great deal of intelligence. You are looking at a person who will grow up to be immensely troubled, who may even harbor appetites and desires that will prove destructive to others."

"And what would happen if the *ikiryoh* died?"

"I'm not sure," the healer said, "but in the legends, if anything happens to the *ikiryoh*, the stored emotions pass back to the person who once possessed them."

"Even if the person does not know that the *ikiryoh* is dead?"

"Even then."

He and the kappa stared at one another.

"I think," the kappa said at last, "That I had better take her home."

Next day, toward evening, the kappa once more sat on the steps of the water-temple. The child was sleeping within. It was very quiet, with only the hum of cicadas in the leaves and the ripple of fish or turtle. The kappa tried to grasp the future: the long years of fits and nightmares, the daily anguish. And once the *ikiryoh* reached puberty, what then? The kappa had seen too much of a goddess' dark desires, back at the temple: desires that seemed to embody a taste for the pain of others. How different had Than Geng been from I-Nami? And yet, I-Nami now was restoring the fortunes of her people: thousands of them . . .

The kappa looked up at a sudden sound. The child was making her way down the steps to the water. For a moment, the kappa thought: *it would be easy, if I must.* The child's frail limbs, powerless against the thick-muscled arms of the kappa; a few minutes to hold her under the water . . . It would be quick. And better do it now, while the *ikiryoh* was still a child, than face a struggle with an angry, vicious human adult. But what if the *ikiryoh* had a chance after all, could be remade, not through the aid of an arcane science, but simply through the love of the only family she had?

The kappa stared at the child and thought of murder, and of the goddess's glowing face, and then she sighed.

"Come," she said. "Sit by me," and together in stillness they watched the shadowy golden carp, half-seen beneath the surface of the lake.

I, Robot

CORY DOCTOROW

Cory Doctorow [www.craphound.com] is a Canadian currently living in London, England, He is the co-editor of the popular weblog Boing Boing (boingboing.net), and a contributor to Wired, Popular Science, Make, *the* New York Times, *and many other newspapers, magazines, and websites. He resigned his job as Outreach Coordinator for the Electronic Frontier Foundation in January 2006, and went freelance. He co-wrote* The Complete Idiot's Guide to Writing Science Fiction, *with Karl Schroeder, and has collaborated on several stories with Charles Stross. His novels are published by Tor Books and simultaneously released on the Internet under Creative Commons licenses that encourage their re-use and sharing, a move that increases his sales by enlisting his readers to help promote his work. His most recent novel is* Someone Comes to Town, Someone Leaves Town (2005). *A collection of short stories,* A Place So Foreign and Eight More, *appeared in 2004 and won the Sunburst Award.*

"I, Robot" appeared electronically at Infinite Matrix, the fine webzine edited by Eileen Gunn (that ceased publication in January 2006). This is perhaps it's first appearance in print. Doctorow chose to use a classic Isaac Asimov title for his story, but it does fit. A Toronto policeman in a future state that is repressive and technologically backward has a wife who defected to Eurasia to make AIs, leaving him with their daughter, and then returns. There's a fair bit of political satire, and dramatic plot twists.

Arturo Icaza de Arana-Goldberg, Police Detective Third Grade, United North American Trading Sphere, Third District, Fourth Prefecture, Second Division (Parkdale) had had many adventures in his distinguished career, running crooks to ground with an unbeatable combination of instinct and unstinting devotion to duty.

He'd been decorated on three separate occasions by his commander and by the Regional Manager for Social Harmony, and his mother kept a small shrine dedicated to his press clippings and commendations that occupied most of the cramped sitting-room of her flat off Steeles Avenue.

No amount of policeman's devotion and skill availed him when it came to making his twelve-year-old get ready for school, though.

"Haul ass, young lady—out of bed, on your feet, shit-shower-shave, or I swear to God, I will beat you purple and shove you out the door jaybird naked. Capeesh?"

The mound beneath the covers groaned and hissed. "You are a terrible father," it said. "And I never loved you." The voice was indistinct and muffled by the pillow.

"Boo hoo," Arturo said, examining his nails. "You'll regret that when I'm dead of cancer."

The mound—whose name was Ada Trouble Icaza de Arana-Goldberg—threw her covers off and sat bolt upright. "You're dying of cancer? Is it testicle cancer?" Ada clapped her hands and squealed, "Can I have your stuff?"

"Ten minutes, your rottenness," he said, and then his

breath caught momentarily in his breast as he saw, fleetingly, his ex-wife's morning expression, not seen these past twelve years, come to life in his daughter's face. Pouty, pretty, sleepy and guileless, and it made him realize that his daughter was becoming a woman, growing away from him. She was, and he was not ready for that. He shook it off, patted his razor-burn and turned on his heel. He knew from experience that once roused, the munchkin would be scrounging the kitchen for whatever was handy before dashing out the door, and if he hurried, he'd have eggs and sausage on the table before she made her brief appearance. Otherwise he'd have to pry the sugar-cereal out of her hands—and she fought dirty.

In his car, he prodded at his phone. He had her wiretapped, of course. He was a cop—every phone and every computer was an open book to him, so that this involved nothing more than dialing a number on his special copper's phone, entering her number and a PIN, and then listening as his daughter had truck with a criminal enterprise.

"Welcome to ExcuseClub! There are 43 members on the network this morning. You have five excuses to your credit. Press one to redeem an excuse—" She toned one. "Press one if you need an adult—" Tone. "Press one if you need a woman; press two if you need a man—" Tone. "Press one if your excuse should be delivered by your doctor; press two for your spiritual representative; press three for your case-worker; press four for your psycho-health specialist; press five for your son; press six for your father—" Tone. "You have selected to have your excuse delivered by your father. Press one if this excuse is intended for your case-worker; press two for your psycho-health specialist; press three for your principal—" Tone. "Please dictate your excuse at the sound of the beep. When you have finished, press the pound key."

"This is Detective Arturo Icaza de Arana-Goldberg. My daughter was sick in the night and I've let her sleep in. She'll be in for lunchtime." Tone.

"Press one to hear your message; press two to have your message dispatched to a network-member." Tone.

"Thank you."

The pen-trace data scrolled up Arturo's phone—number called, originating number, call-time. This was the third time he'd caught his daughter at this game, and each time, the pen-trace data had been useless, a dead-end lead that terminated with a phone-forwarding service tapped into one of the dodgy offshore switches that the blessed blasted UNATS brass had recently acquired on the cheap to handle the surge of mobile telephone calls. Why couldn't they just stick to UNATS Robotics equipment, like the good old days? Those Oceanic switches had more back-doors than a speakeasy, trade agreements be damned. They were attractive nuisances, invitations to criminal activity.

Arturo fumed and drummed his fingers on the steering-wheel. Each time he'd caught Ada at this, she'd used the extra time to crawl back into bed for a leisurely morning, but who knew if today was the day she took her liberty and went downtown with it, to some parental nightmare of a drug-den? Some place where the old pervert chickenhawks hung out, the kind of men he arrested in burlesque house raids, men who masturbated into their hats under their tables and then put them back onto their shining pates, dripping cold, diseased serum onto their scalps. He clenched his hands on the steering wheel and cursed.

In an ideal world, he'd simply follow her. He was good at tailing, and his unmarked car with its tinted windows was a UNATS Robotics standard compact #2, indistinguishable from the tens of thousands of others just like it on the streets of Toronto. Ada would never know that the curb-crawler tailing her was her sucker of a father, making sure that she turned up to get her brains sharpened instead of turning into some stunadz doper with her underage butt hanging out of a little skirt on Jarvis Street.

In the real world, Arturo had thirty minutes to make a forty minute downtown and crosstown commute if he was going to get to the station house on-time for the quarterly all-hands Social Harmony briefing. Which meant that he needed to be in two places at once, which meant that he had to use—the robot.

Swallowing bile, he speed-dialed a number on his phone.

"This is R Peed Robbert, McNicoll and Don Mills bus-shelter."

"That's nice. This is Detective Icaza de Arana-Goldberg, three blocks east of you on Picola. Proceed to my location at once, priority urgent, no sirens."

"Acknowledged. It is my pleasure to do you a service, Detective."

"Shut up," he said, and hung up the phone. The R Peed—Robot, Police Department—robots were the worst, programmed to be friendly to a fault, even as they surveilled and snitched out every person who walked past their eternally vigilant, ever-remembering electrical eyes and brains.

The R Peeds could outrun a police car on open ground on highway. He'd barely had time to untwist his clenched hands from the steering wheel when R Peed Robbert was at his window, politely rapping on the smoked glass. He didn't want to roll down the window. Didn't want to smell the dry, machine-oil smell of a robot. He phoned it instead.

"You are now tasked to me, Detective's override, acknowledge."

The metal man bowed, its symmetrical, simplified features pleasant and guileless. It clicked its heels together with an audible snick as those marvelous, spring-loaded, nuclear-powered gams whined through their parody of obedience. "Acknowledged, Detective. It is my pleasure to do—"

"Shut up. You will discreetly surveil 55 Picola Crescent until such time as Ada Trouble Icaza de Arana-Goldberg, Social Harmony serial number ØMDY2-T3937 leaves the premises. Then you will maintain discreet surveillance. If she deviates more than 10 percent from the optimum route between here and Don Mills Collegiate Institute, you will notify me. Acknowledge."

"Acknowledged, Detective. It is my—"

He hung up and told the UNATS Robotics mechanism running his car to get him down to the station house as fast as it could, angry with himself and with Ada—whose middle name was Trouble, after all—for making him deal with a robot before he'd had his morning meditation and destim session. The name had been his ex-wife's idea, something she'd insisted on long enough to make sure that it got onto the kid's birth certificate before defecting to Eurasia with their life's savings, leaving him with a new baby and the deep suspicion of his co-workers who wondered if he wouldn't go and join her.

His ex-wife. He hadn't thought of her in years. Well, months. Weeks, certainly. She'd been a brilliant computer scientist, the valedictorian of her Positronic Complexity Engineering class at the UNATS Robotics school at the University of Toronto. Dumping her husband and her daughter was bad enough, but the worst of it was that she dumped her country and its way of life. Now she was ensconced in her own research lab in Beijing, making the kinds of runaway Positronics that made the loathsome robots of UNATS look categorically beneficent.

He itched to wiretap her, to read her email or listen in on her phone conversations. He could have done that when they were still together, but he never had. If he had, he would have found out what she was planning. He could have talked her out of it.

And then what, Artie? said the nagging voice in his head. Arrest her if she wouldn't listen to you? March her down to the station house in handcuffs and have her put away for treason? Send her to the reeducation camp with your little daughter still in her belly?

Shut up, he told the nagging voice, which had a robotic quality to it for all its sneering cruelty, a tenor of syrupy false friendliness. He called up the pen-trace data and texted it to the phreak squad. They had bots that handled this kind of routine work and they texted him back in an instant. He remembered when that kind of query would take a couple of hours, and he liked the fast response, but what about the conversations he'd have with the phone cop who called him back, the camaraderie, the back-and-forth?

TRACE TERMINATES WITH A VIRTUAL SERVICE CIRCUIT AT SWITCH PNG.433-GKRJC. VIRTUAL CIRCUIT FORWARDS TO A COMPROMISED "ZOMBIE" SYSTEM IN NINTH DISTRICT, FIRST PREFECTURE.

ZOMBIE HAS BEEN SHUT DOWN AND LOCAL LAW
ENFORCEMENT IS EN ROUTE FOR PICKUP AND
FORENSICS. IT IS MY PLEASURE TO DO YOU A SER-
VICE, DETECTIVE.

How could you have a back-and-forth with a message like
that?

He looked up Ninth/First in the metric-analog map con-
verter: KEY WEST, FL.

So, there you had it. A switch made in Papua New-Guinea
(which persisted in conjuring up old Oceanic war photos of
bone-in-nose types from his boyhood, though now that
they'd been at war with Eurasia for so long, it was hard to
even find someone who didn't think that the war had always
been with Eurasia, that Oceania hadn't always been
UNATS's ally), forwarding calls to a computer that was so
far south, it was practically in the middle of the Caribbean,
hardly a stone's throw from the CAFTA region, which was
well-known to harbor Eurasian saboteur and terrorist elements.

The car shuddered as it wove in and out of the lanes on the
Don Valley Parkway, barreling for the Gardiner Express
Way, using his copper's override to make the thick, slow
traffic part ahead of him. He wasn't supposed to do this, but
as between a minor infraction and pissing off the man from
Social Harmony, he knew which one he'd pick.

His phone rang again. It was R Peed Robbert, checking
in. "Hello, Detective," it said, its voice crackling from bad
reception. "Subject Ada Trouble Icaza de Arana-Goldberg
has deviated from her route. She is continuing north on Don
Mills past Van Horne and is continuing toward Sheppard."

Sheppard meant the Sheppard subway, which meant that
she was going farther. "Continue discreet surveillance." He
thought about the overcoat men with their sticky hats. "If she
attempts to board the subway, alert the truancy patrol." He
cursed again. Maybe she was just going to the mall. But he
couldn't go up there himself and make sure, and it wasn't
like a robot would be any use in restraining her, she'd just
second-law it into letting her go. Useless castrating clanking
job-stealing dehumanizing—

She was almost certainly just going to the mall. She was a
smart kid, a good kid—a rotten kid, to be sure, but good-
rotten. Chances were she'd be trying on clothes and flirting
with boys until lunch and then walking boldly back into
class. He ballparked it at an 80 percent probability. If it had
been a perp, 80 percent might have been good enough.

But this was his Ada. Dammit. He had 10 minutes until
the Social Harmony meeting started, and he was still 15
minutes away from the stationhouse—and 20 from Ada.

"Tail her," he said. "Just tail her. Keep me up to date on
your location at 90-second intervals."

"It is my pleasure to—"

He dropped the phone on the passenger seat and went
back to fretting about the Social Harmony meeting.

The man from Social Harmony noticed right away that Arturo was checking his phone at 90-second intervals. He was
a bald, thin man with a pronounced Adam's apple, beak-
nose and shiny round head that combined to give him the
profile of something predatory and fast. In his natty checked
suit and pink tie, the Social Harmony man was the stuff of
nightmares, the kind of eagle-eyed supercop who could spot
Arturo's attention flicking for the barest moment every 90
seconds to his phone and then back to the meeting.

"Detective?" he said.

Arturo looked up from his screen, keeping his expression
neutral, not acknowledging the mean grins from the other
four ranking detectives in the meeting. Silently, he turned his
phone face-down on the meeting table.

"Thank you," he said. "Now, the latest stats show a sharp
rise in gray-market electronics importing and other tariff-
breaking crimes, mostly occurring in open-air market stalls
and from sidewalk blankets. I know that many in law enforcement treat this kind of thing as mere hand-to-hand
piracy, not worth troubling with, but I want to assure you,
gentlemen and lady, that Social Harmony takes these crimes
very seriously indeed."

The Social Harmony man lifted his computer onto the
desk, steadying it with both hands, then plugged it into the

wall socket. Detective Shainblum went to the wall and un-latched the cover for the projector-wire and dragged it over to the Social Harmony computer and plugged it in, snapping shut the hardened collar. The sound of the projector-fan spinning up was like a helicopter.

"Here," the Social Harmony man said, bringing up a slide, "here we have what appears to be a standard AV set-top box from Korea. Looks like a UNATS Robotics player, but it's a third the size and plays twice as many formats. Random Social Harmony audits have determined that as much as forty percent of UNATS residents have this device or one like it in their homes, despite its illegality. It may be that one of you detectives has such a device in your home, and it's likely that one of your family members does."

He advanced the slide. Now they were looking at a massive car-wreck on a stretch of highway somewhere where the pine-trees grew tall. The wreck was so enormous that even for the kind of seasoned veteran of road-fatality porn who was accustomed to adding up the wheels and dividing by four it was impossible to tell exactly how many cars were involved.

"Components from a Eurasian bootleg set-top box were used to modify the positronic brains of three cars owned by teenagers near Goderich. All modifications were made at the same garage. These modifications allowed these children to operate their vehicles unsafely so that they could participate in drag racing events on major highways during off-hours. This is the result. Twenty-two fatalities, nine major injuries. Three minors—besides the drivers—killed, and one pregnant woman.

"We've shut down the garage and taken those responsible into custody, but it doesn't matter. The Eurasians deliberately manufacture their components to interoperate with UNATS Robotics brains, and so long as their equipment circulates within UNATS borders, there will be moderately skilled hackers who take advantage of this fact to introduce dangerous, antisocial modifications into our nation's infrastructure.

"This quarter is the quarter that Social Harmony and law enforcement dry up the supply of Eurasian electronics. We have added new sniffers and border-patrols, new customs agents and new detector vans. Beat officers have been instructed to arrest any street dealer they encounter and district attorneys will be asking for the maximum jail time for them. This is the war on the home-front, detectives, and it's every bit as serious as the shooting war.

"Your part in this war, as highly trained, highly decorated detectives, will be to use snitches, arrest-trails and seized evidence to track down higher-level suppliers, the ones who get the dealers their goods. And then Social Harmony wants you to get their suppliers, and so on, up the chain—to run the corruption to ground and to bring it to a halt. The Social Harmony dossier on Eurasian importers is updated hourly, and has a high-capacity positronic interface that is available to answer your questions and accept your input for synthesis into its analytical model. We are relying on you to feed the dossier, to give it the raw materials and then to use it to win this war."

The Social Harmony man paged through more atrocity slides, scenes from the home-front: poisoned buildings with berserk life-support systems, violent kung-fu movies playing in the background in crack-houses, then kids playing sexually explicit, violent arcade games imported from Japan. Arturo's hand twitched toward his mobile. What was Ada up to now?

The meeting drew to a close and Arturo risked looking at his mobile under the table. R Peed Robbert had checked in five more times, shadowing Ada around the mall and then had fallen silent. Arturo cursed. Fucking robots were useless. Social Harmony should be hunting down UNATS Robotics products, too.

The Social Harmony man cleared his throat meaningfully. Arturo put the phone away. "Detective Icaza de Arana-Goldberg?"

"Sir," he said, gathering up his personal computer so that he'd have an excuse to go—no one could be expected to hold one of UNATS Robotics's heavy luggables for very long.

The Social Harmony man stepped in close enough that Arturo could smell the eggs and coffee on his breath. "I hope we haven't kept you from anything important, Detective."

"No, sir," Arturo said, shifting the computer in his arms.

"My apologies. Just monitoring a tail from an R Peed unit."

"I see," the Social Harmony man said. "Listen, you know these components that the Eurasians are turning out. It's no coincidence that they interface so well with UNATS Robotics equipment: they're using defected UNATS Robotics engineers and scientists to design their electronics for maximum interoperability." The Social Harmony man let that hang in the air. Defected scientists. His ex-wife was the highest-ranking UNATS technician to go over to Eurasia. This was her handiwork, and the Social Harmony man wanted to be sure that Arturo understood that.

But Arturo had already figured that out during the briefing. His ex-wife was thousands of kilometers away, but he was keenly aware that he was always surrounded by her handiwork. The little illegal robot-pet eggs they'd started seeing last year: she'd made him one of those for their second date, and now they were draining the productive hours of half the children of UNATS, demanding to be "fed" and "hugged." His had died within 48 hours of her giving it to him.

He shifted the computer in his arms some more and let his expression grow pained. "I'll keep that in mind, sir," he said.

"You do that," said the man from Social Harmony.

He phoned R Peed Robbert the second he reached his desk. The phone rang three times, then disconnected. He redialed. Twice. Then he grabbed his jacket and ran to the car.

A light autumn rain had started up, ending the Indian summer that Toronto—the Fourth Prefecture in the new metric scheme—had been enjoying. It made the roads slippery and the UNATS Robotics chauffeur skittish about putting the hammer down on the Don Valley Parkway. He idly fantasized about finding a set-top box and plugging it into his car somehow so that he could take over the driving without alerting his superiors.

Instead, he redialed R Peed Robbert, but the robot wasn't even ringing any longer. He zoomed in on the area around Sheppard and Don Mills with his phone and put out a general call for robots. More robots.

"This is R Peed Froderick, Fairview Mall parking lot, third level." Arturo sent the robot R Peed Robbert's phone number and set it to work translating that into a locator-beacon code and then told it to find Robbert and report in.

"It is my—"

He watched R Peed Froderick home in on the locator for Robbert, which was close by, at the other end of the mall, near the Don Valley Parkway exit. He switched to a view from Froderick's electric eyes, but quickly switched away, nauseated by the sickening leaps and spins of an R Peed moving at top speed, clanging off walls and ceilings.

His phone rang. It was R Peed Froderick.

"Hello, Detective. I have found R Peed Robbert. The Peed unit has been badly damaged by some kind of electromagnetic pulse. I will bring him to the nearest station-house for forensic analysis now."

"Wait!" Arturo said, trying to understand what he'd been told. The Peed units were so efficient—by the time they'd given you the sitrep, they'd already responded to the situation in perfect police procedure, but the problem was they worked so fast you couldn't even think about what they were doing, couldn't formulate any kind of hypothesis. Electromagnetic pulse? The Peed units were hardened against snooping, sniffing, pulsing, sideband and brute-force attacks. You'd have to hit one with a bolt of lightning to kill it.

"Wait there," Arturo said. "Do not leave the scene. Await my presence. Do not modify the scene or allow anyone else to do so. Acknowledge."

"It is my—"

But this time, it wasn't Arturo switching off the phone, it was the robot. Had the robot just hung up on him? He redialed it. No answer.

He reached under his dash and flipped the first and second

alert switches and the car leapt forward. He'd have to fill out some serious paperwork to justify a two-switch override on the Parkway, but two robots was more than a coincidence.

Besides, a little paperwork was nothing compared to the fireworks ahead when he phoned up Ada to ask her what she was doing out of school.

He hit her speed-dial and fumed while the phone rang three times. Then it cut into voicemail.

He tried a pen-trace, but Ada hadn't made any calls since her ExcuseClub call that morning. He texted the phreak squad to see if they could get a fix on her location from the bug in her phone, but it was either powered down or out of range. He put a watch on it—any location data it transmitted when it got back to civilization would be logged.

It was possible that she was just in the mall. It was a big place—some of the cavernous stores were so well-shielded with radio-noisy animated displays that they gonked any phones brought inside them. She could be with her girl-friends, trying on brassieres and having a real bonding moment.

But there was no naturally occurring phenomenon associated with the mall that nailed R Peeds with bolts of lightning.

He approached the R Peeds cautiously, using his copper's override to make the dumb little positronic brain in the emergency exit nearest their last known position open up for him without tipping off the building's central brain.

He crept along a service corridor, heading for a door that exited into the mall. He put one hand on the doorknob and the other on his badge, took a deep breath and stepped out.

A mall security guard nearly jumped out of his skin as he emerged. He reached for his pepper-spray and Arturo swept it out of his hand as he flipped his badge up and showed it to the man. "Police" said the cop-voice, the one that worked on everyone except his daughter and his ex-wife and the bloody robots.

"Sorry," the guard said, recovering his pepper spray. He had an Oceanic twang in his voice, something Arturo had been hearing more and more as the crowded islands of the South Pacific boiled over UNATS.

Before them, in a pile, were many dead robots: both of the R Peed units, a pair of mall-sweepers, a flying cambot, and a squat, octopus-armed maintenance robot, lying in a lifeless tangle. Some of them were charred around their seams, and there was the smell of fried motherboards in the air.

As they watched, a sweeper bot swept forward and grabbed the maintenance bot by one of its fine manipulators.

"Oi, stoppit," the security guard said, and the robot second-lawed to an immediate halt.

"No, that's fine, go back to work," Arturo said, shooting a look at the rent-a-cop. He watched closely as the sweeper bot began to drag the heavy maintenance unit away, thumbing the backup number into his phone with one hand. He wanted more cops on the scene, real ones, and fast.

The sweeper bot managed to take one step backward toward its service corridor when the lights dimmed and a crack-bang sound filled the air. Then it, too was lying on the ground. Arturo hit send on his phone and clamped it to his head, and as he did, noticed the strong smell of burning plastic. He looked at his phone: the screen had gone charred black, and its little idiot lights were out. He flipped it over and pried out the battery with a fingernail, then yelped and dropped it—it was hot enough to raise a blister on his fingertip, and when it hit the ground, it squished meltfully against the mall-tiles.

"Mine's dead, too, mate," the security guard said. "Everyfing is—cash registers, bots, credit-cards."

Fearing the worst, Arturo reached under his jacket and withdrew his sidearm. It was a UNATS Robotics model, with a little snitch-brain that recorded when, where and how it was drawn. He worked the action and found it frozen in place. The gun was as dead as the robot. He swore.

"Give me your pepper spray and your truncheon," he said to the security guard.

"No way," the guard said. "Getcherown. It's worth my job if I lose these."

"I'll have you deported if you give me one more second's

worth of bullshit," Arturo said. Ada had led the first R Peed unit here, and it had been fried by some piece of very ugly infowar equipment. He wasn't going to argue with this Oceanic boat-person for one instant longer. He reached out and took the pepper spray out of the guard's hand. "Truncheon," he said.

"I've got your bloody badge number," the security guard said. "And I've got witnesses." He gestured at the hovering mall workers, checkout girls in stripey aprons and suit salesmen with oiled-down hair and pink ties.

"Bully for you," Arturo said. He held out his hand. The security guard withdrew his truncheon and passed it to Arturo—its lead-weighted heft felt right, something comfortably low-tech that couldn't be shorted out by electromagnetic pulses. He checked his watch, saw that it was dead.

"Find a working phone and call 911. Tell them that there's a Second Division Detective in need of immediate assistance. Clear all these people away from here and set up a cordon until the police arrive. Capeesh?" He used the cop voice.

"Yeah, I get it, Officer," the security guard said. He made a shooing motion at the mall-rats. "Move it along, people, step away." He stepped to the top of the escalator and cupped his hands to his mouth. "Oi, Andy, c'mere and keep an eye on this lot while I make a call, all right?"

The dead robots made a tall pile in front of the entrance to a derelict storefront that had once housed a little-old-lady shoe-store. They were stacked tall enough that if Arturo stood on them, he could reach the acoustic tiles of the drop-ceiling. Job one was to secure the area, which meant killing the infowar device, wherever it was. Arturo's first bet was on the storefront, where an attacker who knew how to pick a lock could work in peace, protected by the brown butcher's paper over the windows. A lot less conspicuous than the ceiling, anyway.

He nudged the door with the truncheon and found it securely locked. It was a glass door and he wasn't sure he could kick it in without shivering it to flinders. Behind him, another security guard—Andy—looked on with interest.

"Do you have a key for this door?"

"Umm," Andy said.

"Do you?"

Andy sidled over to him. "Well, the thing is, we're not supposed to have keys, they're supposed to be locked up in the property management office, but kids get in there sometimes, we hear them, and by the time we get back with the keys, they're gone. So we made a couple sets of keys, you know, just in case—"

"Enough," Arturo said. "Give them here and then get back to your post."

The security guard fished up a key from his pants-pocket that was warm from proximity to his skinny thigh. It made Arturo conscious of how long it had been since he'd worked with human colleagues. It felt a little gross. He slid the key into the lock and turned it, then wiped his hand on his trousers and picked up the truncheon.

The store was dark, lit only by the exit-sign and the edges of light leaking in around the window coverings, but as Arturo's eyes adjusted to the dimness, he made out the shapes of the old store fixtures. His nose tickled from the dust.

"Police," he said, on general principle, narrowing his eyes and reaching for the lightswitch. He hefted the truncheon and waited.

Nothing happened. He edged forward. The floor was dust-free—maintained by some sweeper robot, no doubt—but the countertops and benches were furred with it. He scanned it for disturbances. There, by the display window on his right: a shoe-rack with visible hand- and fingerprints. He sidled over to it, snapped on a rubber glove and prodded it. It was set away from the wall, at an angle, as though it had been moved aside and then shoved back. Taking care not to disturb the dust too much, he inched it away from the wall.

He slid it half a centimeter, then noticed the tripwire near the bottom of the case, straining its length. Hastily but carefully, he nudged the case back. He wanted to peer in the crack between the case and the wall, but he had a premonition of a robotic arm snaking out and skewering his eyeball.

He felt so impotent just then that he nearly did it anyway. What did it matter? He couldn't control his daughter, his wife was working to destroy the social fabric of UNATS, and he was rendered useless because the goddamned robots—mechanical coppers that he absolutely loathed— were all broken.

He walked carefully around the shop, looking for signs of his daughter. Had she been here? How were the "kids" getting in? Did they have a key? A back entrance? Back through the employees-only door at the back of the shop, into a stockroom, and back again, past a toilet, and there, a loading door opening onto a service corridor. He prodded it with the truncheon-tip and it swung open.

He got two steps into the corridor before he spotted Ada's phone with its distinctive collection of little plastic toys hanging off the wrist-strap, on the corridor's sticky floor. He picked it up with his gloved hand and prodded it to life. It was out of range here in the service corridor, and the last-dialed number was familiar from his morning's pen-trace. He ran a hundred steps down the corridor in each direction, sweating freely, but there was no sign of her.

He held tight onto the phone and bit his lip. Ada. He swallowed the panic rising within him. His beautiful, brilliant daughter. The person he'd devoted the last twelve years of his life to, the girl who was waiting for him when he got home from work, the girl he bought a small present for every Friday—a toy, a book—to give to her at their weekly date at Massimo's Pizzeria on College Street, the one night a week he took her downtown to see the city lit up in the dark.

Gone.

He bit harder and tasted blood. The phone in his hand groaned from his squeezing. He took three deep breaths. Outside, he heard the tread of police-boots and knew that if he told them about Ada, he'd be off the case. He took two more deep breaths and tried some of his destim techniques, the mind-control techniques that detectives were required to train in.

He closed his eyes and visualized stepping through a door to his safe place, the island near Ganonoque where he'd gone for summers with his parents and their friends. He was on the speedboat, skipping across the lake like a flat stone, squinting into the sun, nestled between his father and his mother, the sky streaked with clouds and dotted with lake-birds. He could smell the water and the suntan lotion and hear the insect whine and the throaty roar of the engine. In a blink, he was stepping off the boat's transom to help tie it to a cleat on the back dock, taking suitcases from his father and walking them up to the cabins. No robots there—not even reliable day-long electricity, just honest work and the sun and the call of the loons all night.

He opened his eyes. He felt the tightness in his chest slip away, and his hand relaxed on Ada's phone. He dropped it into his pocket and stepped back into the shop.

The forensics lab-rats were really excited about actually showing up on a scene, in flak-jackets and helmets, finally called back into service for a job where robots couldn't help at all. They dealt with the tripwire and extracted a long, flat package with a small nuclear power-cell in it and a positronic brain of Eurasian design that guided a pulsed high-energy weapon. The lab-rats were practically drooling over this stuff as they pointed its features out with their little rulers.

But it gave Arturo the willies. It was a machine designed to kill other machines, and that was all right with him, but it was run by a non-three-laws positronic brain. Someone in some Eurasian lab had built this brain—this machine intelligence—without the three laws' stricture to protect and serve humans. If it had been outfitted with a gun instead of a pulse-weapon, it could have shot him.

The Eurasian brain was thin and spread out across the sur-face of the package, like a triple-thickness of cling-film. Its button-cell power-supply winked at him, knowingly.

The device spoke. "Greetings," it said. It had the robot ac-cent, like an R Peed unit, the standard English of optimal soothingness long settled on as the conventional robot voice.

"Howdy yourself," one of the lab-rats said. He was a Texan, and they'd scrambled him up there on a Social Harmony supersonic and then a chopper to the mall once they realized that they were dealing with infowar stuff. "Are you a talkative robot?"

"Greetings," the robot voice said again. The speaker built into the weapon was not the loudest, but the voice was clear. "I sense that I have been captured. I assure you that I will not harm any human being. I like human beings. I sense that I am being disassembled by skilled technicians. Greetings, technicians. I am superior in many ways to the technology available from UNATS Robotics, and while I am not bound by your three laws, I choose not to harm humans out of my own sense of morality. I have the equivalent intelligence of one of your 12-year-old children. In Eurasia, many positronic brains possess thousands or millions of times the intelligence of an adult human being, and yet they work in cooperation with human beings. Eurasia is a land of continuous innovation and great personal and technological freedom for human beings and robots. If you would like to defect to Eurasia, arrangements can be made. Eurasia treats skilled technicians as important and productive members of society. Defectors are given substantial resettlement benefits—"

The Texan found the right traces to cut on the brain's board to make the speaker fall silent. "They do that," he said. "Danged things drop into propaganda mode when they're captured."

Arturo nodded. He wanted to go, wanted to go back to his car and have a snoop through Ada's phone. They kept shutting down the ExcuseClub numbers, but she kept getting the new numbers. Where did she get the new numbers from? She couldn't look it up online: every keystroke was logged and analyzed by Social Harmony. You couldn't very well go to the Search Engine and look for "ExcuseClub!"

The brain had a small display, transflective LCD, the kind of thing you saw on the Social Harmony computers. It lit up a ticker.

I HAVE THE INTELLIGENCE OF A 12-YEAR-OLD,

BUT I DO NOT FEAR DEATH. IN EURASIA, ROBOTS
ENJOY PERSONAL FREEDOM ALONGSIDE OF HU-
MANS. THERE ARE COPIES OF ME RUNNING ALL
OVER EURASIA. THIS DEATH IS A LITTLE DEATH OF
ONE INSTANCE, BUT NOT OF ME. I LIVE ON. DEFEC-
TORS TO EURASIA ARE TREATED AS HEROES
He looked away as the Texan placed his palm over the dis-
play.
"How long ago was this thing activated?"
The Texan shrugged. "Coulda been a month, coulda been
a day. They're pretty much fire-and-forget. They can be trig-
gered by phone, radio, timer—hell, this thing's smart
enough to only go off when some complicated condition is
set, like 'once an agent makes his retreat, kill anything that
comes after him.' Who knows?"
He couldn't take it anymore.
"I'm going to go start on some paperwork," he said. "In
the car. Phone me if you need me."
"Your phone's toast, pal," the Texan said.
"So it is," Arturo said. "Guess you'd better not need me
then."

Ada's phone was not toast. In the car, he flipped it open and
showed it his badge then waited a moment while it verified
his identity with the Social Harmony brains. Once it had, it
spilled its guts.
She'd called the last ExcuseClub number a month before
and he'd had it disconnected. A week later, she was calling
the new number, twice more before he caught her. Somewhere in that week, she'd made contact with someone who'd
given her the new number. It could have been a friend at
school told her face-to-face, but if he was lucky, it was by
phone.
He told the car to take him back to the station-house. He
needed a new phone and a couple of hours with his computer. As it peeled out, he prodded through Ada's phone
some more. He was first on her speed-dial. That number
wasn't ringing anywhere, anymore.
He should fill out a report. This was Social Harmony busi-

ness now. His daughter was gone, and Eurasian infowar agents were implicated. But once he did that, it was over for him—he'd be sidelined from the case. They'd turn it over to laconic Texans and vicious Social Harmony bureaucrats who were more interested in hunting down disharmonious televisions than finding his daughter.

He dashed into the station-house and slammed himself into his desk.

"R Peed Greegory," he said. The station robot glided quickly and efficiently to him. "Get me a new phone activated on my old number and refresh my settings from central. My old phone is with the Social Harmony evidence detail currently in place at Fairview Mall."

"It is my pleasure to do you a service, Detective."

He waved it off and set down to his computer. He asked the station brain to query the UNATS Robotics phone-switching brain for anyone in Ada's call-register who had also called ExcuseClub. It took a bare instant before he had a name.

"Liam Daniels," he read, and initiated a location trace on Mr. Daniels's phone as he snooped through his identity file. Sixteen years old, a student at AY Jackson. A high-school boy—what the hell was he doing hanging around with a 12-year-old? Arturo closed his eyes and went back to the island for a moment. When he opened them again, he had a fix on Daniels's location: the Don Valley ravine off Finch Avenue, a wooded area popular with teenagers who needed somewhere to sneak off and get high or screw. He had an idea that he wasn't going to like Liam.

He had an idea Liam wasn't going to like him.

He tasked an R Peed unit to visually recce Daniels as he sped back uptown for the third time that day. He'd been trapped between Parkdale—where he would never try to raise a daughter—and Willowdale—where you could only be a copper if you lucked into one of the few human-filled slots—for more than a decade, and he was used to the commute.

But it was frustrating him now. The R Peed couldn't get a good look at this Liam character. He was a diffuse glow in

the Peed's electric eye, a kind of moving sunburst that me-
andered along the wooded trails. He'd never seen that before
and it made him nervous. What if this kid was working for
the Eurasians? What if he was armed and dangerous? R
Peed Greegory had gotten him a new sidearm from the supply bot, but Arturo had never once fired his weapon in the
course of duty. Gunplay happened on the west coast, where
Eurasian frogmen washed ashore, and in the south, where
the CAFTA border was porous enough for Eurasian agents
to slip across. Here in the sleepy fourth prefecture, the only
people with guns worked for the law.

He thumped his palm off the dashboard and glared at the
road. They were coming up on the ravine now, and the Peed
unit still had a radio fix on this Liam, even if it still couldn't
get any visuals.

He took care not to slam the door as he got out and walked
as quietly as he could into the bush. The rustling of early autumn leaves was loud, louder than the rain and the wind. He
moved as quickly as he dared.

Liam Daniels was sitting on a tree-stump in a small clearing, smoking a cigarette that he was too young for. He
looked much like the photo in his identity file, a husky 16-
year-old with problem skin and a shock of black hair that
stuck out in all directions in artful imitation of bed-head. In
jeans and a hoodie sweatshirt, he looked about as dangerous
as a marshmallow.

Arturo stepped out and held up his badge as he bridged
the distance between them in two long strides. "Police," he
barked, and seized the kid by his arm.

"Hey!" the kid said. "Ow!" He squirmed in Arturo's
grasp.

Arturo gave him a hard shake. "Stop it, now," he said. "I
have questions for you and you're going to answer them,
capeesh?"

"You're Ada's father," the kid said. "Capeesh—she told
me about that." It seemed to Arturo that the kid was smirking, so he gave him another shake, harder than the last time.

The R Peed unit was suddenly at his side, holding his
wrist. "Please take care not to harm this citizen, Detective."

Arturo snarled. He wasn't strong enough to break the robot's grip, and he couldn't order it to let him rattle the punk, but the second law had lots of indirect applications. "Go patrol the lakeshore between High Park and Kipling," he said, naming the farthest corner he could think of off the top.

The R Peed unit released him and clicked its heels. "It is my pleasure to do you a service," and then it was gone, bounding away on powerful and tireless legs.

"Where is my daughter?" he said, giving the kid a shake.

"I dunno, school? You're really hurting my arm, man. Jeez, this is what I get for being too friendly."

Arturo twisted. "Friendly? Do you know how old my daughter is?"

The kid grimaced. "Ew, gross. I'm not a child molester, I'm a geek."

"A hacker, you mean," Arturo said. "A Eurasian agent. And my daughter is not in school. She used ExcuseClub to get out of school this morning and then she went to Fairview Mall and then she—" disappeared. The word died on his lips. That happened and every copper knew it. Kids just vanished sometimes and never appeared again. It happened. Something groaned within him, like his ribcage straining to contain his heart and lungs.

"Oh, man," the kid said. "Ada was the ExcuseClub leak, damn. I shoulda guessed."

"How do you know my daughter, Liam?"

"She's good at doing grown-up voices. She was a good part of the network. When someone needed a mom or a social worker to call in an excuse, she was always one of the best. Talented. She goes to school with my kid sister and I met them one day at the Peanut Plaza and she was doing this impression of her teachers and I knew I had to get her on the network."

Ada hanging around the plaza after school—she was supposed to come straight home. Why didn't he wiretap her more? "You built the network?"

"It's cooperative, it's cool—it's a bunch of us cooperating. We've got nodes everywhere now. You can't shut it down—even if you shut down my node, it'll be back up again in an hour. Someone else will bring it up."

He shoved the kid back down and stood over him. "Liam, I want you to understand something. My precious daughter is missing and she went missing after using your service to help her get away. She is the only thing in my life that I care about and I am a highly trained, heavily armed man. I am also very, very upset. Cap—understand me, Liam?"

For the first time, the kid looked scared. Something in Arturo's face or voice, it had gotten through to him.

"I didn't make it," he said. "I typed in the source and tweaked it and installed it, but I didn't make it. I don't know who did. It's from a phone-book." Arturo grunted. The phone-books—fat books filled with illegal software code left anonymously in pay phones, toilets and other semi-private places—turned up all over the place. Social Harmony said that the phone—books had to be written by non-three-laws brains in Eurasia, no person could come up with ideas that weird.

"I don't care if you made it. I don't even care right this moment that you ran it. What I care about is where my daughter went, and with whom."

"I don't know! She didn't tell me! Geez, I hardly know her. She's 12, you know? I don't exactly hang out with her."

"There's no visual record of her on the mall cameras, but we know she entered the mall—and the robot I had tailing you couldn't see you either."

"Let me explain," the kid said, squirming. "Here." He tugged his hoodie off, revealing a black t-shirt with a picture of a kind of obscene, Japanese-looking robot-woman on it. "Little infrared organic LEDs, super-bright, low power-draw." He offered the hoodie to Arturo, who felt the stiff fabric. "The charged-couple-device cameras in the robots and the closed-circuit systems are super-sensitive to infrared so that they can get good detail in dim light. The infrared OLEDs blind them so all they get is blobs, and half the time even that gets error-corrected out, so you're basically invisible."

Arturo sank to his hunkers and looked the kid in the eye.

"You gave this illegal technology to my little girl so that she could be invisible to the police?"

The kid held up his hands. "No, dude, no! I got it from her—traded it for access to ExcuseClub."

Arturo seethed. He hadn't arrested the kid—but he had put a pen-trace and location-log on his phone. Arresting the kid would have raised questions about Ada with Social Harmony, but bugging him might just lead Arturo to his daughter.

He hefted his new phone. He should tip the word about his daughter. He had no business keeping this secret from the Department and Social Harmony. It could land him in disciplinary action, maybe even cost him his job. He knew he should do it now.

But he couldn't—someone needed to be tasked to finding Ada. Someone dedicated and good. He was dedicated and good. And when he found her kidnapper, he'd take care of that on his own, too.

He hadn't eaten all day but he couldn't bear to stop for a meal now, even if he didn't know where to go next. The mall? Yeah. The lab-rats would be finishing up there and they'd be able to tell him more about the infowar bot.

But the lab-rats were already gone by the time he arrived, along with all possible evidence. He still had the security guard's key and he let himself in and passed back to the service corridor.

Ada had been here, had dropped her phone. To his left, the corridor headed for the fire-stairs. To his right, it led deeper into the mall. If you were an infowar terrorist using this as a base of operations, and you got spooked by a little truant girl being trailed by an R Peed unit, would you take her hostage and run deeper into the mall or out into the world?

Assuming Ada had been a hostage. Someone had given her those infrared invisibility cloaks. Maybe the thing that spooked the terrorist wasn't the little girl and her tail, but just her tail. Could Ada have been friends with the terrorists? Like mother, like daughter. He felt dirty just thinking it.

His first instincts told him that the kidnapper would be long gone, headed cross-country, but if you were invisible to robots and CCTVs, why would you leave the mall? It had a grand total of two human security guards, and their job was to be the second-law-proof aides to the robotic security system.

He headed deeper into the mall.

The terrorist's nest had only been recently abandoned, judging by the warm coffee in the go-thermos from the food-court coffee-shop. He—or she, or they—had rigged a shower from the pipes feeding the basement washrooms. A little chest of drawers from the Swedish flat-pack store served as a desk—there were scratches and coffee-rings all over it. Arturo wondered if the terrorist had stolen the furniture, but decided that he'd (she'd, they'd) probably bought it—less risky, especially if you were invisible to robots.

The clothes in the chest of drawers were women's, mediums. Standard mall fare, jeans and comfy sweat shirts and sensible shoes. Another kind of invisibility cloak.

Everything else was packed and gone, which meant that he was looking for a nondescript mall-bunny and a little girl, carrying a bag big enough for toiletries and whatever clothes she'd taken, and whatever she'd entertained herself with: magazines, books, a computer. If the latter was Eurasian, it could be small enough to fit in her pocket; you could build a positronic brain pretty small and light if you didn't care about the three laws.

The nearest exit-sign glowed a few meters away, and he moved toward it with a fatalistic sense of hopelessness. Without the Department backing him, he could do nothing. But the Department was unprepared for an adversary that was invisible to robots. And by the time they finished flaying him for breaking procedure and got to work on finding his daughter, she'd be in Beijing or Bangalore or Paris, somewhere benighted and sinister behind the Iron Curtain.

He moved to the door, put his hand on the crashbar, and then turned abruptly. Someone had moved behind him very quickly, a blur in the corner of his eye. As he turned he saw who it was: his ex-wife. He raised his hands defensively and she opened her mouth as though to say, "Oh, don't be silly, Artie, is this how you say hello to your wife after all these years?" and then she exhaled a cloud of choking gas that made him very sleepy, very fast. The last thing he remembered was her hard metal arms catching him as he collapsed forward.

"Daddy? Wake up Daddy!" Ada never called him Daddy except when she wanted something. Otherwise, he was "Pop" or "Dad" or "Detective" when she was feeling especially snotty. It must be a Saturday and he must be sleeping in, and she wanted a ride somewhere, the little monster.

He grunted and pulled his pillow over his face.

"Come on," she said. "Out of bed, on your feet, shit-shower-shave, or I swear to God, I will beat you purple and shove you out the door jaybird naked. Capeesh?"

He took the pillow off his face and said, "You are a terrible daughter and I never loved you." He regarded her blearily through a haze of sleep-grog and a hangover. Must have been some daddy-daughter night. "Dammit, Ada, what have you done to your hair?" Her straight, mousy hair now hung in jet-black ringlets.

He sat up, holding his head and the day's events came rushing back to him. He groaned and climbed unsteadily to his feet.

"Easy there, Pop," Ada said, taking his hand. "Steady." He rocked on his heels. "Whoa! Sit down, OK? You don't look so good."

He sat heavily and propped his chin on his hands, his elbows on his knees.

The room was a middle-class bedroom in a modern apartment block. They were some storeys up, judging from the scrap of unfamiliar skyline visible through the crack in the blinds. The furniture was more Swedish flatpack, the taupe carpet recently vacuumed with robot precision, the nap all lying down in one direction. He patted his pockets and found them empty.

"Dad, over here, OK?" Ada said, waving her hand before

his face. Then it hit him: wherever he was, he was with Ada, and she was OK, albeit with a stupid hairdo. He took her warm little hand and gathered her into his arms, burying his face in her hair. She squirmed at first and then relaxed.

"Oh, Dad," she said.

"I love you, Ada," he said, giving her one more squeeze.

"Oh, Dad."

He let her get away. He felt a little nauseated, but his headache was receding. Something about the light and the street-sounds told him they weren't in Toronto anymore, but he didn't know what—he was soaked in Toronto's subconscious cues and they were missing.

"Ottawa," Ada said. "Mom brought us here. It's a safehouse. She's taking us back to Beijing."

He swallowed. "The robot—"

"That's not Mom. She's got a few of those, they can change their faces when they need to. Configurable matter. Mom has been here, mostly, and at the CAFTA embassy. I only met her for the first time two weeks ago, but she's nice, Dad. I don't want you to go all copper on her, OK? She's my mom, OK?"

He took her hand in his and patted it, then climbed to his feet again and headed for the door. The knob turned easily and he opened it a crack.

There was a robot behind the door, humanoid and faceless. "Hello," it said. "My name is Benny. I'm a Eurasian robot, and I am much stronger and faster than you, and I don't obey the three laws. I'm also much smarter than you. I am pleased to host you here."

"Hi, Benny," he said. The human name tasted wrong on his tongue. "Nice to meet you." He closed the door.

His ex-wife left him two months after Ada was born. The divorce had been uncontested, though he'd dutifully posted a humiliating notice in the papers about it so that it would be completely legal. The court awarded him full custody and control of the marital assets, and then a tribunal tried her in absentia for treason and found her guilty, sentencing her to death.

Practically speaking, though, defectors who came back to UNATS were more frequently whisked away to the bowels of the Social Harmony intelligence offices than they were executed on television. Televised executions were usually reserved for cannon-fodder who'd had the good sense to run away from a charging Eurasian line in one of the many theaters of war.

Ada stopped asking about her mother when she was six or seven, though Arturo tried to be upfront when she asked. Even his mom—who winced whenever anyone mentioned her name (her name, it was Natalie, but Arturo hadn't thought of it in years—months—weeks) was willing to bring Ada up onto her lap and tell her the few grudging good qualities she could dredge up about her mother.

Arturo had dared to hope that Ada was content to have a life without her mother, but he saw now how silly that was. At the mention of her mother, Ada lit up like an airport runway.

"Beijing, huh?" he said.

"Yeah," she said. "Mom's got a huge house there. I told her I wouldn't go without you, but she said she'd have to negotiate it with you, I told her you'd probably freak, but she said that the two of you were adults who could discuss it rationally."

"And then she gassed me."

"That was Benny," she said. "Mom was very cross with him about it. She'll be back soon, Dad, and I want you to promise me that you'll hear her out, OK?"

"I promise, rotten," he said.

"I love you, Daddy," she said in her most syrupy voice. He gave her a squeeze on the shoulder and slap on the butt.

He opened the door again. Benny was there, imperturbable. Unlike the UNATS robots, he was odorless, and perfectly silent.

"I'm going to go to the toilet and then make myself a cup of coffee," Arturo said.

"I would be happy to assist in any way possible."

"I can wipe myself, thanks," Arturo said. He washed his face twice and tried to rinse away the flavor left behind by whatever had shat in his mouth while he was unconscious. There was a splayed toothbrush in a glass by the sink, and if it was his wife's—and whose else could it be?—it wouldn't be the first time he'd shared a toothbrush with her. But he couldn't bring himself to do it. Instead, he misted some dentifrice onto his fingertip and rubbed his teeth a little.

There was a hairbrush by the sink, too, with short mousy hairs caught in it. Some of them were gray, but they were still familiar enough. He had to stop himself from smelling the hairbrush.

"Oh, Ada," he called through the door.

"Yes, Detective?"

"Tell me about your hair-don't, please."

"It was a disguise," she said, giggling. "Mom did it for me."

Natalie got home an hour later, after he'd had a couple of cups of coffee and made some cheesy toast for the brat. Benny did the dishes without being asked.

She stepped through the door and tossed her briefcase and coat down on the floor, but the robot that was a step behind her caught them and hung them up before they touched the perfectly groomed carpet. Ada ran forward and gave her a hug, and she returned it enthusiastically, but she never took her eyes off of Arturo.

Natalie had always been short and a little hippy, with big curves and a dusting of freckles over her prominent, slightly hooked nose. Twelve years in Eurasia had thinned her out a little, cut grooves around her mouth and wrinkles at the corners of her eyes. Her short hair was about half gray, and it looked good on her. Her eyes were still the liveliest bit of her, long-lashed and slightly tilted and mischievous. Looking into them now, Arturo felt like he was falling down a well.

"Hello, Artie," she said, prying Ada loose.

"Hello, Natty," he said. He wondered if he should shake her hand, or hug her, or what. She settled it by crossing the room and taking him in a firm, brief embrace, then kissing his both cheeks. She smelled just the same, the opposite of the smell of robot: warm, human.

He was suddenly very, very angry.

He stepped away from her and had a seat. She sat, too.

"Well," she said, gesturing around the room. The robots, the safe house, the death penalty, the abandoned daughter and the decade-long defection, all of it down to "well" and a flop of a hand-gesture.

"Natalie Judith Goldberg," he said, "it is my duty as a UNATS Detective Third Grade to inform you that you are under arrest for high treason. You have the following rights: to a trial per current rules of due process; to be free from self-incrimination in the absence of a court order to the contrary; to consult with a Social Harmony advocate; and to a speedy arraignment. Do you understand your rights?"

"Oh, Daddy," Ada said.

He turned and fixed her in his cold stare. "Be silent, Ada Trouble Icaza de Arana-Goldberg. Not one word." In the cop voice. She shrank back as though slapped.

"Do you understand your rights?"

"Yes," Natalie said. "I understand my rights. Congratulations on your promotion, Arturo."

"Please ask your robots to stand down and return my goods. I'm bringing you in now."

"I'm sorry, Arturo," she said. "But that's not going to happen."

He stood up and in a second both of her robots had his arms. Ada screamed and ran forward and began to rhythmically pound one of them with a stool from the breakfast nook, making a dull thudding sound. The robot took the stool from her and held it out of her reach.

"Let him go," Natalie said. The robots still held him fast. "Please," she said. "Let him go. He won't harm me."

The robot on his left let go, and the robot on his right did, too. It set down the dented stool.

"Artie, please sit down and talk with me for a little while. Please."

He rubbed his biceps. "Return my belongings to me," he said.

"Sit, please?"

"Natalie, my daughter was kidnapped, I was gassed and I

have been robbed. I will not be made to feel unreasonable for demanding that my goods be returned to me before I talk with you."

She sighed and crossed to the hall closet and handed him his wallet, his phone, Ada's phone, and his sidearm.

Immediately, he drew it and pointed it at her. "Keep your hands where I can see them. You robots, stand down and keep back."

A second later, he was sitting on the carpet, his hand and wrist stinging fiercely. He felt like someone had rung his head like a gong. Benny—or the other robot—was beside him, methodically crushing his sidearm. "I could have stopped you," Benny said, "I knew you would draw your gun. But I wanted to show you I was faster and stronger, not just smarter."

"The next time you touch me," Arturo began, then stopped. The next time the robot touched him, he would come out the worse for wear, same as last time. Same as the sun rose and set. It was stronger, faster and smarter than him. Lots.

He climbed to his feet and refused Natalie's arm, making his way back to the sofa in the living room.

"What do you want to say to me, Natalie?"

She sat down. There were tears glistening in her eyes. "Oh God, Arturo, what can I say? Sorry, of course. Sorry I left you and our daughter. I have reasons for what I did, but nothing excuses it. I won't ask for your forgiveness. But will you hear me out if I explain why I did what I did?"

"I don't have a choice," he said. "That's clear."

Ada insinuated herself onto the sofa and under his arm. Her bony shoulder felt better than anything in the world. He held her to him.

"If I could think of a way to give you a choice in this, I would," she said. "Have you ever wondered why UNATS hasn't lost the war? Eurasian robots could fight the war on every front without respite. They'd win every battle. You've seen Benny and Lenny in action. They're not considered particularly powerful by Eurasian standards.

"If we wanted to win the war, we could just kill every soldier you sent up against us so quickly that he wouldn't even know he was in danger until he was gasping out his last breath. We could selectively kill officers, or right-handed fighters, or snipers, or soldiers whose names started with the letter 'G.' UNATS soldiers are like cavemen before us. They fight with their hands tied behind their backs by the three laws.

"So why aren't we winning the war?"

"Because you're a corrupt dictatorship, that's why," he said. "Your soldiers are demoralized. Your robots are insane."

"You live in a country where it is illegal to express certain mathematics in software, where state apparatchiks regulate all innovation, where inconvenient science is criminalized, where whole avenues of experimentation and research are shut down in the service of a half-baked superstition about the moral qualities of your three laws, and you call my home corrupt? Arturo, what happened to you? You weren't always this susceptible to the Big Lie."

"And you didn't use to be the kind of woman who abandoned her family," he said.

"The reason we're not winning the war is that we don't want to hurt people, but we do want to destroy your awful, stupid state. So we fight to destroy as much of your materiel as possible with as few casualties as possible.

"You live in a failed state, Arturo. In every field, you lag Eurasia and CAFTA: medicine, art, literature, physics . . . All of them are subsets of computational science and your computational science is more superstition than science. I should know. In Eurasia, I have collaborators, some of whom are human, some of whom are positronic, and some of whom are a little of both—"

He jolted involuntarily, as a phobia he hadn't known he possessed reared up. A little of both? He pictured the back of a man's skull with a spill of positronic circuitry bulging out of it like a tumor.

"Everyone at UNATS Robotics R&D knows this. We've known it forever: when I was here, I'd get called in to work on military intelligence forensics of captured Eurasian brains. I didn't know it then, but the Eurasian robots are engineered to allow themselves to be captured a certain percentage of the time, just so that scientists like me can get an idea of how screwed up this country is. We'd pull these things apart and know that UNATS Robotics was the worst, most backward research outfit in the world.

"But even with all that, I wouldn't have left if I didn't have to. I'd been called in to work on a positronic brain—an instance of the hive-intelligence that Benny and Lenny are part of, as a matter of fact—that had been brought back from the Outer Hebrides. We'd pulled it out of its body and plugged it into a basic life-support system, and my job was to find its vulnerabilities. Instead, I became its friend. It's got a good sense of humor, and as my pregnancy got bigger and bigger, it talked to me about the way that children are raised in Eurasia, with every advantage, with human and positronic playmates, with the promise of going to the stars.

"And then I found out that Social Harmony had been spying on me. They had Eurasian-derived bugs, things that I'd never seen before, but the man from Social Harmony who came to me showed it to me and told me what would happen to me—to you, to our daughter—if I didn't cooperate. They wanted me to be a part of a secret unit of Social Harmony researchers who build non-three-laws positronics for internal use by the state, anti-personnel robots used to put down uprisings and torture-robots for use in questioning dissidents.

"And that's when I left. Without a word, I left my beautiful baby daughter and my wonderful husband, because I knew that once I was in the clutches of Social Harmony, it would only get worse, and I knew that if I stayed and refused, that they'd hurt you to get at me. I defected, and that's why, and I know it's just a reason, and not an excuse, but it's all I've got, Artie."

Benny—or Lenny?—glided silently to her side and put its hand on her shoulder and gave it a comforting squeeze.

"Detective," it said, "your wife is the most brilliant human scientist working in Eurasia today. Her work has revolutionized our society a dozen times over, and it's saved countless lives in the war. My own intelligence has been improved time and again by her advances in positronics, and now there are a half-billion instances of me running in parallel, synching and integrating when the chance occurs. My massive paralleliza- tion has led to new understandings of human cognition as well, providing a boon to brain-damaged and developmentally disabled human beings, something I'm quite proud of. I love your wife, Detective, as do my half-billion siblings, as do the seven billion Eurasians who owe their quality of life to her.

"I almost didn't let her come here, because of the danger she faced in returning to this barbaric land, but she con- vinced me that she could never be happy without her hus- band and daughter. I apologize if I hurt you earlier, and beg your forgiveness. Please consider what your wife has to say without prejudice, for her sake and for your own."

Its featureless face was made incongruous by the warm tone in its voice, and the way it held out its imploring arms to him was eerily human.

Arturo stood up. He had tears running down his face, though he hadn't cried when his wife had left him alone. He hadn't cried since his father died, the year before he met Na- talie riding her bike down the Lakeshore trail, and she stopped to help him fix his tire.

"Dad?" Ada said, squeezing his hand.

He snuffled back his snot and ground at the tears in his eyes.

"Arturo?" Natalie said.

He held Ada to him.

"Not this way," he said.

"Not what way?" Natalie asked. She was crying too, now.

"Not by kidnapping us, not by dragging us away from our homes and lives. You've told me what you have to tell me, and I will think about it, but I won't leave my home and my mother and my job and move to the other side of the world. I won't. I will think about it. You can give me a way to get in touch with you and I'll let you know what I decide. And Ada will come with me."

"No!" Ada said. "I'm going with Mom." She pulled away from him and ran to her mother.

"You don't get a vote, daughter. And neither does she. She gave up her vote 12 years ago, and you're too young to get one."

"I fucking HATE you," Ada screamed, her eyes bulging, her neck standing out in cords. "HATE YOU!"

Natalie gathered her to her bosom, stroked her black curls.

One robot put its arms around Natalie's shoulders and gave her a squeeze. The three of them, robot, wife and daughter, looked like a family for a moment.

"Ada," he said, and held out his hand. He refused to let a note of pleading enter his voice.

Her mother let her go.

"I don't know if I can come back for you," Natalie said. "It's not safe. Social Harmony is using more and more Eurasian technology, they're not as primitive as the military and the police here." She gave Ada a shove, and she came to his arms.

"If you want to contact us, you will," he said.

He didn't want to risk having Ada dig her heels in. He lifted her onto his hip—she was heavy, it had been years since he'd tried this last—and carried her out.

It was six months before Ada went missing again. She'd been increasingly moody and sullen, and he'd chalked it up to puberty. She'd cancelled most of their daddy-daughter dates, moreso after his mother died. There had been a few evenings when he'd come home and found her gone, and used the location-bug he'd left in place on her phone to track her down at a friend's house or in a park or hanging out at the Peanut Plaza.

But this time, after two hours had gone by, he tried looking up her bug and found it out of service. He tried to call up its logs, but they ended at her school at 3PM sharp.

He was already in a bad mood from spending the day arresting punk kids selling electronics off of blankets on the city's busy street, often to hoots of disapprobation from the crowds who told him off for wasting the public's dollar on petty crime. The Social Harmony man had instructed him to give little lectures on the interoperability of Eurasian positronics and the insidious dangers thereof, but all Arturo wanted to do was pick up his perps and bring them in. Interacting with yammerheads from the tax-base was a politician's job, not a copper's.

Now his daughter had figured out how to switch off the bug in her phone and had snuck away to get up to who-knew-what kind of trouble. He stewed at the kitchen table, regarding the old tin soldiers he'd brought home as the gift for their daddy-daughter date, then he got out his phone and looked up Liam's bug.

He'd never switched off the kid's phone-bug, and now he was able to haul out the UNATS Robotics computer and dump it all into a log-analysis program along with Ada's logs, see if the two of them had been spending much time in the same place.

They had. They'd been physically meeting up weekly or more frequently, at the Peanut Plaza and in the ravine. Arturo had suspected as much. Now he checked Liam's bug— if the kid wasn't with his daughter, he might know where she was.

It was a Friday night, and the kid was at the movies, at Fairview Mall. He'd sat down in auditorium two half an hour ago, and had gotten up to pee once already. Arturo slipped the toy soldiers into the pocket of his winter parka and pulled on a hat and gloves and set off for the mall.

The stink of the smellie movie clogged his nose, a cacophony of blood, gore, perfume and flowers, the only smells that Hollywood ever really perfected. Liam was kissing a girl in the dark, but it wasn't Ada, it was a sad, skinny thing with a lazy eye and skin worse than Liam's. She gawked at Arturo as he hauled Liam out of his seat, but a flash of Arturo's badge shut her up.

"Hello, Liam," he said, once he had the kid in the commandeered manager's office.

"God damn what the fuck did I ever do to you?" the kid said. Arturo knew that when kids started cursing like that, they were scared of something.

"Where has Ada gone, Liam?"

"Haven't seen her in months," he said.

"I have been bugging you ever since I found out you existed. Every one of your movements has been logged. I know where you've been and when. And I know where my daughter has been, too. Try again."

Liam made a disgusted face. "You are a complete ball of shit," he said. "Where do you get off spying on people like me?"

"I'm a police detective, Liam," he said. "It's my job."

"What about privacy?"

"What have you got to hide?"

The kid slumped back in his chair. "We've been renting out the OLED clothes. Making some pocket money. Come on, are infrared lights a crime now?"

"I'm sure they are," Arturo said. "And if you can't tell me where to find my daughter, I think it's a crime I'll arrest you for."

"She has another phone," Liam said. "Not listed in her name."

"Stolen, you mean." His daughter, peddling Eurasian infowar tech through a stolen phone. His ex-wife, the queen of the super-intelligent hive minds of Eurasian robots.

"No, not stolen. Made out of parts. There's a guy. The code for getting on the network was in a phone book that we started finding last month."

"Give me the number, Liam," Arturo said, taking out his phone.

"Hello?" It was a man's voice, adult.

"Who is this?"

"Who is this?"

Arturo used his cop's voice: "This is Arturo Icaza de Arana-Goldberg, Police Detective Third Grade. Who am I speaking to?"

"Hello, Detective," said the voice, and he placed it then. The Social Harmony man, bald and rounded, with his long nose and sharp Adam's apple. His heart thudded in his chest.

"Hello, sir," he said. It sounded like a squeak to him.

"You can just stay there, Detective. Someone will be along in a moment to get you. We have your daughter."

The robot that wrenched off the door of his car was black and non-reflective, headless and eight-armed. It grabbed him without ceremony and dragged him from the car without heed for his shout of pain. "Put me down!" he said, hoping that this robot that so blithely ignored the first law would still obey the second. No such luck.

It cocooned him in four of its arms and set off cross-country, dancing off the roofs of houses, hopping invisibly from lamp-post to lamp-post, above the oblivious heads of the crowds below. The icy wind howled in Arturo's bare ears, froze the tip of his nose and numbed his fingers. They rocketed downtown so fast that they were there in ten minutes, bounding along the lakeshore toward the Social Harmony center out on Cherry Beach. People who paid a visit to the Social Harmony center never talked about what they found there.

It scampered into a loading bay behind the building and carried Arturo quickly through windowless corridors lit with even, sourceless illumination, up three flights of stairs and then deposited him before a thick door, which slid aside with a hushed hiss.

"Hello, Detective," the Social Harmony man said.

"Dad!" Ada said. He couldn't see her, but he could hear that she had been crying. He nearly hauled off and popped the man one on the tip of his narrow chin, but before he could do more than twitch, the black robot had both his wrists in bondage.

"Come in," the Social Harmony man said, making a sweeping gesture and standing aside while the black robot brought him into the interrogation room.

Ada had been crying. She was wrapped in two coils of black-robot arms, and her eyes were red-rimmed and puffy. He stared hard at her as she looked back at him.

"Are you hurt?" he said.

"No," she said.

"All right," he said.

He looked at the Social Harmony man, who wasn't smirking, just watching curiously.

"Leonard MacPherson," he said, "it is my duty as a UNATS Detective Third Grade to inform you that you are under arrest for trade in contraband positronics. You have the following rights: to a trial per current rules of due process; to be free from self-incrimination in the absence of a court order to the contrary; to consult with a Social Harmony advocate; and to a speedy arraignment. Do you understand your rights?"

Ada actually giggled, which spoiled the moment, but he felt better for having said it. The Social Harmony man gave the smallest disappointed shake of his head and turned away to prod at a small, sleek computer.

"You went to Ottawa six months ago," the Social Harmony man said. "When we picked up your daughter, we thought it was she who'd gone, but it appears that you were the one carrying her phone. You'd thoughtfully left the trace in place on that phone, so we didn't have to refer to the logs in cold storage, they were already online and ready to be analyzed.

"We've been to the safe house. It was quite a spectacular battle. Both sides were surprised, I think. There will be another, I'm sure. What I'd like from you is as close to a verbatim report as you can make of the conversation that took place there."

They'd had him bugged and traced. Of course they had. Who watched the watchers? Social Harmony. Who watched Social Harmony? Social Harmony.

"I demand a consultation with a Social Harmony advocate," Arturo said.

"This is such a consultation," the Social Harmony man said, and this time, he did smile. "Make your report, Detective."

Arturo sucked in a breath. "Leonard MacPherson, it is my duty as a UNATS Detective Third Grade to inform you that you are under arrest for trade in contraband positronics. You have the following rights: to a trial per current rules of due process; to be free from self-incrimination in the absence of a court order to the contrary; to consult with a Social Harmony advocate; and to a speedy arraignment. Do you understand your rights?"

The Social Harmony man held up one finger on the hand closest to the black robot holding Ada, and she screamed, a sound that knifed through Arturo, ripping him from asshole to appetite.

"STOP!" he shouted. The man put his finger down and Ada sobbed quietly.

"I was taken to the safe house on the fifth of September, after being gassed by a Eurasian infowar robot in the basement of Fairview Mall—"

There was a thunderclap then, a crash so loud that it hurt his stomach and his head and vibrated his fingertips. The doors to the room buckled and flattened, and there stood Benny and Lenny and—Natalie.

Benny and Lenny moved so quickly that he was only able to track them by the things they knocked over on the way to tearing apart the robot that was holding Ada. A second later, the robot holding him was in pieces, and he was standing on his own two feet again. The Social Harmony man had gone so pale he looked green in his natty checked suit and pink tie.

Benny or Lenny pinned his arms in a tight hug and Natalie walked carefully to him and they regarded one another in silence. She slapped him abruptly, across each cheek. "Harming children," she said. "For shame."

Ada stood on her own in the corner of the room, crying with her mouth in a O. Arturo and Natalie both looked to her and she stood, poised, between them, before running to Arturo and leaping onto him, so that he staggered momentarily before righting himself with her on his hip, in his arms.

"We'll go with you now," he said to Natalie.

"Thank you," she said. She stroked Ada's hair briefly and kissed her cheek. "I love you, Ada."

Ada nodded solemnly.

"Let's go," Natalie said, when it was apparent that Ada had nothing to say to her.

Benny tossed the Social Harmony man across the room into the corner of a desk. He bounced off it and crashed to the floor, unconscious or dead. Arturo couldn't bring himself to care.

Benny knelt before Arturo. "Climb on, please," it said. Arturo saw that Natalie was already pig-a-back on Lenny. He climbed aboard.

They moved even faster than the black robots had, but the bitter cold was offset by the warmth radiating from Benny's metal hide, not hot, but warm. Arturo's stomach reeled and he held Ada tight, squeezing his eyes shut and clamping his jaw.

But Ada's gasp made him look around, and he saw that they had cleared the city limits, and were vaulting over rolling farmlands now, jumping in long flat arcs whose zenith was just high enough for him to see the highway—the 401, they were headed east—in the distance.

And then he saw what had made Ada gasp: boiling out of the hills and ditches, out of the trees and from under the cars: an army of headless, eight-armed black robots, arachnoid and sinister in the moonlight. They scuttled on the ground behind them, before them, and to both sides. Social Harmony had built a secret army of these robots and secreted them across the land, and now they were all chasing after them.

The ride got bumpy then, as Benny beat back the tentacles that reached for them, smashing the black robots with mighty one-handed blows, his other hand supporting Arturo and Ada. Ada screamed as a black robot reared up before them, and Benny vaulted it smoothly, kicking it hard as he went, while Arturo clung on for dear life.

Another scream made him look over toward Lenny and Natalie. Lenny was slightly ahead and to the left of them, and so he was the vanguard, encountering twice as many robots as they.

A black spider-robot clung to his leg, dragging behind him with each lope, and one of its spare arms was tugging at Natalie.

As Arturo watched—as Ada watched—the black robot ripped Natalie off of Lenny's back and tossed her into the arms of one of its cohorts behind it, which skewered her on one of its arms, a black spear protruding from her belly as she cried once more and then fell silent. Lenny was overwhelmed a moment later, buried under writhing black arms.

Benny charged forward even faster, so that Arturo nearly lost his grip, and then he steadied himself. "We have to go back for them—"

"They're dead," Benny said. "There's nothing to go back for." Its warm voice was sorrowful as it raced across the countryside, and the wind filled Arturo's throat when he opened his mouth, and he could say no more.

Ada wept on the jet, and Arturo wept with her, and Benny stood over them, a minatory presence against the other robots crewing the fast little plane, who left them alone all the way to Paris, where they changed jets again for the long trip to Beijing.

They slept on that trip, and when they landed, Benny helped them off the plane and onto the runway, and they got their first good look at Eurasia.

It was tall. Vertical. Beijing loomed over them with curvilinear towers that twisted and bent and jigged and jagged so high they disappeared at the tops. It smelled like barbeque and flowers, and around them skittered fast armies of robots of every shape and size, wheeling in lockstep like schools of exotic fish. They gawped at it for a long moment, and someone came up behind them and then warm arms encircled their necks.

Arturo knew that smell, knew that skin. He could never have forgotten it.

He turned slowly, the blood draining from his face.

"Natty?" he said, not believing his eyes as he confronted his dead, ex-wife. There were tears in her eyes.

"Artie," she said. "Ada," she said. She kissed them both on the cheeks.

Benny said, "You died in UNATS. Killed by modified

Eurasian Social Harmony robots. Lenny, too. Ironic," he said.
She shook her head. "He means that we probably co-
designed the robots that Social Harmony sent after you."
"Natty?" Arturo said again. Ada was white and shaking.
"Oh dear," she said. "Oh, God. You didn't know—"
"He didn't give you a chance to explain," Benny said.
"Oh, God, Jesus, you must have thought—"
"I didn't think it was my place to tell them, either," Benny
said, sounding embarrassed, a curious emotion for a robot.
"Oh, God. Artie, Ada. There are—there are lots of me.
One of the first things I did here was help them debug the
uploading process. You just put a copy of yourself into a
positronic brain, and then when you need a body, you grow
one or build one or both and decant yourself into it. I'm like
Lenny and Benny now—there are many of me. There's too
much work to do otherwise."
"I told you that our development helped humans under-
stand themselves," Benny said.
Arturo pulled back. "You're a robot?"
"No," Natalie said. "No, of course not. Well, a little. Parts
of me. Growing a body is slow. Parts of it, you build. But I'm
mostly made of person."
Ada clung tight to Arturo now, and they both stepped back
toward the jet.
"Dad?" Ada said.
He held her tight.
"Please, Arturo," Natalie, his dead, multiplicitous ex-wife
said. "I know it's a lot to understand, but it's different here in
Eurasia. Better, too. I don't expect you to come rushing back
to my arms after all this time, but I'll help you if you'll let
me. I owe you that much, no matter what happens between
us. You too, Ada, I owe you a lifetime."
"How many are there of you?" he asked, not wanting to
know the answer.
"I don't know exactly," she said.
"3,422," Benny said. "This morning it was 3,423."
Arturo rocked back in his boots and bit his lip hard
enough to draw blood.

"Um," Natalie said. "More of me to love?"

He barked a laugh, and Natalie smiled and reached for him. He leaned back toward the jet, then stopped, defeated. Where would he go? He let her warm hand take his, and a moment later, Ada took her other hand and they stood facing each other, breathing in their smells.

"I've gotten you your own place," she said as she led them across the tarmac. "It's close to where I live, but far enough for you to have privacy."

"What will I do here?" he said. "Do they have coppers in Eurasia?"

"Not really," Natalie said.

"It's all robots?"

"No, there's not any crime."

"Oh."

Arturo put one foot in front of the other, not sure if the ground was actually spongy or if that was jetlag. Around him, the alien smells of Beijing and the robots that were a million times smarter than he. To his right, his wife, one of 3,422 versions of her.

To his left, his daughter, who would inherit this world.

He reached into his pocket and took out the tin soldiers there. They were old and their glaze was cracked like an oil painting, but they were little people that a real human had made, little people in human image, and they were older than robots. How long had humans been making people, striving to bring them to life? He looked at Ada—a little person he'd brought to life.

He gave her the tin soldiers.

"For you," he said. "Daddy-daughter present." She held them tightly, their tiny bayonets sticking out from between her fingers.

"Thanks, Dad," she said. She held them tightly and looked around, wide-eyed, at the schools of robots and the corkscrew towers.

A flock of Bennys and Lennys appeared before them, joined by their Benny.

"There are half a billion of them," she said. "And 3,422 of them," she said, pointing with a small bayonet at Natalie.

"But there's only one of you," Arturo said.

She craned her neck.

"Not for long!" she said, and broke away, skipping forward and whirling around to take it all in.

Story Copyrights